LINDA CHAIKIN

Wednesday's
CHILD

A NOVEL

HARVEST HOUSE PUBLISHERS

EUGENE, OREGON

Scripture quotations are taken from the King James Version of the Bible.

Cover by Koechel Peterson & Associates, Minneapolis, Minnesota

WEDNESDAY'S CHILD

Copyright © 2000 by Linda Chaikin
Published by Harvest House Publishers
Eugene, Oregon 97402
www.harvesthousepublishers.com

Library of Congress Cataloging-in-Publication Data
Chaikin, L.L.,
    Wednesday's child / Linda Chaikin
        p. cm. — (A day to remember series)
    ISBN 978-0-7369-0069-0
        1. Children of the rich—Fiction. 2. Poor women—Fiction. 3. Sisters—Fiction. I. Title.
PS3553.H2427 W46 2000
813'.54—dc21

                                                                            00-044988

Printed in the United States of America

LINDA CHAIKIN
is an award-winning writer
of more than 18 books. Her Trade
Winds series includes *Captive Heart,*
Silver Dreams, and *Island Bride.*
Wednesday's Child is the third book
in the popular A Day to Remember
series. Linda and her husband, Steve,
make their home in California.

~

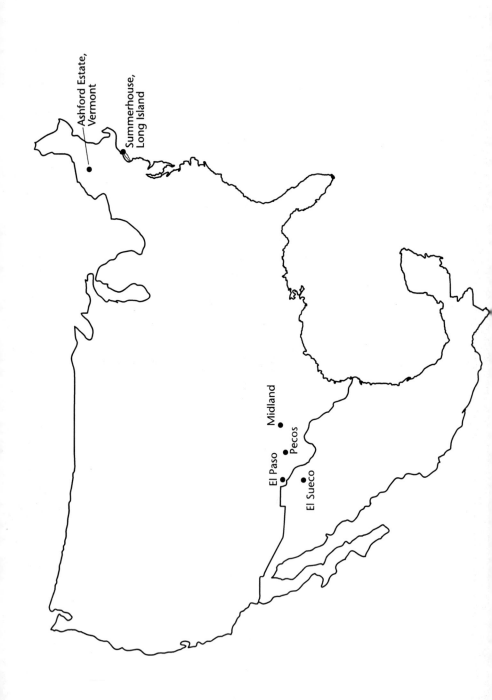

PART ONE

Ashford Summerhouse
Long Island, New York

He that is greedy for gain troubleth his own house...

Proverbs 15:27

1

It was a radiant summer morning at the shore in August 1929. The Ashfords' Long Island summer mansion with brick-and-green-shuttered splendor stood proudly on private beachfront property. Without a doubt, this vacation home was easily as elitist as its third-generation master, millionaire banker and Wall Street mogul Burgess Ashford II.

The Ashford family routinely came to Long Island each year to summer at the thirty-room "cottage." In doing this they joined the tradition of other members of the wealthy aristocracy whose annual pilgrimages from New York and Boston lasted from late May through August. The elite, however, came not only to Long Island, but to the most favorable localities their status permitted: Martha's Vineyard, Cape Cod, Edgartown, Nantucket, and Bar Harbor. Here in their socially isolated Meccas, traditions died slowly and outsiders rarely disturbed those who believed they were born special.

Sharlotte Ashford preferred to fraternize with her equals where the waters rippled cool and blue, and the zesty Atlantic breeze could at times whip up the waves into a meringue-like froth. Lazy afternoons were spent on wide covered porches sipping from tall minted glasses of lime sherbet with red-striped straws. High society debutantes collected fashionable summer tans while watching sailing yachts with white canvas sails snapping in the salty wind. These were the days of huge straw hats, Irish lace collars, and squash games. But this was also the Roaring Twenties, when the Bible and morality had been rejected, and flappers dared to wear short skirts and bobbed hair for the first time in American culture.

Sharlotte had been taught from the age of three that the rich were a special breed of people who, to avoid social disaster, did not deviate from their legacy of proper breeding and lifestyle. One went to the right school, collected only certain friends, and—most of all—married one's "own kind" in order to carry on the status quo.

Sharlotte and her sister, Amanda, did everything expected of them without question: they took piano lessons, ballet lessons, dancing lessons, French lessons, tennis lessons, sailing lessons, riding lessons, and, at the appropriate age, went to Vassar College with other like-minded rich girls from blue-blooded families. Once there they discussed the rich boys from the Ivy League schools who were mythically considered of superior breeding, which went hand in hand with being well-educated, suave, and oh so very rich.

Sharlotte adored coming to Long Island for the summer. At night there were communal clambakes or lobster fries on private beaches. While the men discussed their ever-climbing stock portfolios that seemed to be reaching toward the Empire State Building, their Ivy League sons would sneak away undetected to illegal speakeasies for a few hours of dancing. Here, where the big jazz bands performed, they secretly sipped bootlegged scotch from stylish hipflasks masterfully concealed from their busy, self-preoccupied Daddies and Mummies.

Though Sharlotte avoided such vices, she knew flapper girls who would join the boys after adding mascara to their eyelashes, rouge to their cheeks, bright red lipstick to their pouting lips—and darling little clutch hats to their short bobbed hair.

On this August morning, Sharlotte, a recent graduate of Vassar College, made a pretty picture as she rode her light-auburn mare along the private trail above the beach on her way to the yacht club. Beside her rode Clarence Fosdick, her soon-to-be fiancé, the son of Congressman Franklin D. Fosdick of New York. Clarence was a good eight years her senior, but because his future was already far along a prosperous political road leading straight toward the House of Representatives in Washington, D.C., his determined approach to life had pleased Sharlotte's father. "One must know where he is going in life. And one can never begin too soon," Burgess had said.

Sharlotte's custom-tailored riding habit, the color of hunter green, contrasted nicely with her golden hair. She wore a classy little hat with the private yacht club insignia, and her breeches and hip-length jacket with gold monogrammed buttons perfectly conformed to her envied figure of nineteen years. Indeed, Sharlotte Ashford, granddaughter of the late Alfred D. Ashford (who had been President Coolidge's roving ambassador in Latin America), was the darling of the Long Island social set.

Her debutante coming-out ball had been in the Beacon Hill area of Boston where she was born. She was presented at the annual cotillion, and then afterward had returned to her home in upstate New York where she'd enjoyed three more coming-out balls: the Infirmary Ball, the Junior Assemblies' Ball, and the Junior League Ball. In fact, all summer Sharlotte had been attending a nonstop whirl of parties given by friends of the family. There were teas, exclusive dinners and dances, luncheons, Saturday picnics—and even more extravagant balls with fabulous gowns, food, and performing orchestras. As was customary, her name was announced as she "came out" to be viewed by society: This is Miss Sharlotte Chattaine Van Dornen Ashford, presented by her father, Mr. Burgess Upton Worthington Ashford of New York.

When a debutante first made her appearance on the social scene, brothers, cousins, and virtual strangers were often pressed into service as escorts—and sometimes a young woman had no choice but to go to her ball on the arm of her daddy's Ivy League college roommate's son. For Sharlotte, whose lovely features and charm had made her popular, there was little need for Daddy to work behind the scene to find escorts for her. There were a number of suitable young men eager for her company, most of them handsome, charming, and exceptionally good dancers.

The ball gown for her first appearance had to be white because a wealthy "deb" was as close to a princess as permitted in a democracy. And Sharlotte was determined not to be outdone by her competitive girlfriends. She and her Aunt Cecily Van Dornen had shopped for a month for just the right dress. They had finally found it at Saks after being assured by the grave-faced management that Miss Ashford's gown would be the only one of its kind—there was absolutely no reason to fear that another debutante would appear at the ball in the same dress. Naturally, since Sharlotte was presented at numerous balls, she would need a different gown for each night. How could she possibly wear the same one twice! Afterward, there was yachting at the New York Yacht club, which had as good a social register as Nantucket—except at Nantucket, one needed to be able to play tennis to join, whereas Sharlotte, though she played a fair game of tennis, preferred squash. Although she had barely passed mathematics at college, she was a whiz at the game.

Yes, thus far it had been a wonderful summer—she was becoming the most sought after prize of the year. What fun to have handsome boys outdoing themselves to win one dance with her at the ball.

Now she was vacationing at Long island, and the morning stretched on with lazy cotton puffs dotting the blue sky like feeding lambs. The tangy sea breeze blowing in was congenially warm. If there was a storm approaching, as her father had said at breakfast on the terrace, there was little evidence of it now.

"Jeepers, I hope it doesn't rain," she told Clarence, casting her violet-blue eyes toward the sky. "Not on the day of the picnic."

Sharlotte and Clarence were trotting their horses along the sandy roadway toward the yacht club where family members and friends were meeting to sail to Shrewsbury Landing. There they would picnic, then everyone would dance barefoot for hours on the sand to accordion arrangements of Rudy Vallee's hit songs.

Clarence wore a spotless white yachting suit and a captain's hat on his glossy reddish-brown hair that was carefully parted in the middle according to fashion. He was stocky, with a slightly crooked nose that had been broken in a football game at Harvard. His thick brows were bleached golden by the sun and wind, and his eye color uncannily matched whatever he wore. He loathed picnics because of ants and sunburn.

"Father says my five years of law at Uncle's firm is the most advantageous career move I've made. I'll soon be leaving to join his congressional staff."

Sharlotte agreed that Clarence was acquiring a respectable reputation. His name had appeared in the newspaper recently in connection with his father's bill favoring his congressional district.

"In eight years or less, Chuck Hillier will be retiring from his congressional seat. Then I'll be able to toss my hat in the political ring."

Sharlotte wondered how she would like being a politician's wife. Eight years seemed like such a long time to plan for. By then she expected to have children: a boy first, then a girl. And she wanted to live in either Virginia or Maryland, with a brownstone in New York. Oh, there was so much to worry about. She sighed and looked out toward the sea where the whitecaps were breaking on the shore.

"I can't imagine the boisterous Chuck Hillier not wanting his son Stuart to uphold the family name and run for his seat," she said. "Stuart mentioned to me at the spring country club dance that he intended to run against you. The district seat has been in the Hillier family for generations. Running for his daddy's office is a matter of pride." Sharlotte glanced at Clarence. He usually became upset whenever Stuart was mentioned. Inviting Stuart to the picnic today may have been a mistake on Cousin Pamela Van Dornen's part. But Pamela enjoyed mixing up trouble. "The Hilliers are known for getting what they want in the world of politics," she continued, a vague warning in her voice.

Clarence gave an exasperated shrug. "And so are the Fosdicks. What Hillier wants doesn't matter to anyone except Hillier and his son. There's always been rivalry between our families—for generations. I intend to win that vacated seat. If I didn't think the odds were on my side, I wouldn't risk my reputation."

"Yes, however—"

"There's no however about it, Sharlotte darling. It's understood I'll run at the end of his next term."

"Understood by whom?" She thought of his grandmother, the dictator in the Fosdick family.

"By everyone who matters in politics. A deal's been struck with some of Hillier's backers. They're unhappy about him supporting Al Smith for President. We're all Hoover men," he said, as though there were nothing left to say.

Politics had never interested her, but she understood that she must change her mind if she were to marry Clarence and be content with her calling.

"Does that mean Congressman Hillier's career is over?" she dutifully inquired, wrinkling her brows as though the future of America depended on his reply.

"After backing Al Smith?" he looked at her with amused tolerance. She had her answer. "The decisions I make now have just one end in view," he told her. "And I'll need to prove myself capable during the next few years." He looked over at her. "We both will, Sharlotte."

Clarence left a great deal unsaid, but Sharlotte understood his meaning. The Ashford name carried political implications that were well received in New York. Her grandfather had been an ambassador, and her father was the bank president of Manhattan Security and Loan; a man with high connections in Wall Street. Sharlotte herself was an asset with no scandals attached to her behavior.

Clarence hadn't explained what deal his father had struck with the previous financial backers of Stuart's father, nor was she concerned. It was a splendid morning for a picnic, except for the threat of an unexpected storm...

"Looks like everyone's here, even Sheldon," she commented of her older cousin who was usually late. "I thought he was still eating breakfast at the house."

"You mean mid-morning brunch," Clarence said dryly. "I've never known a fellow who so enjoys sleeping the morning away."

"Well, it is summer," Sharlotte said in Sheldon's defense, laughing.

Clarence looked at her with a raised brow.

"Anyway, Sheldon was waiting for Bitsy," she said of her cousin's new summer love.

"Bitsy," Clarence said wearily, "hasn't a brain cell in her head."

Sharlotte made a face at him. "You're being cynical, Clarence. Come! Sheldon's waving!"

"With a drink in his hand as usual—and he's supposed to sail us to Shrewsbury Landing?"

Sharlotte saw several polished and gleaming roadsters parked in front of the club. She and Clarence dismounted from their horses to turn them over to the young groom who came running from the boarding stables. Sharlotte walked hand in hand with Clarence across the sunbaked sod toward the New England-style clubhouse. Below the sandy slope where some crimson-flowered ice plant bloomed, two flights of wooden steps with handrails led down to the long wooden jetty. She could see the sailboats bobbing at their moorings as though impatient to be off, and several white sails were already out on the water. Seagulls cried, and the salty damp wind playfully tugged at her champagne-colored hair, causing the silken strands to glimmer like spun glass.

Cousin Sheldon's boat, *Captain's Choice*, was anchored and waiting for them to board. Sheldon Van Dornen, blond, sun-tanned, and smiling, was the outdoorsy sort who somehow always managed to be on the winning team, whether it was a boat race or a game of squash. Sheldon's last remaining ambition in life was to win the Bermuda Race, the only one at which he had failed thus far. His sister, Pamela, had told Sharlotte it wasn't due to any lack of skill, but because of his gin and tonics. In fact, he and his rugby friends from Tulane had once been able to come in first in the Edgartown Regatta. Racing was indeed fun, but Sharlotte had seen a friendship or two dissolve as competition made fellow club members feel intimidated. Yachting, for her social strata, was more of a status symbol than a real sport, but her cousin lived sailing.

Sheldon, tall and clean-limbed, waited on the club steps. He wore faded brick-red pants and a shirt with his boat name sewn above the pocket. He lifted a hand and waved again. Sharlotte noticed unhappily that even at the comparably young age of twenty-six, the puffy telltale lines of sinful excess showed on his face.

Once again, without knowing exactly what it was that troubled her, she wondered about the pursuits that everyone else assumed were the essential things in life. No, not everyone. Aunt Livia Ashford, who had married into the Landry family of Texas, had been a maverick. And Livia's nephew, Kace Landry—well, never mind *him*. Her hand closed more tightly about Clarence's.

Then there was that man that her group shamelessly called a "half-cracked" evangelist, Billy Sunday. Perhaps Sharlotte had been intimidated by his wild preaching that many mocked, but phrases from his message on "What Money Can't Buy" continued to pop up in her mind at the most inconvenient times.

It was only by accident that she had heard him. She had been out shopping for a birthday gift for her father and, noticing a large crowd gathering around a man on a soapbox, had paused briefly to listen. At first she mistook Billy Sunday for one of the new Communists who were often in the ritzy shopping districts handing out flyers. Sharlotte soon became caught in the throng around him and was forced to listen to his sermon on the emptiness of riches. His unconventional style had made him a topic of conversation. Sometimes he acted things out, even wrestling, so he said, with the devil. Other than giving her goose bumps, Sharlotte wondered if it were anything to laugh about. After all, she had once heard that Martin Luther threw an inkwell at the devil.

But why was she thinking of such extraneous things now? It must be Sheldon and his drinking. She worried about him and, well, about them all. Clarence was the only one who knew where he was going in life. But did even he really know? He wanted to get to Congress, but after that? One day he would end up just like the older man he wanted to unseat now, Congressman Chuck Hillier. Then what? One retired. Then what? One died. Then what? She frowned. Her father, an atheist, said it was all over. "Like a dead dog. When you die, that's it." She had no reason to question him. Everyone said Burgess Ashford II was a financial genius. Her father mocked Billy Sunday.

The private clubhouse overlooked a small bay, and as they approached the entrance Sheldon sauntered toward them.

"Oh, you kid!" He smiled at Sharlotte and kissed her cheek as all Van Dornen and Ashford cousins did each time they met. Sharlotte noticed the inevitable tall frosted glass clinking with ice that contained something that must have been bootlegged. His tanned fingers flashed with a gold school ring, and there was a masculine gold chain bracelet on his wrist sporting his renowned yacht club emblem.

"It's about time you two showed. Hullo, Clarence, old boy, we missed you last night at the clambake. Politics as usual, I suppose? Well, never mind. Better brace yourself for a rather uncomfortable afternoon."

"Picnics are always miserable. Sand, heat, and lukewarm beer. But what do you mean by 'uncomfortable'?" Clarence asked, a small frown forming between his brows.

Sheldon lowered his glass and looked over his shoulder toward the club. "Your rival, Stuart Hillier. He's joined the gladsome throng. Sorry," he murmured when Clarence's frown deepened. "You can blame Pamela. She says she didn't know you were coming. She happened to run into Stuart last night and asked him to come along on the picnic today. Tough luck, really. It's rather stormy weather for short tempers."

Clarence's lips tightened and he shoved a hand into his pocket, a clear sign to Sharlotte that he was irked by Stuart's presence.

"There's no reason why we can't all enjoy a picnic in peace," she said. "It's only for a few hours."

"True enough," Sheldon murmured, drinking from his glass. "Just between us, though, let's stay off the topic of the congressional race." He looked toward the sky, still mostly blue. "Those are thunder clouds. Is it my imagination, or do they harmonize with the mood of those present today?"

"What's this? A harbinger of danger to come?" Cousin Pamela interrupted, joining them. "Hullo, everyone," but her eyes showed concealed anger when they focused on Clarence.

Pamela was a short, squarely-built golden girl garbed in a white tennis outfit. She knew little about sailing, but she was social president of the club.

"What's this about you inviting Stuart Hillier to the picnic?" Clarence asked her shortly.

"A terrible blunder, Clarence dear, so sorry." Though she smiled sweetly, her hazel eyes were hard. Sharlotte, an unwilling observer, wondered uncomfortably if it had indeed been Pamela's blunder or a deliberately planted burr that she'd placed under Clarence's saddle.

Sheldon too must have picked up the crackling tension between his sister and Clarence because he formed a rueful smile.

"Looks like Stuart isn't the only fly in our happy ointment today. Let's hope this snappish mood doesn't begin infesting all of us, or we'll end up throwing bread scraps at one another."

"Really, Sheldon, go easy on that stuff, will you?" Pamela tapped on his glass. "Remember, you've got to get us all safely to Shrewsbury."

"Big sister!" Sheldon laughed at her, undisturbed, his even teeth flashing white against his suntanned face. "Don't worry so much."

Pamela was known to dote on her younger brother, though their bickering suggested the opposite. She had lost her husband to illness, and after two years of widowhood had emerged again on the social scene. At twenty-nine Cousin Pamela had turned her motherly instincts on Sheldon.

"I just want to make sure you can captain the old boat to our happy rendezvous," she suggested to him.

"I'll have us all picnicking at Shrewsbury by one o'clock once we're ready to leave."

"Say—isn't that Mr. Hunnewell, your father's lawyer?" Clarence suddenly asked Sharlotte.

Sharlotte followed his gaze to a small man rushing toward the club as though late for a business appointment. He carried a briefcase—or, rather, clutched it to his chest, adjusting his horn-rimmed glasses as he went, his sandaled feet beating a path across the sandy yard. He apparently hadn't noticed them yet, grouped together beneath a shady hawthorn tree.

"What's he carrying, his life preserver?" Sheldon joked. "Maybe he doesn't trust my sailing."

"Daddy invited him on the picnic," Sharlotte explained. "Oh dear, I forgot all about Mr. Hunnewell. Daddy asked me to keep him company today. He's not much of a sailor, I'm told."

"I assume he doesn't know your father isn't coming?" Clarence said.

"No. Daddy tried to call him at his hotel room, but Hunnewell had already left."

"Why isn't Uncle Burgess coming?" Sheldon asked.

"He received a telephone call this morning that changed his plans. He didn't explain what it was about, some business of one sort or another."

"Then we'd better let Hunnewell know," Clarence said.

"Yes," Sheldon murmured. "Maybe he'll change his mind too. He looks as if he'll put a damper on our little picnic."

"Shame on you, Sheldon. He's actually a very nice man," Sharlotte said.

"Well, good. Then you can look after him this afternoon."

Sheldon and Pamela wandered away as Sharlotte and Clarence went to intercept Mr. Hunnewell and explain her father's absence. Hunnewell was quite apologetic about his presence, as though it was his fault, and questioned whether or not it might be better for him to return to his hotel until Burgess could meet with him. But Sharlotte assured him he should do nothing of the sort, and that his company was wanted. Whereupon, Clarence launched into a zealous discussion of the laxity and excesses of those in Congress and why it was necessary to vote the self-serving gentlemen out of office.

"And elect men of thrift. Free of graft and bribery, whose sole purpose to serve in the hallowed halls of the United States Congress is to protect and serve the good-hearted American people."

It had seemed a matter of ill-timing for Clarence to be concluding his speech just as they entered the clubhouse with Mr. Hunnewell. Sharlotte saw Stuart Hillier turn his head sharply and gaze at Clarence as his voice carried throughout the room. Muted anger toned Stuart's face a ruddy color as he must have concluded that Clarence was signaling out his father for criticism. His voice cut through Clarence's rhetoric: "And of course, you and your father would know all about ending graft and bribery."

A sudden silence descended upon the group in the clubhouse as Clarence stopped and turned to face Stuart.

Oh no, Sharlotte thought. She must stop this exchange of hot words before the fire sprang out of control. She laid a restraining hand on Clarence's arm, but too late. He walked toward Stuart, who had stopped and was smiling unpleasantly.

"Here we go," murmured Sheldon. "Just two ordinary, red-blooded Americans determined to pounce on each other to prove which is better qualified to represent us in Congress. Aren't you impressed, Sharlotte dear?"

"Oh, Sheldon, do something to stop them," she whispered.

"Nothing I can do," he said lazily, "but get my nose punched."

"Well, hullo Stuart," Clarence was saying. "I'm surprised to see you here today."

"No more than I am to see you, my good fellow. Still gaining access to the bank?" Stuart's gaze meaningfully went toward Sharlotte.

Clarence's smile disappeared and his face turned an angry red. "Speaking of bankers, I would expect you to be out with your father making patriotic speeches. Don't tell me you both have run out of sugarcoated promises to brainwash the good citizens in your district? Or perhaps they've at last seen through your Socialistic lies?"

"Don't you dare call me Socialistic," Stuart fumed.

"I'll go one step beyond. Your ideologies are dangerous to the freedoms of this country. I say your father embraces many of Lenin's Communistic policies."

"Communistic! What about your father's policies? His campaigns have been so larded with money from bank swindlers that J. Edgar Hoover and his G-men ought to come after Fosdick instead of Al Capone in Chicago!"

The caustic rhetoric turned Clarence colorless. He doubled back his fist, but two others quickly intervened.

"Now, now, gentlemen, all's fair in politics and war."

Both Clarence and Stuart backed down and stood silent. The room seemed to Sharlotte to become too humid as the tension crackled. Raw anger had struck out at its victims, leaving poison and paralysis.

Stuart was the first to move, turning his back on Clarence and walking out of the club with a firm stride. Through the windows the shamefaced spectators, who now wondered why they hadn't done more to intervene, watched Stuart walk across the faded lawn toward the boats. Evidently he had no notion of withdrawing from the picnic on Shrewsbury Landing.

Clarence, recovering his dignity, turned on his heel and walked over to the long buffet table where he filled a glass with ice chips and proceeded to make himself a British gimlet.

"My, wasn't that simply awful?" whispered Pamela.

Sheldon turned his head and gave his sister a justifiably long look. "Then why did you invite him? You knew Clarence was coming. Those two have never got on. How did you think it would turn out now that they're both after the same pot of gold?"

Pamela frowned and walked away to where Clarence stood, saying something that he apparently did not accept, for he turned his shoulder toward her and walked out on the veranda. Sharlotte was about to go to him but decided he would probably prefer to be alone until his nerves had cooled. Watching Clarence, she noticed that he gazed out across the lawn to where the sailing boats were docked—to where Stuart was walking on the jetty. He could be seen talking to someone on the wharf.

Sharlotte looked around for Mr. Hunnewell. He was frowning as he stood near the telephone, but he didn't appear to have made a call. She noted something in his hand that looked like a piece of paper. *What's he so agitated about?* she wondered. *The fight between Clarence and Stuart, no doubt.*

Meanwhile, clouds were gathering. Sharlotte noted that the once-bright morning no longer offered the same carefree summer spirit that it had only minutes before.

The wind picked up, and the dappled shadows were heavy with an ominous silence.

2

Pamela plopped into a comfortable wicker chair with a faded red canvas cushion sporting a yachting anchor and the words: "Seascape Yacht Club." Sharlotte noticed that Pamela had that bored done-everything look that her brother Sheldon displayed. The unpleasant discovery prompted Sharlotte to remove a silver compact from her handbag and check her powder. She was relieved to see that cynicism hadn't aged her since she'd washed her face this morning. The flattering appeal of youth and innocence remained. Her vanity was also satisfied with the violet-blue eyes that peered back, the golden hair, and the peaches and cream complexion. Too bad she couldn't have kept Kace...along with Clarence.

Feeling her cousin's stare, she glanced up. A glimmer of dislike showed in Pamela's plain hazel eyes. "Would you like something to drink, Sharlotte?"

"Um, yes, Coca Cola, with lots of ice."

"It's all melted," wailed the favorite date of Cousin Sheldon, who went by the fashionable nickname of "Bitsy." She had movie star "Clara Bow" eyebrows—a thin dark pencil line above lashes thick with mascara that fluttered butterfly fashion. Her bobbed black hair was smoothly molded to her head and glued with sugar water to the sides of her cheeks. "That was some confrontation between Stuart and Clarence," she giggled, chewing her gum. "Why, I thought we'd have an Al Capone shootout any moment." She paused and then whispered, "Is it true Sheldon knows gangsters in Chicago?"

"Don't be a dimwit," Pamela said, bored.

"Yes, well—" and Sharlotte changed the subject to the picnic. It remained a humid day, but the damp wind coming in through the open terrace refreshed her and fingered her tresses.

Sheldon and Clarence joined them at the table, drawing up more wicker chairs.

"What about tonight's dance, Sharlotte?" Pamela asked, her eyes keenly watchful. "Did you invite the Texas cousins?"

Bitsy's eyes widened into fringed circles of delighted excitement. "Texas cousins? You don't mean it."

"She certainly does mean it," Sheldon said of his sister. Don't you, Pamela?" His tone was wry.

Clarence must have picked up a sense of veiled importance from Sharlotte's silence, for he had stopped brooding into his glass about Stuart and gave her a searching look. "More cousins, Sharlotte darling?" he asked with mock dismay. "How many are there in the Ashford family that I haven't met yet?"

There was laughter. Sharlotte's automatic smile had frozen on her lips and she hoped no one noticed. Her heart knew a curious, faster beat. Why would Pamela mention Kace and Tyler Landry? What could be the motive behind her strange query? Pamela would know that she wouldn't have invited Kace and Tyler to the ball.

The others apparently hadn't noticed that Sharlotte didn't answer Pamela's question. Sheldon was saying in a light, humorous vein: "Cheer up, Clarence. We don't even bother to count the Texas hillbillies, and they make up at least half of the twenty-five cousins," and he winked over his glass at Bitsy, as though having cousins from Texas were amusing for one of blue blood aristocracy. Bitsy must have decided it was so, for the term "hillbilly" had caused her to erupt into a gale of uncontrollable giggles.

Sharlotte dimly wondered whether Bitsy's thickly dabbed mascara was going to smear. For some reason it didn't.

"You see, some of us just don't meet the pedigree requirements for the esteemed distinction of being called cousins," Sheldon mocked.

"Not speaking of yourself, are you?" Stuart Hillier spoke from across the room as he opened a bottle of Coca Cola.

There was a moment of strained silence, then Sheldon laughed.

"The great Sheldon Van Dornen? Are you kidding? My family tree goes back to royalty. And the Ashfords have been added to the line and produced blood offspring." He turned to his sister. "But the Landrys are a prickly breed coming from Texas. What should we consider them?"

Pamela raised her fair brows. "Gosh, don't look to me for the answer. Better ask Sharlotte. She's the one who knows Kace Landry." She leaned back in her chair, playing with her drink. "Sharlotte's spent a few weeks' vacation on the Landry ranch every year since she was ten. The last time was around two and a half years ago, wasn't it Sharlotte?"

Sharlotte reached for her Coca Cola and sipped, giving herself an extra moment to answer the subtly needling question.

Sheldon frowned at Pamela. "Why is it I think you know more than you're willing to tell?"

Pamela raised both brows in innocent confusion. "Me?"

Clarence looked at Sharlotte, clearly bewildered.

Sharlotte was still trying to muster her poise and keep herself from giving anything away that would alienate Clarence.

"I didn't know you had relatives in Texas, Sharlotte," he repeated.

Sharlotte's throat felt unexpectedly tight. She tried to make light of the situation. "You've heard of Sherman Landry, haven't you? Well, he married Daddy's sister."

"He's the cattle rancher?"

Pamela watched them. "And now Uncle Sherman's nephew Kace is dabbing in oil exploration," she offered unexpectedly.

Clarence appeared anything except bored. "Oil," he repeated thoughtfully, and a hungry fire smoldered in his faraway look.

"Yes, they call it black gold," Sheldon added with an understanding smile.

Even Bitsy ceased her giggling and looked a little awed. "I never heard of black gold, only yellow gold."

"Brilliant," Sheldon patted her shoulder. "Well, you have now, toots."

Even Sharlotte paused to consider. Oil? Since when had the Landrys become involved in oil exploration? She watched Pamela and Sheldon, wondering how they knew what the Landrys were doing. The Van Dornens had even less communication with the Texas relatives than did the Ashfords.

"Looks as if the joke may have been on us," Sheldon suggested.

The mood at the table turned from lightheartedness to somber reality.

"What joke is that?" Clarence asked, curious.

"Years ago, the family thought Livia Ashford was foolish to marry that ol' cowpoke, Sherman Landry. Just a minute ago we were all laughing at the hillbillies. Now, a little dab of black crude has made them smell like rare perfume."

"You're the one who called them hillbillies," Pamela corrected over her glass.

"Every family has its black sheep they say. Livia was the Ashford's wayward lamb. She committed an unforgivable deed: She refused Great-Uncle Hubert's choice for her from the Pickford family and then went off secretly and married a Landry."

Bitsy's brow puckered. "I don't get it."

Sheldon reached over and put an arm round her shoulders. "Meaning, my dumb cluck, that as soon as I mentioned black gold, a sanctified hush descended. It just shows how money and power can clear the air of all snobbery."

Sharlotte moved uncomfortably. Kace had once come to the same conclusion, only when Kace said such things she bristled.

"Back when Aunt Livia married Sherman Landry, he was nothing except a big handsome Texan with a poor rancho near the Rio Grande—or is it Midland?" Sheldon asked Sharlotte.

Sharlotte shrugged indifferently, avoiding Clarence's eyes, and took a sip of warm Coke.

"Now his nephew's slick with oil! Livia will be a millionairess. Quite a contrast from the woman Great-Uncle Hubert swore would end up in a south-of-the-border poorhouse."

"She wasn't rebellious in the way we think," Sharlotte said coming to the defense of her aunt. "She was never disrespectful; she merely broke away from the family's dominance and decided she'd rather have a man she loved than an arranged marriage with affluence."

"And now she has both," Sheldon repeated.

"I think both you and Pamela are wrong," Sharlotte said stiffly. "If Uncle Sherman struck oil, Aunt Livia would have written me by now, 'hooping and hollering' as she would put it. She just wouldn't have held back news like that from me and Amanda," she said of her younger sister.

Clarence looked from Sheldon to Pamela, then to Sharlotte. Bitsy was wide-eyed and crunching the last melting chips of ice in her glass.

"All this chatter about the Landrys and oil is pure presumption," Sharlotte continued. "There's no proof."

"True," Sheldon admitted grudgingly.

"You sound as if you don't want them to find oil," Pamela said, watching her alertly.

"Even if the Landrys did discover oil, so what?" Sharlotte said firmly.

" 'So what,' she says, " groaned Sheldon. "Money, honey."

"We Ashfords already have money." She looked from one to the other. "For that matter, another million in oil wouldn't make us any more able than we are now to pursue our narrow little dreams."

"Ouch," grimaced Sheldon, "what's been added to your Cola, anyway?"

"Jeepers," sorrowed Bitsy. "I can't dream at all. My daddy isn't a millionaire yet." Her eyes brightened hopefully. "But he's trying. Why, just last week he bought a whole hundred shares of something or other."

"Sharlotte was only being sarcastic, Bitsy," Pamela said, bored. "A girl can spin golden daydreams anytime she cares to. As for me, I gave up a long time ago." She set her empty glass down on the table.

"Poor little rich girl," Sheldon lamented with a grin in his voice, looking at his sister.

Clarence flushed, and avoided looking at Pamela.

Sheldon got up and shoved his hands in his white trouser pockets. He walked to the windows. "Say, why not ask Mr. Hunnewell about Landry oil? He's a lawyer, and he works for your father." He turned toward Sharlotte. "Did you see that fat briefcase he was carrying? Seemed a little odd on an afternoon for a picnic."

"Maybe he was bringing his own sandwiches," Bitsy said innocently, and then giggled at her joke.

"Yes, why is Hunnewell here?" Pamela asked curiously.

"He had expected to meet my father," Sharlotte explained, happy to change the subject away from Kace Landry.

At the mention of her father and his lawyer friend, Mr. Hunnewell, Sharlotte once again came aware of her social failings and glanced about the club room as if expecting to see him somewhere about. "Oh dear, I'd forgotten about poor Mr. Hunnewell. I suppose I'd better go search for him."

"You're looking for Mr. Hunnewell?" Bitsy asked her. "He was standing right over there by the telephone. Soon as the quarrel broke out between Clarence and Stuart, he turned pale as a Halloween ghost and left. He must've gone back to his hotel room."

With the unpleasant way things were turning out, Sharlotte couldn't blame Hunnewell for preferring to lunch alone.

"I'll just have a look around the club, just in case he's hiding." She smiled, imagining Mr. Hunnewell crouching in the shadows, clutching his thick briefcase.

Pamela got to her feet and settled her dark sunglasses on her pug nose. "Tuh dah! I'm on my way. If we don't get going soon, we might as well eat here among the wicker furniture." She walked to the big window. "Look at those clouds, Sheldon. If that doesn't mean rain, I don't know what does."

Clarence followed Pamela to the window. "How far to Shrewsbury Landing?"

"Forty-five minutes up the coast. Fifteen to Seagull Point," Sheldon said. "No need to worry."

Pamela looked toward the road leading back to the Ashford's summerhouse. "I wonder what's keeping Amanda?"

"It takes her longer, for a good reason," Sheldon remarked soberly. "Well, come on, Bitsy sugar. Let's go."

She cooed up at him. "You know how afraid I am of water, Boopsy. Sure you have life preservers on board?" She looped her arm through his, smiling as sweetly as her sugared curls.

"Now, would I ever fail you?"

Bitsy giggled.

"Horses are coming," Clarence told them in a bored voice. "Could that be Amanda and her boyfriend?"

Sharlotte tensed. George would do almost anything to cheer her younger sister, but he wouldn't dream of bringing her here on his horse—not after the traumatic accident two years earlier.

Sharlotte left the clubhouse and stood on the steps glancing toward the sandy road. Yes, horses' hooves—galloping! Her heart beat faster. Anger at George gave way to runaway fear. Her thoughts went racing backward in time to that last summer in Texas…

She and Amanda were galloping back toward the ranch. They were laughing, the hot wind in their hair. Kace and Tyler were behind, letting them win…then Amanda screamed…Sharlotte's eyes widened with horror. She saw her sister thrown from the saddle, lost in a cloud of dust and thundering hooves—

Tyler had reached Amanda first. Kace had caught Sharlotte by the shoulder and swung her around. "Don't look, honey." But she had looked, and she would never forget. She would always blame herself for her sister's twisted spine and her crutches, because if it hadn't been for what she'd done that afternoon—

A Long Island sea breeze brought her back to the present. "Stop!" Sharlotte heard herself speaking uselessly into the wind, her voice raspy with fear. She started to rush down the clubhouse steps as if expecting to see Amanda on the ground, unconscious, dusty, and bleeding. Sharlotte found that she was clutching her hands into tight fists.

Clarence came hurrying down the steps. "What is it, darling?" He turned her toward him, frowning. The light caught his reddish-brown hair. She looked at him blankly. "I thought I heard you yell," he said.

"I'm sorry—" she stopped and turned to look toward the road again where someone was galloping from the direction of the summerhouse. The tall gray-green cypress which hid the Ashford house on the hill screened the rider from clear view. She left Clarence and walked forward.

The sun momentarily peaked out from behind a cloud. The wind had cooled and there was a hint of early autumn in the air. She could sense it in the sad sigh of the sea when the sunlight began casting longer shadows. Summer was almost over, leaving her with a sensation that her life, like the carefree summer days and evenings, was also changing, merging with oncoming autumn.

George came riding up to the club with Amanda sitting in front on the saddle. Amanda grinned and waved a delighted greeting at Sharlotte, who stood silent and tense. The exhilarated smile on her sister's face and the glow in her eyes surprised Sharlotte.

Why, Amanda's loved every moment of her ride, she thought, astounded. *She looks happier than I've seen her all summer.* Sharlotte's relief welled up within. *Maybe George is right. He keeps telling me and Daddy that Amanda needs more activity, that we're smothering her with too much protection. And I have to admit he was right about this ride. I'd never have agreed to it had I known, nor would Daddy.*

Sharlotte smiled up at her sister. "You enjoyed it?" she cried with shocked dismay.

"Oh, it was wonderful! I was suddenly free again." Amanda turned in the saddle to smile adoringly at George. "Darling George gave me wings, and we flew together like a mystical prince and princess."

Sharlotte glanced at the handsome young man with masked concern. If Daddy heard her speak that way he'd never let her see George again. Burgess Ashford was totally against any match with George. He had plans for Amanda to marry Albert Gosling.

"Prince, nothing doing," teased George. "It's King George, at your service, madam." He swung down, bowed, lifted Amanda from the saddle, and carried her to the club steps.

Amanda was laughing and trying to stop him. "I've got to talk to Sharlotte first—alone." She turned, waving, and called: "Sharlotte, over there, at the bench." She pointed off toward a shade tree.

Sharlotte followed them, smiling, wondering what might be so important. After George had deposited her on the bench, he left and walked over to talk with Clarence.

Sharlotte came up, still smiling. "What is it? A secret?" she teased.

The look on her sister's face caused Sharlotte to pause.

Amanda, seventeen, was a pretty girl with light red hair and a heart-shaped face. Her unplucked brows were too wide for 1920s fashion, but they added a comely emphasis to the widely spaced pale blue eyes that was all her own. Since the accident she had grown thin, and she wore her hemlines long. Although she could walk around the house with crutches, she tired easily and spent part of each day in bed. For an outdoor girl who had always indulged in riding, swimming, tennis, and dancing, her crippled condition remained a heartbreak. Before meeting George last summer, her health had steadily declined. Now, she even envisioned walking again one day—without crutches.

She had upset their father by declaring her undying love for George Fieldstone, who was an aviation student taking flying lessons and presently learning stall recoveries.

"He's a radical," Burgess had said. "No Ashford daughter is going to become involved with a stunt flyer."

Sharlotte lowered her voice: "You're late. I could have used your moral support earlier."

Amanda wrinkled her nose. "Pamela's here?" she asked with insight.

"Yes, and as usual she is trying to stir up controversy. She seems awfully mysterious about something."

"Well, she still has a crush on Clarence. She blames you for stealing him away from under her nose, though she won't admit it. As I always say, if she couldn't keep him on her own, that's no reason to blame you."

Sharlotte felt a pang. She wasn't as certain as Amanda that her reasoning was right. But…"I didn't steal him—" Sharlotte began with a little wince, and Amanda must have seen it, because she hurried on: "Oh well, Sharlotte, let's not worry about *that* now." She glanced off toward the road. "You're going to need even more support. Wait till you hear the news."

Sharlotte bit her lip "Oh dear, what is it?

"Kace has arrived from Texas. I wanted to warn you. He'll be here any moment now. He's driving George's new roadster."

Sharlotte stared at her sister. Blood pounded in her temples and her heart thudded.

"I can't believe it either, but he's here," Amanda said. "He arrived on Long Island last night and came over to the house a few minutes after you and Clarence rode down here. I've no idea why. Daddy insisted he come to the picnic. Daddy's coming too. He's decided to keep the meeting with Mr. Hunnewell at Shrewsbury Landing. It's all a bit daffy, isn't it? Wonder what's going on?"

Kace, here? Even before her wits were in order she heard the sound of a motor.

"Smile," Amanda whispered urgently. "Good luck." And grabbing up her crutches, she stood and slowly began making her way toward the clubhouse. George saw her and left Clarence to help her.

The others were beginning to come out onto the steps to walk down to the jetty to board the sailboat. Amanda called up: "Morning, everyone. Wonderful end-of-the-summer picnic!"

"Looks like rain," Pamela called.

"Pamela—you were in charge of the picnic baskets?"

"Yes, why?"

"You didn't bring those awful cucumber and watercress sandwiches, did you?" Amanda cried.

"No—liverwurst. Why?"

Amanda groaned. "Liverwurst! Now I'd even prefer the cucumber. Maybe we ought to call this whole fiasco off."

"Not on your life, girl," Sheldon called cheerfully, coming down the steps. "Just as long as you remembered to bring what quenches my thirst."

"Not me. George did. He brought boxes of soft drinks in the back of his roadster."

"Soft drinks!"

"There's other stuff too," George said.

"Where's the fancy roadster, George?" Pamela asked.

"Kace Landry's driving it here. Said he was tired of horses. Wanted to try something fast."

"Kace? Oh really! Interesting…" Sheldon looked at his sister on the steps. "So that was your little secret. You knew he was here. Why didn't you tell us?"

Pamela didn't answer. She was looking toward the road.

"That's him now…" Sheldon called to the others.

Amanda glanced back at Sharlotte.

Sharlotte had stood from the bench and was already watching the shiny Niagara Blue roadster approaching. She was remembering the last time she'd seen Kace on the Landry ranch.

Sharlotte's troubled emotions churned with the clouds gathering above the sea. Her mind again went back to Texas, not to the horror of her sister's accident and the hot smell of dust and horses, but to the turbulent memory that surrounded her goodbye to Kace. To this day she could not bear remembering the overwhelming sweet fragrance of the honeysuckle vines that had been their secret sanctuary.

Against her will, Sharlotte was again remembering…

3

Kace Landry was the sort of young man that women were easily smitten by. They found his warm green eyes and dark brown hair irresistible, his independence and restless spirit intriguing. Though his cousin, Tyler, was also attractive, everything about Kace was more noticeable. He could be ardent at times, and maddeningly aloof at others. A girl just never knew where she stood with him. So far, Kace hadn't fallen in love with any of them. At least not for keeps, which was an aspect of his mystique that made him dangerous, but to some women, an interesting challenge.

Sharlotte was now ashamed to admit that when she was younger she had been out to win him just for winning's sake. Capturing Kace's heart each summer, just to break it before she left for New York, had been an exciting game. But he hadn't played seriously enough—at least not until that last summer. By her seventeenth birthday she began to think that she was winning, but it hadn't been as much fun as she had thought. Even when winning, she had discovered that he was still free and wouldn't surrender to her the way others like Clarence had.

Romance was no longer a game she wanted to play with Kace Landry. She wanted life to be safe and predictable—and Kace was neither.

Until recently, Sharlotte had known little about his background, for she had never previously taken the time while visiting Aunt Livia to find out. Then again, they had been so young back then, and the summer month of July too full of discoveries to wade into the distant, murky past. Since then, however, she'd learned from Aunt Livia that Kace was the son of Uncle Sherman's younger brother, Austen. No one apparently knew who his mother was. But after Austen was killed in France during the war, Kace was brought to Texas and placed in a boys' orphanage near the Rio Grande on the outskirts of El Paso. During the next two years, Tyler, the son of Austen's sister, Rose, had become the favored nephew and possibly the heir as Livia and Sherman's only child, a baby girl, had died in her first year. Several years after this disappointment they refused to wait any longer. Sherman wanted sons, strong ones, so he made the decision to go to El Paso to get his late brother's illegitimate boy. When he arrived at the orphanage, he learned that Kace had run away. Sherman found him working in a cantina and brought him to the Landry ranch on family probation where he worked as a hand with the cattle and horses.

Surprisingly, Kace had gradually won Sherman's heart and was brought into the house where, at Aunt Livia's insistence, he began taking his meals with the rest of the family. He was given a room next to Tyler's, which immediately produced rivalry, and at times, skirmishes, but by the time Sharlotte arrived for her first summer visit the boys had bonded as brothers and turned their attention on their "funny and strange-speaking cousin from the East."

Sharlotte had long been expected to make the trip West to visit her father's sister, Livia, even though she had heard most of her life about the terrible mistake Livia had made by leaving the esteemed Ashford family to marry Sherman Landry. Naturally,

Sharlotte hadn't wanted to go to Texas, but regardless of the Ashford family's disinheritance of Livia, Sharlotte's father had quietly kept up a relationship with his younger sister, unconventional though her life may have been in his eyes. Burgess rarely mentioned his contact with Livia to the others in the family, especially Great-Uncle Hubert Ashford. Still, he made certain that Sharlotte and Amanda went to the Landry ranch in West Texas each summer.

As Sharlotte grew into her mid-teens she protested these summer trips as a "horrendous waste of her life" and persuaded her father to shorten her visits to one month instead of all summer. "The people there are uncultured," she had said, "and Uncle Sherman's cattle and horse business is smelly and undignified."

The only time Sharlotte and Amanda appreciated a cow was at a Texas barbecue, and even then it wasn't the civilized picnic she and her sister were accustomed to. The dinners were rowdy and there was too much food. Instead of sandwiches with the crusts cut away, there were large slabs of smoking meat at burning temperatures. Even under the oak trees it was hot, with thousands of flies. Sharlotte had even seen tarantulas and rattlesnakes. And the people were too loud, the chili and Mexican tamales had too much hot pepper, and the servants, all Spanish-speaking, were simply too different.

One thing Sharlotte and Amanda did like was the attention they were getting. Sharlotte was accustomed to being treated with deference, and the more special the treatment, the more delightsome life became. She had brought an extravagant feminine wardrobe and secretly enjoyed the surprised glances she would get from Kace and Tyler when she came down to breakfast or dinner in one of her expensive little gowns.

In New York she would never have accepted the attention of the sons of Texas ranchers, but while visiting far from home, she had. It had all seemed amusing and harmless to her and Amanda.

Sharlotte and Amanda had traveled to Texas thereafter, spending a dreadful six weeks each July and early August. Sharlotte had complained the most, especially in front of Kace. As far as she was concerned, July was the hottest, dustiest, most disagreeable month in Texas. And whenever she compared the Texas ranch to Edgartown or Martha's Vineyard, she disliked everything about it. She had especially been nettled by Kace, because he'd flat out told her she could have Martha's Vineyard and her daddy's summerhouse, that he wouldn't go there if she begged him to come. Naturally, she had wanted to prove to him that her life was better, that his life was "poor and cracker." And on and on the feud had grown until she suddenly decided that Kace was the cutest boy she'd ever seen. From then on she had wanted to win him, plain and simple—but on her terms. She was the special one, he was an outcast. As long as he recognized that distinction, she was willing to flatter Kace by making him her first love. But Kace, having his own ideas added to Texas pride, had insisted she come off her "high horse" and admit she wasn't superior at all.

She thought of the first time she met Kace and Tyler on a bright, hot July morning.

"Well, girls," Sherman had said to Sharlotte and Amanda, "these are your new cousins."

Sharlotte had tried not to show her disdain in front of her uncle. They were no cousins of hers. No indeed, nor would they be! She had scanned them. They weren't much older than she. They were, as uncle Sherman bragged, "the finest-looking young bucks in the county you ever laid eyes on," but Sharlotte was not impressed. The two Landry boys looked at each other while she stood eying them, licking her lollipop—a very large one her father had given her before the long, arduous trip on the train. She immediately sensed rejection. Tyler had grinned mischievously, and Kace, sitting on the porch rail, studied her as though she were a frog.

Amanda had been the one to reach out. "What's your name?" she had asked Kace.

He had smiled. "Kace."

"Kace Ashford?"

"No. Just Kace."

"He's got no last name," Sharlotte had said. "He came from a poor school by the border of Mexico."

He had looked at her. Even then, his eyes could be a hard green.

"Can you ride that horse, Kace?" Amanda asked.

"No, he can't ride," Tyler had said. "But I can."

"'Course I can ride," Kace said. "I've even tamed a horse once."

"All I get to ride is a pony with a tether," Amanda said. "We go round and round a pole."

"That's sissy stuff," Tyler had said.

"No it isn't," Sharlotte spoke up.

"Yes it is," Kace said. "Only girls from the East ride a tethered pony round and round a silly pole. I feel sorry for the horse to have to put up with it."

"Are you really our cousins?" Amanda asked.

"No," Sharlotte said in a snippy voice. "That one on the porch is low-class trash. I heard the governess, Miss Hopper, say so on the way down here." And she made a face at Kace and crossed her eyes.

Kace had slipped down from the rail and walked toward her. "You're a snooty little brat, you know that?"

"No I'm not. I'm a good girl. But you're a bad little boy. Miss Hopper said so, and I don't like you—ow! You pulled my hair."

"I didn't pull it. I was just looking at it."

At first he had ignored her. Tyler was anxious to begin a verbal exchange, but Kace had tried to stop him.

"She'll be going back home where she belongs soon. She's only a snob. Forget her, Ty."

His indifferent response to her barbs only provoked her. "You're worse than those funny-looking Indians we saw on the train with hats and Mexican ponchos. You're probably a half-breed."

But once she had broken through his barrier of restraint, Sharlotte found no peace. Kace looked behind him toward the house to see if a beaming Uncle Sherman was looking on. He had gone inside. He looked at her and smiled. "Hey Ty, I know just the thing to do with bratty little rich girls."

"Yeah?" Tyler said, his blue eyes shining. "What, Kace, what?"

"Dunk her in that horse trough yonder."

Tyler doubled over with laughter.

"Oh—" cried Sharlotte," her violet-blue eyes narrowing. "If you ruin my dress I'll—"

He grabbed her, and before she knew it, drug her to the trough and tossed her in. It was only a few feet deep, but Sharlotte could still recall the horror of the cold stinky water seeping into her eyes, nose, and mouth, and she could still hear his laughter as she sat up with her dress floating on the surface like a balloon.

Thereafter, the only time she found herself safe from his taunts was in the presence of Uncle Sherman or Aunt Livia, when Kace behaved the perfect young gentleman. Once, even at breakfast, Sharlotte was greeted with a toad on her covered plate, though Kace vowed to Sherman he hadn't done it, but Tyler. One night he had placed a tarantula under her pillow—just so he could make her scream. But she refused to surrender. In private she lashed him with barbs and often got the best of Tyler, but her usual tactics didn't seem to work with Kace. "Ignore her, Ty. She isn't half as nice as the girls at Pastor McCrae's church. Clothes don't make a lady."

His condescension troubled her even more than the horse trough. Then, as suddenly as the childhood war games had begun, they ended as Kace and Tyler reached their early teens and were sent to fine schools in Virginia. When they returned one summer she found them restrained from their malicious behavior and gentlemanly in the extreme, and even more handsome than the boys back home.

Sharlotte was now a fashionable young girl, and instead of making faces, she had discovered the wonderful world of feminine wiles to get the best of them. It not only worked better, but turned out to be intriguing, especially with Kace.

Between themselves, Kace and Tyler had agreed that Sharlotte had emerged as the prettiest thing they had ever laid eyes on.

"Still an insufferable brat," seventeen-year-old Kace had said, "but a beautiful one."

He had summed up the situation quite well for Tyler.

Sharlotte was smugly satisfied to learn this. What insults she had endured from them! What misery from Kace's boyhood jokes! Now Tyler was easily defeated with a dimpled smile and a flapper dress. Kace wasn't quite so easy to topple. He was on guard as the dangers of warfare changed from dunks and tarantulas to sweet smiles and fluttering lashes. The war came to a head on her seventeenth birthday when she firmly made up her mind that Kace would fall in love with her.

"Oh, you're not so bad," she had told Tyler and Kace. "A little education in Virginia seems to have tamed your rebel spirits. Mind you, Virginia isn't Boston, and all the boys I know are *real* gentlemen with lots of money and good blood, but you're endurable, at least for the month of July."

But she had smiled sweetly and laughed when she said it so that her dimples and violet-blue eyes would magically remove the sting from her words. When she directed her charms toward Tyler, he seemed willing to become deaf to the sense of her words. Just to sit with such a lovely girl and talk during the warm Texas nights, or escort her to a dance at one of the other ranch houses, was enough.

Kace, however, whom she later learned had been going to see the pastor's daughter, Elly McCrae, had unexpectedly backed off.

This puzzled her, and when she asked Tyler about Elly, he had shrugged.

"Elly's a sweet girl. She's aiming to help her father teach Bible stories with the children at church. I guess Kace is pretty impressed with her character. Can't blame him. He's been seeing her ever since he came home from Richmond."

Sharlotte lapsed into silence. She decided to go to church that next Sunday morning to take a closer look at Elly. But Elly had been ill and Sharlotte was forced to listen to Pastor McCrae preach about sin and the need for Christ's forgiveness. Sharlotte felt terribly guilty. On the way home a small voice seemed to question what she'd heard: *Your father doesn't believe in God, why should you? Remember when he removed the only Bible from the house and said that faith was for weak people who don't know any better? Your father is rich. The Ashford name is mentioned among the elite families in the East. Surely your father is wiser than this poor preacher or the hillbilly Landrys! Don't listen to them. Listen to Burgess Ashford II.*

This wasn't the first time that Sharlotte had attended Pastor McCrae's little church or heard about Jesus. Every summer she stayed in Texas Uncle Sherman had taught them Bible stories and insisted she and Amanda go with the family to Sunday school. Sharlotte hadn't minded; it gave her an opportunity to wear her prettiest dresses and flirt with the boys. Not one of the ranchers' daughters wore anything as stylish as she and Amanda, and there was one girl who even wore an old-fashioned calico dress made from flour sacks.

Although Sharlotte was curious about Elly, she was more curious about why Kace would be attracted to her. She didn't have nice clothes, and she certainly didn't go to Vassar College or have a family name like the Ashfords. Sharlotte's vanity was injured, and capturing Kace before she went home became her most important goal for the summer.

Amanda, now a pretty and mature fifteen, had joined her in this enterprise, and the two of them had whirled their way through barbecues, dances, and rides in the country beneath the starry Texas sky. Sharlotte had dressed up all summer, showing herself superior to all of the ranchers' daughters who wisely wore shirts and pants when working about their father's stables. Later Sharlotte had learned through Tyler that Kace had told him he thought she was enough girl to take his breath away. That was all she needed to know.

"There's a dance this Friday night at the Nelson ranch," Tyler had said on Wednesday after supper when the four of them were out front of the huge white ranch house.

Sharlotte had already known about the dance. Aunt Livia had mentioned it to her that morning, and Sharlotte had innocently inquired whether Kace would be going to bring Elly. Livia had said she didn't know, that he hadn't mentioned it.

"Sherman got the new Spanish mustangs this morning, and Kace is so busy with them that I don't think he plans to go at all," Livia had told her.

"Aunt Livia seems to think one of you should escort me to the dance," Sharlotte said, smiling at her cousin.

"Obviously me," Tyler said cheerfully.

Sharlotte glanced beneath her lashes toward Kace. He had been mostly silent all evening, and was sitting on the railing.

"What about taking me," Amanda said.

"Oh, well you're included," Tyler hastened. "The first and last waltz is mine, honey."

Amanda scowled and spoke as Sharlotte had asked her to earlier: "But you already asked me, Tyler. At least I was sure you had. Now I won't have anyone to go with."

Silence. Sharlotte glanced toward Kace. She fanned herself. "Too bad Kace is taking Elly—he could bring you, Amanda," Sharlotte said innocently.

Kace said nothing.

"But Tyler already asked me," Amanda pretended to be hurt.

"I did? Well…sure I will, Amanda. I was just teasing Sharlotte."

"But now Sharlotte won't have anyone to take her," Amanda said and looked at Kace.

Sharlotte lifted her fan to cover her smile and avoided looking at Kace.

"Maybe Kace could take Sharlotte," Amanda said.

"Kace is taking Elly," Tyler said. "He and Elly are as good as engaged, so that's out, even if Elly is sick tonight."

Engaged…Sharlotte felt a strange, sickening plop in her stomach. She looked at Kace.

Kace smiled at Tyler and rose to his feet. "Don't believe him. It's Tyler who is almost engaged—to Abby Hutchins."

"No, I haven't decided," Tyler said, glancing hurriedly toward Amanda.

"My, you two have been busy," Sharlotte said, trying to keep her voice casual. She felt frustrated and even angry. "Aren't you both rather young to make up your minds so quickly?"

"We marry young in Texas," Tyler said with a grin.

"If Abby finds out you're flirting with Amanda, you'll be in deep trouble," Kace goaded Tyler.

Tyler glared at him. "What do you mean? I did no such thing."

"Better make up your mind," Kace teased him as he went down the porch steps. "I have to check on those mustangs. Good night."

He's retreating, Sharlotte thought, lashes narrowing. As he walked away, she sat listening to his fading footsteps in the hot night. A sense of disaster enveloped her. She sat in strained silence while Amanda chattered to Tyler. After fifteen minutes Sharlotte stood up from the wicker chair and stretched as if tired and sleepy. She faked a yawn, then murmured that she'd had enough Texas moonlight and was going inside.

But after she'd made certain no one noticed, she slipped out the backdoor and took the long path toward the stables.

She found Kace inside with one of the new horses. He was still in his white shirt and dark trousers from the dinner hour. Aunt Livia always insisted the family dress up for the evening meal, one of her very few holdovers from being raised in the Ashford family.

"You'll get your nice clothes soiled fooling with that horse," Sharlotte told him.

"You sound like Aunt Livia. Better stay by the door," he stated, not looking up, but cautiously touching the mane of the mustang. The beautiful animal was still nervous and whinnied, throwing up his head.

"Is he wild?" she breathed.

"Just needs the right handler. He'll calm down after a few weeks. I've tamed wilder horses than this one."

She was impressed. "Have you? I'm not afraid of horses. I've had the best riding instructor in Maryland. I want to come closer."

He hesitated. "Seems like you've had the best of everything."

His remark set her off guard. "I suppose I have," she admitted.

He smiled. "All right, but approach slowly. No sudden movements, and keep your voice soft."

Sharlotte *was* afraid but pretended differently. She wondered if Elly was afraid of horses. Probably not. Elly was one of those girls who appeared to have been raised right. She had lots of charm and confidence, which seemed unusual because she had few earthly goods. The paradox bewildered Sharlotte.

Sharlotte walked slowly toward the stall. It was the first time she had ever known what it was like to be envious of another girl. That Kace spent so much time at her residence nibbled at her heart. Was it pride, or did she really care?

"He's magnificent," she whispered, taking in the shiny mane, the flashing eyes.

The mustang snorted, his nostrils flared. Kace slowly closed the stall door for safety and they edged away.

"That's enough taming for tonight," he said.

After a moment she looked at Kace. She found his direct gaze troubling and couldn't seem to think of anything witty to say.

"Why did you come here?" he asked.

She shrugged easily. "To see the horse."

He was smiling now, watching her with that very straight, disconcerting look of his.

For once she read it for what it was, a challenge, and accepted.

"You spend so much time with horses and cattle, how do you find time to court Elly?"

There was only a slight alteration to the look he gave her. The silence grew uncomfortable, and she was sure he felt it too. It seemed they were avoiding each other, as though afraid of something.

"Who told you about Elly?"

"Tyler mentioned her."

He smiled. "Has he married me off to her yet?"

"Something like that. He intimated that you were impressed by her."

"I see. And you're curious. Why?"

She flushed, but tried to avoid being cornered. She laughed. "All girls are fiercely curious about such things."

"Are they?"

"You know that. It's a weakness of ours. That, and what the bride will wear."

"Is that the only reason? Curiosity about my schedule and bridal gowns?"

She smiled, this time refusing his challenge. "What else would it be?" she said evasively.

His green eyes were amused, and yet, somehow serious. "I could think of a few things."

She returned the look he gave her. "Only a few?"

"Why did you come this summer? You didn't have to. You hate Texas and you're old enough now to refuse your father. He doesn't seem to concern himself all that much with your plans anymore, except with whom you'll marry."

"I don't know why I came. This may be my last summer here. Maybe I just wanted to…to say goodbye to everyone for the last time. It hasn't been all that bad, not really."

"You're being generous," he said with teasing gravity.

"I know I sound like a snob. I can't help it."

"I think you can. You'll need to make up your own mind about your values. You'll soon be all grown up. It won't be what the Ashfords think anymore, but what Sharlotte thinks that matters."

"You must have learned that from Elly's father."

"You're being evasive."

"Why did I come this summer? Maybe to find out something important."

"Is that why you came here tonight?"

The laugh in his eyes died away. And Sharlotte felt the mask drop from her face. The wind had picked up and sent a scattering of gravel against the side of the stable. A sudden, unexplainable panic seized her heart. "Oh!" She turned. "I must go now." She was running outside. She didn't look at him. "Good night, Kace." Her steps quickened across the soft new straw on the ground.

Kace left the mustang and followed her out into the windy night, the moon as bright as silver shining down over the Texas landscape. He turned, closed the door, and bolted it.

For a moment they stood together, then he took her hand and they walked through the orchard to Aunt Livia's arbor. Wrapped in the dense fragrance of honeysuckle, warmed by the prairie wind, and illuminated by the full moon, he took her into his arms. He held her tightly, sending her heart thudding.

"Does this answer your question?" he murmured and then his lips were on hers. A low roaring in her ears seemed to send her into a dizzying spin.

A voice could be heard in the near distance. It was Aunt Livia from somewhere on the front porch calling: "Sharlotte, honey, are you out there? Better come inside. It's ten o'clock. Sharlotte? It's time for prayers. And if you see Kace, tell him to come too. We're all waiting!"

It took all of their wills to tear apart. Gasping, Sharlotte stared at him, backing away, and then she turned and fled from the honeysuckle toward the sweet, wise voice of Aunt Livia and the open door above the porch.

~

What had begun as simply escorting her to the Friday night dance grew steadily through the weeks of outings and barbecues. Sharlotte had planned on a simple, uninvolved summer romance that would inevitably end when she packed her trunk and boarded the train. She had not intended to come back to Texas. And, naturally, she could never marry someone like Kace, not when it was her father's will and her family duty to marry her "own kind of people." She thought Kace understood that it must be that way. Goodbye was the only sensible way their brief infatuation could possibly end. So she had thought.

But Kace didn't see it that way. And Sharlotte found that the longer their relationship went on, the more intense it became. She was discovering that goodbye was not going to be as easy as she had thought. Her game had turned upon herself. Kace wasn't a young man she could easily forget. Though he was enamored with her, she didn't have the upper hand she thought an Ashford should have. He was just as independent and opinionated as ever. When he engaged her in debate he usually won, which left her pride badly wounded.

While Sharlotte was willing to enjoy his attention, she always knew it must eventually end. However, she wouldn't tell all this to Kace until the end of July, just a few days before she and Amanda would catch the train home, where they would spend the rest of their summer on Long Island.

The day before she left she gave him back the school ring he had given her weeks earlier.

"You're not being fair, Sharlotte."

She knew that now and avoided his gaze. "Surely you knew this had to be," she said defensively.

"I thought you'd see the truth and have the courage to act upon it."

"I don't know what you mean."

"I think you do. You'll be leaving tomorrow, and you're just now telling me we will end it here and never see each other again?"

She had steeled herself against the emotion of this moment and refused to face it. "You knew what's expected of me. I'll soon be finishing up at Vassar. I have a longtime obligation to become engaged to someone who is approved of by my father and great-uncle. I've always meant to marry my own kind."

"Well if you still do, you've recently kept it from me."

"I thought you knew!"

"Knew what, that you were only interested in playing a summertime game?"

"Something like that," she said flatly. "Besides, did I ever promise anything? And have you? Well? Have you?"

"I thought that's what we were doing each time you allowed me to kiss you. I guess you really didn't mean it. And I allowed myself to become gullible."

She turned her head away, furious with herself and him. Why had she done it? "I...I did mean it," she said softly.

"For a season," he said coldly. "And to think I was fool enough to trust my heart to you, to hurt Elly because I believed you were playing for keeps."

"Now you're being unfair, Kace. What we had for so short a time obviously couldn't last between us."

"Why couldn't it, Sharlotte?" He held her by the shoulders so she had to look into his eyes. Now she felt a wave of regret, of more pain than she had thought she could ever feel. She had been the fool, not him. He had believed in her and she had crushed the beauty of that first love.

"I...I can't be like Livia," she whispered.

"Because you don't love me, Sharlotte?"

The look in his eyes was breaking her heart. She dropped her forehead against his chest. She shook her head silently. "I don't know. My family's wishes are very important," she said in a tight voice. "I've always been honest about that."

"Yes, you have told me, with childish insults when you first arrived, and with aristocratic rejection now."

"I...I didn't mean to hurt you, Kace, honest I didn't. I...I wanted you to want me, to love me—" her voice cracked.

"You couldn't stand it if a man didn't, is that it? You couldn't stand for me to turn to Elly. And yet when you saw that I turned away from her for you—it didn't register upon your heart that I was playing for keeps?"

"No, no! At first that was how I felt, but later—"

"So you didn't want to hurt me?"

"No, oh no, I didn't—"

"I don't believe you, Sharlotte."

He was so matter of fact that she looked up at him, stunned. The look in his eyes did more to make her draw back, loathing her own actions, than anything he could have said.

"You're still the same spoiled brat."

"Please, Kace, don't be that way. I could—we could never marry even if I wanted to, and you know that. I don't fit here in your life, and you don't fit in mine. Except for an attraction...we share so little in common."

"I don't believe that either. If I did, I'd never have allowed this to happen. I thought you'd grow up."

Grow up. In place of pain came anger. "And I suppose Elly is grown up?"

"Yes, she is. You're both the same age and she's twice the woman you are. She's mature, sensible. Even now, after I've treated her shamefully, she's willing to take me back, while you turn your back and return to your shallow, ritzy parties."

"Oh, is that right? And just how do you know what she'll do if you haven't already been seeing her behind my back?"

"Come off it, Sharlotte. Naturally I see her. She's the pastor's daughter.

"And you dare call me unfair?"

"Yes. Elly has never been mean-spirited about you, though she had a right to be."

"Well, that was very good of her," she said tartly. "So you think she's better than me?"

"She's dedicated to the purposes of God. I thought you at least believed, but now I wonder. Looks like I've been wrong about too many things. I wasn't careful."

She turned her back, troubled by more than their parting, more than about Elly. She didn't know if she believed or not…

"You knew as well as I that it would end between us, Kace, so don't pretend I'm the only one to blame. We both knew we'd have to forget a lot of things when the summer ended. But I didn't think it would end this way."

"No, you thought you could have your 'fun' with no responsibility, that you could walk away freely without feeling guilt."

"That isn't all true."

"How did you want it to end?"

"I—I don't know. Friends, I suppose—with memories to take with me into life."

"Memories," he said dryly.

She whirled, tears in her eyes. "Yes, memories."

"Memories to keep while you return to your *dignified* life and marry someone you really don't love but is *right* for you? So that in later years you can look back and remember what love was really like?"

She turned away again. "Yes," she barely breathed. "Something like that."

"Then, Sharlotte Ashford, you're a fool." He turned her around to face him, his eyes blazing.

"Fool or not, my mind's made up. I'm going! And I can't see you again, Kace, not ever." She tore away, looking at him sorrowfully. "I'm sorry… I wish you'd believe that. I *have* done some growing up this summer, Kace. I wish you'd believe that," she repeated. "If I'd known a few weeks ago what I do now, I'd never have let this happen. I'd never want for you to care."

"Thanks, but it's too late."

"Oh, Kace…"

He looked at her uncertainly. There was a sadness, a sincerity in his face that twisted her heart.

"Goodbye," he said, and he turned and walked away.

She looked after him. *No!* She took several steps in his direction, her heart aching, for she did love him in her own way. She wanted to call out—I love you, Kace, I could adore you. But her lips were cold and silent, and he was already gone. Youth had loved but a short time, had loved, had parted. It would never be the same for either of them.

When Sharlotte arrived home at Long Island the rest of summer rolled by as though it were a dream. She would wake up at two in the morning and think of Kace. In the fall she returned to Vassar College. Aunt Livia continued to write about the goings on at the ranch, but she would usually skip these portions of her long, diary-like letters to read the sections dealing with Kace and Tyler. Tyler was helping his uncle run the huge cattle business and seeing Abby Hutchins; but Kace had packed up and left. He was drifting, Livia wrote. He had gone into Mexico with friends to do some oil exploration. Then, a year later, Sharlotte heard from her aunt that Kace was back again, and he and his friends were forming some sort of company and hoping to buy oil land.

Sharlotte wrote secretly to Livia asking in a roundabout way whether or not Kace was still seeing Elly. Livia wrote that Elly was in correspondence with him, and that if she wished to know anything about what Kace was doing now, that Elly was the person to ask. Naturally, Sharlotte had not written to Elly. Then, as the New Year of 1929 rang in, and Sharlotte graduated from Vassar and began her coming out extravaganza, she sent all of her photographs and newspaper pictures to Livia. Livia wrote telling her that they had arrived just in time for her to show to her Texas "cousins." Tyler had been quite taken by them, Livia wrote, but Kace had made no comment.

"Kace is working long days with the handful of partners in the little company they started over a year ago. Two of the men want out, and Kace is looking for businessmen to buy in."

Sharlotte found all this interesting, but the last line of Aunt Livia's letter rankled her nerves: "Elly is such a sweet, Christian girl. She's so supportive of Kace in everything he's hoping to accomplish. Kace is very protective of her. He loves her so much."

Sharlotte got up from the bed emotionally stunned. She crumpled the letter and tossed it into the wastebasket. By now she should have forgotten all about Kace, but the fact was, she hadn't.

Sharlotte turned to go downstairs and caught sight of her flushed cheeks and gleaming violet-blue eyes in the mirror. Her own image shocked her.

Why, you're jealous, Sharlotte Ashford, she thought, surprised.

Sharlotte was burdened by a sense of disaster. So he was seeing "wonderful little Elly," was he? Well, that news shouldn't surprise her. He'd been going with her off and on since they were sixteen. *But he doesn't love her*, she thought firmly. *He couldn't. He loved me once, enough to walk away from Elly. He couldn't have forgotten me all that quickly, could he?*

"Oh, Kace! Kace!" she whispered, and her heart ached. She walked dazed to the window of her Vermont home as the snow came down white and glistening in the moonlight, bathing everything with purity. She leaned there, hurting, yet fully aware she had no right to be hurt, no reason to feel loss this painfully. She had made her choice. There was no turning back now. Regrets could not change the past, nor could they reach out and arrange the future. Sharlotte looked out and saw a servant coming across the front yard of virgin white. He stamped his boots on the walk and came indoors, but left behind his footprints in the new-fallen snow. In the distance she heard the bells of Christmas ringing from the small New England church. Soon afterward came a group of carolers. Their sweet voices drifted to her through the icy windowpane with words of invitation from "It Came Upon a Midnight Clear":

> All ye, beneath life's crushing load,
> Whose forms are bending low,
> Who toil along the climbing way
> With painful steps and slow,
> Look now! for glad and golden hours
> Come swiftly on the wing:
> O rest beside the weary road
> And hear the angels sing.

4

But all that was in the past, and now Sharlotte stood outside the yacht club and watched as Kace drove George's shiny roadster into the club drive. Kace looked toward the clubhouse and removed his sunglasses. Sharlotte's heart gave a dreadful lurch as their gazes met. That look had once been disconcerting, and it was no less so now as the same feelings came rushing back to her like the hot, dry Texas whirlwinds, bewildering her. She pushed a windblown strand of hair away from her face.

Now she knew why Pamela had asked if she'd invited her Texas cousins to the ball tonight! Pamela must have known Kace was here, yet she hadn't come out and said so. How had she known before anyone else? More importantly, what had brought Kace to Long Island? Neither he nor Tyler had ever been to the Ashford estate before. *It must be my soon engagement to Clarence,* she thought.

There was trouble ahead. Sharlotte could feel the emotions crackling in the air. Worst of all she could feel it in her own heart as it thudded, and she realized she was staring too long at Kace. He was watching her with calm scrutiny, and his masculine confidence was having its effect. Unlike the comfort she felt with Clarence, she became flustered.

Kace got out and walked around to the trunk. George went to meet him to ask how he liked driving his roadster. Sharlotte didn't move and was calling on all her learned social proprieties so that she could appear calm and collected.

Clarence had come up beside her, and she wondered if he could sense the troubling emotions that radiated about them. He too watched Kace as if he'd begun to realize that this exceptional-looking young Texan with dark green eyes was a rival, not a cousin. Sharlotte thought words had formed on Clarence's lips so that she could just barely make them out: "Over my dead body."

She turned and looked at him sharply, then became bewildered. His face showed nothing, and she thought she must have imagined that he'd spoken.

Sharlotte took hold of his arm, speaking a little too tensely: "Clarence darling, I've just learned from Amanda that Daddy is coming on the picnic after all. I promised him I'd make Mr. Hunnewell comfortable—and there he is now, down on the jetty. Would you tell him Daddy's on his way?" Clarence looked away from studying Kace Landry toward the wooden jetty where sailboats waited at anchor. He shaded his eyes.

"Very well," he said reluctantly.

"I'll be around here," she said. "I need to find out from Amanda what she did with the case of bottles and soft drinks."

She didn't think anyone else had heard her, but Kace spoke up matter of factly: "Is this what you're looking for? There's a box of bottles back here."

She felt the heat rise in her cheeks. Forced to turn and face him, she found him standing at the back of the motorcar, its trunk lifted. She scanned the six-footer with the firm, muscled body dressed in casual clothes. He seemed comfortable seeing her again. Much more so than Sharlotte felt in his presence.

"Where do you want me to put them?" he asked almost too helpfully, a smile in his resonant voice.

Fearing she was the object of everyone's watchful stare, Sharlotte mustered her sagging courage and walked to the back of the car. She looked gravely at the goods piled in the trunk.

Sharlotte felt his gaze, but stared at the boxes of bottles as if she'd never seen them before. The moment of silence lingered, torturously long.

"Hello, Sharlotte."

"You shouldn't have come," she whispered. "There's nothing you can say to change family plans. Daddy expects me to marry Clarence Fosdick. It's all but settled."

He had the nerve to laugh. Sharlotte wanted to squirm as every head turned in their direction with speculative interest. She was glad Clarence had already left.

"Dear Sharlotte," Kace said. "As spoiled and self-centered as ever."

She was taken aback. "I am not!"

"Then why jump to the conclusion that I'm here to see you?"

His blunt question stunned her. She turned to look directly at him for the first time. Her bewilderment arose from more than peering into the warm depths of his eyes. His gaze seemed to threaten the undoing of her private, comfortable world as a grumble of thunder sounded out at sea where clouds gathered.

"I assumed—" she began, then faltered as the warmth stole up into her cheeks.

Kace wore a slight smile. "How quickly the things we think we want when standing beneath a honeysuckle vine melt away with boredom as we mature," he said lazily. "So much for young, boyish love."

Stung, she didn't know what to say. Boredom!

She searched his eyes. They refused her admittance. "Are you saying that you don't…ca…" she couldn't bring herself to say the words.

Kace appeared as calm and controlled as though he'd been discussing nothing more emotional than the weather. "Why should it matter? Was that the noble Clarence Fosdick by your side?"

"Yes…"

"Are you disappointed I didn't come to plead?"

"Two years *is* a long time," she floundered, "but you did tell me on that last night that you cared—" she added with emphasis, "deeply."

A flicker stirred in his eyes. Her assertion broadened his amused smile. "Am I to understand you grieve over the loss of my ardor because of some deep emotional need, or because your vanity abhors losing an admirer?"

"Don't be presumptuous." His suggestion seemed dangerously close to the truth. But if he hadn't come to attempt to dissuade her from marrying Clarence, then why?

"Did you think I've been lamenting my loss for the last two years while wandering the wastelands of Mexico and Texas?" he goaded.

She looked at him cautiously. Kace watched the heightening color in her cheeks with matter-of-fact interest.

"What a child you are, Sharlotte," he said thoughtfully. "I've a notion you don't know what you want in life. You're a slave to what's expected of you."

Slave! She ruffled indignantly. No one of her wealth and position was ever in slavery.

"Well, someday you're going to have to discover your own heart and grow up."

That he thought she might not be grown up riled her. She did know what she wanted. And just because she found Kace attractive didn't mean that he was the right man for marriage. Kace wasn't like Clarence. She and Clarence understood the same things. Kace was a foreigner to her world. What's more, he laughed at and demeaned her family.

For a moment she mistook the glimmer in his gaze for pity and it angered her. "Are you saying you haven't thought about me since that night?" she whispered heatedly, unable to keep silent gracefully. She had given him much thought, more than she would admit—and she had expected it to be mutual. But Kace was admitting to nothing now, and behaving as casual and indifferent as a cold fish.

"That enamored boy under the honeysuckle no longer exists. Elly and I are going to become engaged soon."

Abashed, Sharlotte said in a small voice: "Oh!" What she wanted to say was: "But you can't." She realized just in time how foolish it would sound to him when she became engaged herself. It would strengthen his conviction that she was indeed frivolous. Was she a spoiled child? With a trunkload of toys, refusing to give one up? So, she was spoiled, was she! Or was she merely trapped because she was an Ashford?

She had no hold on him now, she reminded herself. She had said her goodbye two years ago and walked away. It was the only thing she could have done under the circumstances, and yet…was she being immature and unfair to think she could hold onto him just because—her mind fumbled. Because of what? If she truly cared about Kace wouldn't she want him free of her so he could marry Elly and have a happy life of his own? But she didn't want him to marry Elly.

She stood looking at him. He watched her face with interest.

Murmuring voices could be heard behind them discussing whether they should even risk the picnic now that thunder had been rumbling over the sea. Suddenly the picnic didn't matter. Nothing mattered. The sun had disappeared behind the clouds.

Sharlotte was so upset by Kace's presence that she could think of nothing to say. *Soon…he was going to marry Elly.*

She felt foolish, believing she had misread that look he'd given her when he first arrived in the roadster. Or perhaps he still found her attractive even though he loved Elly. She realized something else: how shallow attraction was from a man when it was only physical. She suddenly, almost fiercely, envied Elly and yearned for the concern and kindness that Kace poured upon her. She wanted Kace to think of her that way. Instead, he thought her vain and shallow…but pretty. Elly had depth and character and sweetness—and she, Sharlotte, had none.

She fought hard to contain her outward demeanor while her heart demanded release for pent-up emotion. She couldn't let Kace know how much the news about Elly hurt. She became aware that he was watching her alertly. His eyes softened a little and he looked as though he wanted to say something, but Sharlotte swallowed hard and rallied.

She lifted her chin. "Well, I hope you'll be happy. She'll fit your lifestyle sufficiently. All she knows is that little church, and—" she stopped, for she found she really didn't mean what she was saying, and she was certain Kace would know. She turned to walk away. Kace's word's stopped her dead.

"I know it must wound your pride to learn you are not the cause for my being here, but you needn't attack Elly."

Her nails dug into her palms but she kept her rigid back toward him. Had he seen her face, he would have been moved by the paleness that came with the crushing pain piercing her soul. *He doesn't know. Kace thinks he knows me, but he really doesn't. Until now, I haven't even understood myself.* She was thankful he couldn't see into her heart.

Kace lowered his voice. "I came to see your father on business and got lassoed into hauling some picnic items up here to the club. Then your father decided it was best if we all came on this outing planned by your cousins. Because I need to see him and Hunnewell, I agreed."

She turned slowly to look at him again, her face revealing nothing of the depth of her emotions. He too was unreadable.

"Surely you're jesting about meeting my father and Mr. Hunnewell."

"He's coming to the picnic, isn't he?"

"Well, yes, but to see his lawyer. Not you."

"Maybe I should say Hunnewell *was* his lawyer."

Odd that he would say that. "Mr. Hunnewell's been working for my father for most of my life. Not only that, but they're friends."

Kace didn't explain. "I know this will rankle you, but I've come to meet with both men at your father's request."

This news was so uncharacteristic of her view of Kace that it jarred her. "What business could you possibly have with my father?"

"Debt resolution," he drawled silkily.

Sharlotte felt she understood, and was now less on the defensive, thinking of her father's generosity to keep the Landry ranch operating in the black. Little had changed, after all. Uncle Sherman must have sent Kace.

Sharlotte smiled ruefully. "So Sheldon was right."

Kace looked interested. "What did your cousin tell you?"

"Oh, just that my father—whom you tend to scorn in spite of his business savvy—is the helping hand you depend upon to bail your uncle out of his financial woes. How like the less fortunate to berate the wealthy, yet look who you turn to when in need. He's lending money for Livia's sake, of course. I suppose you've been sent to arrange for delayed payments?"

She meant to goad him, because he had so hurt her, and was surprised when she saw him suppressing a smile.

"Ah yes, the generous hand of the benevolent Ashfords. However, I wouldn't pay all that much attention to what Sheldon may have told you. He drinks too much and his world consists of his yacht. He doesn't have all the facts. It's your father who is in debt," he said, watching her expression, "to me."

"To *you!*" The notion was absurd. Kace wasn't smiling now, however.

"Yes. And to our oil exploration team."

She had fully intended to laugh at his preposterous joke. Her father owed *him*? It was like Kace to tease her. Instead, she felt vaguely frightened, not knowing why. The confidence she had marshaled had dissolved. How and why would her father owe him, of all people?

"I don't believe you. It can't be true."

"Life does have its surprises, doesn't it?" he said wryly. "And its disappointments. Even for the rich."

Yes, he appeared quite serious. So much so that Sharlotte again found herself on a crumbling foundation. Could he possibly be just enjoying this absurdity?

"Disturbing, I know," he said. "The fact that Burgess Ashford II owes me a sum that he is unable to pay is unnerving."

Unable to pay? Sharlotte couldn't even imagine what it was like to have a second thought about the cost of anything she ever wanted. The Ashfords could go anywhere, and just on their name alone have anything they wanted. She never carried much cash. There was no need. Her life consisted of accounts, and businessmen smiling and treating her with a tender hand, giving her and Amanda anything from dinner to a new outfit to wear to the beach.

"Can't pay?" she laughed. "Kace, you are amusing."

"I'm not here to entertain you, Sharlotte. If you care to learn more, you'd best discuss it with your father or his lawyer." He straightened from where he'd been leaning against the trunk and looked toward the jetty. "Where's Hunnewell now?"

"I don't know," she managed, suddenly sober. The fight had gone out of her. Her mind was unable to sort through all the unpleasant things that were beginning to happen to her so unexpectedly.

He looked at her strangely. "You don't know?"

"No…" she said absently.

"I think I'll wait for your father on the jetty. He should arrive any minute now."

"It's fine with me," she managed airily.

He watched her a moment, his gaze scanning her demeanor, then he turned and walked toward the wharf.

Sharlotte watched him go. Her mind churned. She must speak to her father alone. If possible, before he came and boarded Sheldon's yacht. By now the others had all gone down to the jetty. Sharlotte turned and looked toward the sandy road leading back up to the summerhouse. Her father must be on his way.

On the spur of the moment she glanced behind her, then made up her mind. Even if they all left without her, it didn't matter now. Not as much as speaking alone with her father.

Sharlotte turned and ran toward the road.

Her heart raced from more than her sprint on a humid day. She knew a frustration she'd never felt before and she wanted it relieved. Yet somehow her pain seemed as though it would not be soothed by seeking comforts to take its place. Nor could she, by arranging anything, have what she wanted. Circumstances prevented her from having Kace. Perhaps the bitterest cup of all was learning that he no longer wanted her. She felt helpless and afraid realizing that even if she could tear down the wall keeping them apart, he no longer wanted her. He could now dismiss her with an aloof smile. He wanted Elly.

Sharlotte was too dazed to cry. She had discovered in a hard and painful way that the feelings she had for Kace were more than girlhood fancies that had not faded with the passing of summer. The troubling emotions remained alive, reminding her with each beat of her heart that she was as vulnerable to the hurts of life as the girl who cleaned her room or the boy who worked cleaning the stables. She didn't even know their names. What mattered now was that she was little better off than they. In fact, if they had what they wanted, they were better off than she was. This didn't seem right or fair. But maybe it was fair. Sharlotte was becoming acutely aware that she had been wrong to think she deserved to be different. She *wasn't* different. With a start, she realized her riches had woefully deceived her.

Suddenly she was afraid. The walls of illusion were slowly crumbling around her. What would be left in their place? What did reality offer to soothe dismay, to answer questions of need and longing that she as yet could not even form into questions?

Out of breath, she slowed her stride to a walk, hand at her aching side. There was a tree ahead, a dark-green pine that cast a tall shadow across the narrow road. A low rambling fence ran along the road. She sat down on the rail to catch her breath and wait.

A blue jay squawked in the trees and looked down at her boldly. In the distance some crows called: ha, ha, ha. Not all her esteemed social status, nor all her daddy's wealth, as great as it was, could give her satisfaction. The thought of all the things she could buy to ease her disillusionment only added to her discontent. And when she thought of all the places she could go in the world, there was no place that beckoned strongly enough to light a glow in her heart. Yet, Elly was contented. She was dedicated to God, Kace had once said. If there was a God, could He truly bring satisfaction?

Sharlotte ran a sweaty palm along the embroidered monogram of her name and riding club on her expensive jacket. There was an empty feeling in her stomach, a hollow ache that couldn't be filled. Her hands knotted on her lap. Against her will tears blurred her eyes. The crows continued: ha, ha, ha, and the blue jay lifted its graceful wings and boldly soared away, leaving her sitting alone. Even the blue jay was free, but she was not. Kace had dared call her a slave to her world and she'd been indignant, but perhaps there was truth to what he'd said. Sharlotte blinked hard and raised her eyes toward the tops of the spruce trees to where a ribbon of blue-gray sky filtered through. Is there a God? A stillness settled over her fevered brain. The rush of wind in the trees seemed to call, speaking her name over and over. A strange tug pulled at her heart.

The wind continued to blow. The warmth touched her hair and tearstained cheeks. It seemed to play gently with the ribbon on her hat, pulling it affectionately with unseen fingers. She sighed wistfully and dried her eyes with the handkerchief from her jacket pocket.

It seemed a long time before she heard a motor from the direction of the house. Sharlotte stood, brushing her habit clean of pine needles and straightening her perky hat. She stepped out toward the road and saw her father's motorcar coming with its top down, old Henry at its wheel. They were late for the jetty. Would the others have boarded and left without them? No one would dare leave Burgess Ashford behind if he intended to go on a picnic. Her father was not the sort of man who enjoyed picnics, however. Like Clarence, he disliked the troublesome wind. He was vulnerable to swellings from certain summer insects and he complained for weeks afterward, vowing never to sit outdoors again on a summer evening. In many ways, her father and Clarence were much alike.

Sharlotte put on her prettiest smile, hiding her emptiness, and lifted a hand. "Over here, Daddy!"

The motorcar pulled to a stop at the roadside and Sharlotte opened the door and climbed in beside her father.

Henry drove on. Sharlotte sank back into the comfortable seat and turned to look at her father, but his smile was as fixed as hers. Something had changed. Something was different from when she'd left him that morning seated at the garden dining table in his crisp white summer outfit reading the newspaper. She had left him leisurely sipping coffee from a blue china cup with the silver urn on the table beside a platter of cakes.

Yes, something had changed.

"You're late," she said, reaching over and patting his hand, with its protruding veins and slightly swollen fingers. The pat was a little too energetic because she noticed a quiver in his cheek. He suffered from gout. She noted that his fingers shook ever so slightly. *He's not well*, she thought worriedly. She mentioned the argument between Clarence and Stuart. He grunted disapproval.

"And Mr. Hunnewell arrived." She didn't say anything about Kace.

He didn't respond at first. "Where is he now? Has anyone seen him?"

"Not since he first arrived. No, actually I did see him down on the jetty. I asked Clarence to go down and tell him you were on your way."

"Has Clarence returned?"

"No. That is, I didn't stay to find out. I came to meet you. I thought you might walk here."

"It's a fine day for it, but I was late. I rang down, but the boy that works there didn't pick up the telephone. Then I remembered this is a holiday, and he had the day off. Now, what's this I hear about an argument between Clarence and Stuart?"

"Oh, it was foolish, Daddy. They behaved like a couple of boys trying to insult each other. Poor Mr. Hunnewell slipped away, looking upset."

"Did he?" Burgess glanced at her, his stylish Panama hat matching his white summer suit. His eyes were a glittering pale blue and his once-dark hair was now mostly gray. He had a fine English nose and stately eyebrows that sometimes bristled, reminding Sharlotte of a squirrel's bushy tail. He was tall and slim, and his shoulders were still set well, evidence that he'd been quite a handsome man in his younger years. He was a widower, for Sharlotte's lovely mother had died soon after Amanda was born, and her father had never remarried.

"Too busy with business," he had confessed. "And I doubt there's another woman anywhere in our society who would be willing to put up with my weaknesses the way your mother did so graciously."

There had been other women in his life, but these he had kept a secret from Sharlotte and Amanda. Once, recently, a woman in Mexico City had written him, but he'd been very upset over the letter and had burned it just as Sharlotte had walked into the library of the brownstone mansion in New York. He had refused to discuss the matter, even though Sharlotte had brought him the letter, noting the name of the señora on the envelope.

"Troublesome woman," he had breathed angrily, and walked out of the library.

Sharlotte had been tempted to walk over and salvage what she could from the fire, but her conscience had smitten her. What right did she have to spy on her father? She had let it burn. There had been no more letters from Mexico City.

He looked at her now as the motorcar shuttled down the road with the clubhouse in sight. A moment later she could see the blue-gray bay with triangular white sails bobbing in the water.

"This foolish argument between Stuart and Clarence, what was it about?" Burgess asked.

"The congressional seat belonging to Stuart's father. Daddy, I almost wish Clarence wouldn't run for that office. Maybe you should—"

"Never back down to opposition, Sharlotte. The plans are all made. Brace up, my dear. Life is little more than a competition anyway. You play hard to win. Losing only shows weakness. One must persevere to accomplish anything worth keeping. If Clarence can't fight and win, then he won't be a good husband for you. In which case we'll need to look elsewhere."

"Yes, Daddy."

She glanced at him. She had grown up on such speeches, and coming from her father she had embraced them as great words of wisdom. After all, he was a millionaire. And if one believed that financial success proved a man smart, then her father was one of the wisest. And besides, she had been taught all her life that his vast resources provided all things.

"Did the fuss come to blows?"

Sharlotte sighed. "No, but it might have."

Her father was thoughtful. He reached into his jacket pocket and removed a cigar, lighting it expertly against the wind. "Interesting," he said.

"Daddy! You've been bitten by a mosquito again. They make you swell terribly."

He looked at the back of his hand where a pink mark flamed. "Oh, that. It's nothing. If that were all my worries I'd be a happy man." He reached into his pocket for his gloves and brought out just one. "That foolish Peter is a miserable valet. I don't know why I keep the man around."

She smiled. "Because you're attached to him."

Peter had served as valet since her father was a very young man. He was old now, and forgetful, but still her father wouldn't let him go. He complained, but Sharlotte learned long ago that his bark was far worse than his bite.

Sharlotte laughed. "Keep your hand in your pocket, Daddy. No one will notice." She scowled playfully and reached over to check the time on his gold vest watch. "That old watch! It's broken again." She smiled. "It's a good thing I bought you one for Christmas."

"You're not supposed to tell me your secrets," he said with a grim smile, and lifted the watch by its chain. "At last it's given out," he said, slipping it into his pocket as Sharlotte laughed. Then, as if on second thought, he handed it over the back of the seat to his chauffeur, Henry, who had served him for more years than Sharlotte could remember.

"You can sell it by the ounce, Henry old boy. Sell it and play the market. My grandfather started off with far less, and through wise investing turned it into a dynasty."

"Yes, sir, Mr. Ashford. Thank you, sir."

Sharlotte smiled at her father and watched him settle back more at ease now, enjoying his Cuban cigar.

5

Henry brought the motorcar to a standstill on the yacht club drive, and even before Sharlotte and her father got out, George was pushing Amanda in her wheelchair towards them.

"Hello, Daddy. We've been waiting for you. It's time we sailed, but none of us can locate Mr. Hunnewell," Amanda said.

"Hello, Mr. Ashford," George said precisely.

"Hello, George." Burgess gave him a brief nod that was more of a dismissal. Amanda's eyes faltered.

"What's this about Hunnewell?"

"We can't find him, sir," George repeated.

Burgess frowned. "What do you mean can't find him? Sharlotte just informed me he was here." Henry had come around and opened his door. Burgess stepped out onto the gravel.

"He's since disappeared," George explained.

Sharlotte descended from the motorcar on her own and closed the side door, remembering that Kace had gone to Sheldon's boat to find Hunnewell. Then evidently he hadn't been able to locate him. She glanced casually about for Kace and saw him further down on the jetty, hands on hips and looking up in their direction. Sailboats bobbed at their moorings like wooden ducks against the backdrop of the gray water. The thought of the sail up to Shrewsbury upset her equilibrium. Clouds churned above.

Kace, apparently seeing that Burgess had arrived in his chauffeured motorcar, left the jetty and came bounding up the wooden steps toward the club. As he walked up, Sharlotte turned away. Amanda was still explaining the group's dilemma.

"Do you suppose he grew tired of waiting for us and went on to Shrewsbury Landing? He may be there now, expecting us."

"He couldn't have done that, the boats are all here," Sheldon said, walking up with Bitsy and Pamela. "Anyway, he wouldn't have taken off by himself with a storm blowing in. A man of his age?"

"Maybe he asked one of the boys up at the old boathouse to bring him there," Pamela suggested.

Clarence shook his head. "It's a holiday. There's nobody there."

"Those old wrecks?" Sheldon scoffed. "They haven't been used in years. Do you suppose the old fellow is off somewhere snoozing under a tree? He may have given up on us. And with that squabble earlier inside the club we may have frightened him off as a pack of rabble-rousers."

Sharlotte saw Clarence and Stuart glance at each other, then Stuart walked a few feet away and looked out toward the bay, a glum look on his ruddy face.

"Why don't you young folks go on with your plans and Henry and I will locate Hunnewell," Burgess said.

The others seemed inclined, until Kace spoke for the first time. "If something has happened to Hunnewell, we'd better locate him as soon as possible."

Everyone glanced at him. Sharlotte felt her breathing tighten.

"Why jump to conclusions that something happened to Hunnewell?" Clarence asked shortly.

"His age is a factor we need to take into consideration," Kace said casually.

"He's probably snoozing like Rip van Winkle under some shady tree," Sheldon remarked dryly.

"I don't think so," Pamela mused. "He looked upset when he left the clubhouse, wouldn't you agree, Bitsy?"

"Well, yeah. He did. Sharlotte was the last to see him. Right, Sharlotte? You said you were going to look for him."

Sharlotte felt their glances turn her direction. "Yes, but I was delayed. Amanda rode up just then."

"Then I gather we can assume no one has seen Hunnewell since he left the clubhouse soon after the, er, minor disagreement between Clarence and Stuart," Burgess said tactfully.

Clarence turned his head slightly toward Sharlotte, but Kace said: "No. None of us saw him. So he left the club about forty-five minutes ago, Bitsy?"

Bitsy frowned and looked at Sheldon as though the question were too difficult for her to think through.

"Longer than that," Sheldon said. He looked down at her. "I'd say a good hour, maybe more, wouldn't you?"

Bitsy nodded her bobbed head. "Yeah," she said. "At least. When we walked down to the jetty later, no one was there except Stuart."

Stuart shrugged. "There wasn't anyone on the jetty when I got there. Just a little boy."

"This is private property," Burgess stated. "It must have been one of the vacationer's children wandering too far afield."

The wind blew more strongly, and Sharlotte folded her arms, feeling chilly. Clarence noticed and placed an arm around her shoulders. She avoided looking at Kace.

Clarence said with bored impatience: "Does it really matter so much? The man is free to come and go. No one invited him except—" he abruptly stopped, looking embarrassed as he glanced at Burgess.

"Yes, Daddy invited him," Amanda said, putting her hand in his. "He felt sorry for him. After all, it is a holiday when families get together, and poor Mr. Hunnewell is far from his home in New York."

Sharlotte thought, *According to Kace, my father invited him for business reasons. Kace has also come for that meeting.* Kace, however, gave no indication that suggested he was thinking the same thing.

"Do you suppose the weather changed his mind?" Sharlotte addressed her father. "He may have decided you weren't coming."

"Yes," Clarence said. "Anyone can see this is foul weather for a picnic. He may have returned to the house, or even to his hotel."

"You have a good point there. I'll call the house from inside the club and find out," Mr. Ashford said.

The wind was strengthening and the clouds thickening.

"Well, we can't very well go on the picnic now," Amanda said, looking sorrowfully at George. "Even if Hunnewell's up at the house or his hotel room, the storm has foiled our plans."

"What do you say about the weather, Sheldon?" Clarence asked.

Sheldon looked out at the bay's roughening gray waters. "It's too chancy now. Once out in the open one of those waves could turn the boats over and we'll all be swimming to shore."

"I can't swim," Bitsy said with a shudder.

"Let's wait and see what Uncle Burgess finds out," Pamela suggested.

"If there's anything worse than an indoor picnic," Amanda groaned, "it's an indoor picnic with liverwurst sandwiches."

"Yes, but we'd better settle for unpacking Pamela's picnic baskets inside the clubhouse. By then, with this rising wind, Hunnewell is bound to report in from whatever jaunt he decided to take."

Sharlotte glanced at the trees as they began to sway and moan. Hunnewell didn't seem the kind of man to enjoy a hike in stormy weather. Even if he had wandered too far, by now he should be back. Kace must have been thinking the same thing, for while the others reluctantly agreed to unload the boat of their lunch, he said: "I don't think we should delay a search party to eat. That storm is coming in fast. We may not have another opportunity until it blows over tomorrow."

They all looked at him grimly.

"Search party? Do you think Hunnewell's lost?" Clarence asked cryptically.

"He's a fairly old gentleman. He may have tripped and fallen," Kace said, looking at him evenly. "We can't take chances."

No one said anything. The wind was soughing through the tops of the trees, and the rough swells lapped against the jetty pilings.

Sheldon looked thoughtfully toward the water. "There are a few precarious places around here to hike, all right, if that's what he decided to do. As you say, Kace, someone his age could have slipped easily enough."

"If that's true," Sharlotte said, "what are we waiting for?"

"We're waiting for your father's report," Kace reminded her quietly. He looked toward the club steps. "He's coming now."

Her father wore a grim face as he walked up. "He's not at the house."

"Did you call his hotel, sir?" Kace asked.

"Yes. The desk clerk assured me he hasn't returned."

The mood sobered. Mr. Ashford looked up at the sky and frowned. "It's going to be a bad storm. I don't like the looks of things. I think we'd better form a search party. Kace, why don't you take one group and I'll lead the other. We can meet back here at the club in an hour, though we may get drenched before then."

"If you'll pardon my saying so, sir, I'm not the most efficient guide. I'm not acquainted with the territory. My suggestion is to spread out on our own, or at the most, two by two. We'll cover more area that way. It's faster."

"Yes, yes, you're right, Kace. I should have thought of that. I guess I'm a little upset over this. Hunnewell wasn't feeling well when I saw him last night."

"Daddy, why don't you wait inside the clubhouse with Amanda," Sharlotte urged. "The rest of us are more than enough to form an adequate search party. Who knows? Mr. Hunnewell may come back before we do, or he may call the club telephone. Someone has to be here."

"Yes, Daddy, she's right," Amanda urged. "Let's go inside and wait. There's hot coffee waiting."

"Well, if the rest of you won't mind." He looked around at the dismal faces.

Sharlotte glanced at Kace and saw that he was watching her father.

"It's already beginning to sprinkle," Pamela said.

"Come on, Bitsy, we'd better hurry," and Sheldon went off toward the trees. A trail was there that wound along the cove.

"George? Why don't you go with Stuart?" Amanda said.

The group began to scatter, and Sharlotte was left alone with Clarence. She watched her father walk wearily back to the club, his chauffeur pushing Amanda's chair. Sharlotte had a sick dread in her heart. She glanced to see where Kace had gone and found that he'd already disappeared.

"Which direction are you going, Sharlotte?" Clarence asked.

"I don't know yet," she replied briefly. She looked deliberately toward the stable area and the trail that wound around behind it, though she had no intention of going in that direction. She didn't want Clarence going with her, for there was something she must do alone.

"Mr. Hunnewell could have wandered anywhere his fancy took him," she suggested.

"Then I'd better come with you and make sure you get back safely."

"No, Clarence, it's best we do this separately. We'll accomplish much more." She urged him to search the area around the immediate woods that grew along the sandy road.

He scowled. "You don't mean the road where you met your father just now? Don't be silly, Sharlotte! Why do that? You would have seen him, or your father would have spied him on his way down in the motorcar."

"Mr. Hunnewell enjoyed bird watching," she protested. "He could have wandered off the road onto the hiking trail that winds up to Shorecliff. There's a magnificent view there. Whenever he'd come to spend a week visiting my father, he'd always take an early morning walk there."

Clarence didn't appear convinced. "He knew we were waiting for your father. Was he so irrational as to go wandering off that far when he could see one atrocious storm blowing in? He wouldn't have gone without telling someone."

"Maybe not, but what's the use searching if we don't look everywhere? We've got to try. Kace may be right. What if he did trip and injured his ankle or something?"

"Then come with me," he urged, as though concerned she might go off with Kace.

"I'm sorry, Clarence, but I'd rather not. This is too important, and there's something else I must do." Without waiting to hear further protests, she walked toward the jetty, leaving Clarence frowning and walking moodily in the direction of the sandy road and the woods.

~

Once Sharlotte was down on the jetty, she looked back up at the clubhouse on the hillside. The front windows and wide balcony looked down over the inlet. She could see her father walking to and fro. He paused to relight his cigar and appeared to notice her. He waved. She smiled and lifted her hand. Burgess stood there for a moment longer, as though concerned with her being out in the coming storm, then he apparently walked over to where the telephone sat on a table, and was waiting with Amanda for a call that could end their concerns about Mr. Hunnewell.

Sharlotte turned away and gazed out at the choppy gray water. The wind was picking up and the sky was completely overcast. Although it was barely one o'clock, the day had taken on a twilight gloom that matched her spirits. Gusts of wind were blowing across the water, washing boiling foam onto the jetty. The boats rolled and pulled restlessly against their lines.

She walked to the place on the wharf where she'd last seen Hunnewell, and looked across at Sheldon's boat, the *Captain's Choice*, which was larger than the other sailing boats. Of one thing she was almost sure, that Mr. Hunnewell had come this way. Unexpectedly, her misgivings gave way to a wry sense of humor. What if he were below in Sheldon's boat, dozing contentedly?

"Little chance of that," she sighed. With the boat bobbing on the water, no one could sleep, unless, she thought with apprehension, he was unconscious. She could look, but Clarence would have already done so, and Kace. They had both come here looking for Hunnewell. As neither of them had said anything, he probably wasn't there.

There was something else she must do while there was time before the storm struck, another place where Mr. Hunnewell may have gone, and although she hadn't said anything to her father or the others, she had an inexplicable notion that he'd been looking off in a certain direction when she'd last seen him on the jetty. She only knew she must go there and check it out for herself.

Sharlotte glanced about and didn't see anyone watching her. The others must have scattered up shore or along the back trails, she decided. Good, she preferred it that way. She wanted to follow her own hunch without explaining her reasons for doing so. Satisfied she was alone, she turned away from the boats and quickly made her way up the jetty, walking away from the club.

She reached the point where the yacht club's property ended. Here, just below the gently rolling hillside facing the bay, there were steps rising to a seldom-used path belonging to the Ashford estate. There wasn't much chance Mr. Hunnewell would have taken this route, but she wouldn't be convinced otherwise until she looked for herself. Had she seen him turn this way? The path hugged the hillside. Above the path, tall gray-green cypress trees made a thick windbreak for the house during the winter. The house stood a comfortable distance away from the hill's edge so that when looking up, she couldn't see the roof at all. Between the house and the hillside a half-acre garden was protected by a brick retaining wall.

Sharlotte knew that for Hunnewell to reach the house from the jetty area, he would need to take the hillside trail, which eventually passed a view of the old abandoned family boat landing.

When she reached the top of the steps she came to a short rocky path overgrown with clumps of wild daises that followed the hillside around toward the other side of the bay. Because the hillside was eroding in places, slides had sporadically gullied the path. She stepped around these and hurried forward. The path was rarely used by family or guests and had not been kept up. However, she knew of occasions in past years when Hunnewell had walked it with her father. She was remembering that the gardener had approached her father several times about the rock slides, but he usually became too distracted when he returned to his work at the New York bank to remember all the springtime maintenance items for the summerhouse.

She glanced up from the bay at the lowering horizon. There were darker clouds coming in. It was indeed wise not to have tried sailing to Shrewsbury. Below the gray billows, the heaving swells surged upon the rocks with curling foamy fingers that she imagined could snatch her and pull her out to the deep. Seagulls screamed in ecstasy and effortlessly rode the updraft above the turbulence.

Sharlotte followed the trail until it opened onto a cypress-lined lane wide enough for a single motorcar.

An odd feeling settled upon her. The wind had picked up. It was beginning to sprinkle again...slowly at first. As the force of the wind increased there was soon little cover from the rain that was now pummeling her riding clothes and dripping from her hat. She lowered its brim and pulled it down, but it offered scant cover. She was soon completely soaked and shivering in the chilling sea wind. She had ceased to ask herself why she was doing this as she pressed toward the old boathouse. Something was driving her. A compulsion?

As the abandoned boathouse came into view she saw the decaying wooden steps that went down to the boat landing. They were slimy green in places where moss grew in constant dampness and shade. They led down to the floating wooden launch where a few sunken and decaying boats of various sizes were tied. The inlet cove was gray and choppy, with some swells reaching the landing. The old boathouse was built on pilings. Her skin knew a shiver as she looked at it, seeing a shadowy window watching her as though she were suspected of some hidden malice.

She went down the decaying steps precariously, and paused before the floating platform, riding the swells. The wind struck her. The old pilings groaned like deep voices in the pull of the water. A wave splashed up across the warped boards. On the other side of the cove a steep flight of wooden steps led up the hillside to a tree-shrouded path toward a large stone gate and the estate garden, but before going there, she needed to check the boathouse—her main reason for coming.

Sharlotte tried to bolster her courage by telling herself she would at least be out of the rain. She knew the door had not been locked for years.

She made her way across the platform, feeling the unsteadying pull beneath her feet. She lifted the bolt and pushed the door cautiously as it creaked open. Suddenly, daunted by the twilight shadows, the room smelling of rotting seaweed—or something very much like it—she nearly turned and ran like a frightened child. She gritted her teeth and counted calmly to five, then stepped over the threshold into the silent room where ghostly ropes, chains, and boat tackle were stacked and piled in confusing shapes and bundles.

She reached for the lantern and the box of matches. She hoped they weren't so old and damp that they wouldn't light—

She shuddered. There were *fresh* matches on the dusty table, right beside the lantern. Then someone had been here, and recently. So— Mr. Hunnewell himself? But why?

Sharlotte controlled her runaway nerves with considerable effort and lit the lantern with shaking fingers. She closed the door and looked at the chair. Though everything else was covered with a fine layer of dust, the seat had been wiped clean, as though someone had just been sitting. The lantern light fell across the wooden planks. She stooped, her heart in her throat. Yes, someone had been here. There was ash on the floor. She examined it closely in the lantern light. A piece of it had fallen without crumbling; it looked as though it was lying above the old layer of dust. She looked down through wide gaps in the floor boards at the dark waves below as the boathouse swayed and groaned. Her teeth chattered convulsively.

She had a dreadful sensation that Mr. Hunnewell was not only dead, but that his body was somewhere inside the boathouse. Her skin crawled. She shut her eyes and took several deep breaths, trying to steady her nerves. But how had the body gotten here?

Stop this at once, Sharlotte, she told herself. *If you don't pull yourself together you'll end up screaming, and there's no one to hear you!*

There is really no evidence that Hunnewell is dead! she thought. And common sense told her that if he'd had a heart attack or had fallen and injured himself, his body would be in plain view. If it was hidden—but it couldn't be, unless—someone had brought it here. Her nerves tingled at the back of her neck. It was so unthinkable she immediately rejected the idea. *Why would anyone put his body inside an old abandoned boathouse?*

Although she knew this, she stood with the lantern, her eyes searching. There had been rats. Ugh. She felt a cold plop on the back of her neck and looked up. The roof leaked, no wonder the room was musty. She tensed. In the far corner there was a dark mound covered with a tarp. Her breathing came shortly. Carefully she approached and mustered her courage. She slowly drew it back. She let out a sigh of relief...almost giggling hysterically. Nothing but old tackle and a life preserver.

As she turned away a low growl of thunder rumbled in the distance over the bay. A sharp gust shook the boathouse and the pilings groaned eerily, rattling the windowpanes and whining through the wide cracks. Sharlotte looked about slowly and intently, and again at the tobacco ash beside the chair—cigarette or cigar?

She was still stooping when above the wind and water she heard something quite different and far more frightening, the sound of someone just outside the door. Pausing again, she looked over her shoulder. It must have been the wind. Some loose pebbles sliding down the hill behind her? Or had someone followed her? Her mind went blank as her emotions suddenly recoiled in fear and denial. What had come over her? Why was she thinking the unthinkable?

She knew it was too late to put out the lantern. Surely it had already been seen. Then, before she could stand, the door opened...

"Looking for something?"

She rose breathlessly, both relieved yet feeling consternation when Kace stood there in the pouring rain.

"Mind if I join you?" he asked wryly.

She must have appeared pale and frightened, for his expression lost its cynical amusement as he entered the gloomy room. He took hold of the lantern, put it on the table, and searched her face.

"What is it," he asked soberly, "what did you find, the weapon?"

"Weapon?" she squeaked. His concerned voice offered just the assurance needed, and spoken by the right man, she collapsed with a small muffled sob into his arms. "Oh, Kace, you nearly frightened me to death," she wailed.

"Sharlotte, I'm sorry. I thought you heard me coming across the landing. I certainly wasn't trying to sneak up on you. Hey, it's all right now. Pull yourself together. Here, wipe your eyes."

She nodded dismally as he slipped the hanky from her riding jacket and handed it to her. She dried her face as he looked down at the floor where she'd been stooping when he entered.

"Careful where you step. Those boards are rotting through. We don't want to end up in the grip of a giant squid."

She looked down through a wide gap in the floorboards. The dark swelling sea pulled at the pilings beneath them, making her feel a little dizzy. She gripped him tighter, then noticed that his shirt was sopping wet and he was without his jacket. She came aware again of her fears and looked up at him searchingly. Her lashes squinted. "Did you follow me?" her teeth chattered.

"Of course." He smiled. "The trick was to stay far enough behind so you'd lead me to the right place on your mind." He looked up at the roof. "Well at least we'll be out of the worst of it. In the meantime you can explain."

She grew taut, pulling away, for she didn't dare explain. "W-what is there to explain?" she asked innocently, shivering.

"You can begin by telling me what compelled you to come and search this old boathouse."

"I—don't know what you mean. I came to get out of the rain."

"Crawling about the floor with a lantern?" he suggested doubtfully. "You'll need to do better than that. It's not exactly what I'd call a place conducive for reverie, or even a rendezvous with Fosdick," he said wryly. "You're nearly engaged. I wouldn't think you'd need to hide in this musty spot to steal a wee kiss. A honeysuckle arbor is much more aromatic."

"Don't be silly," she accused mildly, blushing.

"Curious is all, about why you'd be searching through rusty old piles of tackle and rotting rope?"

She avoided his insistent gaze. "I wasn't searching."

"No? You were down on your hands and knees with this lantern. Not an appropriate activity for a newly introduced debutante. At least you knew better than to wear white gloves."

She turned, lifting her chin, her violet-blue eyes taking on some of her old fighting spirit. "And I thought you were being so nice. I should have known it wouldn't last."

He laughed and looked around. "What earthly reason did you have for thinking Hunnewell would be stashed here?"

Sharlotte caught her breath.

"Ah, so you did think you'd find his corpse. Interesting, indeed. Come, Sharlotte, don't look so shocked. I know you well enough to believe you wouldn't have come here if you hadn't shared the same suspicions I did."

The same suspicions. Then she wasn't losing her mind, she thought, finding justifiable relief in knowing someone like Kace had considered the same thing. No sooner did she think this, however, than she grew alarmed, for if he did think Hunnewell was dead and his body hidden here in the boathouse, then it was much more likely to be true. Realizing he also held little sympathy for her relatives, she was reluctant to tell him anything that would cast them in a poor light.

"Suspicions?" she whispered, eyes wide. "What same suspicions?"

He studied her for a long moment, as if weighing her sincerity. "Those limpid blue eyes of yours are trying to convince me of guilelessness. However," he drawled, "I also know you're a clever young woman when standing on the brink of disaster."

The word "disaster" brought a new rigidity to her spine and she stepped back. "I'm completely baffled by whatever you're trying to suggest."

His back was to the lantern light and his face was in shadow, but she could sense his sober stare, and could imagine the determined line of his mouth and jaw.

"You're not baffled at all. You know, don't you?" he persisted.

"Know *what?*" she asked in a shaky voice.

"We both think there's a strong chance the man is dead. That's why we both came here. But why did you think peeking under some old tarp might disclose his body?"

Her hand flew to her mouth. She sat down quickly, breathlessly.

"You did think he might be here."

She couldn't find her voice. Kace stepped closer, caught her arm and drew her to her feet, his eyes searching hers. "Yes, you get the picture all right. We both know a dead body isn't likely to come here of its own accord and hide under a tarp."

"He—he might have been ill, needing rest, seeking to avoid the rain—until he felt better."

"This is the last place he'd come. If he was ill he'd want to draw attention to the fact, not hide under a tarp and lengthen the time to when someone located him."

"Maybe he injured himself, twisted his ankle…and…" her weak excuses trailed off as Kace slowly shook his head.

"That won't do either. He would have found a tree to wait under until someone came looking for him. He'd want to stay as near the road as possible. You know that as well as I. So why did you come in here, searching, so frightened that you nearly jumped out of your skin when I spoke?"

Trapped, she pulled away, her strength rallying. "I didn't know for sure that he came here," she said stubbornly.

"Maybe not, but why did you think to look in here in the first place?"

"We're all out searching for the man, remember? Naturally it's wise to look everywhere."

"Everywhere within reason, yes. Somehow, an abandoned boathouse isn't very probable if he were either injured or ill. If he were dead, then obviously he couldn't place his own body in here. Someone else would have to do it—deliberately. So let's have it,

Sharlotte. I want to know what made you think he was dead and his body under that tarp."

"I told you already! I've nothing more to say."

"So far you've said next to nothing."

"I'm going up to the house—" she said in dismay and started for the door.

He caught her hand. "Not yet, please."

She wanted to continue to deny that she had thought Hunnewell was dead, but Kace's steady gaze wouldn't allow it—and her own behavior in coming here had betrayed her. "Maybe I was looking for something else."

"Jewels? I hardly think so. The murder weapon? Now that's a possibility." Her breath stopped and their eyes held.

"Well?" he asked softly after the moments crawled by.

Her gaze faltered. She had entertained a gross suspicion that Hunnewell's body would be inside the boathouse, just as Kace insisted. But at the same time her strange suspicion had made no sense to her. She envisioned again someone carrying Hunnewell's body up the path. The thought was so grotesque that she immediately took to shivering. No. Impossible. Who would have done it? Her heart felt the vise of cold panic. And why?

Sharlotte found she was swaying on her feet, but whether from the pull of the swells, or her brain spinning, she couldn't tell.

Kace steadied her, his arms around her waist as he searched her face, then frowned.

"All right, never mind for now," he said softly. "You look a little sick…better sit down."

She knew that Kace would not be satisfied with her denials, and that he was perhaps even more interested in the reasons for her fears. She must think of something that would not implicate the Ashfords and Van Dornens—but would he allow her to get by with it?

6

Wet and cold and sitting on the squeaking, hard-backed chair, Sharlotte wrapped her arms about herself, trying to stay calm.

Kace looked around, rummaging. "I don't suppose there's an old jacket in here."

"If there is, it's rotten by now. The family hasn't used this place since I was a little girl."

He went on rummaging and only casually remarked: "Interesting."

She glanced at him, remaining silent. What was?

He found something, gave it a whiff, and handed it over with a smile. "Not too bad. Someone's old towel from yesteryear. Here, dry yourself off before you catch cold and miss your next coming out ball."

She noticed the same old amused glimmer in his green eyes. She snatched the old towel, removed her ruined hat, and began drying her hair, face, and arms as best she could. Kace watched her thoughtfully.

"Since you haven't been here in years, why show up now, in a storm?" he asked.

So that was what he found interesting. "You asked me that before."

"Yes, and you didn't explain, so I need to ask again until I get a reasonable answer."

She smiled too sweetly. "Yes, Inspector. But I can play that game too. Why did *you* follow *me*?"

"You were behaving so strangely, I wanted to see what you were up to. And protect you."

Her brows arched, and her lips formed a little smile. "From the rain?"

"From a murderer, maybe."

Her lips parted and her fingers tightened about the towel. She stared at him.

"Not so amusing now, is it?" came his grave reply.

She glanced around the eerie room uneasily. Was Kace serious? Yes, of course he was.

"And, your reason for coming here aroused my curiosity." He took the towel from her and dried himself. "If anyone in the family noticed your odd behavior, your coming here wouldn't have remained a secret very long. And that in itself could be dangerous."

She tensed in the chair, searching his face for clues. *Could I be in danger?* she wondered, dazed. *Impossible…*

"Fortunately, no one else followed you. I made sure of that. Even Fosdick, who claims to know you well enough to become your 'Ever Loving,' didn't seem to notice your apprehension."

She stood abruptly, anxious to divert him. "You're trying to frighten me. Just the same nasty way you did in Texas. Throwing me in the horse trough, placing that tarantula beneath my pillow, but it won't work this time."

He jammed his hands in his pockets. "How many times must I apologize for all that? Are you ever going to forget?"

"No," she stated, thinking of that hairy, long-legged tarantula. She stepped back as if one might be creeping across the floor.

He laughed softly and spoke her name, "Sharlotte—" but she took another step backward. "Stay away."

He held up both palms. "Okay," he said. "I promise to *never* put a tarantula under your pillow again. There, can you forgive me now?"

"Maybe," she said with the faintest smile, "except now you follow me and accuse me of some nasty business concerning Hunnewell."

"I've accused you of nothing. I noticed you were frightened about something. Naturally, wanting to make up for my notorious boyhood pranks, I decided to follow you and offer my service for your protection. And the only thing I'm accusing you of at the moment is holding back the truth from me."

"The truth? It's just that I was concerned, is all," she countered evasively. "If something happened to Mr. Hunnewell, it would not only be a tragedy, but…well…it would ruin everything for me."

"Another of your social events ruined? Forbid."

"You're being sarcastic. I think you resent my friends and their social status."

"Don't go overboard complimenting your stuffy friends. I wonder how many would come buzzing about your door if you became a pauper overnight?"

"Well, I've no intention of finding out. And if you really mean to accuse Clarence of buzzing about just because Daddy is a millionaire—"

"I'd never go that far. If he's buzzing about you, I'd be generous enough to give him credit for being able to appreciate violet-blue eyes and golden hair, among other things of noted value. But we're getting way off track, aren't we? The topic for today is Hunnewell and why you thought he might be hidden here."

She sat down again, vaguely pleased about his indirect compliment, even if Elly stood in the way, but the seriousness of the situation over Hunnewell ruined it.

Kace continued in a low voice, "Believe it or not, I can be sympathetic about the destiny your ball will take tonight. Murder has such a ruthless tendency to cast a pall over a happy gathering and turn it into a funeral."

"It couldn't have been murder. Someone might have come upon his body, feared the consequences of the police being called in, and panicked, hiding him in here." She looked around with distaste.

"He isn't in here," he stated. "He never was. Be truthful. You imagined he was, not because you thought someone panicked and brought him here to save the Ashford name from a scandal of having a dead body on their property, but because you feared the murderer concealed him here, purposely."

"No!" She jumped to her feet. "How can you say that? You don't even know for sure he's dead. He may be at the house now—yes, laughing at all of us for chasing about for him in the rain while he's safe and dry."

"I'm afraid he's neither safe nor dry, and I doubt he's doing any laughing."

The boathouse creaked and swayed. The awful realization began to set in. "W-what do you know that makes you so certain?"

"Elementary, my dear Sharlotte. I know he's dead because I found the body. It *appears* as though he'd fallen in an accident and drowned. I have my reasons for doubting that."

For a moment she didn't speak, just looked at him. Fear tightened about her heart like a python. It was certain. There was no escaping the horrible fact now. He was dead. And Kace didn't think it was accidental.

He remained quiet after his declaration. His silence meant that he wasn't willing to say any more, but perhaps he suspected more than he could prove.

Her throat was dry and her heart beat tensely. "It can't be," she breathed. "It had to be an accident. Yes, Kace, an accident." Her eyes pleaded with his. "Heart failure—he was an old man. Or, he might have fallen. That's it, isn't it! Say that's all it was."

"An accident involving a heart attack or a serious fall could explain what has happened," he said. "But it doesn't satisfy me. And it doesn't explain why you'd think he was here at the boathouse, dead."

"I didn't know for sure," she managed at last in a low, tight voice. "I thought I saw him looking in this direction when he was on the jetty. I thought he might have returned this way to the house, because the route is shorter, though abandoned by the family. I knew he was anxious to see my father."

"How much shorter?"

She read his sparked interest. "Maybe seven or eight minutes," she admitted reluctantly.

"Go on."

"I thought when he reached the house and realized they'd missed one another by minutes—that Hunnewell would turn around and come back to the club using the same shorter route."

"Most of us would have, but not Hunnewell. He was an old man. Think about it. If he did go up to the house, which I don't think he did, the servants would have told him Mr. Ashford had already left for the club by motorcar. What would Hunnewell do next? Turn round and come right back this same way? No. He'd be a little winded from rushing. He'd sit down with something cool to drink. He'd call down to the club to tell your father where he was and ask that the motorcar be sent back for him. By then it would have begun to rain."

Sharlotte lapsed into uneasy agreement. She didn't like the way things were being construed, not at all. It only made more questions—unpleasant ones. Kace was making too much sense.

"You haven't told me where you found him," she whispered.

He looked at her. "Right across from the dock, below the stairway for the path to the house. It looks as if one of the rotting steps gave way and he fell, breaking through part of the rail. Perhaps he grabbed the rail and it broke away, and that was it. It looks as if he hit his head on some rocks."

"You took him out of the water?"

"Yes. His body was floating near the shoreline. I pulled him out and covered him with a tarp."

Sharlotte sat very still, hardly daring to breathe, visualizing the scene all too clearly. Her mind refused to go any further down that dark, troubling path.

She watched Kace musing, trying to fit the puzzle pieces together, but certain key pieces were missing.

"Very well, he's dead. That doesn't mean he was murdered. You say the step was rotted through, that he grabbed the rail and fell. Why can't that be sufficient to explain what happened? Accidental drowning," she said.

"But you didn't think it was accidental when you came here searching."

She shook her head in dismay, palms pressed against her temples. "Oh, I don't know what I was really thinking, or why. I had an unexplainable fear," she admitted. "I can't even explain it to myself."

"Maybe because you find the answer too painful."

She looked at him sharply, but fell off in confusion when she saw his restrained sympathy.

"For me there's just one reasonable explanation. He must have expected to meet someone here," he said.

A shiver inched up the back of her spine. The boathouse creaked and moaned suggestively. He walked over to the smudged window and looked out, hands in his trouser pockets, but she didn't think he was even noticing what he was looking at. Sharlotte glanced toward the tobacco ash on the floorboard, the chair seat that had been wiped clean. When she looked up he was watching her steadily.

"So you noticed that too?" he said quietly.

"One of the workmen. Probably a few days ago."

"Or left by someone today waiting for Hunnewell. The next unhappy question is who among us would wish Hunnewell dead?"

"You don't really mean that?" Sharlotte asked in a dry whisper.

"I wish I didn't. Have you a better explanation?"

Her own thoughts, churning around in her soul, gripped her painfully. She looked at him quickly, now remembering what it was that had been troubling her earlier about Kace finding Hunnewell's body.

"If you're so sure it wasn't an accident, then maybe that doesn't speak so well for *you*. As far as I know, Mr. Landry, you might not have followed me here at all. You may have been the one Hunnewell came here to meet."

"I don't smoke for one thing."

"I've seen Hunnewell with a cigarette. Those ashes could have been left by him as he waited for you to arrive."

He frowned, watching her alertly. "Not bad at all, and certainly not impossible."

She gained more confidence and stood, walking toward him. "What about your own disappearance at the yacht club? Isn't it true there was about twenty-five minutes when no one saw you?"

"I would say that was true of most of us," he said with a bored tone.

"Yes, but 'most of us' did not arrive at the scene of the crime, only you."

"Then you admit a crime's been committed."

"You said so yourself. You might have come here and... silenced him. When you saw me coming, you hid until I entered the boathouse. Then you came to the door and frightened me half out of my wits."

He looked thoughtfully through the soiled window again, trying to peer out at the mounting dark swells that were even now entering the cove. "Yes, someone could hide easily enough, maybe among the trees up there. And Hunnewell, unsuspecting, sat down and lit a cigarette, waiting for his appointment to be kept with whoever asked him here. Minutes later the murderer arrived. And any one of us had time and opportunity to make this walk, perform the ruthless deed, and return without suspicion." He turned toward her. "But, not all of us wanted to see Hunnewell dead."

Sharlotte stood, hand at throat, watching him.

A shadow of a smile showed on his face. "So you think I'd do in old Hunnewell?"

"You said you had an appointment with him," she said stubbornly, though she didn't believe it. "You told me so when we were standing by George's roadster. You were really the person Hunnewell had come to see. No one else even knew he was coming to the picnic, so they couldn't have planned anything."

"Not quite accurate. Your father knew. So did Sheldon and Clarence. And Sheldon most likely told his sister, Pamela. Besides, I'm the outsider, the disinterested party."

"The perfect candidate for mayhem," she corrected, folding her arms and looking smug.

He laughed shortly. "We are all candidates, but I'm the only one who didn't need to worry about the news Hunnewell was bringing the Ashford and Van Dornen families."

"You've mentioned that news before, but you haven't bothered to explain," she said, apprehensive.

"I will, in time. Or your father will. I also admitted I was here to see your father, not just Hunnewell. It was your father who arranged the meeting, a meeting that will now never take place."

Sharlotte was still curious about that. Why would Kace come to meet with her father and his lawyer? He had mentioned something about debt, but she didn't believe that tall tale for a moment. It must be just another one of Kace's little jests.

He walked over to her. He was saying quietly, "But, if I did as you suggest, you're not being very wise in accusing me. It must surely occur to you that if I was desperate enough to kill Hunnewell, I would also be capable of a second murder to cover my tracks. And you, my charmer, are not only alone, but no one even knows you've come here. And this old boathouse could collapse at any moment."

Sharlotte heard the creaking, felt the boards moving beneath her feet, and had to struggle to keep herself from bolting toward the door.

He laughed softly. "I commend you for keeping your nerve. Is it because you don't really believe a word you've been saying about me?"

Her eyes faltered and she turned away.

"You're perfectly safe—with me. I was merely pointing out that you'd best be cautious in what you say to the others. As I told you, it was my concern for your wandering off that caused me to follow you. Now sit down, please. We haven't much time and there's still a few more things I need to ask you before I notify the others about Hunnewell."

She did so slowly, watching him. His smile turned rueful. "All right, with that suspicious look of yours, I owe you an explanation of my actions before I arrived. I went looking for Hunnewell at the yacht club jetty just where you suggested, but he wasn't there. I even checked your cousin Sheldon's boat. I ran into Stuart, who'd also been on the jetty, but he hadn't seen Hunnewell either. As I was looking around, I noticed the old path and wondered if the house could be reached from that direction. When I got here to the boathouse, that's when I noticed the broken step and rail. It didn't take long to guess what had happened." Sharlotte had to agree that his explanation was convincing.

He watched her thoughtfully. "Sheldon's girlfriend—what was her name, Bitsy?—suggested to everyone you were the last to see Hunnewell leaving the club before he vanished. Did you also tell Clarence?"

"Yes. I asked him to go to the jetty to find Hunnewell and tell him my father was coming on the picnic after all. Clarence said he wasn't there. You also forcefully interrupted before I had the chance to explain to my father."

"I didn't want you to admit it just yet, not in front of the others. One of them is likely to have killed Hunnewell."

No, her mind shouted, *no.*

"I don't like what you're suggesting." She stood abruptly, intending to leave. "To think any of us had cause to harm Hunnewell is…is ludicrous, reckless, and very self-serving on your part. So let me by."

"Self-serving? Where do you get that? It was I who followed you to this musty, dilapidated place, with the idea of keeping a protective eye on you. This is a perfect location to hide evidence if one was in a hurry. It's also dangerous. If someone did hide something, they're likely to come back for it."

"It's quite obvious you don't like any of us. You'd find some nasty pleasure in pinning Hunnewell's death on one of us."

"Sharlotte, I'm just trying to keep you from getting involved in something that's far above your head. That's why it's important to answer my questions. After I went down to the jetty to find Hunnewell, would you mind telling me where you met your father?"

"My father?" she stammered.

"Yes, you came back to the club with him. I saw you in his car. Did you return to the house?"

"No, I decided to walk partway up the main road and wait for him. He usually walks down. And I thought I wanted to discuss some things with him." She looked at him evenly, letting him know she wasn't about to share those particulars with him.

"You say he usually walks, but this time his chauffeur drove him."

"Yes, what are you getting at?"

"How long did you wait?"

"A few minutes," she said stiffly.

"More like half an hour, wasn't it?"

"It could have been." She knew what he was getting at, and she hotly rejected it. Yes, there'd been enough time for her father to have left the house and walk down to the boathouse to meet Hunnewell. No one would have missed him, because everyone by that time was at the club waiting for his arrival. But her father *hadn't* met Hunnewell here, she was sure of it.

"Then you saw the motorcar coming?"

"And stepped out to ride down with my father. I told him about Hunnewell, and he was a little concerned that he might have wandered off with the storm coming on."

"Is there a gate to the garden grounds from this boathouse?"

"Yes, by way of the upper path. It's a very large stone gate, with an old-fashioned gatekeeper's cottage, but it's abandoned now. As I said, no one uses the route much now. In horse and buggy days Grandfather used it. Since then there's been rock and mud slides cutting off the path down to the club jetty."

"This old boat launch lies in the middle of the path?"

"Yes."

"The shorter distance up to the house is reason enough for Hunnewell to have walked this route," Kace agreed. "It's also reason enough for the murderer to have wanted him to come by this way. Then there's the obvious advantage of not being seen."

"Hunnewell could have come to meet a woman as well as a man," she interjected.

"Yes. We can't leave out Pamela or Bitsy. I'm now thinking perhaps Hunnewell didn't come here expecting to meet someone, but went first to the gate you mentioned. You say it enters the garden."

She shuddered. "Then both of them walked back here to the boathouse? But that's pure speculation," she said in a shaky voice. It was too terrible to accept.

"True. But you'll agree it makes sense."

She wouldn't agree to anything, not now. Not after he'd suggested one of them may have murdered Hunnewell.

"Hunnewell could have received a message down at the club, telling him to come to the gate. What he was told to lure him to this wretched place is anyone's guess."

Sharlotte was imagining Mr. Hunnewell trudging along that lonely, shadowed way until he came to the gate where fallen leaves rustled in the wind...

"But who would send for him?" he mused, and looked at her.

Sharlotte's lips tightened. Her handkerchief had been turned into a wad in her damp palm.

"If we had the answer to that question, we'd most likely know everything," he said. "Until there's a postmortem, we'd best keep any ideas we have between ourselves. Any other course is bound to prove very prickly for you, and maybe dangerous."

He walked to the door. She was on her feet, clutching his arm. "Kace, what are we going to do?" she whispered.

He looked down at her thoughtfully, and she saw the gravity in his eyes. He placed his hand over hers, comfortingly.

"At the moment? Nothing. Hunnewell tripped, hit his head, and fell into the water. Accidental death by drowning until evidence to the contrary convinces the police. I'm sure there'll be an inquest. In the meantime, we'd better get up to the house so I can call your father at the club. And Sharlotte, I think it's wiser if you didn't mention coming here until the authorities arrive. Your father will need to call the police. So let's keep this simple."

She stared up at him white and shaking. She knew what he meant: don't mention a suspicion of murder to anyone. He didn't need to warn her. She wasn't about to do so.

"Why are you willing to involve yourself?" she whispered.

He smiled unexpectedly. "With my past reputation for horse trough dunking, what else would a Texas gentleman do to make up for his faults? I've discussed things openly and bluntly with you, but I mean to keep it between us until something more turns up. You and I are the only ones who were suspicious enough to come here. That doesn't bode well for either of us should the murderer learn about our meeting."

His suggestion would have frightened her except that she was already overly distraught, but she drew some needed courage from his calmness and unexpected concern for her well-being. She looked at him curiously, trying to read his thoughts unsuccessfully. At times he seemed cynically amused with her, yet at other times genuinely interested. He baffled her.

He smiled as though understanding her attempt to gauge him.

"And now I think we'd both better brave the storm before this whole thing comes down and washes us out to sea."

With a last glance about the murky room, he opened the door, took her arm, and they stepped together into the wind and lashing rain, leaving the dilapidated boathouse to keep its dark, ugly secrets.

7

Kace and Sharlotte ran together across the landing to the far side of the cove onto the stairway that led toward the Ashford summerhouse. The storm had increased and angry swells were rising as though trying to impede their progress.

He halted her at the stairs. "Watch for that broken step," he warned above the wind, "and don't touch the rail. The police will want to see it."

Sharlotte shuddered from the windy blast, but she was thinking of Hunnewell on these very steps, losing his footing on the broken step above her, and then desperately grasping for the rail only to have it break away.

"Don't look down, honey. He isn't there now."

She clutched his arm. "Where did you put him, Kace?"

"Does it matter?"

"Yes!"

He hesitated, as if to shrug off an unpleasant thought, then gestured across the landing. Sharlotte followed with her eyes and saw what must have been Hunnewell's remains wrapped in a tarp away from the water. She turned away, and Kace put his arm tightly around her as they went carefully up the steps where the unfortunate accident—or murder—had happened that very morning.

When they reached the top, the path turned away from the landing toward some cypress and made a gradual climb.

Sharlotte noticed that he had looked at his watch and was timing the walk. An unsettled feeling blew against her with the strong wind and rain. Kace was looking at the wet dirt lane, as though checking for prints, but she was relieved to see only the well-worn path made through the years. Perhaps there was nothing to worry about there, she thought.

The lane was turning muddy, ruining her expensive riding shoes from Spain. Her riding habit too, she feared, was looking wrinkled and maybe even a bit shrunken. Kace laughed. "That feather in your hat looks like it was plucked from a drowned rooster."

She glared. "You loathe everything that sets my life apart from everyone else's, don't you." She pulled her arm loose from his.

Kace slipped his arm tightly around her waist and grinned down at her. "Don't be difficult. If I don't keep you on your feet you'll likely end up in the mud. Think what a sight that would be."

"If I didn't need you—" she began furiously.

"Ah, nothing like the terrors of nature to prove to a woman how she desperately needs a man." He helped her forward against the wind and rain. "Whose cottage is that ahead by the gate?"

Sharlotte looked up at the large graystone gate overgrown with tangled ivy. An ancient-looking oak tree formed a giant umbrella, but on a day like this, she decided it appeared ghostly and dark, with crooked branches resembling elbows. The wind groaned through its leaves. Beside it stood a small building with a thatch roof.

"It belonged to the old gatekeeper," she said.

"Anyone there now?" he asked curiously.

"No. A gatekeeper stayed there years ago in my grandfather's youth. I never saw him. Pamela, Amanda, and I used to play in there when we were children. I suppose by now it's as full of cobwebs as the boathouse. But I think the telephone is still connected. We used it to call up to the kitchen and have Nana bring us down cookies."

"Let's have a look inside. With this downpour we've a good excuse."

Reluctantly, she went with him toward the shadowed cottage where tangled vines whipped in the wind.

The paved drive, covered with a layer of decaying leaves and seedpods, ended at the solitary gate where squirrels darted for cover at their approach. The poignant smell of sodden earth and molding leaves, beaten down by rain, hung thickly on the air. There was an uneasy mutter in the wind that set her already tender nerves on edge.

They went through the tall gate. The old cobbled carriageway ran ahead through park-like grounds of flowering pink rhododendron bushes and chestnut trees. The cobbled way continued around a corner and up to the main house overlooking the bay toward the yacht club, but from here at the gate the house could not be seen.

The cottage appeared empty and shrouded with eerie silence as had the boathouse.

"Someone's been here recently," Kace said.

There was an overgrown bush covered with red ornamental berries near the front door. Many of the berries had dropped off onto the ground in front of the threshold. Some had been stepped on and squashed recently, their juice staining the cement. Kace tried the door.

"Locked."

"There used to be a skeleton key under that geranium pot."

He looked, and a moment later turned the latch on the front door, opening it. The same musty smell greeted them. Sharlotte followed Kace over the threshold into the darkened room. She loitered by the open door, and saw him look at a crushed berry that had been tracked indoors.

"Who'd come here?" he asked.

"I've no idea, unless it was Mr. Hunnewell. I don't see how that—" she stopped, wrinkling her brow.

"Yes, that does put a crunch on our boathouse scenario, doesn't it. He may have met someone here instead. Then the question is what brought him down to the boat landing steps where he fell?"

Sharlotte closed the door and stood waiting while Kace began a search. She shivered. The overstuffed furniture, a divan and several winged-back chairs that she remembered as a girl, were still in their places. She saw some of her playthings piled in a box in a corner, and a teddy bear belonging to Pamela on a braided rug on the floor. She heard Kace moving around in the small kitchen. The window rattled, and the draft sent the edge of the curtain fluttering. The trees and shrubs that huddled closely beside the walls scratched and tapped and whispered.

A gray mouse ran across the floor and her eyes followed it, her heart in her mouth. Spotting something on the floor, she glanced quickly toward the kitchen door, hearing Kace. He was still occupied in his search. She crossed the room and knelt, reaching for a glove. She examined it, heart thudding. Yes. Her father's glove. The mate to the one he'd had with him in the motorcar that morning when Henry had pulled over to let her in. He had dropped it here, why? What had her father been doing here just before he rode down to the yacht club? Her heart went cold and her stomach felt sick.

"No sign of anyone having been in the kitchen," Kace was saying from the other room.

Sharlotte quickly pushed the glove further beneath the divan and jumped to her feet just as Kace came to the doorway between the two rooms. She didn't trust herself to speak yet, or to look at him, and pretended to be lifting a small embroidered pillow from the seat.

"Whoever came here stayed in this room, I think," he said. "See anything?"

"No," she managed. Did her voice sound strained?

She felt his gaze but she did not turn. If she moved away from the divan now it might draw his attention. She eased herself onto the cushion and looked at him, afraid her face was white, or worse yet, flushed. *If only he didn't notice everything about me,* she thought desperately.

He scanned her, then the floor at her feet. Her heart paused. *This might be a good time to faint,* she thought, *to distract him.* But if she did it would only give him ammunition to later suggest she lacked courage. His gaze held hers and she stared back. Then, he walked over to the telephone and picked up the receiver.

"It's working," he said. He dialed zero. A minute later he spoke to the butler. "Has Mr. Ashford called up from the club? Then ring him, will you? Tell him to call off the search for Hunnewell. He's dead. Ask him to inform the others to come up to the house. Looks as if he fell from the old boathouse steps. Probably hit his head on the way down and drowned…yes, an unfortunate accident."

Kace glanced at the telephone receiver a moment, then slowly replaced it in the cradle. He turned toward Sharlotte, who sat still and cold, staring at him.

He walked over to the divan. Looking down at her with a frown. "You look as if you've seen Hunnewell's ghost."

"I'm tired, is all…can we go now?"

"Sure. Can you walk?"

She nodded.

"I don't think so. What's come over you?"

"Nothing…I just don't feel well."

His unexpected look of concern was mollifying at this wretched moment and she surrendered to it.

"I'd better carry you."

"Yes…"

He reached down and helped her up from the divan. His gaze softened. "This has been one miserable day for you, hasn't it?" He cupped her chin, and despite her woe, her heart lurched when he looked at her lips. She saw his jaw flex and his hand lowered to his side. "The sooner you can change into dry clothes and get something hot to drink, the sooner you'll feel better." He propelled her toward the door, then swung her up into his arms.

"To the house, I think," he said.

~

The Ashford summer "cottage" was a huge, old, two-storied, and rather imposing house, full of rooms and mellowed furnishings of antique quality, most of which remained from the years of Sharlotte's grandfather and great-grandfather, both of whom had been sociable with railroad tycoons Jay Gould and Jay Cooke.

The ground floor was almost entirely an entertaining room— or ballroom, as Amanda called it—with a wide glassed-in porch that encircled the entire lower floor. Potted palms and overflowing greenery hovered lushly over white rattan chairs, benches, and cozy tables where two or three guests might wish to loiter alone. There were three exits from the porch: one led into the big garden, a second into a walkway to the hillside overlooking the bay and yacht club, and the third onto a sweeping driveway that led to the sandy road where earlier that day Sharlotte had waited for her father.

Behind the ballroom were a number of other rooms, including a morning room, a sitting room, and a musty old library that was never used except by Mr. Burgess Ashford, who also kept his office there for meetings with Mr. Hunnewell and other business associates from the New York banking system. A wide but shallow-stepped stairway accessed the rooms on the top floor. It was to her bedroom that Sharlotte escaped upon her arrival with Kace.

In a daze, Sharlotte went through the steps of taking a warm bath and putting on dry clothes without relishing either. Her mind jumped from one horrid incident to another, never quite settling on one long enough to sort through the consequences or the meaning. The image of her father's glove dangled like a skeleton in the dark recesses of her mind. A thousand times the same question arose in fearsome agony: What was it doing there in the old cottage? How had he lost it? What did it mean? Could he have met Hunnewell there? But surely he had nothing to do with Hunnewell's accident? Accident? Kace had said murder. But she knew her father was no murderer! There was some other explanation for the glove, but if the authorities found it they would be suspicious. She couldn't allow that to happen because he was innocent. Why should the scandal in the newspapers touch either her father or herself? It was going to be dreadful enough to have Hunnewell's death associated with their summerhouse and party. She could see the scoop in the newspaper now. Odious. And what would Clarence's grandmother, Lady Fosdick, say to this? She guarded Clarence's unsullied reputation like a bulldog. Any hint of scandal, and it might ruin her future.

I must get Daddy's glove from the cottage and put it safely in his room, she thought. *Tonight will be the perfect opportunity. Tonight at the ball. The ball must go on, Hunnewell's death or not.*

Kace *had* to be wrong about it being murder. When she thought of her friends and relatives, it was unthinkable. She knew all of those gathered at the house, her blood kin, her friends. There certainly wasn't a murderer among them. How could he have concluded that Hunnewell's death was deliberate? Perhaps Hunnewell had ended his own life. No, an accident, she thought again. It was the only acceptable conclusion she could come to, one that the police *must* come to as well.

There was a gathering in the sitting room late that afternoon. Her father had come rushing back to the house as soon as the news of Hunnewell's death had reached him by telephone. He had left word with the servants at the club to alert the others as they came wandering back dripping wet from their vain search. Her father had made the dreaded call to the town authorities almost at once, as soon as Kace had explained about finding the lawyer's body below the stairway.

"Great scot," her father had breathed, shaken. His valet had handed him a brandy and he had lowered himself into a chair looking old and withered. Sharlotte noticed that Kace watched him with intense interest, but also with pity. She was surprised to see the emotion in Kace. She had always felt the Landrys disliked her father, especially Kace.

"Do you have a personal physician?" Kace asked him.

Sharlotte answered: "Yes." She turned to the butler. "Owen, call Dr. Lester, will you?"

"I've already called him, miss. He's on his way."

"Poor old fellow," her father was saying. "I should have warned him to stay away from that area, but how was I to suspect he'd go there?"

Sharlotte took her father's hand between her cold palms. "There wasn't any way you could know, Daddy. Everyone realizes that."

Kace was polite and attentive to her father. Sharlotte was relieved to see that if he did hold suspicions they were not blatantly displayed.

"I understand he likes to take long morning walks, sir."

"Yes, yes, that's true."

"That trail to the old boathouse from the club jetty must have held some attraction for him. Solitude, most likely. He could have been worried about something."

Mr. Ashford and Kace exchanged glances.

"Yes, that's true," her father repeated. "Debt, I think. It terrorizes us all, I'm afraid." Her father frowned and ran his fingers across his wrinkled forehead. "Worried, yes, I wonder…"

Sharlotte looked at him, then at Kace. Why did she have the strange feeling that Kace was guiding the conversation down an acceptable path, and that her father was gratefully following?

"I guess we'll never know why he was worried," Kace said. "I've a notion he's the only one who could tell us."

"Yes…yes, you're probably right. A tragedy."

Burgess stood. "Thank you for your help, Kace. If you don't mind, I'll be up in my room until the authorities arrive."

"Yes, of course, Mr. Ashford. You'd better rest a while. I'll send Dr. Lester up as soon as he gets here."

Her father walked unsteadily toward the stairs, and Kace came alongside him. "Can I help you to your room?"

"Thank you, no. I'll be all right."

Sharlotte followed her father to the stairs and watched him slowly climb upward. Kace came up beside her, and they exchanged glances.

The others arrived two and three at a time, uncertain whether they had heard the bad news correctly and wondering how such a thing could happen on their holiday. First the storm, and now a sudden death. They all rushed off to change into dry clothing before the police inspector arrived, and Sharlotte wandered about trying to take control and falling short.

"What is it you're trying to accomplish?" Kace asked.

She looked at him, dazed. "Everyone needs something to eat and drink. The police, too."

"Go sit down, will you? I'll handle it," he said in a low voice as Clarence sullen, glanced their way.

Kace gave the kitchen help orders to bring in hot coffee, tea, and roast beef sandwiches.

The food was set out buffet style on a long table on the glassed-in veranda and Sharlotte, dressed in sedate white linen, her damp hair pinned on top of her head, sat silently in a chair. Kace brought her a cup of strong black coffee. When Clarence walked up, Kace casually left her side.

Clarence was pale and fidgety. "Revolting business," he told her in a whisper. "For something of this nature to happen when we're all gathered for the weekend at your father's residence. Hunnewell's suicide could become a regular feast for the gluttons of journalism."

Amanda had been listening. "Suicide? What makes you think that, Clarence?"

"Use your head, Amanda. What else would it be?"

So Clarence noticed the unusual set of circumstances too, but instead of murder, he had opted for suicide, thought Sharlotte.

"Why couldn't it have simply been an accident?" Amanda said.

"I suppose it could be that, but suicide is more likely. Dreadfully embarrassing for all of us."

Kace said dryly: "Yes, it was rather inconsiderate of Hunnewell to ruin everyone's summer yachting event."

Sharlotte was prepared for fireworks. She didn't have to wait long. Clarence turned to him sharply, taking him in with a measuring glance. "I find it strangely curious, Mr. Landry, that you found the body."

"Do you?"

"Yes. You're a stranger here, and all that sort of thing. How did you know to go to the old boathouse launch?"

Sharlotte tensed. Her gaze cautiously moved to meet Kace's. How was he going to explain his reason for going there?

Kace smiled lazily. "I didn't know, actually."

Clarence looked smug, as if he'd deducted some important bit of information that the authorities would need to look into.

Then Kace offered: "The back trail up to the house was Sharlotte's choice for a secluded walk for our private reunion. We hadn't seen each other in over two years and we had so much to say." Sharlotte caught her breath silently. She looked from Kace's amused green eyes to Clarence, who was turning an ugly burnt color. He turned on his heel and strode into the sitting room.

Kace walked up and Sharlotte stood, whispering heatedly: "How could you? You might have come up with *anything* better than that."

Kace smiled. "I doubt it." He plucked a sugary donut from a large platter. "Besides, he had it coming—between his loaded question about knowing where the body was and his superior attitude."

"You know what he thinks now, don't you?"

"Yes, he's worried. And very uneasy about why I've come to Long Island on the summer of your coming out. That should benefit you in the long run," he said lightly. "He's more likely to fight a little harder to get an engagement ring on your finger. That's what you want. Anyway, I had to come up with a good reason for both of us being up there. It's not a good idea for anyone to think you went on a hunch, or that I followed you because I had one. This suicide idea isn't new. I put that bug in your father's ear an hour ago. I also let it slip to him that we were recovering from something rather like a Texas prairie fire romance just a few years ago."

"You *what?*" she breathed.

"So when I arrived this morning, lightning struck. Wham! Cupid's arrow sizzles again. We took a stroll on the back trail together, just two innocents driven by old romantic embers. Your father is so worried about Hunnewell he didn't have the heart or the courage to rebuke me." He smiled.

"No!" Sharlotte flushed. But some of his drama wasn't too far-fetched, including the "wham" and "sizzle" part. She turned and left him at the buffet table with his donut.

Cousins Sheldon and Pamela had arrived in the large sitting room when Sharlotte entered. Bitsy was also there, even more wide-eyed than usual (and staring at Kace, Sharlotte noticed with irritation). Kace had come in from the veranda and removed himself to the far side of the room beside the Victrola and a stack of records. Clarence had his back toward him and was eying Sharlotte unhappily.

The room darkened from the thickening clouds, and rain lashed the glass, sealing them all in gloom. Sharlotte sat twisting a gold bracelet round and round, her eyes restlessly moving from one person to the next.

"Ghastly," Pamela was saying. "Amanda dear, you're seated by the light switch, can you turn it on? Or are we broke and saving electricity?"

Amanda reached up and flicked the switch. "Oooh—how glum and sour you all look." She turned it back off.

"Stop that, kiddo," Cousin Sheldon said with a wry smile. "This is our interlude before the funeral—a dress rehearsal. Someone needs to mourn old Hunnewell."

"You're right. Poor Hunnewell, why did he even go up there? And in a storm!" Amanda said plaintively.

"I agree it's not what I would call a friendly jaunt," Sheldon said. "Strange, isn't it?"

"Not so much really," Clarence said sourly. "Many honorable men choose the easy way out of an impossible pitfall by taking their own lives."

"As long as one doesn't end up in a worse pit," Amanda said. She turned. "Sharlotte? Didn't you tell me that preacher Billy Sunday said that if you don't believe in God you will go to hell?"

"Jeepers! That means all of us," Bitsy wailed.

"Speak for yourself," Pamela snapped. "I happen to believe in God."

"He didn't say God," Sharlotte corrected uneasily, aware that everyone was looking at her, no doubt wondering if she listened to Billy Sunday. "He said a person must believe in Jesus Christ as the only Savior from the penalty of sin."

"I wonder if poor old Hunnewell believed?" Bitsy crooned.

"'Please,'" Clarence said with strained boredom, "can we change the subject?"

"Sure, let's talk about murder," Sheldon said with mock cheer.

"Murder!" Bitsy squeaked.

Sharlotte glanced at Kace. He regarded Sheldon with a pensive look. This was the first time anyone had mentioned anything other than suicide. Why had Sheldon said that?

"If Hunnewell didn't end his life, then it must be murder," Sheldon said with a shrug. "Say! You should see your faces, everyone. You all look like yesterday's breakfast. Ha! That's funny. As if anyone here could murder old Hunnewell. Ha, ha, ha."

Clarence scowled at him. "You're not even faintly amusing, Sheldon. I think you've had too much to drink, as usual."

"Yes, this isn't vaudeville," Pamela groaned to her brother. "Do keep quiet, Sheldon."

"Sharlotte walked up to the old boathouse," Clarence said stiffly. "At least someone thought it a favorable stroll, even with the storm blowing in. Isn't that right, Sharlotte?"

Sharlotte, aware that everyone looked at her, and then at Clarence, baffled by his nettled tone, remained silent and embarrassed, which was what Clarence had meant to accomplish. She looked at her hands, biting her lip.

"What Clarence means," Kace drawled, "is that Sharlotte and I walked the back trail together. Although we didn't run into Hunnewell, we did find it conducive to a…quiet chat."

It was clear from Clarence's face that he hadn't banked on Kace admitting such a thing in front of everyone. "Oooh, romantic," cooed Bitsy with a giggle.

"I admit we were only halfheartedly looking for Hunnewell," Kace said. "As it turned out, we got the shock of our lives. Poor Sharlotte. She nearly fainted."

Sharlotte didn't look at Kace, and she also ignored Clarence's furious stare. So that was the story Kace wanted everyone to accept.

Silence settled in the room, then Amanda said: "I know of at least three times when the family's talked about redoing the old launch and boathouse."

"Too bad we're all a pack of procrastinators," Sheldon sighed. "If Hunnewell could get in touch with us like Houdini, he might sue us."

"Or admit Billy Sunday's right about the afterlife," George said.

"That's in horridly bad taste," Pamela said, bored.

"I didn't mean it to be," George said. "Did you ever hear him preach? No? Well, I have. He gave me a lot to think about."

Amanda looked at him, but Pamela made a gesture of dismissal and reached for a cigarette from the box on the table. She turned toward Clarence, who stepped forward and flicked the lighter, then sat down beside her, being overly attentive, Sharlotte noted. *This is all Kace's fault.* She watched Pamela and Clarence talking together in a hushed tone, as though the others were too immature for their dignity.

Amanda wheeled to the window. "As the British say, keep a stiff upper lip everyone. Here come the police investigators."

Pamela looked over at Sharlotte curiously. "Where's Uncle Burgess?"

"In his room." Sharlotte stood from her chair. "He isn't feeling well. Mr. Hunnewell's been a friend for years. He feels dreadful about not fixing those steps."

"Crying over spilt milk and all that," Sheldon said.

Sharlotte turned away. "I'd better go up and tell him they're here." She crossed the room to the stairway and started up. Kace soon joined her, ignoring Clarence, and when they were out of view she halted.

"Did you really need to say all that in front of everyone?" she whispered heatedly, but he interrupted: "Better get used to it. Your father snapped it up like a hungry trout."

Sharlotte caught her breath in a hard gasp. "He did?"

"We need time to develop the truth. I don't know what that is yet. But neither does anyone else. One thing's clear—it isn't looking good for your father."

"If you mean—"

"The sooner you accept that the better," Kace told her in a low, but firm voice. "You're in no position to behave foolishly. If you hope to cover for your father you won't do it by letting them know you went there alone. They'll soon catch on. Once they figure out you're trying to protect him they'll turn on him like a pack of wolves."

"You can't really believe he had anything to do with it. You can't! If it wasn't an accident, then it *must* be suicide."

"Maybe. I have my doubts, but I can't say why now. Look, Sharlotte, you have only your own word for what happened up there, and why you went there alone after sending Clarence on a wild goose chase. If they decide that Hunnewell's death is criminal, they may think you're harboring evidence to protect your father."

Sharlotte leaned against the banister. Kace watched her alertly. He stepped closer. "Did you see anything in the gatekeeper's cottage that frightened you? They'll search there eventually."

Chilling panic rolled over her soul, but she couldn't tell him about her father's glove. She must get it back, tonight. "I—I don't know."

"Sharlotte, you have no idea how really difficult things can get for you if you find yourself involved in a police inquiry. Unless you have a credible motive for wanting to search the old boat landing after Hunnewell's disappearance, the police will suspect that you were privy to something important that preceded his death. From there, it would be quite routine for them to get you to make a slip, especially if they thought you were trying to protect your father. Now you know why I have been setting the stage and promoting our being together on a romantic quest. So you see, I am asking you to trust me and go along with it for now, and—you can always patch things up with Clarence later when this has all blown over."

They both looked upstairs as footsteps sounded. Burgess Ashford came into view. He looked weak and drawn and was still wearing his jacket, but there was an animated glow to his eyes. *Why?* she wondered. *What happened to give him a little courage while up in his room? Was it the rest?*

Sharlotte didn't think he had heard Kace's words, so she said in a rush: "Oh, hello Daddy…"

"The police are here, sir," Kace said quietly.

"Yes, I saw them from my window. Good. About time. The sooner this tragedy is cleared up the sooner we can get back to matters at hand." He came down the stairs, and Kace stepped aside so that he could pass between them.

Burgess stopped. "By the way, Kace, it may be wiser if we didn't mention you came here to meet Hunnewell on money matters."

Sharlotte was taken by the expression on Kace's face. He looked at her father, long and hard.

Burgess removed a Cuban cigar from his pocket. "Naturally you'll stay on? We have so much to talk about once this unsightly mess with Hunnewell is cleared up with the police." Her father turned toward Sharlotte. "There should be plenty to do to keep you two busy over the next few days. If at all possible, we'd better go on with that ball tonight. There's no time to inform all the guests that it's been postponed."

"Yes, Daddy…of course." She glanced up at Kace. His face revealed nothing of his thoughts.

Burgess went on down the stairs.

Sharlotte stood silently, wondering. She didn't think it had been his first intention to ask Kace to stay the week, let alone suggest that she favor him with her company.

Kace was staring thoughtfully after her father with eyes that appeared to be gazing past him. When he said nothing, she whispered: "What he said was important?"

"Just remember what I told you." He went down the stairs. She followed a moment later, dazed.

Sharlotte neared the sitting room doorway where Kace waited for her. Glancing about, she saw that her father wasn't there yet. "Where's Daddy?" Sharlotte asked Amanda quietly.

"He's coming. I saw him hanging his coat in the hat room," and she glanced down the hall. Kace also looked in that direction, then, taking Sharlotte's arm, they entered the room together.

8

Dr. Lester, soon to retire from his general practice and adamant that he'd had sufficient experience throughout his career to make a determination on accidental death by drowning, reported briefly and with calm certainty to the gathered authorities that such had been the fate of the late Mr. Hunnewell. This event hadn't surprised him, he stated crisply.

"Would you comment further on that please, Dr. Lester?" asked Inspector Browden.

"Certainly. I've been treating him recently for a heart ailment. He's complained of dizziness. In fact, he'd told me only last week that he'd taken a tumble getting out of his cab to enter a hotel lobby. I was called to see him in his room, and he had a bruise on his right knee and on the palm of his hand."

Sharlotte, sitting quietly beside Amanda, contained her surprise and glanced briefly at Kace. He was watching Dr. Lester.

"It is my medical opinion that Mr. Hunnewell had another of those dizzy spells and tried unsuccessfully to regain his balance by holding onto the rail. Unfortunately, it was too rotten to provide support. It appears that he struck his head going down."

"He was unconscious when he hit the water?"

"I can't determine that for certain, but it is my opinion that he was."

"Death by drowning?"

"Yes, Inspector."

However, Dr. Lester admitted he was somewhat puzzled about why Mr. Hunnewell would be climbing those precarious steps. He suggested a possible suicide. "He was an ill man and he knew it."

"Doesn't it appear a little strange, Doctor, that a man contemplating suicide would choose such a difficult way to go about it?"

"Well, yes, there is that…but men under duress are known to make bizarre decisions, Inspector."

Mr. Burgess Ashford, distraught, said with self-incrimination that he should have hired builders to fix the rotting wood long ago.

Duress, the police inspector asked, because of ill health?

But Dr. Lester stated that Mr. Hunnewell had been in poor spirits since his arrival on Long Island. Hunnewell had called him to his hotel two days ago highly upset. No, he hadn't explained what he'd been distressed about, but Dr. Lester assumed it had something to do with debt, and that Mr. Ashford would be better able to explain the matter.

The word "debt" stirred Sharlotte's memory. The doctor's explanation sounded familiar. Kace had said much the same thing, except it was her father instead of Hunnewell whom Kace had claimed was having trouble. Then, there'd been that strange conversation between her father and Kace on the stairway only an hour ago.

It was true, her father was saying reluctantly, Mr. Hunnewell did have a reputation for making poor investments in the market. He'd recently mentioned losing a "great deal of money due to some margin calls."

Inspector Browden then turned to Kace, asking him to repeat his story of how he found the body, what he was doing there, and had he seen anything curious when he'd brought him up from the rocky shoreline. They went over the same questions several times, and Sharlotte grew tense, wondering if they would ever be satisfied. Kace refused to become ruffled. He was calm and cool, and the inspector at last turned to Sharlotte, whose handkerchief was balled in her sweaty palm. She was pleased to answer her questions after Kace. He had set the tone, and the agenda, and she merely followed the well-worn path of what had happened.

"Then you and Mr. Landry deliberately walked that solitary trail to the old boat launch because you wanted to be alone together?"

Sharlotte felt Clarence's hard stare, and looking past him encountered Kace's gaze. Yes, he seemed to say. Sharlotte turned her eyes away. "Yes." She added, trying to turn the idea away from romance: "We had so much to talk about. The family in Texas, the ranch—" she stopped. "I used to visit in the summer."

Sharlotte was surprised when her father reached across and took her hand into his as though he understood about some past relationship between her and Kace and was fully supportive. Kace wore a ghost of a smile. After the way the Ashfords had rejected him all these years, he must have found the sudden change amusing. Sharlotte was anything but amused. Especially when Clarence said testily: "And you just *happened* to notice Hunnewell dead below the steps, is that it, Mr. Landry?"

"No. It was the broken step I noticed first. Then the damaged railing," Kace said calmly. "Even though Sharlotte and I weren't especially looking for Mr. Hunnewell, we were well aware that he was missing from the picnic party and that he may have injured himself. And when I looked down the steps toward the water, I saw him." He looked from Clarence's tight face to the inspector. "He was floating face down and his coat appeared to be caught on the rocks. When I brought him up to the bank, there were no signs of life, not so much as a heartbeat. With the storm coming in I knew if I didn't get him away from the shoreline we could lose his body to the sea. By then the waves were stirring up and it was beginning to rain. When I got him up on the launch I wrapped him in a tarp that I found in the boathouse. Then Sharlotte and I walked toward the house and used the phone in the old gatekeeper's cottage to get in contact with Mr. Ashford at the club."

"Pardon, Mr. Landry?" a voice interrupted politely.

They looked at the butler who stepped forward with a bow and a straight face. "I do believe, sir, you called *me* from the gatekeeper's cottage and asked me to call down to the club for you."

Sharlotte tensed. Her eyes swerved to Kace. She held her breath. He, however, remained outwardly calm.

"Yes, you're quite accurate, Owen."

Clarence looked pleased. "So you *forgot* whom you called?"

"Mr. Fosdick," the inspector spoke out, "you'll need to exercise restraint, or I'll ask you to leave the room, sir."

Clarence walked to the other side, but he looked back at Kace, watching him.

"Go on, Mr. Landry."

"Sharlotte and I were in a hurry to call her father. She mentioned a telephone in the old cottage by the gate, and thought that it might still be connected. We stopped and found that it was working, and I called Owen with the unfortunate news for her father. Mr. Ashford must have called the police as soon as he got our message. Then we came up to the house to wait for him."

Sharlotte didn't move. She thought she knew what was going on in her father's mind. Then, again, perhaps he didn't know where he'd lost his glove. Now, her father knew she and Kace had been in the cottage.

The inspector seemed satisfied even if Clarence did not, and her heart slowed its frantic beating.

It must have been another hour before each of the others testified to what they'd seen and heard at the club earlier that morning, which was very little. Bitsy told of seeing Mr. Hunnewell leave hurriedly, looking upset, and this appeared to interest the policeman.

"It was right after the argument between Clarence and Stuart," Bitsy said. "I don't think he liked it one bit."

Clarence flushed and explained that he and Stuart had disagreed over politics. He would be opposing Stuart for the congressional seat occupied by Stuart's father.

"Naturally, we disagreed over which one of us would make the best Congressman for the district."

The inspector looked at Stuart, who also looked embarrassed. "That right, Mr. Hillier?"

"Yes. It was politics as usual, Inspector," he said with a smile. "We'll argue again over it, I'm sure, until it's settled by the voters."

"Neither of you have any idea why this argument would upset Mr. Hunnewell?" the inspector asked.

Both Clarence and Stuart agreed that they didn't. As neither of them knew him very well, perhaps Bitsy had misread his demeanor?

Bitsy shrugged. "I suppose I could have. But I mentioned it to Sharlotte and she was on her way to find him when the roadster pulled up with Mr. Landry and, well, we all got sidetracked until Mr. Ashford showed up. Mr. Hunnewell hadn't been seen, and the storm was blowing in. That's when we split up and began to search."

The inspector remained courteous and sympathetic, and after taking their names and addresses and completing other formalities, he stood and turned with hand extended to Mr. Ashford. He assured him that the matter would be seen to with the utmost promptness. As far as he was concerned, the death of Mr. Hunnewell had been accidental, but they couldn't rule out suicide. There were enough questions remaining to warrant an inquest, and he would be contacted along with the others at the appropriate time. No one was to leave Long Island until after the inquest was held.

An inquest, Sharlotte thought worriedly. It wasn't over yet. Her hopes that the matter would be quickly closed were dashed.

The inspector went on to tell her father that all would be done with consideration for family privacy. And with that, the imperious Dr. Lester took charge again, worrying aloud that his patient was tiring. Mr. Ashford was under medical supervision for his blood pressure, and he must have adequate rest until the funeral several days hence. He would give his patient a sedative and then file all the medical papers.

After the inspector left, Mr. Ashford was taken up to his room where Dr. Lester presided over his medication. The others loitered, discussing the proceeding in low voices, and then Kace was at Sharlotte's elbow saying quietly: "I need to speak with you alone. Where can we meet without Clarence breathing fire down my neck?"

She could see Clarence watching them. If anything he appeared more upset than earlier.

"Daddy wants the dinner party to go on uninterrupted tonight. There'll be some new guests driving in if the storm doesn't discourage them from coming. We can meet then."

Kace left her, and she wondered if he'd gone up to the room arranged for him, or out into the pouring rain. A minute later she heard the distant roar of a motor.

Sharlotte went to the window in time to see him driving away in George's roadster. Where had he gone, and why? "Daddy's really taking Hunnewell's death hard," Amanda worried. "He feels responsible for those old steps giving way."

"That's nonsense," Sharlotte hastened. "Daddy had no idea Hunnewell would go up there. And you heard what Dr. Lester said about Hunnewell's debts and his worries about his health. He must have taken his life."

Just then, George and Stuart walked up.

"You girls going to be all right?" George asked, looking at Amanda. "What can we do to cheer you up?"

"We're hale and hardy," Amanda said with a short laugh. "And you can help me call the other guests to see how many can make it tonight in this storm." They went off together to find a telephone in one of the private rooms.

Stuart was looking into his empty cup with a frown. Sharlotte smiled at him and said lightly: "Still angry with Clarence?"

He looked at her surprised, then grinned. He glanced in his political opponent's direction, but Clarence was once again in deep, quiet conversation with Pamela, and his back was toward them.

"No, he's a fair chap, but a little testy at times. Sorry," he hastened when Sharlotte raised a brow. "I forget you and he—" then he stopped, and glanced to where Kace had been earlier, curious. Sharlotte quickly changed the subject to the dinner party, asking whether or not Lucille Farnsworth would be his date. His eyes brightened, and he explained he would be going after her around four o'clock that afternoon. "It's nearly that time now," Sharlotte told him. "That reminds me, I have much to do before six." She was about to excuse herself when Stuart said in a quiet voice: "What I wanted to ask you concerns the boy I saw at the jetty this morning. I'm a little confused about him, and wondered if you knew his family. His last name was Drummond." Stuart's eyes were inquisitive. "At the time I didn't think much of it, but with this accidental death, or suicide, however the police see it—I wondered about that boy."

Sharlotte's brows went up. "You don't think a little boy had anything to do with it?"

"No, naturally not, that's not what I meant."

"What did you mean?" she asked, keeping her voice casual.

He shrugged. "Oh, I don't know, maybe all this has gotten to me, first with Clarence this morning, then the storm, and now this scandal breaking over your father."

"I'm sure there won't be a scandal," she said firmly. "Everyone understands a man can be mentally—well, very upset, and do something rash. The police seem to think that's what happened. So does Dr. Lester."

"Seems a little rash to me, to have taken his life like that in such a blundering way. I could think of an easier way out."

"About the boy," she hurried. "Drummond runs the stable down at the yacht club. I believe the boy you saw is his son."

"Oh…I see. Well, that makes sense."

"It's quite normal for someone his age to be attracted to the boats," she added.

"Yes, I suppose you're right." He looked thoughtfully at his cup. "But thinking back with hindsight now that we know what happened to Hunnewell, I could almost believe the boy was there waiting for someone. Oh, well. I don't suppose there's anything to it."

There was a brief moment of silence. She collected herself with an effort. "You must have your doubts as well. You didn't mention it just now to the inspector."

Stuart's brows drew together in a frown. "No use adding more hay to the straw man. I just thought I'd ask to see if you knew who he was." He glanced at his watch. "I'd better be running. If I'm late to pick up Lucille she'll be upset all evening. Look at that rain! See you later, Sharlotte."

Sharlotte, anxious to escape to her room to think through all that was happening, replied suitably, and Stuart dashed off.

She walked to the window. Outside, the daylight had given way to stormy shadows. Where had Kace gone in George's roadster? Aware that the others had drifted away, she too left the parlor and climbed the stairs to her room to ready herself for the dinner party. Thunder mumbled overhead and the electric lights flickered for a moment, then came back on. She hoped they wouldn't go out tonight.

And then there was the matter of the glove beneath the divan in the cottage. She would need to go there late tonight and retrieve it. The lonely jaunt in the wind and rain would not be pleasant.

9

If the picnic had been a failure, the dinner party and dance could well be classed as a dark and sober dirge. Mr. Ashford informed Sharlotte and Amanda to put up a "front" and to go through with the entertainment that night. With a house full of family and still more guests on the way, there was no time to postpone the long-planned event which was the last dance of the summer season. The gathering might even serve to take everyone's minds off the ordeal. Sharlotte, however, didn't think anything could free her of her nagging fears and dreaded suspicions.

"It does seem a little ghoulish to throw a party the night someone drowns," Sharlotte was telling Amanda in her room as she dressed. She looked lovely in a silvery-blue gown and her mother's sapphires.

"Daddy says Hunnewell wasn't family," Amanda said. "So our friends won't find it necessary to don black and mourn. Still, I think you're right. It doesn't quite seem appropriate considering we've known Mr. Hunnewell all our lives."

Sharlotte remained uneasy. She slipped on her silvery satin slippers. She was sure her unrest had something to do with Kace and the suspicions he had aired at the boathouse, not to mention the disturbing emotion of seeing him again.

"If this storm continues we may not have too many guests to explain things to," Sharlotte said wistfully.

"Oh! You're right. There's been a phone call. Skip and Julia and Benton and Muffie begged off. The wind will ruin their hairstyles. And Muffie's taffeta dress will shrink if it gets wet. They're staying home and dancing to the Victrola—they've got her little brother Tommy to stand on a stool and keep it cranking."

Sharlotte breathed a little easier. At any other time she would have been upset by their blasé treatment of her dinner dance, but not tonight. She counted on her fingers thoughtfully. "Smashing. That leaves just three other couples coming, and they probably won't know a thing about what's happened today with Hunnewell."

Amanda frowned thoughtfully. "It still seems curious why Hunnewell would go to that musty old boathouse the way he did."

"Oh *don't*," Sharlotte groaned. "Let's not get on that horrid subject again."

Amanda looked sheepish. "Yes, you're right."

"The police already asked all their questions and left satisfied."

Amanda's eyes were thoughtful. "Did you think they were?"

Sharlotte unconsciously frowned. "Well…yes! Didn't you?"

Amanda shrugged and watched Sharlotte walk back to the mirror, smoothing her golden hair into place.

Sharlotte was still thinking of the police. What if they weren't satisfied?

"Do hurry, Sharlotte. We'll be late—" she stopped, turning to look toward the window facing the drive.

Sharlotte too heard a motor and hurried across the highly polished wood floor and Persian rugs and drew the fluff of pink curtain aside.

Below, Owen was walking swiftly to the shiny wet motorcar with an umbrella, holding it to protect the passengers who emerged from the backseat. A flash of satin, diamonds, and platinum hair told her it was Gloria.

"Too late," Sharlotte said, hurrying to the bedroom door. "If we can just keep the others quiet at the dinner table we might make it through the evening without mentioning Hunnewell." But she feared that was very much like trying to silence a flock of crows. Especially Pamela, she thought miserably.

Sharlotte went into the hall and down the staircase, her long silky skirt floating behind.

Chandelier light poured gracefully upon the wide, glossy stairway as she came down, aware that her entrance caused a flattering stir as the male guests turned in her direction. For once, she hardly noticed or cared. She glanced about for her father to handle the awkward evening.

Mr. Ashford was not in the large square hallway to welcome the guests. From the corner of her eye she noticed Kace leaning in the dim doorway of the library, as though separate from the scene playing out before him.

Where had he gone earlier? He had returned just a short time ago and went straight up to his room to change. Sharlotte hadn't time to query him about where he'd been in George's borrowed roadster. He looked terribly handsome in a dinner jacket and impeccable white shirt.

Sharlotte's plans to escape responsibility fell through when her father, who normally would have sat at the head of the table and presided, sent word down through his valet that he'd become ill and developed a state of "the shakes" as he called the condition. "Ill? Poor Uncle Burgess," Pamela spoke out boisterously. "Do you suppose he still blames himself for Hunnewell's drowning, Sharlotte?"

Pamela! Sharlotte looked into the sea of stunned faces turned in her direction. Both Clarence and Sheldon were in the next room, and Sharlotte had to face curious gasps from her guests all alone. It seemed to her that every eye had suddenly turned to scrutinize her response to Pamela's horrid revelation.

She stood, momentarily floundering, before she realized Kace had come up beside her, his hand warm and steady on her elbow, saying calmly to the valet: "Does Mr. Ashford have medication for his illness?"

"He does, sir," came the crisp voice, "but he's out of it at the moment."

"Then put a call through to his doctor—what was his name, Lester?—and have the prescription delivered to the house," Kace said patiently.

"Yes, sir."

When the valet left, Kace looked down at Sharlotte and she blushed, realizing that she should have known what to do, and that it was all quite simple. She saw a faint glimmer of amusement in his green eyes. His fingers tightened on her arm. "Why don't you introduce me to your new guests, Cousin Sharlotte?"

Her lashes lowered. *It looks like I'm going to need his help, and where's Clarence?*

"Yes...this is my father's nephew, Kace Landry—from Texas," she told them.

When Kace turned with polished manners to fulfill his social obligations, she realized he had smoothly given her opportunity to gather her wits and prepare for the ordeal ahead. A glance toward Pamela showed a rather smug look on her face as she turned and walked into the next room where Clarence and her brother Sheldon had appeared in the doorway. Sheldon, seeing a friend who shared his passion for sailing, entered into conversation with enthusiasm and soon the awkward opening to the dinner had been replaced with voices and laughter, as everyone appeared to have moved past Pamela's odd remark.

In a moment of brief respite Kace leaned toward her and whispered: "Is Burgess really ill?"

She looked at him, at first surprised and then a little indignant. She whispered back, "Are you suggesting he might be only pretending?"

"Just a suspicion. I also suspect that this is one gala affair you wouldn't mind missing. If I gave you half a chance you'd fly up to your bedroom like a little butterfly."

"I have more composure than that, thank you." She pulled her arm from his steadying grasp.

He laughed. "Just don't leave me to entertain your elite society friends."

"I'd hardly wish to ruin their evening," she retorted.

"Good, then now's your chance to show your courage. Your cousin is secretly enjoying watching you wilt."

She glanced toward Pamela. Kace was right. She was watching them both with a bright, curious gaze.

"I gather she's your rival for dear, dear Clarence," he said. "Very popular fellow. But I always thought little girls didn't like boys with horn-rimmed glasses."

Sharlotte's lashes narrowed. She fumed silently.

"Maybe they don't mind when his daddy owns millions."

"I think you're appalling," she whispered. "And you're a fine one to talk. Bitsy hasn't taken her eyes off you since you arrived."

"You mean Sheldon's girlfriend? How did she get included in this circle of blue bloods? I'd have thought mama wouldn't approve." He scanned Bitsy in her short flapper dress with bangles. Bitsy wrinkled her nose at him and twitched the cigarette she held, suggesting he come and light it.

"Sheldon's twenty-seven," Sharlotte said stiffly. "He does what he wants."

"Until his allowance runs out."

She wondered how Kace understood them so well, though she did not find his analysis comforting. At present, however, she was merely looking for the least painful way to make it through the evening. Self-preservation and avoidance of unpleasant things remained her goal. Kace stirred up too many embers and threatened to reignite slow burning fires. She was determined to keep her distance in more ways than one.

"Kace? Can I speak to you for a moment?" Stuart spoke out from the library doors behind them.

What's that about? wondered Sharlotte. She left them and joined the guests in the sitting room until the messenger boy arrived from Dr. Lester bringing Mr. Ashford's prescription. Worried about her father, Sharlotte took it upon herself to bring the medicine upstairs to his room.

Arriving a moment later, she tapped on the door.

Silence greeted her. Not even his valet appeared to be in the room. Her poor father must have fallen asleep. Should she let him know his medicine was here? But what if he wasn't asleep…what if he had passed out?

The very thought that she might find him unconscious alarmed her. She could afford to lose many things in life, but *not* her father. He was her towering bulwark of security and wisdom. The great mind that had built the Ashford financial empire. The notion that he could become vulnerable to the mindless twists and turns of life gave her a pang. Her father had always said there was no God. The Bible was myth. Man made his own heaven and hell. He even created his own gods, not that they were real, but man needed something bigger than himself to believe in. But now she had a terrifying feeling that she might find her father, like the Wizard of Oz, a mere illusion of the power and security she had trusted in.

Her hand shook slightly as she turned the brass knob of the massive oak door, only to find it locked from the inside. She was almost relieved. She could delay looking inside for fear of finding that her trepidation had turned to harsh reality.

She was behaving irrationally. Her anxiety must be prompted by the glove in the gatekeeper's cottage. The question must eventually be answered: What was it doing there? The question accused her of cowardice. Answer if you dare. Why had he lost it? Doing…what?

Sharlotte closed her eyes tightly, as if by doing so she could obliterate the question from her mind. She turned and fled back to the stairway, rushing down without stopping and colliding breathlessly into Kace coming out of the library where he'd been talking to Stuart. The butler had soberly announced dinner and Kace was on his way to the dining room.

He caught and steadied her. He glanced up where the chandelier light fell upon the stairs as though expecting to see someone she was fleeing. The wind hammered at the door, personifying evil to her frightened heart.

His frown deepened. "Are you all right?" he asked quietly.

"Y-es. I—" she stopped. How could she say she was terrified of something unknown and not clearly understood? That "something" waited for her in the future and she believed it threatened to destroy her. She had no one to turn to, because Kace disliked everything she stood for. He wanted to see the Ashford empire ruined. He wanted to see her trembling before him.

A skeptical brow lifted as he tilted his head, scanning her. "Running from Clarence?" The wind groaned around the door and porch pillars as if trying to invade the house.

She jerked away, her gaze accusing. Kace represented some of what she feared. He was unspoiled, and she believed he tolerated the society of those she mingled with only because it also amused him at times to watch their lives played out before him. She even suspected he found her father's situation amusing.

"There is nothing wrong," she said heatedly, "except your presence. I wish you'd go back to Texas!"

His eyes flickered with something she did not recognize. "I intend to do just that. Don't worry. I'm not here to try to convince you not to marry Clarence. I told you that before. I came to see your father. I'm not leaving until he and I discuss what I came here about."

"He's ill. You know that."

"Do I?"

"What do you mean by that?" she asked, hiding her fear.

"Is he in his room?"

She stared at him. "Yes. But you can't go up there."

"I've no intention of barging into his room just now." Again, he frowned. "In another moment you'll be throwing a tantrum or lapsing into a faint to get your way."

"Oh!" she sputtered, too furious for words. She flounced away, leaving him in the dim shadows of the library door.

She wished ardently that she had never laid eyes on him. The important thing now was to not lose Clarence to the suspicion and jealousy that Kace had baited with his explanation of why they'd walked together to the old boathouse. Cousin Pamela was already using that situation to her own advantage.

I can't lose Clarence, she thought. *A marriage and everything that will come with it are too important for my future.*

10

Sharlotte paused just outside the dining room door for a moment before entering, composing herself before facing the well-lighted room which would present her with many searching eyes. When she walked in, she did so with grace, her dress shimmering. The men stood and Clarence came toward her, his hand outstretched, his expression seeking information.

"We've been waiting for you, Sharlotte darling."

Though her heart ached, she managed the practiced sweet smile she had been taught to display. "So sorry I'm late, everyone."

"Is Burgess all right?" Clarence asked.

"Of course he is," Sheldon said with a laugh before Sharlotte could answer. He stood by a window streaked with rain, a cocktail glass in hand as usual. Although there was a smile on his tanned face, his pale blue eyes had a weariness about them.

Stuart, looking thoughtful, said: "I doubt it was Hunnewell's death that made him unsteady."

Sharlotte looked across the brightly lit dining room at the mahogany furnishings and glistening white linen tablecloth. The backdrop of the glassed-in veranda had lost its tropical glow of greenery and flowers, and they stood darkly silhouetted as a flash of lightning crackled across the ocean.

There came a slight pause and everyone looked at Stuart, who was gazing thoughtfully into his glass, stirring its contents with an olive on a toothpick.

Cousin Pamela shrugged her pale shoulders with fateful forbearance. "You mean he's worried about the stock market?"

Stuart looked over at her, but made no reply.

"The tumble on the market yesterday has given us all the jitters," Pamela continued. "The radio said margin calls were prompting an avalanche of selling with no end in sight. Before it's over we'll all be bleeding. We've lost a ton of money."

Sheldon toasted his sister. "Tons," he corrected, and emptied his glass.

"You can always count on Pamela for encouragement," someone offered dryly.

"But Uncle Burgess isn't the type who'll waste much time hanging about his bed," Sheldon said. "He'll be wanting to board the train back to New York for Monday's opening. He's a real fighter."

"No one can leave until after the inquest," Stuart said glumly.

Sharlotte became aware that Clarence was speaking to her in a low voice and looked at him quickly. "Yes? I'm sorry, Clarence…"

He looked at her oddly. "I asked if Dr. Lester sent the prescription over yet?"

She looked down and saw that she was still holding the small paper bag with the prescription bottle inside. "Oh—yes…he did."

"Here," he reached for it. "I'll bring it up to your father."

She gripped it. "No, I already went up. He's asleep. I don't want to wake him until after dinner."

Clarence took her hand, holding it for a moment. He lowered his voice again as he glanced toward the dining room doorway, his countenance reflecting restrained dislike. "Where's Kace?"

"I don't know," she said stiffly. "Never mind about him."

"I'm happy to hear you say that, darling. I was beginning to wonder."

"Wonder? About what?" she said, though she knew what he meant.

"Us."

"Don't be an old silly," she whispered. "I don't care a thing about Kace Landry."

Clarence appeared pleased, but still uncertain. He glanced around the room. "They're waiting." He brought her toward the head of the table and seated her where her father would have sat. Amanda entered with Kace and offered a lighthearted apology.

Dinner proved to be a somber affair despite Sharlotte's intentions to keep the conversation entertaining. There was so much on her mind that she often lapsed into silence without realizing it.

The rain worsened her mood, for Sharlotte couldn't help thinking of the gatekeeper's cottage. Perhaps she'd only imagined seeing a glove. No, she couldn't pretend, she must face the harsh reality of returning to that horrid spot tonight when everyone was asleep.

Her eyes moved around the table. They were all laughing and talking pleasantly. They didn't suspect anything abnormal, so why was she so tense?

I must relax. It must have been one of the gardener's gloves.

But no. She knew better. The gardener couldn't waste money on expensive gloves from Italy. The police would know that too. And her father…

Her father always had his gloves monogrammed.

The bite of soufflé was tasteless and sank like a quarry rock to her stomach. She set her fork down, her appetite dead, and reached for her small crystal water glass and sipped, feeling faint. What if B. A. were embroidered on the glove? What could she do to change things? How could she keep silent? This was her beloved father. The question repeated itself over and over.

Somehow aware of Kace's lazy stare, she glanced in his direction. *He knows what I'm thinking,* she thought. She realized then that he couldn't know. He was watching her, silently warning her to snap out of her thoughts. Sharlotte quickly glanced about and found several people noticing her curiously. She smiled until her lips felt stiff from forcing an expression she didn't feel. Amanda was talking her head off trying to cover for her. Even Kace was more talkative than she remembered from the past, entertaining those around him with a story of an oil gusher that had blackened an entire Texas town, eventually making everyone who lived there rich, even the rattlesnakes. It was the kind of story he would never tell, but which was typically expected of a Texan, and why Kace was cooperating now, sending the women into fits of laughter that rankled the men, was a curiosity even to Sharlotte. The Ivy Leaguers obviously disliked him, but it didn't appear to bother Kace. This was one of the first times she had seen him go out of his way to capture female attention, and she was suspicious of his motives. Bitsy was disgustingly mesmerized, and the attractive Lucille, Stuart's date, was laughing with delight at his tale. Stuart was scowling, but Sheldon was too busy discussing the Bermuda boat race with Harvey to notice he had lost Bitsy.

At last dinner was drawing to a close. The conversation had nostalgically turned to the fact that this was the last summer dance of the Long Island season. In the next two weeks they would all scatter like autumn leaves, and in September some would depart for private colleges and Ivy League universities. A few, like Clarence, would pursue success as a junior lawyer in a New York firm.

"I can't believe it's really our last gathering for the summer," Amanda sighed, looking at George, but intending her remark for everyone else as well.

"Gosh! It's awful," Bitsy chipped in, and looked hauntingly at Kace. Her meaning was clear. *Now that I've found you, how can I let you slip through my sweet little fingers?*

Kace merely lifted a eyebrow at this apparent wonder.

"And what a disastrous way for the grand old summer to come to an end," Pamela announced. "Somebody drowns."

Sharlotte's spine stiffened. *There she goes again*, she thought angrily. *Now no one will be able to stop her.*

"Yes, what's this all about, Sharlotte? There's been several mentions of Mr. Hunnewell, and no one's told us what really happened," one of Sharlotte's New York friends asked.

"Yes, isn't it dreadful? He actually drowned," someone said.

Amanda made an attempt to alter the course of the conversation, but it was too late. Pamela's little bomb had at last captured everyone's attention.

"Oh, it was dreadful," Pamela was saying. "You didn't hear about it yet? Well…"

"This is no way to begin an evening of music," Kace said to her. "I think your band has arrived, Sharlotte. I hear them tuning up their instruments."

"Yes," Amanda said, turning to George. "If only I could waltz again."

"We'll manage something," he said.

"They're right," said Sheldon, pushing back his chair and standing. "We're about to try our feet on a light fandango before we're all blown our separate ways like clouds before the wind. Up, girl!" he called to Bitsy. "The haunting clarinets do call!"

Sharlotte slowly released a breath.

"Yes," Amanda said, catching George's hand. "Rather than balmy summer winds and warm beaches next to a glittering sea, we shall have our romantic waltzes amid the sigh of brooding rain, with fevered flashes of brilliant lightning and gloomy grumbles of thunder."

George laughed. "Come along, Sweets."

"Yes, you too, Sharlotte," Sheldon said. "The first dance is mine. Looks like my Ever True is fully occupied," he gestured toward Bitsy, who was hanging on Kace's arm and steering him toward the ballroom.

Pamela was left with Clarence and Sharlotte vaguely wondered if that hadn't been Sheldon's plan. He had always approved of his older sister marrying Clarence before Sharlotte's formal entrance into society.

The small band had arrived late and wet, but in a short time managed to go on with the show. Light flowed becomingly from the chandeliers and the singer, who took great pains to sound like the popular nasal crooner Rudy Vallee, was already singing Mr. Vallee's monumental hit "My Time Is Your Time."

Sheldon was looking past Sharlotte's shoulder with a rueful smile. "Looks like Kace and Bitsy have discovered one another."

Sharlotte tried not to show her irritation. Bitsy was holding onto Kace like glue. Just then, Clarence and Pamela joined the others on the dance floor. Sheldon glanced over at them.

"I was surprised you gave the police the impression of a romance with Kace," he said. "It wasn't very smart in front of Clarence. And Uncle Burgess shocked me totally. He looked as if he were agreeing with the hand-in-hand jaunt on that old back trail to the boathouse."

Yes, odd, Sharlotte thought. He had *never* approved of Kace before, or of any Landry, for that matter, including his brother-in-law, Sherman.

Sheldon looked at her curiously. "What was it all about anyway?"

Caution, she thought. She let her gaze drift casually about the floor at the others. "I'm sure it wasn't that way at all. You must have read more into it than what either Kace or I intended. It was a walk, that's all. We talked about old times."

Sheldon smiled. "You weren't all that excited about old times in Texas this morning at the club. We all got the impression you practically detested the Landrys, Kace in particular. But all that talk about you and Kace having so much to discuss sure convinced Clarence. He's still worried about Texas competition."

She laughed tensely. "What is this, Sheldon? Another police grilling?"

He looked a little embarrassed. "Sorry. It's just that Pamela still has a glow for Clarence, and naturally she'd like to try and patch things up with him if she can."

"Naturally."

"Now, don't be that way. I've really no interest in the matter at all, except that she's my sister. And, well, if you and Kace have something going secretly, we'd like to know about it, is all."

Sharlotte was too upset to want to discuss either Kace or Clarence with Sheldon, and she was grateful that the imitation of Rudy Vallee had come to a faltering end, and even more grateful when Clarence tapped Sheldon on his shoulder. "This dance is mine." He smiled and took Sharlotte away. Unfortunately the tempo speeded up to a rousing, "Yes, sir, that's my baby! No, sir, I don't mean maybe, Yes, sir, that's my baby now!"

Clarence grimaced and threw up his hands. "No Charleston for me. Anyway, I want to talk to you," he said above the music. "Can we go out on the veranda? I realize it's not a nice night for it, but..."

Sharlotte, wanting to escape, took his hand and swept across the ballroom with him. She couldn't resist looking back at Kace. There was Bitsy putting on quite a show of doing the Charleston and making eyes at Kace. It was quite obvious: Yes, sir, she wanted to be his baby now!

Kace had gradually stepped away, letting Bitsy have the floor solo. He looked up to see Sharlotte and Clarence about to step out on the veranda. Bitsy, however, was soon joined by a strutting Sheldon, who had a cigarette dangling from his lip and a hat deliberately tipped low, and the two, a perfect match, were soon tearing up the floor. Bitsy looked to be happy once more, reunited with her dapper yachting enthusiast who loved the Charleston as much as she. Her spangles bounced in the chandelier light and the red feather in her snug little cloche hat quivered.

Sharlotte looked for Kace. He had disappeared.

Curious, she cast a quick glance about the ballroom to see if she could spot him, but Clarence drew her away onto the shadowed veranda.

The muted music drifted to them as Clarence walked her to one of the tables and pulled out a chair. He looked across the table at her with worried brows.

"Sheldon confuses me sometimes."

This wasn't what she had expected him to say, and she looked back, surprised.

He shrugged his shoulders uncomfortably as if bothered by something. "At the club this morning, why did he make such an issue about your Texas cousins and oil?"

"Hm? I'm sorry, Clarence, I didn't notice." Now why was he asking about oil?

He scowled. "Really, Sharlotte, you aren't paying attention. Why was Sheldon trying to make trouble?"

"Trouble? Was he?"

"Of course. You mean you didn't notice?" Clarence looked dubious.

"I don't think he really wanted to make trouble," Sharlotte said, trying to convince herself. "I've always gotten along well with my cousins, especially Sheldon."

"Maybe so, but he was trying to heat up the flames of dissent this time. Tonight before dinner he kept insinuating there was something between you and Kace Landry that I don't know about. After what you and Kace told the police this afternoon about the boathouse, Sheldon seems to think he was vindicated for what he said about Texas."

Sharlotte was angry with Kace for forcing her into that story but realized that it may have shielded her father from some very embarrassing questions.

"It's not Sheldon, but Pamela," she said. "She still hasn't gotten over my having—" she stopped, catching her thoughts from spilling over, and Clarence had the grace to appear a little embarrassed. He was looking into the ballroom. Sharlotte followed his gaze to Pamela. A waltz had struck up and she was being whirled about by Stuart.

Sharlotte pretended she didn't notice Clarence's look of concern over mentioning his past relationship with her cousin. The same unrest she had felt about Pamela returned. She felt a little guilty in being placed in a position whereby she had come between them. She loved her cousin and wanted her to have a chance at a second marriage and finding a father for her five-year-old son, but if Clarence had really loved Pamela he wouldn't have stopped seeing her.

She knew Pamela secretly begrudged her for taking Clarence away, nor could she blame her. No matter what she told herself, it did trouble Sharlotte's conscience that Clarence had once been Pamela's beau, until Sharlotte's father had decided that Clarence Fosdick would make an even better match for his eldest daughter. At first Sharlotte had resisted coming between her cousin and Clarence, but when her father had shared his financial worries with her a year ago, and earnestly implied that the Fosdick gold mines in Australia would save the Ashfords from heavy financial losses, she had allowed herself to be molded by his fears. If there was anything she could do, she had to cooperate.

She had salved her stinging conscience by telling herself over and over that Clarence had assured her three months ago that his relationship with Pamela had only been one of friendship. Sharlotte had doubted that was totally true, but willing to please her father, and raised to believe that parents were always correct when it came to arranging for the best match—she had gone along and settled on Clarence in her mind, if not her heart. Her heart, she'd been told, could not be trusted. But the mind was another matter; especially the financial mind of her father and great-uncle

Hubert. How else could the Ashford family have been able to keep their fortune intact all these generations?

And for Sharlotte, the fact that Clarence was so precise in his attitude toward the marriage was just another evidence of the reasonableness of the matter—an engagement, then marriage within a year or two.

Because very few of Sharlotte's friends or family had deviated from this pattern and married for love alone, everything must be taking its normal course. Except...Sharlotte remembered Aunt Livia Ashford and her maverick marriage to Texas rancher Sherman Landry. She sensed that this was a happy marriage, which reinforced things Kace had said about what true marriage and love was all about. It secretly made her debate the wishes of her father. But she wouldn't allow any of Kace Landry's rebellious words to permanently lodge in her heart and grow to harvest.

"I'm sure Sheldon didn't mean to imply there was anything between Kace and me," she said.

Clarence turned and looked at her quizzically. "You've never told me about your summer visits to the Landry ranch."

"There's not much to tell. They were very hot and boring."

"How often did you go there?"

"Oh—unfortunately, every summer since I was ten."

"Why is it I've never heard about the Landrys until Sheldon and Pamela mentioned them at the club this morning?"

Sharlotte tried to laugh pleasantly. "Darling, there's good reason for that, as Sheldon explained. The Landrys weren't accepted by the family in New York. Great-Uncle Hubert has a terrible grudge against them, especially Uncle Sherman, for marrying Livia against his will."

"But you went there," he persisted. "Every summer."

Sharlotte frowned. It was difficult to explain. She had never talked much of her father's sister living in Texas, but now found herself in the position where she must. She sighed and stood, taking his hands and looking seriously into his eyes. "Aunt Livia contacted my father when I was around ten, and asked that he begin sending me and Amanda to the ranch to spend a month, usually in July or August. Ugh! The worst of months," she said dourly.

Clarence squeezed her hands as though he understood.

"Your Aunt Livia gets along with your father?" he asked curiously.

"More so than with Great-Uncle Hubert. Yet Daddy rarely discusses her. She hasn't been home since she ran away and married Sherman. Hubert will never forgive her. She knows that too. He's ill and bedridden, but even so, the mention of Livia turns him green! It was my father's love for his sister that caused him to send me and Amanda to visit her. Otherwise Amanda and I would never even have met her. After Mummy died, Daddy felt we needed contact with a mother figure, though Aunt Livia was always far too unconventional to be that." She could smile now, but back when she was younger she had disliked everything about Livia and Sherman Landry.

"Livia used to get up at the crack of dawn to saddle one of her horses and join the hands in the roundup. She wore jeans and boots and bobbed her hair long before it was considered acceptable or fashionable. I used to wonder how she could stand such a hard, boring life.

"I haven't been back there since I graduated Vassar. And believe me," she laughed, "I've no intention of ever going again, though I like Aunt Livia. Even Uncle Sherman is a good man. He took us all to church and we had what he and Livia called 'private devotions' each night after supper."

Clarence laughed. "What in the world are private devotions?"

"Bible reading, prayer, and gingerbread," she said with a reminiscent smile. "Nobody makes gingerbread like Livia..." She stopped, realizing there was a slight wistfulness to her voice.

"Good grief, Sharlotte, Bible reading and prayer? Burgess would have a fit over that. He doesn't believe in God."

No, he didn't. He didn't believe in anything except himself and those like him, and the solid foundation of gold upon which to build one's life. People fail you, government fails you, but gold is solid, he had often said. Prayer is a waste of time, but gold can get you anything you need or want. But was that true? she wondered. Gold wasn't helping her now.

She quickly changed the subject. "Mostly I remember the heat, dust, and rattlesnakes." She shuddered. There had been more to Sharlotte's stay with the Landrys, of course, but she had little incentive to describe any of the positive details to Clarence, especially when she wanted to forget the past as much as Clarence wanted Kace back on the next train to Texas.

He smiled with a hint of bored superiority. "That story Kace was telling the girls tonight about a whole town getting rich on oil is utter nonsense. I doubt if he's got a dollar to his name. Why else would he be here except to try and borrow off your father? Probably thinks he can worm himself into the Ashford family and be left something in your great-uncle's will. Relatives are all the same."

Sharlotte was remembering Kace's suggestion that her father owed the Landrys money. He had probably said that to rankle her.

"Kace belongs to Texas," she stated. "To an entirely different life. He'll be leaving again soon, and I've no plans to ever see him again."

Clarence was watching her, and despite the sincerity of her declaration, he looked concerned. "At the club it was suggested that Kace wasn't blood related. If so, then whose son is he, if not your Uncle Sherman's?" he persisted.

Sharlotte turned her back against the lashing rain beating on the window glass, hoping the conversation would soon end.

"He belonged to Sherman's brother, Austen Landry."

"Belonged?"

"Austen is dead. He died in the war. In France. Kace spent his early years in an orphanage near the Mexican border."

"I see," he said stiffly.

She didn't think he understood at all. "Don't be silly, Clarence," she said in a hushed voice, putting her arms around him. "There is no romance between me and Kace. I cannot endure even thinking about him. You and I belong together. We're alike, with the same goals and background. What was it we discussed on the way here this morning? Politics. We know what we want, and we were born lucky enough to have the power to get it."

Even her own words rang hollow in her heart. The words she had heard in Sunday school as a girl in Texas came to mind: "What is your life? It is even a vapor, that appeareth for a little time, and then vanisheth away. For that ye ought to say, If the Lord will, we shall live, and do this, or that…"

She had not wanted to go to the Landrys' church or to Sunday school. Her attitude was typical of the rest of the Ashford family. Her great-uncle was an agnostic, and her father never mentioned God. As for her beloved mother—that was another matter…but Livia and Sherman had made her and Amanda go, along with Tyler and Kace. Even so, the things she'd heard as a young person were fixed in her mind, if not in her soul. At certain times words would come back to her, almost startling her, just as they had now.

She found she was staring up at Clarence, unable to go on with her boast.

He frowned. "What is it, Sharlotte? What's wrong?" She shook her head and turned away. "Nothing. I was remembering something…sitting in a wooden church on a bench, and a dust devil was swirling around outside. For a moment I could even smell the dust."

Yes, she thought, and see Kace and Tyler sitting across from her. Both just as rebellious as she and Amanda. But Uncle Sherman had a Bible that he could find anything in. He would look at Kace and Tyler to see if they were also finding the passage. They would search, and Kace would squirm uncomfortably and ask if he could go get a drink of water from his canteen, and

Sherman would level that steely gray gaze at him and whisper: "You settle down, boy."

And Kace would become silent and open his Bible.

Sharlotte shuddered. She was always glad to come back home and felt comfortable when her father would make himself a gin and bitters, that is—for a time. As she grew older and the Scripture lessons settled in her mind, she became more disturbed. Sometimes, even afraid. Such as now. She rubbed her arms and walked over to the window and looked out at the storm.

"Someone ought to speak to him about the danger he's causing everyone," Clarence murmured with disdain.

Sharlotte turned quickly to see Clarence looking inside the ballroom at Sheldon, still dancing with Bitsy.

"What do you mean?"

"His drinking," Clarence said. "He's becoming a lush."

He said this, Sharlotte thought, not because of moral or spiritual convictions, but because he disliked seeing him wasting his time and talents. Nor was Sheldon interested in politics, and this offended Clarence, who believed political involvement was a democratic duty, even a religion. He believed in the past President Woodrow Wilson's New World Order.

"And that girl is foolish. She's been making an indecent spectacle of her body all day. She's low class and lacks a college education. Except for the obvious, what does he see in her?"

Sharlotte felt uncomfortable with his harshness, even though she agreed that Bitsy was silly.

Sharlotte simply shook her head and wearily turned away. "I don't know," she murmured, "about a lot of things. I used to think…" she stopped, and Clarence came up beside her, studying her a moment. "You thought what?"

She sighed. "Oh, I don't know…that our kind were just a little superior to ordinary people."

"And you no longer think that?" he laughed. "You're superior to Bitsy, that's certain."

"You're right about Cousin Sheldon wasting himself on drinking—and girls like Bitsy. But if we throw stones at Sheldon, we'd better have a close look at ourselves as well. We're all guilty of excesses of the affluence we were born into."

"At least the world of politics offers me a way to do some good for the masses out there."

"Yes, with taxes from the middle class. That's very generous of the rich."

Clarence's brows shot up. "Good grief! You've been listening to George the radical! Soon he'll have you converted to the Communist party."

She was about to snap at him and accuse him of being a Socialist, but when she saw his smile she realized he had softened his denunciation of George's politics.

"George isn't a Communist," she said flatly. "Amanda says—"

"Amanda, bless her seventeen-year-old heart, wouldn't be able to differentiate a Communist from a Fascist, so let's not bring little sister into this. In fact," he said with another smile. "Let's not discuss politics right now." He reached for her arm.

Sharlotte laughed. "Not discuss politics? Is that possible?"

"Very," he said meaningfully, pulling her into his arms.

Sharlotte stiffened automatically, then seeing the look in his face, she relaxed and smiled, putting her arms around him. "Someone will notice us," she said quietly.

"I hope they do. I want everyone to know you love me. *Everyone* meaning one Texan."

She didn't want to think about Kace Landry.

"Sharlotte," he said seriously, "you've never actually said you love me."

Surprised by this unexpected query, she hesitated and stammered: "Why...of course I—we love each other."

He looked at her a long moment, then laughed. "That's not very convincing."

This is what she wanted, she told herself. She needed Clarence. The entire family needed a union of fortunes in marriage.

"Our families think we're perfect for one another."

"Only our families?" he said.

"No," she said softly, "not just our families. We know it too. We understand what's expected of us. You needn't be jealous of Kace. He's a nettlesome piece of cactus, that's all."

"Well, darling, I'm pleased you see it that way. They're different from us all right."

"Tyler is more friendly, more like a real cousin by birth—like Sheldon," she said thoughtfully. "Suffice it to say that Kace is… well—" she shrugged, unable to find the right word. "He's completely unacceptable to Daddy and to our way of life," and she wrinkled her nose with distaste to show her displeasure.

Clarence looked pleased. "And unacceptable to you as well?"

"Need you ask? Goodness! I just told you he rankles me something terrible. He even threw me in a muddy river flowing so swiftly I almost drowned."

"Why that cur!"

"He did rescue me though." She smiled ruefully as she remembered how frightened he'd looked when he realized she couldn't swim. He'd jumped in, and she almost drowned him before he got her to safety.

"He ought to have this—" and he made a fist—"a right on the chin."

She laughed nervously. "No, no, Clarence darling, you mustn't even think that. He's as strong as a bull—you wouldn't stand a chance."

"Well!"

She laughed and hugged him. "Don't be silly. Anyway, you needn't dislike him. He's a drifter, too. Aunt Livia wrote that he'd 'struck out on his own' and was wildcatting somewhere in Texas or Oklahoma. I can't remember which. Maybe both."

His eyes narrowed. "Wildcatting? You mean oil?"

"I guess that's what it means."

"You say he was raised at an orphanage?"

Sharlotte had heard about his orphanage days from Aunt Livia. "Yes, until Uncle Sherman finally brought him to live on the ranch."

He looked pleased. "Could his mother have been a foreigner?"

Sharlotte thought of Kace's warm green eyes. She didn't think so, but it suited her purpose at the moment.

"It's certainly possible." She smiled. "Now, let's not talk about unpleasant things anymore. And believe me, Clarence darling, Kace is—well, quite unpleasant." She pursed her lips and permitted a brief kiss. "Unlike you, he's dull and uninspiring…" she stopped. Leaning in a doorway in the shadows, Kace wore an ironic smile. Her face turned hot and her lips parted slightly. He'd been eavesdropping, but for how long?

Clarence hadn't seen him, and to keep him from turning to discover Kace standing there and risking a fight, she reacted instantly by throwing her arms around his neck. Clarence, thoroughly surprised, willingly kissed her as they stood locked in an embrace.

A minute later she gasped, and glancing toward the ballroom floor, saw that Kace had gone.

Sharlotte jerked away from Clarence and fled from the veranda.

Inside the bright ballroom she slowed her steps and walked straight to the staircase, her heart beating unhappily. She told herself that happiness waited too, just down the road of matrimony. Becoming Mrs. Clarence Fosdick would solve so many problems.

She hurried up the stairs telling her heart that it was so, though unease persisted. *Go away*, she told the small voice of conscience. *I can't listen to you. Not now. Why, I have everything I want and more.*

11

As Sharlotte ascended the stairs to enter the empty hall she listened to the muffled strains from the band playing "Ain't she sweet, just a walkin' down the street, now I ask you very confidentially, ain't she sweet?" A section of the upper hallway looked down over the ballroom, and she quickly glanced below, letting her gaze sweep the room where the chandelier light reflected on the glossy oak floor. Apparently no one had noticed her going upstairs. She saw Amanda seated prettily in a chair near the veranda, her long skirts carefully concealing her legs. Her crutches were behind the drape, easily within reach, but hidden. George came up with a lemonade and two plates of white cake with pink frosting, and said something that made Amanda laugh.

Kace was nowhere about. Her memory of his eavesdropping still stung. He was worse than a scoundrel. She must avoid him now.

Neither did she see Clarence, who must have remained on the veranda. Pamela was just slipping through a doorway, probably in search of her lost quarry. Sharlotte's lashes thinned. *Cousin Pamela would make the perfect Sadie Hawkins. It doesn't bother her in the least to race after a man! Well, she isn't going to get Clarence, no matter how hard she runs.* Too much was at stake—not just for herself, for all of them if she didn't manage to secure the family fortune and good name through marriage into the Fosdick family. Sharlotte glanced at her younger sister, bravely chattering and laughing with George as though her invalid state was of no consequence to her future. They both knew that it was. Now, with the dreadful things that were happening, the future loomed even darker and more dubious.

The heavy burden upon her heart intensified. She slowly became aware that she was still carrying the prescription bottle belonging to her father inside the small fashionable wrist-bag connected to a gold chain bracelet. She left the banister and walked hurriedly down the hallway to his bedroom.

She paused, listening. Was he awake now?

From the beaded bag that contained a powder puff, lipstick, and lace handkerchief, she removed the medicine bottle and prepared to tap on the heavy oak door, still reluctant to disturb him. What was that sound? Dresser drawers opening and shutting? She envisioned the large secretary desk that he kept near the side door leading into the dressing room. She tapped. "Daddy? It's me, Sharlotte. Can I come in?"

There was only silence as she waited for his footsteps.

"Dr. Lester sent over your medication. I'm sorry to disturb you, but you'd best take it now, Daddy."

Silence. Her brows tucked together. She hesitated, then tried the door knob and found it still locked.

Odd. She tapped a little louder. Had she imagined those drawers opening and shutting? Maybe they hadn't been drawers at all but—? But what?

How could she make certain he was all right without causing a commotion by enlisting help from downstairs to get inside? A commotion now, after the day's debacle, would assuredly cause more gossip. Nor did she want to bang on the door. If he was sound asleep she would only frighten him.

Perhaps her father's valet kept a spare key. Of course, Peter was the man to see. She turned to go back down the stairs to the servants congregating in the kitchen area when she remembered.

Her mother's room. There was a large double bath and dressing chamber adjoining her father's room. The doors between were usually unlocked. The less anyone else was involved, the better it seemed to Sharlotte, who wanted as little attention to her actions as possible.

A minute later she entered the vacant bedroom that once belonged to her mother, Lauren. She had been killed in a train accident when Sharlotte was five. Along with her mother, Sharlotte had lost her baby brother, Charles, and Grandmother Ashford, all who had been on their way to visit the family in Vermont for a few weeks of summer vacation. Tragically, her father never recovered from that devastating loss. During the months that followed the accident her father had pined away, closing himself up in his room, and seemed hardly aware of Sharlotte and Amanda, who'd been left in the care of their governess.

Sharlotte discovered when she grew older that if it hadn't been for a case of the chicken pox just before the scheduled trip, she and Amanda would have been on that very same train. But her mother had worried about the long trip, and at the last hour decided to leave them home with the governess, who was to have brought them to Vermont after they'd recovered.

Sharlotte quietly closed the door. Strange, how events as common as chicken pox could totally redirect one's life. Was there a cause behind such events, or was it just fate or chance? Or, was there a plan behind the fortunate or unfortunate circumstances of life? A plan would imply a Planner, a God who directed these things. And if there was, why did God leave her and Amanda, but remove her mother, grandmother, and her seven-month-old brother?

Sharlotte stood at the foot of the huge canopied bed and looked up at her mother's portrait. The room had become something of a sanctuary for her, though no one in the family or among her flighty friends knew this side of her heart. She had stolen away here a multitude of times while growing up when feeling frightened, alone, and bewildered.

The painting of her mother, with her flowing copper-colored hair across one shoulder and her violet-blue eyes so much like Sharlotte's, was always there to welcome her back with serene confidence. Sharlotte had always wondered if her mother had believed in God. There'd been no answer to that curious question that haunted her until Sharlotte's sixteenth birthday, when she'd come here all dressed up in her ball dress to look up at her mother. It was on that night that Sharlotte had discovered a small white Bible tucked away in the drawer of the bedside stand. Why she had not found it sooner remained a question she couldn't answer, for she was almost certain she had gone through all the drawers and trunks and nooks and crannies of her mother's room while growing up. But on the night of her ball she'd found it, a Bible with her mother's maiden name "Lauren Marie Chattaine" imprinted with gold below the words "Holy Bible." Since finding the Bible, Sharlotte was nearly certain her mother had been religious, although her father had never told her so. She supposed it was because the Ashfords had never been what were called "church people."

Poor Daddy, she thought, thinking of her mother's death. He had lost himself in his work, becoming cynical at the mention of religious issues, following zealously the newspaper accounts of the hottest trial of the decade, called the "Scopes Monkey Trial" taking place in the state of Tennessee. Clarence Darrow, defending evolution, had become a hero, and William Jennings Bryan, defending the Genesis account of creation, a cause for ridicule.

After that, while growing up, Sharlotte had only heard the name of the Deity spoken in unbelief. If there's a God, why does He allow *this*? And if there is a God why does He allow *that*? And why do good people suffer, and if God is truly good as the preachers say, why did He allow my wife and baby son to die a horrible death trapped in a fiery train crash?

And on and on the questions went, expecting no answers; indeed, wanting none, but merely seeking to vent his anger and justify his rejection of the church. Christmas cards sent by Aunt Livia showing baby Jesus were never put up. Carols were scoffed at. Indeed, Sharlotte's heart had been filled with doubts, until—

Until the odd situation between her father and the Landrys that had arranged for her and Amanda to begin visiting the Texas ranch each summer. Then, from ten years old onward she'd heard stories from the Bible about Jesus feeding the 5,000, and how he had raised Jairus' little girl from the dead. These stories had been wonderful, and she wondered why her father hated them so, because she had begun to understand God in a different light.

But were these stories true? Her father insisted they weren't when she'd come home and told him about Jesus. "Fairy tales," he had said. "The only heaven, my child, is the one you make for yourself in this life. That's why you must strive to get what you want while you are young and strong, because when you grow older it will be too late. And after that, well...better is a live dog than a dead lion. If Livia keeps up this religious training stuff, you and Amanda won't be going back next summer."

But she had been back to the Landry ranch, again and again, until her seventeenth birthday.

Sharlotte remembered asking Uncle Sherman why Jesus hadn't raised her "Mummy and baby Charles from the dead, and her grandmother too," after they'd died in the train accident. Tyler had snickered behind his uncle's back until Kace snapped him with a rubber band during chapel time.

Sharlotte smiled sadly, reminiscing about those childhood incidents. Little by little she had heard things about God from the Bible that impressed her. She had smuggled her mother's white Bible to Texas the summer of her sixteenth birthday and displayed it calmly to Kace, then to the others. But she had never actually become a Christian by asking Jesus Christ into her life. Somehow she had held back, perhaps influenced by her father.

She looked again at the portrait and wondered if it had been her mother's faith that made her look so serene, or was it because she was beautiful and wealthy, without a material care in the world? And that reminded her of why she was in her mother's room.

She turned, intending to go through the adjoining dressing room to reach her father's door, when she was startled to see a rugged leather suitcase open on the dainty rosebud-and-ivory rug, partially unpacked. There was a recognizable jacket draped around the back of a hard-backed chair. Kace! Had the housekeeper dared give him her mother's room?

Resentment boiled up. That would be the day when Kace Landry slept in her mother's bed. He was intruding into the one sanctuary that Sharlotte had made her very own. She fought off the urge to take his things and dump them into the hallway. Reason prevailed, however, as she remembered that the housekeeper had worried about all the other spare rooms being occupied. She must have brought Kace here as a final resort. Her breathing quieted. After all, Kace hadn't asked to be put here.

She looked again at the masculine leather suitcase, then at the frills of the pink comforter, and whiffed the fragrance of gardenia coming from bowls of potpourri. She noticed that Kace had placed a book on top of the largest bowl. Her resentment turned to a grudging smile, and then she stifled a laugh. Good! Served him right. She hoped it made him sneeze. Coming here to Long Island to snoop on her and her father—for that's exactly what she felt he was doing. Just as he had snooped on her and Clarence on the veranda. And for what reason? She didn't know, but she didn't trust him.

She imagined the expression on his face when the housekeeper brought him to the room—with her mother's painting above the bed looking so much like herself. She laughed as she went over to the dresser. Picking up the bowl of gardenia petals, she pulled back the pink satin cover and then sprinkled the petals evenly on the sheet and neatly drew the cover back into place. *This will be as good as the tarantula,* she thought.

Then she looked at his jacket hanging carelessly on the back of the chair.

Hmmm…her eyes narrowed. Well, well…If he could snoop, then…She sped to the open suitcase. She glanced guiltily toward the closed door. She turned back to the suitcase, dropping to her knees. Maybe there was something that would explain why her father had asked him to stay for the remaining holiday. There must be something unusual behind all this. Her father would never accept him into the house otherwise.

She began her quiet search for anything that might look as if it had been sent from New York to Texas. Ah, a small black leather folder. She hesitated, feeling a prick from her conscience. Then, setting her jaw, she went ahead and opened it. She leafed hurriedly through some papers, seeing addresses both in New York and Long Island, but none of them familiar or concerning banking or the stock market. She paused. Mr. Hunnewell's home address and telephone number was written in Kace's hand. Had he known him so well? Had Hunnewell sent it to him, and if so, why? Maybe it was true that Kace had really come here thinking to meet Hunnewell.

An envelope fell from the folder. She picked it up, seeing the Texas postmark and a familiar name, "Miss Elly McCrae," in the left-hand corner.

Sharlotte bit her lip, then quickly removed the single sheet of plain paper and read the pretty handwriting.

Dear Kace,

I received a wonderful surprise today. A leather-bound edition of Charles Dickens' Great Expectations. What a wonderful birthday present. I don't need to ask how you knew I wanted it so very much. My collection is growing with each passing year, thanks to your thoughtfulness.

We all miss you here, especially me. The moonlit walks, the long conversations, I especially miss being in your arms...

There was more, but Sharlotte couldn't read it. She looked at the end to the last words, *Love, Elly.*

A bewildering jealousy bit savagely into her heart, leaving bitter anguish. "I especially miss being in your arms." Oh, she did, did she?

She frowned, unhappily. Had he signed the book *Love, Kace?*

In a surge of rage she nearly crumpled the letter, then caught herself. She bit her lip instead and replaced the letter inside the envelope, almost tearing the flap. Careful, or he'll know someone read it.

Elly! The pastor's daughter. Does her father know she was out taking romantic walks with Kace, kissing in the moonlight? I'll wager he doesn't!

Sharlotte tried not to remember what his kiss had been like under the honeysuckle arbor. "I ought to tell on her," she thought, then she was smitten.

Why so jealous? a small voice seemed to say. *You could have had Kace two years ago and you turned him down. What right do you have now to resent his loving relationship with a kind girl like Elly McCrae? And you have to admit she is worthy of his attention.*

Yes, and that was part of the pain. She was worthy. Sharlotte felt disappointed with her own lack of Christian graces. Compared to Elly, she was spoiled.

The ticking clock sounded too loudly in her ears. *Life is rushing by,* it seemed to warn. *How are you spending these precious years? When will you decide to know God?*

She had Clarence. Wealthy, influential, going somewhere in life—straight to the United States Congress. She had her path forged and the race must be finished. She couldn't permit confusing emotions to get the best of her, to detour her from accomplishing the goal that waited, a goal with a great reward. And the reward would not just benefit her future, but her younger sister, even her father. All the Ashfords. Maybe even the Van Dornens.

Rejecting the jealousy and the pain, she once again steeled her emotions and shut the door of her heart. Her position in society and her pedigree demanded she marry her own kind.

She listened. All was silent in the hallway. She continued her search through a stack of clean shirts, trousers, and underwear for anything that might tell her why he had come. There was nothing more of interest except the fact he had Mr. Hunnewell's home address.

She quickly left the suitcase and went to his jacket, feeling flushed. She looked through the inner pockets. Her heart leaped when her fingers felt the edge of a folded envelope. Surely this one wasn't from Elly. She sensed that its contents might hold something interesting, maybe even important. She rushed to the desk, spreading the fine linen stationery carefully under the lamp. Her breath caught when she read the printed stationary: Mr. Hubert Ashford, Manhattan.

"My great-uncle," she whispered, staring at the carefully written letter. Her heart began to race. Her eyes darted to the door, then back to the letter. She began to read...rushing past the elementary greetings to the content:

> *Although I can sympathize with your situation, I have no incentive to sustain your present enterprise as long as you are unable to present adequate collateral to justify Ashford backing for more prolonged drilling. I advise you to accept your loss and disband the company. The unproductive property is better left to the Apaches and jackrabbits. If you want sound advice, get into the banking business.*
>
> *Hubert Ashford*

Well, Sharlotte thought coolly. So the family owed him money, did it? He'd lied to her. He had come to get a loan from her great-uncle. Whatever possessed Kace to think he could accomplish such a thing?

Clarence was right, she thought, putting the letter back into its envelope and returning it to the jacket pocket. Kace was a scoundrel. He probably didn't have a dollar to his name. He had a lot of nerve coming here! He had wasted her time and tried to frighten her about bad debts and her father's reputation. Why? Did he think by doing so she would help him get the loan from her great-uncle, or even her father? She had half a mind to confront Kace tonight and let him know she knew the truth. That idea, however, faded fast when she heard quiet footsteps coming down the hall. Any notion of confronting him gave way to the horror of being caught snooping, and she held her breath, waiting to hear if the footsteps stopped outside the door.

The footsteps did indeed pause. She waited a moment longer, then prepared to flee. He was outside in the hall. She rushed to the dressing room door. What if it was locked? It opened silently. She sighed with relief. Sharlotte managed to slip into the dressing room and close the door just as the hall door opened admitting Kace.

She stood still as a statue in the darkness of the dressing room, whiffing the fragrance of spice. Her hands went cold and damp as she heard Kace moving about on the other side of the door. What if he noticed that someone had been in his things? She'd been careful to replace everything the way she'd found them, but—

What if he decided to enter the dressing room?

She heard his footsteps cease as though he were looking at something that caught his attention. She decided not to take any chances, and she moved stealthily across the darkened room to the door that led to her father's bedroom.

Her trembling hand quietly turned the doorknob…it was unlocked. She pushed the door open a crack. One lamp glowed beside the bed with rumpled blue satin coverlet. There was a sound—as though someone had moved quickly. "It's me, Daddy," she whispered, afraid she'd startled him.

She entered, trying to keep her skirts from rustling, and closed the door behind her, slipping the oiled bolt through the lock. She turned and glanced about expecting to see her father in his bathrobe.

Burgess Ashford wasn't in his room. She stood staring, first at the empty bed, then her gaze darted around the room to the floor, expecting to see his body crumpled in a heap, unconscious. Her father was nowhere to be seen. *But I heard him.*

Seeing was believing, or was it?

Then I must have imagined that sound. The wind, probably. He must have begun to feel better and walked to the upstairs morning room to get some tea and maybe a book or newspaper to read in bed. But if so, why hadn't she seen him in the hall? And he should have returned in the interval she spent looking through Kace's suitcase.

Her brow wrinkled and she felt a gust of chilling, damp wind. She saw the veranda door standing open and the curtains fluttering. So *that* was the sound she had heard.

Would he step outdoors on a night with torrential rains and wind? Hardly, yet she walked over to make certain, picking up the flashlight that lay on the stand.

She pushed the doors open wide and stepped out into the darkness, squinting against the wind lashing the rain into her face, chilling her, and wetting the front of her dress. In her concern over her father's disappearance she felt no regard for her silk gown. She leaned over the veranda railing and held out the light. The darkened shrubbery below shook and swayed. She noticed the fire escape had been let down against the side of the veranda. Could that scraping sound she'd heard earlier in the hall have been the fire escape? But could she have heard it in the hall with all that wind and rain? She didn't think so. Then what *had* she heard? Even now her best guess was that it had been the heavy drawers on the large secretary nearer the hall door.

Her father had obviously gone down the fire escape. He must not have wanted anyone to see him. Perhaps he hadn't been ill after all, and while everyone else was busy with dinner and the dance, he—

Her heart felt like a stone. Had he left in search of the missing glove? Did he know it was at the cottage, or would he also search the old boathouse? She shuddered, fearing that he, like Hunnewell, might put his weight on a rotting step. In this weather her father might meet with the same horrid fate! She trembled, and her light flickered and went out. One hand went to her face.

She drew back from the railing, bumping into a wrought-iron chair. She turned quickly as panic seized her and rushed blindly into the room leaving the door ajar as her father had left it. She didn't want him to find her waiting here. It would force him to make up some excuse for returning by the fire escape, an uncomfortable confrontation. And what if he didn't know where he'd lost the glove? What if he hadn't found it? Should she risk going there to make sure?

What a dilemma she found herself in! If only it was someone else instead of her father, she would ignore it.

She stood shaking.

Footsteps again. This time making scraping sounds against the side of the house. Her father was returning up the fire escape. She couldn't go back into Kace's room!

She rushed to the door that opened to the hall, reaching for the bolt, then stopped. If her father noticed that it was unbolted he'd know someone had been here.

Now what? She looked behind her toward the veranda, desperation seizing her. She sucked in her breath, her knuckles going to her mouth, then—

Kace stepped out from the shadows of the tall secretary, and glanced toward the veranda. Sharlotte barely silenced her cry. So he was the one she had heard in her father's room. Then *who* was in Kace's room?

Kace caught her arm and silently dashed with her toward the dressing room. He pulled her inside, shutting the door without making a sound.

She stood shaking, her heart beating in her chest as though it were anxious for flight. Leaning against Kace was strangely comforting, as though he were a refuge from the storm raging without and within. She heard her father coming into his bedroom, heard the veranda door close, and his wet shoes squeaking as he walked slowly across the floor. Her eyes closed, and a sick feeling churned. *Daddy…Daddy…what have you done?*

She felt Kace's arms tighten and wondered if she were going limp.

"Don't faint now," he whispered in her ear.

She sensed he was reaching blindly for the doorknob to her mother's room so they could make their escape. She tensed and grasped his arm, "No! Someone else is in there."

She thought he was about to enter anyway and confront whomever it was, then must have decided it would alert her father. If her father saw her rain-soaked dress, he would realize she'd been on his veranda.

But now Burgess was likely to come to the dressing room to change out of his wet clothing.

Trapped!

A moment later Kace slipped the bolt into place on the door to her father's bedroom, switched on the light, and began boldly whistling "Ain't She Sweet," while turning on the water in the washbowl.

Sharlotte slumped with relief against the wall. Of course! Her father would think nothing of Kace using the dressing room as he had the adjoining room. If her father hadn't known the housekeeper had given Kace her mother's room, he knew it now. Silence fell, and then she thought she heard the bolt slip quietly into place on the other side of the door. He didn't want to take any chances of Kace coming through.

Kace looked over at her with a wry smile, but Sharlotte, feeling pale as well as weak, sank onto a stool and froze.

He made more noise, then apparently confident that he could enter his room, he opened the door and stepped in.

Sharlotte listened to water running in a daze. It must have been only a minute later that Kace reappeared, took one look at her, then frowned. He reached for her hand and brought her into her mother's room. He went back and she heard him turning on the bath water.

He returned, shutting the door. "That should give us a few minutes," he said in a low voice. "Have you any idea who was in here?"

She shook her head no. Her eyes followed him to his suitcase. He stooped down and rummaged, then went over to his jacket and looked inside the pocket. His dark head turned slightly and he looked at her evenly. Her eyes wavered. His narrowed.

"So you went through my things."

"Ha! Listen to you. You were searching my father's secretary desk. I heard you from the hall."

"So you did. We can't talk here, though. Where can we go without being disturbed?"

Her lips thinned uncooperatively.

His gaze shot over her. "You'll need to get out of those wet clothes. If you catch pneumonia you'll miss your engagement ball."

"Very amusing. I'm sure you're concerned about my engagement."

"Not half as much as your daddy."

She flounced toward him. "Now what do you mean?"

"We can't talk here, unless you want to whisper. Do you want the facts or don't you?"

"Of course I want the facts, *if* I can trust you."

"*If* you can take the truth, you'll have it now," he challenged.

She was furious with his arrogance. "I can take the truth as well as you can."

"That's what I'm counting on. Your room may be the safest place we can talk without being disturbed," he said matter-of-factly.

Her eyes widened over his temerity.

Kace frowned at her, clasped her arm again, and guided her toward the hall door. "Relax. Your bedroom interests me not at all. Come along, and don't give me any trouble. I'm in no mood for your spoiled antics."

She glared, but he ignored it, opened the door quietly and looked out, then stepped back and bowed her past. "After you, Princess."

Sharlotte swept past him into the hall and walked briskly toward her room with Kace following.

12

Sharlotte entered the small parlor connected to her bedroom, switched on the lamps, drew closed the white organdy curtains to mask out the storm, and shut the door leading to her bedroom. Kace bolted the door to the hallway.

She turned, arms folded, and looked across the room at him. He glanced about, taking in the ivory damask love seat, two matching chairs, and dark-wood tables with spindle legs. There was a glass bowl filled with pink rosebuds and a dozen *Vogue* magazines scattered on the fringed upholstered bench near one chair.

"Very nice," he commented smoothly. "It's not every young debutante who has her own parlor connected to her bedroom."

Sharlotte whipped about and went to her bedroom door. With her hand on its golden knob she glanced back over her shoulder. "Do make yourself comfortable, Mr. Landry. I'll only be a few minutes." She closed the door behind her and locked it with an abrupt "click" so Kace couldn't miss it.

"Texas coyote! I ought to—to—" but she didn't really know what she ought to do about Kace. Indeed, there was very little she could do except endure his barbs until she knew how this entire deplorable situation with Hunnewell was to be settled by the inquest.

She went to her huge closet and leafed through a dozen lovely ball gowns, then chose instead a white flapper dress with deep fringe. She was trying with difficulty to smooth her long wavy hair into a tight roll in order to wear the matching hat with its little white fluffy goose feather, when Kace tapped.

"C'mon, Princess, we haven't all night."

A few moments later she flung open the door and met his gaze, then came out, banging it shut.

Kace lifted a brow. "Well, well. Kinda short, isn't it? Scandalous!"

"Oh, be quiet. I dress for my fiancé, not *you*. What you think matters very little." She breezed over to the window. Folding her arms, she turned and looked at him.

"All right, let's get down to the facts," he said.

"I'm waiting."

"First, what were you doing searching through my luggage and jacket?"

"You're a fine one to act offended, sneaking about my father's bedroom, pilfering his Cuban cigars probably—"

"Pilfering cigars! You're kidding."

"Well, what were you doing, looking for the club you think was used on poor Hunnewell?"

"Ah," he said softly, walking toward her. "A telling remark. So that's how you think dear old Dad did it, eh?"

"Don't be absurd. And if you're going to stand in my private room insulting my father, you can leave at once."

"Now, now, I've made no accusations…yet."

"No? Then what were you searching for? And by the way, just what proof do you have that I searched through your things? Someone else was in there."

"Probably Clarence," he said.

She watched him out of her corner of her eye as she picked a pink rosebud and plucked a velvety petal loose, rubbing it between her fingers thoughtfully.

Kace leaned toward her and whiffed her perfume. "Expensive, and vaguely familiar from the past. It has a way of lingering in the room…even on my jacket."

She pushed her palms against his chest and walked past him over to a chair, but she didn't sit. Her nerves were too on edge.

"Did you read the letter from your great-uncle?" he challenged quietly.

"You haven't told me yet why you were searching the desk in my father's room," she countered. Did he wonder if she'd also read Elly's letter? She noted he watched her, but didn't pursue that path, as though wanting to avoid it.

"Better sit down, Sharlotte."

She did so, hoping to resolve the events in her father's room.

He stood there frowning, driving his hands into his pockets. "Are you going to be all right? You're pale."

"I doubt it matters to you."

"Let's not debate that. Earlier, you wanted to know why I came here to see your father."

She tensed, waiting. He must have decided circumstances warranted an explanation now that she'd read the letter.

"Now that I know the truth I suppose you have little choice except to come clean," she said.

"That letter leaves the wrong impression, but we won't argue that now."

"Wrong impression, indeed," she scoffed, scanning him. "You're in debt up to your neck to *my* family. I suspected it all along."

"Yes, you did. That's the first conclusion you'd jump too. It suits your agenda."

She started to rise to her feet, but Kace stopped her. "Stay put. I won't have you fainting. I don't suppose you have anything in the room to calm your nerves? Burgess is a bootlegger. Has he ever given you a flask?" He glanced toward a cupboard.

Now she did manage to jump to her feet. "Bootlegger—oh!" she squealed trying to hit him, but Kace held her wrist, putting a finger to her lips. "Shush. Do you want someone to hear you?"

She tried to nip his finger with her teeth. He gently pushed her away, stepping back. "High society, my foot. I think Apaches raised you. Too bad your daddy didn't paddle you well when he had the opportunity."

"And I suppose you think another dunking in the Rio Grande would do," she accused, tears prickling her eyes.

"It's too late for that now. You still haven't learned anything from the first time." He scanned her.

"I've learned that you still don't have any manners, Mr. Landry. You're stuck in your old Texas boots."

He laughed, his hands back in his pockets. "This is getting us nowhere. Shall we call a truce so we can get through all this or not? In a week I'll be out of your life permanently and you can cuddle all you want with dear Clarence. And I—"

"Can make sweet little Elly swoon in the moonlight," she said, unable to keep silent.

"Keep Elly out of this," he said too quietly.

"Oh, yes, you rush to her defense but intimidate me."

"Intimidate? With those feline claws extended, you don't need a defense."

His contrasting attitude between her and Elly stung. She lapsed into silence.

Kace watched her thoughtfully as he seemed to ponder her reaction, but she turned her back so he couldn't see the hurt in her expression.

"All right," he said laconically, "I apologize. And now—as I was saying—you wanted to know why I came here to see Burgess, and I told you it might be wiser to ask him."

"The horrid circumstances of the day have precluded doing that. I doubt if he'd tell me much anyway. He has a terrible habit of thinking of me as a child."

"I'm inclined to agree at times. You do have a tendency to shrug off business matters that don't pertain to your personal goals."

Her personal goals were important and pertained to more than her so-called selfish interests, yet Kace didn't know that.

"I wasn't trying to insult you," he said, reading her expression. "Merely making a comment on how things are."

She doubted he actually knew how "things are."

"I want the truth, Kace. You made an earlier statement outside the club that my father owed you a debt of money. That wasn't true, according to Great-Uncle's letter."

His eyes were veiled. "It wasn't a joke. What your great-uncle failed to say was that 'my situation,' as he called your father's debt to me, was none of his concern and that he had no intention of paying your father's bills."

"My father has millions," she said. "He could buy the Landry cattle ranch with the change in his piggy bank if he wanted. Why should he owe you money? You have nothing he wishes to buy even if what you say were true."

A restrained look of impatience crossed his face at her glib response. Perhaps she had been a little snobbish, but Kace had asked for it.

"Your father is a heavy loser in the stock market."

"First a bootlegger, now a loser. Anything else?"

"Maybe," he said quietly.

She knew what he meant and was awash with silent horror. Lies, lies. They had to be.

"These millions you feel so secure about were nothing more than unrealized gains on stocks he's bought using deep margin loans from New York brokers and banks. In the last few weeks, however, he's had many of those margins called because of the recent stock market drop. Unfortunately, he's had to sell off assets heavily in order to cover the margin calls, and still he's in debt."

She had feared that, and that was why her marriage to Clarence was now so important. She suspected Kace knew that was part of the reason she was becoming engaged.

"And my father owes you too. Is that the story you want me to believe?"

"Whether you do or not won't change the fact. My partners in oil drilling exploration believed in the Ashford name and gave him what he came to Texas to get: forty-eight percent of the company."

Her father owned part of the company? When had he gone to Texas? She decided it must have happened when she and Amanda were away at college. That he would be interested in doing business with any of the Landrys, especially Kace, still intrigued her.

"So far the enterprise hasn't hit anything," he said, frowning.

She laughed deliberately.

Kace shot her a glance. "We've got a chance to survive, but it depends on Burgess putting up the rest of the venture capital we agreed upon. We need it in order to continue operations as well as to protect his own investment."

She watched him, finding his interest in oil drilling curious. How and when did he acquire this passion? How different Kace was from Clarence.

"That's the subject mentioned in the letter. I'd written Hubert asking that he come through for your father the way he has in the past. But he's fed up with your father's investments and has no intention of giving him more Ashford money. His estate is unsound, to put it mildly."

Sharlotte remained locked in unbelief, unable to accept that such a thing could happen. There just had to be some mistake.

"My father has always been a financial genius when it comes to wisely investing the Ashford fortune. Do you really expect me to believe this?"

"Don't be an ostrich, Sharlotte. His financial 'genius,' as you put it, isn't all what it's cracked up to be. He's lost money in a Florida land deal and in another oil venture in Bakersfield, California."

She knew about that fiasco, and it embarrassed her.

"Even the Ashford aristocracy is susceptible to mistakes," he said dryly. "Actually, his unconventional sister hasn't done so badly after marrying my uncle. Who knows, the Landrys may unexpectedly become quite respectable. I suppose I then shall emerge as quite the gentleman."

She laughed. "No amount of wealth will buy you good breeding, Kace. Do you think it's only financial power that made the Ashfords what they are today?"

He smiled, holding her gaze until she felt the warmth in her cheeks. "Without the slightest doubt. Lose it, and you'll be back at the bottom of the heap."

She found the idea not just unpleasant, but frightening. She thought of the secret reasons why her marriage to Clarence was being rushed.

"You don't really believe it's pedigree that holds aristocracy together, do you?" he asked. "If you do, then you're self-deceived, my dear girl. It's money first, last, and always. Unfortunately, some of the finest people in the world wear hand-me-downs and boil a second pot of coffee with used grounds. Shocking, isn't it? What did Solomon say in Ecclesiastes 10:7? 'I have seen servants upon horses, and princes walking as servants upon the earth.'"

She had enough concerns of her own, so she shrugged off his controversy. "Oh, well…" she managed airily. "I suppose my father has finally decided you should be treated as a relative."

Kace laughed. "The austere Mr. Ashford thinks nothing of the sort, and neither do your friends. Oh, they're polite enough on the surface, but their civility is born of necessity. That's one of the things I like about you, Sharlotte. You're open and honest with your snobbery. You put me in my place and don't bat an eyelash."

His eyes glimmered with malicious amusement as she cast him a dour look.

Sharlotte felt more than dour. She was beginning to worry about the calm confidence with which he spoke. Could there be something as seriously wrong with the Ashford estate as he was saying? She preferred to think that he was just being horrid, finding her dilemma amusing.

"I'm not sure that I've put you in your place at all," she said. "And if you're suggesting the Landrys' present affluence means that I, or any member of my family, can be bought—you're dead wrong."

He winced. "Can't you think of another word to use after what's happened?"

Another of Kace's innuendoes that played upon her own fears. "I think you're positively horrid, Kace Landry." She swept toward the door. "I demand you leave my room at once—"

Kace intercepted her with a slight smile. "I apologize. Do sit down, Sharlotte."

She fumed: "We have a culture that goes far beyond any sudden rise to fortune that you intend to create in Texas. We have our history," she lectured, "our pedigree, our pride."

"Surely the Ashfords are a race above other mortals, but what good will your pedigree do for you when the bottom falls out and the great Ashford estate comes tumbling down like a ton of bricks?"

What good will it do? His blunt question, so unlike anything she'd expected, shook her to the core, and she had to clench her teeth to keep them from chattering. The burden of her father's financial blunders, and even Amanda's bleak future, came pouring in on her like an avalanche. Her position in society had never prepared her for the possibility of basic survival, and now she was feeling unusually young and inept, her shoulders too small for carrying burdens.

"I want you to listen to me whether you like what you're about to hear or not," Kace announced. "Just this year alone, Burgess has lost a fortune."

There was a sudden angry sparkle in Sharlotte's eyes and she lifted her chin. "How can you possibly know of such private matters! Who would dare tell you about my father's finances?"

"Hunnewell."

"Hunne—" she stopped. "Mr. Hunnewell told you these things?" she asked suspiciously, liking this less and less. She remembered what Kace had said about her father being a bootlegger—of all absurd things! She didn't take any of his wild tales at face value, but she was listening and weighing his words with a good deal of distrust.

"Hunnewell stopped in Texas two weeks ago on his way back from Mexico. He delivered your great-uncle's letter to me with an explanation as to why your father wouldn't be paying for the rest of his investment in the oil company."

"He told all this to you?" she asked crossly. "Practically a stranger?"

"Not so. I am perceived as the nephew of Livia, your father's sister."

"So that's it," Sharlotte said annoyed. "You managed to *trick* Mr. Hunnewell into giving you information that was none of your affair."

"Not exactly. He came to his own conclusions about my relationship to your great-uncle."

"And you did nothing to correct him."

"Don't get ruffled. I had a right to some of that information."

"Some?" she said irritably.

"Yes. I wasn't kidding when I said your father owes a bundle to those of us making up the oil partnership we got going a couple of years ago," Kace said reasonably.

She gazed back hotly, refusing the fear that clamored for control. Kace had to be exaggerating, and the implications were wildly untrue.

"Something must have caught Hunnewell's attention and caused him a sleepless night or two," Kace mused, sitting down on the edge of the love seat and frowning thoughtfully at the bowl of rose buds on the table. He glanced up at her. "That's when he mentioned his financial concerns for you and Amanda."

Sharlotte began pacing, clasping and unclasping her hands, trying not to allow her thoughts to take his suggestion about Hunnewell too seriously.

He frowned. "Will you sit down? That fringe dancing about is distracting."

Sharlotte did so weakly in the nearest chair and dejectedly removed her little hat with its precocious feather. "This can't be happening to me. If only I'd spent the summer vacationing in Europe!"

"Poor girl," he drawled. "Life gets tough so she wants to run away to Paris. But if you smother all your troubles with French éclairs you won't fit into your thousand dollar dresses."

"Ohhh!" She threw her hat at him. "I'm not running away," she said with a sob.

"That's a girl," approved Kace. "If you want my opinion—"

"I don't," she sniffed.

He leaned forward. "I think Hunnewell was going to talk to your father this morning about something important, though I've no idea what it was. The poor fellow lucked out on the picnic as well."

She stared into his brittle green eyes, her heart quavering, mortifying heat beginning to burn her cheeks. "You cad," she whispered.

"Now, now," he lulled, twirling her hat on his finger. "Let's see those polished finishing school manners, Miss Ashford. A few dimples wouldn't hurt either. They always did get to me."

She sat up straight. "You don't believe any of this anymore than I do. If you did, you'd go straight to the police. You're just trying to get even with me—"

"Petty revenge? That's just your conscience speaking. Well, you can expect that. Chickens come home to roost as the old saying goes. Better yet: 'Whatsoever a man soweth, that shall he also reap.' That's from the Bible, in case you wondered. Harvesttime includes girls with dimples too, even ones with sapphires dangling around their throats like millstones." He stood. "It's your vanity, pure and simple, that wants to think I've been carrying a burning torch for you these last few years."

As the terrible day's events continued to mount, Sharlotte's mind began to feel as clogged as a saturated sponge.

"After Hunnewell's death this morning, I feel it my duty to pass on his concerns to you and Amanda." Kace regarded her with an inquiring look. "He had a soft spot in his conscience for the two of you."

Sharlotte glanced up. She was surprised by that. Mr. Hunnewell had never shown any particular interest in them before.

"What is there to be concerned about?"

"For one thing, he mentioned Amanda's accident."

Sharlotte stood abruptly and walked a few feet away, her back toward him.

Kace's voice softened. "He worried that her condition would worsen, affecting her future and yours." He had some wild notion about your feeling responsible for the injury."

Her throat tightened and ached. She fought bravely to hold back the prickling of tears. "It was my fault," her voice was so quiet she didn't think Kace heard.

A moment later his hands took hold of her shoulders. He turned her around to face him.

"Amanda doesn't believe that."

"Y-yes she does, secretly, though she'd never say it to me."

"That's nonsense, Sharlotte. She's always loved horses. Even when she was a child she used to beg and plead with Livia to let her ride. She was reckless that afternoon when we all went riding. We both called her back. She refused to come."

Sharlotte had relived that horrifying moment many times in the last two years. No matter what Kace said, she was convinced of her blame. What Kace didn't know was that she and Amanda had argued over Tyler, and it was only after Sharlotte had threatened to come between them that Amanda burst into tears and ran off to mount her horse and gallop away.

"You're punishing yourself with false guilt. Hunnewell thought your sisterly devotion and self-sacrifice would lead you to do most anything to protect her."

"Amanda might never walk again, but even if she does, she will always need a crutch. And she will need the most expensive physicians money can buy."

Kace lifted her chin until she was forced to meet his searching gaze. "Is that why you're marrying Clarence?"

She couldn't admit that marriage into the Fosdick family would end all of their financial worries. Kace would scorn that kind of decision and think her foolish. She couldn't face the fiery trials and disappointments of life unless she had a feather cushion to lean back on. Kace was tough and took risks. If he was knocked down he got back up again and tried even harder. He wouldn't understand her fears of poverty and rejection by the society into which she'd been born, raised, and educated. Life outside of that society was a jungle of intimidating shadows.

Kace was silent and she felt his alert gaze studying her. "I confess you have me bewildered."

"Bewildered?" she asked, trying to delay him from pursuing his scrutiny of her motives.

"Yes. The Sharlotte I've known since she was a young girl wouldn't risk her plans to benefit anyone. Not even sister Amanda. Could it be there's another Sharlotte Ashford I haven't met yet?"

Her eyes lifted to his, finding them a riveting gray-green, gently but consistently wrapping her in a cocoon from which she couldn't escape. Her heart beat uncontrollably faster. She knew the dangers of vulnerability, and the impossibility, of caring for Kace. She pulled her gaze from his.

"You still haven't explained Mr. Hunnewell's concerns, or why I should take your bleak explanations about my father seriously. As far as I know you're making all this up." She walked away.

Kace's voice turned abrupt. "Hunnewell wanted to make sure your inheritance would be there when the two of you reach the age to claim your patrimony."

Her brows lifted. "You're not suggesting it won't be? Because if you are, I've never heard of anything more absurd."

"Maybe not so absurd. I went to see your great-uncle today after I'd received a last-minute invitation that allowed me to darken the door of his sanctuary."

So that's where he went after borrowing George's roadster.

"To put it mildly, he emphasized again what he'd already written in that letter you spied in my jacket: he was finished bailing your father out of his losses in the market. Your father will need to come up with the money to pay off his own debts. What your great-uncle didn't tell me is what Hunnewell worried about." He walked up to her. "That he'll need to start dipping into your inheritance."

"I don't believe it…"

"Now that Hunnewell is dead you'd be wise to find yourself a lawyer willing to work for your best interests and Amanda's. Ask him to check the status of your financial estate. The one your mother's side of the family left you as an inheritance."

Sharlotte reached to slap him. Kace caught her hand a fraction of a second before it reached its mark.

"Sharlotte be sensible, be realistic for a change. Do you think I enjoy telling you this? Do you think I take some immature satisfaction in unmasking the grandiose image that you carry of your father?"

"Yes! You're jealous of his dignity, his name, and his status as a respected gentleman in the financial world. You enjoy trying to insult us because I've turned you down for Clarence."

"You're wrong. But marriage to Clarence is also for your father's benefit, not yours. Admit it. You won't be happy, Sharlotte. You don't love him and he doesn't love you. He too is under the grip of his family, especially his rich grandmother. Is that what you really want?"

He understood more than she had thought, and the idea was mortifying.

"How Clarence and I feel about each other is none of your affair. It's immaterial."

"Oh, is it? You're taking marriage a little lightly, aren't you?"

She turned away. "Marriages were always arranged by parents in past generations."

"The fact that he's rich is the deciding factor."

"Yes."

"Just like that—'yes.' It's that simple?"

"Yes." She bit her lip and marveled that her voice was steady and indifferent when her heart groaned with fear.

"Then you're being extremely foolish. You're selling yourself into a loveless marriage. And cheaply, at that. You'll live to regret your decision."

She turned. "Cheaply!"

"That's right."

"The Fosdicks are millionaires."

"I'm referring to the fact you're willing to sell your future in exchange for a man's bank account."

She flushed as his rebuke stung like a whip. Down deep in her heart she knew he was right. "Well, I would rather marry into wealth and power than to struggle to make a piece of Texas dirt produce oil," she countered defensively.

"Fine. Better get that coveted Fosdick ring and hang onto it like a bulldog. Because," he said quite calmly, "once the financial foundation begins to crumble beneath the mighty Ashford empire, your father is likely to use whatever he can get his hands on to pay off his creditors, including your personal baubles and beads."

She sucked in her breath. "How dare you say these vicious things, or…or even suggest he'd take what belongs to *me* and use it to pay debts."

"He may, if he hasn't already sold them. Better check your safe."

"I will hear no more of this. I don't ever want to see you again." She hurried across the room to the door, unbolted the latch, flung it open, and pointed. "Leave my room at once, or I will scream for help."

Kace looked at her for a thoughtful moment, his jaw tensing. Then abruptly he walked to the door.

"If my father owes you anything," she declared, "which I doubt, you'll get every last penny."

He smiled a little. "I feel better already. You'll see to that, of course?" he asked dryly.

"Yes," she said with firm dignity, but wondered at her impulsiveness. "Even if I must sell some of my jewels. In fact—" their eyes held steadily as she reached behind her neck and unlatched the gold clasp to her sapphires. She also removed her earrings and held them out. "I don't know if he really owes you anything, or how much, but it can't be much more than what these are worth on the London market. Here, take them and go," she said loftily. "The sacrifice is worth getting you out of my life."

For a long moment he looked at her, and she grew uneasy as his gaze hardened. She reached for his hand and pressed them into his palm. "There. Goodbye, Mr. Landry."

Sharlotte turned her back toward him.

The jewels struck the floor with a tiny crash. She whirled to face him. His eyes blazed. She took a step back. She had never seen him this angry. He turned suddenly and strode away down the hall.

Sharlotte stood for a moment without moving, biting her lip, her fingers tightly closing about her skirt. She looked down at the blue sapphires winking in the lamplight. She stooped to the floor and gathered them up. Why had he become so angry? She'd been willing to part with them and pay the debt he insisted her father owed. Were they not enough? Or had something else angered him?

A moment later she arose and closed the door, still looking at the shimmering blue gems dangling across her palm that he had rejected.

13

It wasn't until well after midnight that Sharlotte realized that Kace had done a thorough job of getting her to defend her own actions, but he hadn't explained why he'd been in her father's room or what he'd expected to find. Even so, she suspected his search had been little more than a fishing expedition to try to learn about her father's business dealings with Hunnewell. If Mr. Hunnewell had written her father, more than likely he'd have kept any letters in his bedroom desk.

She listened at the stairway, making sure everyone had gone to their rooms.

I must get Daddy's glove, she thought.

She started down the staircase in her stocking feet, rain boots in hand. She wore a long dark coat with a hood and carried a flashlight in her pocket. The clock clanged two A.M., causing her to start, catching her breath. How could she have ever thought it sounded musical? The woodchopper with his hatchet brought goose bumps to the back of her neck as she envisioned the clock in the hall below.

She went down silently into the darkness, feeling as though she were descending into a well.

At the front door she paused, but except for the loud ticking the house was deceptively silent and at rest. She sat down on an upholstered bench and slipped on her boots and gloves, then carefully unbolting the brass lock, she stepped out onto the doorstep. The eaves offered little escape from the rain as the wind drove it against her. She closed the door silently and, wrapping her coat about her snugly, went down the steps to the graveled drive and followed it around the house toward the garden.

Sharlotte's heart was thudding in her ears. The tops of the trees hissed liked weaving serpents. Black bushes reached out at her with spiny fingers that snagged her coat. The gravel crunched and water slopped about her boots as she rushed through the garden toward the gatekeeper's cottage, perhaps five minutes ahead. Fear ran along beside her like speeding wolves, and it was her own rasping breath she heard warning her not to get caught. *There's no reason to fear,* she kept repeating to herself. *Everyone is asleep. No one except Daddy knows about that missing glove. All I need do is retrieve it and return to my bedroom undetected. By morning this nightmare will all be over. Once the inquest is held, this horrible day will fade away forever.*

The wind slapped the rain into her face and took away her breath. One of her boots slid in a small puddle of mud near the cottage, and she reached out and steadied herself on the frontal post near the door. Branches were sprawling along the wall below the narrow front window.

Sharlotte cautiously tried the doorknob and found it as she and Kace had left it, unlocked. Had her father come here? Clenching her teeth to master her faltering courage she pushed the door open and stood trembling on the threshold.

A musty smell of old wood and dampness wafted over to her. She switched on her flashlight and swept its beam across the floor to see if there were wet footprints. She was relieved to see nothing. He probably hadn't come here, but had gone down to the old boathouse. Envisioning the creaking and groaning of the decaying wooden structures in the darkness brought a shudder. If he'd gone there, it had been in vain.

Removing her boots at the threshold, Sharlotte was about to step inside, then decided to place them behind the bush growing close by the porch.

She switched off her light and stepped into the dark room, breathing the close, damp air. She closed the door and leaned against it.

The wind yanked at the roof shingles and buffeted the side of the cottage. Dank odors hung in the air, but there was something else. The faint odor of...smoke. A candle? Yes, that was it. A snuffed wick, and not long ago from the smell of it. Her father?

She stood still. The tempest-driven deluge smothered any sounds that might come from behind the closed door of the next room. Her heart began to race so that she had to force herself to breathe slowly and quietly. Had her father come back? Not likely. He wasn't well enough to take on two treks into the stormy night. Who, then? Someone had obviously lit a candle recently. Her hand shook as she clutched her flashlight, not daring to switch it on again. She stood frozen like a pillar of salt in the deep shadowy gloom.

Maybe...maybe she could find the glove without the flashlight. *Hurry. Do it quickly.*

She controlled herself with considerable effort, then tiptoed toward the darker image of the divan against the backside of the wall. A white flash of lightning flared outside the upper window, briefly illuminating the room. It lasted just long enough to allow her to gain her bearings. She moved swiftly toward the divan, knelt, and thrust her hand beneath the dust ruffle, moving her palm alongside the floor for the glove. Her fingers traced across the dust, but where was it? She then heard the door to the next room opening softly...very softly.

Sharlotte fought the panic that threatened to shut off her breathing.

A moment later she felt the movement of someone walking, the faint stir of the musty air, the slight creak of the floorboards as footsteps silently passed. Terror mounted inside her until her lips parted to scream, but instead she prayed silently, *God, please help me.* Her reason went blank, and she had no impressions until she was aware again that the movement had glided past without stopping. Whoever it was had apparently not seen her.

The door opened and the sound of loud rain filled her eardrums as fresh wind cooled her perspiring throat. Then, with the barest trace of noise, the front door shut again.

Darkness enfolded her once more within its secretive grasp.

Her eyes shut with overwhelming relief and tears slid down her cheeks. Slowly, as one recovering from a long-distance run, her heartbeat slowed, leaving her clammy and weak.

And to think, she had almost left her boots in plain view on the step!

The thought horrified her. Who could it have been? Someone from the house, a stranger? She was relieved she had heeded Kace's observation and washed away her perfume before dressing to come here tonight. If she had smelled the candle smoke, the stranger passing by her as a breath of shadowy wind might have caught a whiff of perfume.

Kace! No, it couldn't have been him, she thought. She had passed his room before going downstairs, and his reading lamp had still been on.

Then who? Who had been inside the cottage? And why? Who else beside herself and her father would know about that glove? Or had there been something else the stranger was looking for?

Yet, thought Sharlotte, bewildered, there was nothing of value in the rundown cottage. She was certain of that. Certain too, that whoever had come here earlier had been searching for something related with Hunnewell's accident, though she couldn't explain her reason for believing it. The glove was the one item she could think of, but was there something else she didn't know about? The weapon used? Could it have still been here?

She shuddered. Her wet clothes and the emotions she had just experienced made her feel cold and a little sick. She marveled that she was brave enough to have come here. Despite the anguish, she was learning new things about herself. For one thing, she could be driven to face danger if she believed someone she loved was in jeopardy. For Sharlotte remained sure that her father, though he had his weaknesses, was no murderer. If he had met Mr. Hunnewell at the boathouse to discuss his gambling debts, or some mysterious goings on in Mexico, she was positive that he had not caused his lawyer's death.

She waited, still kneeling on the floor and too afraid to move, her imagination thinking that whoever had been in the room might be waiting just outside to spring upon her when she switched on the flashlight. Reason told her to either go back to the house or to leave by the back garden gate for the road that wound past the boathouse. The thought of that lonely path beneath the swaying trees sent shivers along her spine. She almost wished she had told Kace about the glove just to have his company now. Naturally, she couldn't tell him. He already held her father in a web of suspicion. Anything else, especially his glove, would convince him he was right.

After a few moments, she realized that the rain was easing and the wind settling, as were her emotions. She counted to five, placed her hand over the flashlight to weaken the beam, then switched it on and darted to the front door and locked it. Breathing easier, she shone the light to the divan and looked beneath. Ah. There it was! She reached under and pulled the glove out.

The expensive Spanish leather was sadly familiar. She had seen the same style too many times on her father to believe it could belong to anyone else.

Then Sharlotte caught her breath. She stared, unbelieving. There were initials, but they weren't her father's. She stood to her feet, stunned. A brilliant streak of lightning dazzled her eyes, followed a moment later by a menacing growl of thunder. Sharlotte's nerves began tingling. The initials *K.L.* were revealed under the close beam of the flashlight. Kace Landry. The glove belonged to Kace.

Quite suddenly Sharlotte's thoughts were astir, putting strings of events together. Kace had been the one to find Hunnewell. He had made an alibi for himself by joining her on the way to the boathouse. He had decided to stop here at the cottage to get out of the worst of the downpour, but had that been the real reason? What if he'd met Hunnewell here earlier, instead of her father? Perhaps he'd suspected he might have dropped it here and needed an excuse to look before the police arrived. But she had found it first and pushed it under the divan before he'd seen it. Perhaps all that talk tonight in her room had just been to see how much she knew, or how much he could get away with by shifting the guilt on her father. He had met Mr. Hunnewell here, then walked back with him to the boathouse, maybe convincing Hunnewell they should use a boat to get back to the club for the picnic. And…and when Mr. Hunnewell told him that her father did not owe him anything and would not—what? Be blackmailed?—they had argued and…

And now Kace was trying to turn her against her father by planting seeds of suspicion about his tremendous debts. And just why had he been in her father's bedroom searching through his desk?

She looked at Kace's glove again. What should she do? Confront him with it? Turn it over to the police? And yet, what did it prove except that he'd been here and dropped it? He could come up with any excuse. Nor was there proof Mr. Hunnewell had even visited this cottage or met anyone at the boathouse where he'd met his death.

Her scenario against Kace was mere conjecture. Weren't the police satisfied it had been an accident? Yes, there'd be an inquest, but Dr. Lester was confident Hunnewell's death had been accidental drowning.

Sharlotte stuffed the glove inside the pocket of her coat and forced herself to unbolt the front door and step back out into the rainy night. She retrieved her boots from where she'd stashed them and leaned back against the door to wrestle them back on. Maybe it had been Kace who came here just now. Perhaps she'd been mistaken about his being in his room. What did a burning lamp prove?

Sharlotte trudged back through the bleak garden amid ghostly branches waving their spindly arms. The house was ahead and looming grim in the baying wind. Her mind continued to be filled with apprehension; there was still the reason that had compelled her father to go out into the night after convincing everyone that he was ill.

Perhaps it was best not to ask such questions, or mention to Kace that she'd found his glove. The secrets that loitered in the shadows might be better left to darkness.

⌖

Five minutes later, soaked and buffeted, shaken and feeling utterly alone in her fears and suspicions, Sharlotte reached the house.

She arrived just in time, for as she left her boots and coat hidden behind the large rhododendron bushes growing alongside the front porch and slipped in through the little-used side door on the left wing of the house, she thought she heard someone in the darkened library. She stopped in her stocking feet, holding her breath. The sound did not repeat, but it was the last straw. Her nerve broken, she turned and sped to the dimly lighted staircase and rushed up without stopping until she reached her room and ducked in, thrusting the bolt through the lock.

If I wasn't such a coward I'd have hidden and waited to see who was in the library. Nine chances out of ten it was the same person who was in the gatekeeper's cottage.

She waited by her door, listening to see if she could discern what bedroom the person in the library would enter. Five minutes later the one discernible sound was still just the rain on her veranda. Either he hadn't come upstairs or the person had come up in stocking feet as she had. She waited another minute, then cold and shivering, she turned away and readied herself for her warm, dry bed with the lamp off.

Sharlotte huddled under the covers thinking of Kace's glove hidden in the bottom drawer of her bureau. Disturbing thoughts ran helter-skelter through her mind. She thought she would never fall asleep. When at last she did, she dreamed of Sheldon's yacht tossing on a violent sea. Amanda's picnic basket slid off the deck and began bobbing up and down in the water with Kace's glove inside of it. She yelled and sat up with a terrified start. The gray morning light was peeping shyly through the window. It was another rainy day.

∾

The storm lasted another twenty-four hours before it blew itself out. A day later Mr. Hunnewell was buried in a civil ceremony with few in attendance. A poet read from Shakespeare's *A Midsummer Night's Dream,* and another speaker from the Great Minds of the Century Club read snatches from Darwin, Voltaire, and Bertrand Russell.

They have no hope, Sharlotte thought, desolation filling her heart. *This is the best they can do—a plastic copy of a Christian funeral without the Bible and without Christ. If death ends it all with nothing to offer except a few ideas that have no meaning beyond the grave, then life also holds no meaning.* She glanced at her father and realized with unexpected dread that one day this would be his fate also. *Then why was he striving so, and for what, if it all ends in death?*

Sharlotte shuddered. Not just her father, but she too would die, and Amanda.

Kace was standing across from her on the opposite side of the casket. *He doesn't believe any of this hopeless philosophy,* she thought, *not if he's going to marry Elly. Her father would never permit her to marry an unbeliever. He must think we're fools. Or does he pity us?*

Like a flash she remembered a story Uncle Sherman had read to them on the ranch. It was about the rich man who had built larger barns for his goods, yet ignored God. Jesus had labeled him a fool. Uncle Sherman had then read a verse from the Psalms: "The fool hath said in his heart, There is no God."

Disturbed, Sharlotte plucked at her handkerchief with damp hands. She didn't want to think about death or rich fools, but this time there was no escape: It was all laid out before her, staring her boldly in the face. *I'm afraid. I wish Aunt Livia were here.*

Aware that Kace was looking at her, Sharlotte turned her head away and felt Clarence's hand reach over and take hers, giving it a squeeze. Perhaps he understood.

On the way back to the house in the limousine Clarence had hired she commented: "That was a silly funeral."

"I haven't attended one yet that I liked."

"That's not what I meant. It was senseless. The words, I mean."

"Oh, I don't know…what were his associates and friends supposed to say?"

She looked at Clarence to see if he were jesting, but his somber face convinced her otherwise. His eyes were calm and his jaw line immobile. The black suit he wore made his face especially pale, vaguely reminding her that he'd worked all summer in New York except for the week he'd been on Long Island.

"Most funerals have a minister," she said, "who reads from the Bible."

"He didn't believe in either, so he might as well have quotations from Voltaire."

"Don't you find that dreadfully dismal and hopeless?"

Clarence reached into his jacket pocket and removed a cigarette case and lighter. "Most of us would rather not think of death. We're too busy living."

She watched the flame dance on the lighter. "It's hard to live happily when you know the path you're taking leads to a dead end."

"That's why most people don't want to think about it."

"Do you, Clarence? Think much about it?"

He frowned at the end of the glowing cigarette, then glanced toward the sky. "It may not be a dead end. Not the way you mean anyway. Some think we go on living happily on one of the planets out there."

"People can think anything," she murmured, "but that doesn't mean it's true."

At least the Bible claims to be truth from God, she thought. *And it gives the answers to life's questions. Maybe I should start reading Mummy's Bible.*

"Who knows?" Clarence said. "We may even come back to earth as someone or something else. Houdini is convinced of it anyway. What a marvelous magician."

A starling squawked and landed boldly on the grass not far ahead of them, picking up a worm. "Meet Mr. Hunnewell," Clarence joked. "The only question is, which one is he, the starling or the worm?"

"Clarence, shame on you! The poor man isn't even buried yet."

"The sooner he is, the better. His demise really upset your father. Took straight to his bed over it."

Could Clarence have gone down to the library the night before last? she wondered. Perhaps, but wouldn't he have turned on the light? "Well, we're not through yet. The inquest is on Friday," she said.

~

The coroner's inquest on Mr. Hunnewell was unexpectedly brief. The perfunctory questions undergirded Dr. Lester's theory that it was accidental death by drowning. The pathologist's report and the police findings were gone over carefully, while Sharlotte wondered uneasily if everyone was deliberately being lulled into a false sense of security.

Everyone was there because they had no choice: Burgess Ashford, Sheldon and Pamela, Bitsy, George, Amanda, Kace, Stuart, Clarence, and Sharlotte. Amanda had been carried in by Kace, and Sharlotte watched as he placed her in a chair, then sat down beside her and George. Amanda turned and looked for her, then smiled bravely.

Sharlotte found herself watching them all with furtive speculation. She especially watched Kace. Wasn't he worried at all about not finding his glove?

Sharlotte and Kace described finding Mr. Hunnewell's body near the boathouse, and Burgess told of his broken appointment with his lawyer earlier that morning and that he had seemed a little agitated by something on the telephone. At that, Sharlotte shifted in her seat and glanced at Kace. His expression revealed nothing, nor did he look at her, but she remembered what he'd told her about why he thought Hunnewell had come to see her father. No further questions were put to Mr. Ashford beyond asking him why he'd needed to break the appointment and why he'd asked his lawyer to the house for the weekend. The answers to these questions were corroborated, according to the police, by his butler, his chauffeur, and his valet.

The room had been stuffy and the day long, and it was a relief to get in the open air again. The late afternoon had the feel of fall and the smell of late-blooming roses. With the inquest over, they all drifted toward waiting automobiles while talking in low voices.

"Well," Clarence said matter-of-factly, as he walked beside her across the lawn, "that's that."

She looked at him quickly. "It seems they're convinced it was an accidental drowning."

"What else could it be?" he cast her a glance. "Unless he committed suicide."

Cousin Sheldon overheard, for he came between them by putting an arm around both their shoulders. "Listen to the would-be lawyer."

"'Would-be'?" Clarence offered a sour grin.

"Destined to become another Clarence Darrow, I hasten to add. Now, Sharlotte, listen to my take on this ordeal. The old fellow went hiking where he shouldn't have for a man his age, stepped on the rotting stair, began to fall, reached for the banister but didn't have the strength to maintain his balance—down he went. There you have it. Tragic, but life marches on."

Sheldon turned to Clarence again. "As they say, summer is past and dreary autumn is in the air. That does it for me in these parts. Pamela and I are going home to Boston. I suppose you're going on to New York?"

"Yes, work begins at my uncle's firm. I'll be helping him on a case."

"You too, aren't you, Sharlotte? Going to New York?"

"I haven't completely made up my mind yet," she admitted. "Amanda and I were thinking of spending a few weeks in Vermont."

The weak sunshine did little to warm Sharlotte, who put her hands in the pockets of her long blue coat and wondered why she hadn't remembered to bring gloves. Gloves. She shuddered. From the corner of her eye she saw Kace walk up to the roadster and

wait for George, who was pushing Amanda's chair. When George
had placed her in the seat he turned and shook hands with Kace.

"Guess this is goodbye, Kace. Come look us up if you ever get
to New York."

"Thanks, I will. Right now it's back to Texas. Goodbye,
Amanda. Write to Livia. She loves hearing from you."

"Oh, I will. No chance of any of you coming to Vermont this
Christmas?"

"No. Hard work cracks its whip. Come see us in Texas."

"And ride—Oh, if only I could! Such beautiful horses."

"Another time," Kace said with a smile and tweaked her chin.
"That is, if George lets you out of his sight."

Pamela came up rubbing her pink nose and looking chilly and
morose. "Dreadful end to a lovely summer. 'Bye, Sharlotte,
pleasant journey. See you at Christmas. Goodbye, Clarence…
coming, Sheldon? Oh! Kace, it was fun seeing you again. Do come
for the holidays! We've a splendid skiing holiday already planned
around Christmas and New Year's…'bye, Amanda, honey. I
promise no more liverwurst sandwiches next summer."

Amanda laughed as George called: "If you do, we won't come."

"You've got to come," Sheldon said cheerfully. "I'm going to
win the Bermuda Race this year. I'll have my cup to brag about."

"Odd to think summer is over," Sharlotte sighed. "It all went by
so quickly."

"And ended so tragically," Pamela said moodily, and looked
sadly at Clarence. He flushed and took hold of Sharlotte's arm.

"Come along, Sharlotte. I'll run you back to the house. Is your
father coming with us?"

"No, he's catching the train to New York."

Clarence walked with her to the car, and the chauffeur opened
the passenger door.

Sharlotte glanced over her shoulder, but Kace, with his back
toward her, was leaning lazily against the side of George's roadster.
His hands were in his pockets and Bitsy was talking and flirting

with him. *If he doesn't want to say goodbye, that's fine with me,* Sharlotte thought, annoyed. She got into the rear passenger seat and Clarence slipped in beside her.

"Whew," he muttered again, "I'm relieved this week is over," and he glanced, not at Kace, but at Pamela. Sharlotte agreed with him as the chauffeur released the brake and drove away.

They left the others standing in the breeze among the sighing elm trees, all of them scattering to their various pursuits like leaves blown by the winds of change.

PART TWO

Ashford Brownstone, New York

Wealth gotten by vanity shall be diminished...

Proverbs 13:11

14

Sharlotte and Amanda returned to New York in September, where their father had immersed himself in his endless duties as bank president of Manhattan Security and Loan. As for Sharlotte, she resumed her social debut with a new round of activities ranging from afternoon teas and picnics to bejeweled balls. Life in the spacious brownstone mansion in Manhattan was luxurious and pleasant, but she wished for 1929 to come to an end so that she and Clarence might announce their engagement at a gala New York ball.

With the engagement in mind, Sharlotte proceeded to make plans for her grand tour of Europe that was expected of someone from her background. She chose her wardrobe and made arrangements to visit with friends of other elite families in London, Paris, and Rome. Then, once she returned from Europe, her engagement to Clarence would be publicly announced, followed by marriage in September, 1931.

Marriage seemed too distant to Sharlotte, who wanted the Fosdick name as soon as possible, but the Fosdicks were not to be rushed, and because they were on a higher social strata than the Ashfords, Sharlotte had no choice but to go along with their wishes.

Sharlotte had never particularly cared for Mrs. Fosdick, Clarence's grandmother. The older woman held the puppet strings of the rest of the members of the family, and she was shrewd and exacting. Grandmother Fosdick didn't approve of her as heartily as Sharlotte would have liked, so she went out of her way to behave discreetly when in her presence, which was as seldom as possible.

The Fosdick dinners were especially cumbersome to attend. As Mrs. Fosdick claimed to be a blooded granddaughter of a British lord, she expected to be treated with precise deference. Her guests were not merely the new wealthy, but people with names of renown and blood connections to old families esteemed in Europe.

When attending these dinners with Clarence, Sharlotte would walk on eggshells in trepidation of saying something that would raise the eyebrows of Lady Fosdick.

"The old woman is exceedingly wealthy," her father stated. "She owns fabulous jewels, most of which are never seen by the public. She hoards them away in a vault at the bank. So we want to make certain we do nothing that will rankle her sensibilities."

Clarence adored her. "There's nothing she wouldn't do for me," he bragged. "And there isn't anything I wouldn't do for my grandmother. She's a smart woman, darling. She deserves our respect and obedience."

It was on the tip of her tongue to ask if he'd feel that way if Grandmother Fosdick was poor, but she bit back her words. After all, she was marrying Clarence for his family name and wealth. Sharlotte would naturally show the needed respect, but love? It was difficult when Mrs. Fosdick's steely blue eyes surveyed her with the composure of a biology professor contemplating the dissection of a dead rat. She told this to Clarence, thinking he would laugh the way she knew Kace would have, but Clarence was shocked.

"But," Sharlotte said defensively, "I think she could carve up a rat without blinking an eye."

Grandmother Fosdick was also a member of a newer religion called "Christian Science," although Sharlotte had read a minister's comments in the newspaper that said it was neither "Christian," nor "scientific." Once, when Sharlotte had a migraine, Mrs. Fosdick coolly claimed that "actually there was no such thing as illness."

"Your pain merely proves that you are too giddy. If you believed in God enough, my dear, you wouldn't get ill. You should munch fewer bonbons and drink minted barley water. I credit my good health and longevity to drinking a quart of minted barley water a day."

As for sister Amanda, Sharlotte's worries had only increased since the summer vacation on Long Island. Amanda had a year remaining at Vassar College, but a change in the seasons and the oncoming chilly fall weather appeared to weaken her system. A cold that Sharlotte shook off in a week had become a severe lung malady in Amanda that kept her coughing through the night. Burgess was seeking the advice of an expert in the medical profession, not merely because of the cold, but also for her spinal injury.

It hurt Sharlotte to see Amanda grow more depressed when the new physician, Dr. Helmer, refused to let her return to Vassar even with a nurse companion. Maybe next year, he had told Burgess.

"I'll be too old," groaned Amanda.

"At eighteen?" he looked at Burgess and smiled.

"Next year I expect to become engaged to George," Amanda said bravely, glancing at her father.

Sharlotte saw her father's face lose its smile and become adamant.

"We won't discuss George now. Here, I have something for you. It will make you happy." He handed Amanda a sealed envelope.

Sharlotte leaned toward the side of the bed to see whom it was from.

"It's from Aunt Livia," Amanda cried.

Sharlotte sat down on the edge of the bed as her father and Dr. Helmer left the room, talking quietly together about Amanda's condition.

Sharlotte hadn't heard from Aunt Livia since before Kace had come to Long Island, and she curled up on her sister's large bed to hear the latest gossip from Texas.

A second sheet of paper, included with Livia's letter, fell out as Amanda unfolded her aunt's letter.

"It's from Tyler. I wonder what he has to say," Amanda said weakly, her red-gold braids outlining a pale face. Even so, Sharlotte noted a faint glimmer of interest in Amanda's blue eyes. Before George had come along, her sister had had quite a crush on Tyler Landry.

"Probably wondering about your improvement," Sharlotte said, putting an emphasis on improvement. The more she encouraged Amanda that she was getting better the happier she became. "But I'll bet Daddy didn't know Tyler's letter was in there. He might have confiscated it."

Amanda sighed. "Daddy doesn't like *any* of the young men I find interesting. Not George or Tyler. He keeps talking about Albert." She made a face.

Albert Gosling was the youngest son of a bank president in Boston.

"What does Aunt Livia say?" Sharlotte asked.

"Here…you read it to me," Amanda said with a weak voice. "Tyler's note too."

Sharlotte happily obliged her, wondering if there might be some bit of news about Kace. She was not disappointed.

"Kace has returned home to the ranch after making a trip to the Christian boys' orphanage near El Paso," Sharlotte explained. "Livia doesn't say what it's about."

"She never does," Amanda said with a sigh. "She drops these little explosions and you're left with all sorts of questions stirring round in your mind. Oh well…" she smiled. "It keeps up our correspondence. I need to write back to find out what she meant."

Sharlotte couldn't help but agree. Livia always accepted Kace's bare explanations at face value without probing into his affairs. Livia must trust him explicitly, she thought.

Tyler was another matter. Aunt Livia and Uncle Sherman watched him as carefully as a mother bobcat with a kitten.

"Go on, Sharlotte, read more."

Sharlotte finished Livia's letter, but she had no more to say about Kace. She spoke of the ranch and about some disease that was killing the cattle. Sherman was up day and night trying to save the calves, and a new shipment of medicine was to arrive on the train from Chicago. They would need to borrow against the ranch to support their losses. Once the disease was considered by Texas authorities to be under control, they would buy new cattle to take their place. Sharlotte went on to read: *Sherman had to go into debt again. Seems like we can never win. No sooner do we get things paid off and the ranch debt free, then something hits us hard and we're down again. Sherman says the Lord wants us to trust in Him and not in our assets. Every good gift comes from His gracious hand, but so do the trials. We expect our faith is being tested. Sherman read from the Book of Job last night after supper. You remember, don't you, how he lost everything he loved, even his health? Satan told God that Job would curse Him to His face if He removed His blessings. Well, you know how it ended. Job didn't curse God. He continued to trust Him. "Though He slay me, yet will I trust Him," Job said.*

Sharlotte finished reading the letter, then glanced at Amanda. She was staring toward the window where the mulberry tree was fast losing its old summer foliage. Big yellow leaves fluttered down to the cold autumn ground like falling butterflies, there to be buried beneath a sod of snow for the winter. Sharlotte saw her sister's jaw clench, and her heart went out to her. She thought she understood her feelings: what if Amanda never walked again?

Sharlotte reached over and squeezed her hand. "See that tree out there? There's a certain sadness when fall sets in and the bright green summer leaves fall away. But the tree isn't injured by this at all. It's merely making room for the new in spring. Sometimes our lives are like that. Our disappointments make room for new and different blessings."

Amanda turned her head and offered a smile. "Where did you learn that?"

"Uncle Sherman used to tell us that, don't you remember?"

Amanda shook her head no. "Guess I wasn't listening—but I am now."

Sherman's words were wise, Sharlotte thought, *but do I really believe them?*

She quietly folded the letter. "Aunt Livia sends her love. Says she's praying for your health and she hopes we'll visit next summer."

"You'll be gone," Amanda reminded her, a blank look coming into her eyes. "You'll be taking the grand tour through Europe. And I'll be here alone."

"No, you won't," Sharlotte said cheerfully, "because I'm going to ask Daddy to have your nurse come along so that you can go with me."

"Oh, Sharlotte, I couldn't. That would be selfish of me. I'd be such a nuisance—someone would either need to carry me or push me about." She tried to giggle. "Can you imagine good old George carrying me into the Louvre? Or around Versailles?"

Sharlotte laughed. "George would love it. He's always game for anything. That's what you like about him."

"Yes." She sighed. "I wish Daddy did. If only George were rich. Then Daddy wouldn't mind."

"Might as well forget that. Daddy will *never* accept George."

"I suppose not, but—"

"Anyway," Sharlotte hastened, "by next year you're going to be so much stronger you won't need George to carry you around.

Why, with a new doctor and a whole year to recover, you'll be feeling much better. You'll either want to come with me or go back to Vassar and be with your friends."

"I wish. My friends, as you say, will have graduated by then. They'll move on to a university. And I won't be a part of the group."

"Then you'll make a whole set of new friends. Stop worrying. Listen while I read Tyler's news. I wonder how he managed to sneak it into Aunt's letter without her knowing?"

"Maybe she knew."

"Seems she would have mentioned that he was including a message."

"Tyler always comes up with ways to get what he wants," Amanda said with a smile.

Sharlotte wondered what she meant. "He certainly took it hard when you told him goodbye that last summer we were on the ranch."

Amanda winced. "Yes, it was awful telling him. Not that he became angry. It was odd, actually. I'd have preferred it if he had gotten mad, like Kace did with you. Instead, Tyler didn't say a word. He just looked at me. I walked back to where you and Kace were at the barbecue, and he finally arrived."

Sharlotte remembered back to that hot, fateful Texas afternoon, comparing it emotionally to the stormy picnic day on Long Island. The picnic ended with Mr. Hunnewell's death; the Texas barbecue had ended with Amanda's tumble from the horse and an injury to her spine. Things had never been the same since.

Sharlotte absently rubbed her arm, thinking of Long Island. The moment after arriving home from there a month ago, almost everything connected with that fateful day of the picnic had been neatly packed away to the back of her mind, just the same way she had put away her swimsuit. Escaping home to her familiar life in New York had been a relief. The events surrounding Mr. Hunnewell, Kace's warning about her father's finances, and the glove had all been mentally boxed away. Until this moment, she had succeeded in discarding those shadows, exchanging them for the sunshine of social gaiety. Nor did she have any wish to conjure up old ghosts from the boathouse or the gatekeeper's cottage. It was far better to forget.

"Sharlotte, what does Tyler say?"

Sharlotte snapped out of her reverie and hastened to read Tyler's letter wishing Amanda a happy birthday. He hoped she was improving day by day to a point where she would regain her ability to walk. He was seeing Abby Hutchins, the daughter of a rancher whose property bordered the Landry ranch.

She read the remainder of the letter without actually hearing his words. She was thinking again of Kace and what he had said about her father gambling on the stock market. To prove Kace wrong she would need to understand more about the market and what her father was doing. It was then that she made up her mind. The truth, she decided, was all important. If she were to learn it, then she must seek it.

In the days that followed, Sharlotte, who had never before paid the least attention to the business of Wall Street, forced herself to garner as much information as she could. She bought the *Ladies Home Journal* to read the article "Everybody Ought to Be Rich." The article pointed out that if everyone saved fifteen dollars a month and invested it in good common stocks, allowing the dividends to accumulate, at the end of twenty years one would have at least eighty thousand dollars and an income from investments of at least four hundred dollars a month. The gateway to fortune was standing right open.

She heard her father discussing on the telephone frequent new mergers of companies and banks. Every rumor of a new merger was an automatic signal for a leap in the prices of the stocks. It was becoming very tempting to the managers of many of the concerns to arrange sweetheart deals for their own speculative fortunes. Prices were going up. That was all that mattered.

Her father's business associates, mainly brokers and their wives, often came to parties at the brownstone mansion. Sharlotte found herself paying closer attention to their conversations in the parlor as they sipped bootlegged scotch: "Prosperity due for a decline? Why, we've scarcely started!" And the puns: "Be a 'Bull' on America." "Never 'sell' the United States 'short.'" "I tell you, some of these prices will look ridiculously low in another year or two." "Just watch that stock—it's going to five hundred." "The possibilities of that company are 'unlimited.'" "Never give up your position in a good stock."

Sharlotte heard about how many millions of dollars a wise fellow could have made if he'd just bought a hundred shares of General Motors in 1919 and held on. "Look at the big names that never sold anything. They're rich today because of it."

She even visited the stock exchange and watched the men in the pits shout for hours on end in what she considered sheer pandemonium. The arteries bulged in their necks, and she wondered why they didn't get migraines. A noisy bell clanged at the end of the day's trading, then someone pounded the podium with a big wooden hammer. Everyone looked at one another, smiled, applauded, and then left the floor which was covered with ankle-deep ticker tape. She understood that on the next morning it would began all over again.

"Daddy, how can you stand this? It's confusing and terribly boring."

He laughed. "Boring? It's the most exciting game in the world! It's the source of great fortunes for people like the Ashfords, the Morgans, the Rockefellers, the Kennedys, and many thousands of others."

Naturally, she knew it took more wisdom and business sense to understand the inner workings of the market than her surface perception allowed. She was bound to appear naïve to the professionals. However, after Kace's private warning that her father was gambling on deep margins, she was determined to try and understand.

"What are margins?" she asked casually.

Her father shot her a look as they ate lunch at an upscale restaurant before going home.

"Margins? To simplify the explanation, my dear, it means to borrow money from your broker to buy a stock. He's paid back when you sell that stock at a profit."

"I see…what happens if the stock goes down?"

"Then the broker issues a margin call—meaning you either pay him more cash to maintain the value of the broker's loan, or he has the right to sell the stock."

"Even at a loss?"

"Yes. Especially at a loss, because that's when the broker starts to worry that your stocks may be worth less than what he loaned you. But the Big Bull isn't going to die." He smiled. "By the end of this year the prices will be even higher."

"If the broker does sell the stock—what about the borrowed money? Must it be paid back right away?"

"Of course. He sells the stock to get his loan back, and there is usually next to nothing left over. Men have been known to lose a fortune on margin calls." He leaned over and laid his hand on hers, his serious blue eyes searching her face. "What's this all about, my girl? Why the sudden interest in the doings of Wall Street? Has Kace Landry been filling your mind with unreasonable fears?"

"Daddy, yes! He insists you owe him a lot of money in a deal with an upstart oil company."

"Oh, that…," he said as though it were trivial, waving his hand. "Yes, I did invest in an oil exploration company of which he was a member. It's since gone broke. But that's not for you to worry about. Kace has gotten his money back. I made certain of that as soon as I returned to New York from Long Island."

"You…paid him?" she asked, surprised.

"Yes. Several weeks ago. The matter is closed." He smiled thinly and reached into his pocket. "You see, I suspected he told you about our little deal last month during his visit to Long Island. All this interest of yours recently could mean only one thing, that you were worried. Yes, he's been paid. Now, then, bury your concerns, my dear."

Surprised, Sharlotte smiled with relief. "Oh, I'm glad, Daddy."

"Kace is a fine boy with a bright future. If he'd come from one of the better families here in the Northeast he would make a name for himself. As it is, he'll forge what he can down there in Texas where he belongs. Now, smile prettily and enjoy your luncheon." He turned and caught the attention of the waiter. "The usual, boy."

"Yes, sir, Mr. Ashford."

A minute later her father was sipping what looked like an iced tea, but it had the smell of something much more wicked. She didn't dare ask him about Kace's other charge that he was involved with Chicago bootleggers. Anyway, she didn't believe a word of it. The fact that her father had told her the truth and had now settled matters with Kace was enough. Her old sense of pride in her father returned.

Now she could turn her full attention to her future marriage with Clarence and forget all about Kace Landry and the unfortunate accident of Mr. Hunnewell. The past was buried; the future bloomed brightly.

15

As the money boom of the reckless 1920s rolled on with no end in sight, Sharlotte read about certain ministers who were warning Americans that they were in danger of becoming like spoiled children. Now that they had plenty of bread to eat, their entertainments were becoming more and more immoral as they abandoned their parents' and grandparents' faith in God and the Bible.

America's growing desire to be entertained found satisfaction in following the lurid details of high profile murder cases. Although Sharlotte was uneasy about anything hinting of murder after Mr. Hunnewell's death, her society friends, like millions of other common Americans, were fascinated by details about Al Capone in Chicago, or a Wall Street tycoon and his movie star mistress who had poisoned his wife for her millions.

Day after day Sharlotte witnessed hordes of Americans waiting in line just to buy the latest edition of the newspaper that carried the drama of the court trial in serial form.

But perhaps even more telling of the changing American culture was the way Americans breathlessly tuned in their radios from coast to coast to follow the New York electric chair execution of Nicola Sacco and Bartolomeo Vanzetti.

Americans weren't merely enthralled with big murder trials, however. The boxing fight between Jack Dempsey and Gene Tunney sent people's blood pressure rising, as did the World Series games playing to the biggest, noisiest crowds in American history, raising millions of dollars from hundreds of thousands of dedicated fans. There was a new craze in movies as well: lower and lower standards was the common rule of the day, as was the topic of illicit relations in the new popular "confession" magazines that filled the newsstands. Fashion, too, reflected the decade's loose values. Sharlotte was astounded to see a picture in the newspaper of the first bathing beauty contest in Atlantic City, New Jersey, where the contestants displayed their bodies for the cameras in skintight bathing suits.

"Look," she said to Amanda, showing her the photo. "We've already raised our hemlines from our ankles to our thighs! What's next?"

"You know what Pamela will do, don't you?" Amanda asked. "She'll rush to buy one and wear it to the beach. That will give her an advantage she'll use to snag Clarence from you."

"She would," Sharlotte said indignantly. "Well, I'm not about to follow her into that arena."

Meanwhile, America's interest in making money on the ever-prospering stock market was also "inching up" to new heights.

There seemed to be firsts in almost everything, including the colors of automobiles. When Henry Ford's new Model A came out in a color other than black it was immediately the rage.

As 1929 and the roaring decade was nearing a close, the new American culture could be summed up by what captured the emotional interest of the population rather than their intellect. While Sharlotte listened to her favorite band on the radio and painted her nails, planning for her engagement to Clarence, she heard little important news from other sections of the world that might eventually affect her life. For the most part, the news strangely omitted warnings that imperial Japan was invading

China and massacring millions of people in their quest to gain control of the Pacific trade routes, or that a group with the strange political name of the "Nazi" party was making strong gains in Germany. Nor did she hear that a new dictator in Italy by the name of Mussolini had declared his intention to create a new Roman Empire. The American economy was booming, so who cared? And who wanted to be bothered by members of the U.S. military establishment that were warning Congress that America's defenses were the weakest in its history. After all, hadn't Americans just helped liberate Europe from World War I? Democracy was on the rise. America no longer had any real enemies, so why waste money on military equipment?

Americans were too busy to worry about such mundane things. Nor did they have time to attend church the way their grandparents had done. Young flapper girls, who saw themselves as the "It" girl, wanted to show how grown-up they were by using profanity and lighting cigarettes in public. They would even drink from their boyfriends' flask of bootlegged scotch and sleep with them before marriage.

However, neither did Sharlotte have much time to worry about the decaying culture, as Amanda did not seem to be improving as they all had hoped.

"What she needs is a little sunshine and the good outdoors," Dr. Helmer briskly suggested to Burgess as they went down the stairs, with Sharlotte remaining behind on the top landing. "What about your sister in the Southwest? Texas, isn't it?"

"Livia? I don't think so, Doctor. Neither of my daughters think much of the Landry ranch. They're city girls."

"Well Burgess, there's always Palm Beach."

"Yes…"

But unexpectedly, suddenly, irrevocably life changed. October rolled around and the worst financial crisis to strike the nation and Europe brought a selling panic on Wall Street. At first Sharlotte paid little attention, for she'd heard of several previous drops in the market in March and May of that year and as recently as last month, in September. She therefore expected, as did most everyone else, to see the market bounce back again. But the market continued its sell-off as panic increased. What was happening she wondered uneasily? She listened to the radio of accounts of bleak stories of certain investors losing all their wealth. But surely *that* couldn't happen. There soon would be bargain hunters buying up stocks in companies at ridiculously low prices.

She was especially listening to a radio news commentator explaining that margin calls were now driving investors to the brink. As prices dropped, worried brokers who had lent their clients' money and held their stock as collateral were demanding to be paid back at once, otherwise they would sell their clients' stock for what they could get before prices dropped even further. But the margin-call selling was of such high volume that stock prices were collapsing. Those who had borrowed heavily had not only lost any hope of gain, but were now hopelessly in debt to the brokers, who in turn could not repay the banks.

Sharlotte knew something important was happening, something very threatening to investors and bankers like her father.

Over the next few days the market continued to vacillate wildly, then crashed further. Some stocks that had sold for a hundred dollars a share were now worthless. Investments and assets had vanished, disappearing like summer fog when the sun rose to burn it away. For many, everything was gone—everything, that is, except debt. Debt remained.

"Did you hear?" Amanda cried as Sharlotte came into her room. "The radio says businessmen are jumping from high windows or shooting themselves."

How had the crash affected the Ashfords? Sharlotte wondered, horrified. She rushed to the telephone to call her father at the bank office, and was told that he was in urgent meetings at Wall Street. At last he called her, and his voice seemed normal and calm.

"Everything is all right, daughter. Don't worry."

"Daddy, how much did we lose?"

"We're fine. Just fine. I can't come home now. There's a meeting of bankers who hope to stabilize the market by pumping money into it and buying back company stock. This will bring the market up to normal and stop the hemorrhaging."

Most of the losses that Thursday, October 24, happened to small investors: working men and women who had dabbled in the market hoping to gain enough to buy a house or send their son to college. But in boardrooms all over the country the moneymen stood shoulder to shoulder for hours watching the ticker flash spot quotations, each one lower than the last. No one could sell fast enough as the telephone lines were overloaded.

In small towns everywhere people poured in from the tree-lined streets as though in a daze. They invaded newsrooms to watch the wire-service ticker. No one spoke. Silence walled them into frightening isolation. The impossible was happening. The Big Bull Market was mortally wounded. The boom of the Twenties was over. All the money gained in the long process had vanished, leaving broken dreams.

Sharlotte remembered something Billy Sunday was reported to have said. His disturbing words troubled her even more, now—

"What do you want most of all? A man in Chicago once said to me, 'If I could have all I wanted of any one thing, I would take money.' He was a fool, and you would be too if you made a similar choice. There are many things money can't do. If you had all the money in the world, you couldn't go to the graveyard and put your loved ones back in your arms and have them sit once more in the family circle."

Americans from every walk of life lived to see the loss of everything they had hoped to one day enjoy. As they stood before the ticker, bleary-eyed, now and then there came a groan as some family man realized his ruin as his stocks hit bottom.

The following Tuesday cleaned out the professional speculators. "Black Tuesday" the newspapers called it. The big bankers publicly admitted they could no longer support the market from falling by interjecting more money to prop up company stocks.

Sharlotte, waiting for her father's arrival from a meeting at the exchange so she could learn the condition of the Ashford estate, heard some commoner on the street yell to a taxi driver: "Hey, I hear the Vanderbilt's are out of yachts."

"They richly deserve it," the taxi driver quipped back.

Sharlotte perplexed, wondered aloud: "Why don't Americans cry out to God?"

A thought came back: *Why don't you?*

∾

Sharlotte continued to follow the foreboding financial news carefully during the following weeks. Though no single day was as bleak as Black Tuesday, prices continued to fall after brief rallies. By mid-November the total loss for the New York Stock Exchange alone was $30 billion. This was wealth that had been destroyed, never to be regained. Bank failures rose from 642 in 1929 to over 1,000 the following year, and double that in 1931. When Sharlotte met her father at the stock exchange he was gray and drawn, with dark shadows beneath his eyes. He needed a shave and his clothes were soiled and smelled sour. Sharlotte had never seen him like this before, and it did more to unsettle her nerves than even the scary headlines she'd been reading in the papers and listening to over the radio.

"Daddy," she whispered, taking his arm and propelling him toward the taxi. "You're ill."

As the taxi driver maneuvered in and out of New York traffic, Sharlotte turned to face her father with trepidation. He sank back into the seat and stared straight ahead. Sharlotte's breathing tightened with anxiety. She took his arm protectively, her hand on his. He felt cold and damp.

"Is it worse than you first thought?" she whispered.

He nodded. His gaze swerved out the side window at the tall, gray buildings.

"We've lost everything. Everything…" his arm trembled.

Sharlotte's knees were weak. Surely not *everything*.

"But…that's impossible…" she said, numbly.

"Not impossible," he snapped, looking at her, his eyes glazed. "It happened. They tightened the noose around me."

"They?" she said, confused.

"The brokers. You might as well know. I borrowed heavily from them and some overseas lenders. When the margin calls flooded in, I was trapped like an animal in a slaughterhouse." He shook his graying head, his free hand covering his eyes. His shoulders shook. "I had to sell assets to cover the calls. Everything is lost."

"Oh, Daddy," she gasped, in panic. To see her father like this was most frightening of all. He'd been a financial bulwark. An invincible giant among the tycoons. Now he was a broken man, his pockets empty, and there was nothing left of the one she had thought she knew except an empty, defeated shell. The terrifying warning of Scripture kept running through her mind: "Lo, this is the man that made not God his strength, but trusted in his riches…"

Pale agony was written across his face. "I can't pay them back. I can't raise any money. I've got to give up the Long Island summerhouse, the brownstone, everything…"

Her trembling fingers reached up to touch the ruby pendant at her throat. She couldn't speak. Even the mansion? Everything…

His voice dropped so low she could hardly hear him, and his speech sounded like mumbling. She stared at him.

A realization that there was no one to turn to in crisis, no source of hope, no stronghold of refuge, pierced her soul like a flash of lightning. Those who had faith in a heavenly Father had everything. She had nothing. Nothing but this poor broken earthly father who, in a moment of disaster, shook and swayed and groaned like the old boathouse ready to come crashing down into the black, swirling sea. How frail was her foundation. How utterly hopeless the darkness closing in around her. And Amanda! What would befall her sister and her tremendous medical bills? What lay ahead? Nothing but uncertainty...

Sharlotte's breath caught on a small sob.

Burgess looked at her, anguished, but did not seem to be able to reach out and put his arms around her to provide comfort. He gripped the back of the driver's seat. "Let me off here," he ordered the taxi driver. The car swerved out of the traffic to the curb. Burgess fumbled to open the door.

"Daddy, where are you going?" she cried.

"Go home, daughter. Go home."

As he walked into a drab building, the taxi driver, chewing gum, said over his shoulder: "That's a speakeasy, miss. He's gone to drown his troubles in Al Capone's bootlegged whiskey." He held out his palm. Sharlotte realized her father had left her to pay the fare. The simple predicament drove home with embarrassing clarity the fact that she had no money.

"I...I'm not getting out here." She gave him the address to the brownstone.

When they reached the drive, he waited while she hurried inside and scrounged together enough change to pay him. Her cheeks were red when she came back out and counted it out. This was her first experience with her new reality. Her secure, quiet harbor, her father, was breaking up before her very eyes.

For the next two weeks, Sharlotte stood by hopelessly as her father relinquished the mansion and the heirloom paintings that had been in the family for generations, and still the debts were not paid. As painful as the material losses were, the wounding of pride and prestige stung even more. Kace's words of warning, once seeming derisive, now reflected the times.

On an afternoon in November, the weather turned crisp and windy and the burnt gold maple leaves shook as though the wind was determined to bring them down. Burgess had locked himself in the library, and Sharlotte went to talk to Amanda. She clutched the bedpost as she gazed down at her sister's drawn face. Amanda's eyes fluttered open. Seeing Sharlotte, she tried to smile.

"You frightened me."

"I'm sorry…I thought you were asleep."

"I was…it's okay. How's Daddy?"

"The same."

"The change in him scares me. It's dreadful, isn't it? Will we be paupers?"

Sharlotte put on a brave front. "Daddy's been through other financial crises and snapped out of them. Remember that Florida land deal he bought into a few years back?"

"Oh, *that*. Wasn't it terribly embarrassing? Everyone kept asking if our new estate had sunk into the Everglades yet. And that silly alligator joke of Sheldon's."

"Daddy lost tons of money, but we survived to gain it back. He'll manage again."

Amanda looked doubtful as she sat up, leaning on an elbow. "I hope so. But the stock market didn't crash back then."

No, thought Sharlotte with a tightening in her chest, *it hadn't, but things will change for the better soon. They have to.*

Amanda looked sadly around her room. "We were raised here. It's going to be awful to pack our things and move out."

The thought of leaving the brownstone mansion tore at Sharlotte's heart. "Let's not think about that now." *There must be something I can do*, she thought desperately, *but what?* There was Great-Uncle Hubert of course. She couldn't imagine the skinflint, who counted his millions once a week and ate peanut butter sandwiches, ever possibly losing a dime. He was much too shrewd for that. He seemed, however, to have little tolerance for his nephew's financial blunders. Her father had tried to borrow money from Great-Uncle Hubert before, only to be turned down, even as Kace had when he appealed to him. *Still,* thought Sharlotte desperately, *I must try, even if Daddy will not.*

Sharlotte remembered why she had come to Amanda's room, and leaving the bedside she walked over to the vanity table. She caught her image in the mirror and wondered that her fears hadn't changed her face into a brittle mask of lines and wrinkles by now. In the last six weeks she felt as if she'd aged thirty years. Her complexion was still young and supple and the innocent glamour was still there. Even her golden hair hadn't prematurely grayed!

Sharlotte opened the drawer.

"What are you looking for?" Amanda asked curiously.

"Grandmother's diamonds. Where are they?"

Amanda's brows lifted. "In the jewelry box. Do you want to borrow them?"

"Yes, if you don't mind." She didn't want to borrow them to wear, but to protect them from being sold should her father resort to the unspeakable. The words of Kace that she had once mocked were now words of wisdom. She must hide their jewels.

"I…" Sharlotte didn't go on to explain. Upon lifting the lid, she stopped.

Amanda wrinkled her nose. "Something wrong?"

Sharlotte bit her lip. She swallowed. Gone. "Are you sure they were here?"

"Yes. Always. Why? Oh no…don't tell me Daddy took them!"

"Yes. They're gone." Thinking of her deceased great-grandmother from France, Charlotte Margot Chattaine, her hand formed a fist. Sharlotte had been named after her mother's grandmother, but the spelling had been changed for uniqueness. There were still Chattaines in Paris, but the French family had been against Sharlotte's mother leaving France to marry Burgess, and they had cut off relations. From what Sharlotte knew of the Chattaine family, they had disliked her father because in the Great War of 1917 her father had refused to fight when shipped to France with General Pershing's soldiers. When he became ill he was released from active duty, and the Chattaines, historically a military family, had shunned him thereafter. The diamonds were the only precious gift her mother had received from them. Now they too were gone.

Amanda groaned, burying her face in her pillow. "Grandmother Chattaine's diamonds! I wanted to wear them at my wedding."

Sharlotte realized she'd been too late, but what about her own jewelry? She closed the lid to the empty jewelry box and sped to the door, opening it. "Hush, don't cry. Say nothing to Daddy, understood?" She hurried out and down the hall to her own bedroom.

She wouldn't give them up. She'd hide them if necessary, even bury them like pirate treasure! Anything to save them. But were they still there?

She went to her walk-in wardrobe. Unlike Amanda, she kept her jewelry locked up, with the key in the toe of her brown riding boot. She found it, unlocked the box, and let out a sigh of relief. Everything was still there. She scooped her fingers through the assortment of necklaces, pendants, earrings, and bracelets.

Voices downstairs in the hall interrupted her thoughts, and she went to the landing to see who it was.

A tall, age-shriveled man with hunched shoulders stood with hat and cane in hand. His knee-length black woolen coat seemed too large for his frame, and his shock of wispy iron-gray hair was windblown and swooped in a V shape over his yellowish forehead.

Great-Uncle Hubert. Although he lived in New York she hardly knew him. He held little interest in the doings of what he considered his foolish nieces and nephews—except for which family they married into. Great-Uncle had inherited the bulk of the huge Ashford financial enterprise from his father, and he managed it with an eagle eye. While the rest of his younger brothers and sisters had married and raised families, Hubert had no time to waste on romance. His one true love had been the Ashford legacy, and woe to anyone in the family who threatened its loss by unsound business practices. He had never approved of her father, calling him reckless, and he'd refused to turn over any Ashford money to him to manage.

"The younger generation is all the same," he had rasped. "You think money multiplies like rabbits from Houdini's hat. You waste what my generation labored to build by idiotic decisions. The Ashfords are one generation away from becoming taxi drivers."

When Great-Uncle Hubert looked up and saw her standing on the stairway, he commanded: "Tell Burgess I wish to speak to him in the library."

Sharlotte was about to answer when the butler appeared from another room. "He's in the library now, sir. I'll tell him you're here." The butler reached for her great-uncle's hat and coat, but Hubert waved him aside with a black-gloved hand. "No, no," he said impatiently, "I won't be staying. Be quick about it. I'm not as young as I used to be."

"Immediately, Mr. Ashford." The butler hurried toward the library when Hubert goaded:

"What's Burgess doing keeping you on if he's broke? Putting on a show again, is he? Or does he expect me to pay your wages?"

"Er…I've been dismissed, sir. I'm leaving in the morning. This way, sir."

"I'll wait here."

Sharlotte's feet remained glued to the landing. She ought to go down, but she knew he wouldn't care if she did or not.

Servants dismissed, she thought, mortified. Wait until her friends heard that bit of shocking news. How could she hold her head up? Anyone who held any kind of social importance in New York had at least one servant.

The library doors swung open and her father hurried out, a tight smile on his face. The nervous tick at his left eye seemed overactive today. Sharlotte's heart went out to him. Her anger over the removal of Grandmother Charlotte Chattaine's diamonds ebbed. He was in an ominous predicament. What else could he do? Nevertheless, she must protect the rest of their jewelry.

She loathed seeing her father squirming before Great-Uncle Hubert, asking for a loan. She turned away, not wishing to watch his humiliation.

"Hubert, how good of you to come," her father's voice was saying, sounding shallow and tense. "You'll stay for lunch? The girls would be delighted to see you. It's been a year, you know."

"Stay for lunch? And have arsenic put in my tea?" he crackled.

"Hubert, that's a horrible accusation—even joking—"

"Who is joking? Horrible, you say? Is it?"

Sharlotte winced. She sped down the hall. This was her chance to hide her jewelry.

The room greeted her pleasantly, denying the nightmarish circumstances. Even so, the ghost of Kace seemed to hover with words that mocked her dilemma. Hadn't he warned her of this? And now, she was desperately doing just as he had said.

She went into the wardrobe and removed the jewelry box. She slipped her mother's diamond and ruby wedding ring on her right hand, then dropped the other pieces into a silk stocking and tied a knot. She stuffed it inside her skirt pocket, then studied the bedroom for a place to hide it. Her father knew of her little safe in the wardrobe and might insist she turn over the key. She didn't want to keep anything back from him when they were in such financial straits, but neither did she want to lose her jewelry. What excuse could she come up with if her father asked for it? She'd think of something later. She placed the jewelry box on her dresser and left it unlocked, replacing odds and ends of less expensive pieces inside. Perhaps he wouldn't inquire about the missing items.

Again, footsteps creaked behind her. She turned, breathless.

Amanda stood there leaning on both crutches. She was white and thin. "What's happening?" she said in a weak voice. "Did I hear Uncle Hubert's limousine pull up front?"

"Amanda, you'll overtire yourself. You shouldn't have walked this far." She helped her to a blue brocade chair. Amanda sank into it, short of breath. "Is he here?" she asked again.

"Yes, to see Daddy," Sharlotte managed calmly. "Don't worry. Everything's all right."

"Don't say that when it isn't so," she said with chattering teeth. "Daddy always says that, but his eyes are full of anguish. Things are falling to pieces, or Uncle Hubert wouldn't have come."

Sharlotte grabbed a throw and laid it around her sister's shoulders, hoping to stop her shivering. "Never mind old Hubert. He's still an Ashford, as are we. He'll have to do something to help us. He won't want to see this mansion out of family hands. We've had it for generations. Even Jay Cooke, the railroad baron, was entertained downstairs once."

Amanda drew the throw around her. "Don't count on it. Uncle Hubert is like Charles Dickens' Scrooge. Even the ghost of Christmas past won't frighten him into sudden charity." She paused for a moment to catch her breath. "I hate being like this," she groaned. "It's horrible being an invalid."

"Don't say that. It's only temporary."

"Is it?" Amanda said rather bitterly. "It already seems like a lifetime."

"You're still my sister. You haven't changed."

"Yes, I have—"

If she keeps this up I'll burst into tears too, Sharlotte thought. She scolded: "Stop that, Amanda. No self-pity. You know what Dr. Helmer said."

Amanda wiped her eyes on the back of her hand. "I know, but sometimes I can't help it."

Sharlotte leaned over and hugged her. "Oh, I know you can't help it, Sis—I hate to think how I'd be acting if I were in your place. Still, you must be optimistic." Sharlotte went to her closet for her slippers. "Here, put these on. You need to stay warm. Remember what the doctor said? You will walk again." But would she?

"You'd be brave if this had happened to you," Amanda said.

"Me?" Sharlotte gave a laugh that was on the verge of hysteria. "I've never been brave."

"Oh, yes you are," Amanda insisted. "You just don't know yourself as well as I do. Kace knows it too."

At the mention of Kace, Sharlotte paused. She'd like to think there was something about her, besides appearance, that Kace Landry admired, but her own lack of optimism precluded that. He was in love with Elly, and in comparison to Elly, Sharlotte lacked all the Christian graces he most admired. Kace was the first to tell her so. Elly's love for God and her dedication to serve Him had won his respect and his heart.

I don't care, she thought resentfully, but knew she was deceiving herself. She found that she did care, more than she had realized.

"What's bulging in your pocket?" Amanda asked. "Is that a silk stocking hanging out?"

Sharlotte looked down at her skirt, where part of the stocking showed. She casually placed her hand over it and smiled crookedly. "Oh, it's just our Christmas stocking."

Amanda wrinkled her nose. "Kind'a early, aren't you?"

"No," she murmured gravely. "A little too late."

"What on earth are you talking about?"

Sharlotte smiled wearily. "Not a thing. Just rambling. Look, let me get you on the divan and then I'll go see Uncle Hubert and Daddy. I'll bring us up some hot cocoa later and tell you everything I've learned."

"Hubert never comes here," Amanda whispered uneasily. "So Daddy's finances must be on a precipice. Nothing else would drag Uncle Hubert out of his Manhattan house."

"Let's just hope dear Hubert isn't playing Old Scrooge this season. Here, lean on me. And bring the throw."

"What would I do without you, 'Mummy'?" Amanda teased.

"You have George," Sharlotte quipped lightly.

"Do I?" Amanda said dully. "He hasn't called in over two weeks. The last I heard he was preparing for a solo flight in that airplane that mimics Charles Lindbergh's."

"He'll call again. He's in love with you."

Amanda's eyes brightened. "Do you think so?"

"Why, it's written all over him."

Amanda appeared to lapse into some memory that brought a summer glow to her otherwise wan face. Sharlotte left her to her dreams and reluctantly went downstairs to face unpleasant reality.

16

Sharlotte neared the library where the double doors stood open. Angry voices sounded, along with Great-Uncle Hubert's cane thumping for emphasis on the burgundy rug. She stopped beside a potted palm—

"When Kace came to see me, I told him he was wasting his time if he thought I was going to pay off your debts. He then wanted me to back him on his oil drilling. I just may do it. But I'll not come in and bail you out this time, Burgess."

"Now Hubert—"

"No! You've created your own disaster. You'll learn your lesson this time, even if you have to go to jail for it."

"You don't mean that," came her father's cracked voice, shaking with frustration.

"I most certainly do. You'll not get a dime from me this time. I've made up my mind. I'm cutting you off as of today. The bulk of the Ashford inheritance will be left to scientific research, not to support your gambling schemes."

"You can't do that!"

"Don't tell me what I can and cannot do." He came out the door and seeing Sharlotte, stopped. "If you have an ounce of Ashford wisdom, you'll marry Clarence Fosdick as soon as he'll have you." He walked toward the front hall, his cane thumping and sounding a death knell to all their hopes.

Her father came out, consternation distorting his face. Sharlotte cringed at the sight. She watched as he stalked after Hubert.

"You must let me talk sense into you, Uncle."

"I have more sense than you'll ever have. You're wasting your breath and mine. After what you've done this time, the die is cast."

"Hubert! You old fool! Stop—"

Sharlotte's hands flew to her mouth. Her father had grabbed him, but Hubert swung his cane and cracked him alongside the head. Her father staggered backward catching himself on the hall table. The vase of yellow mums crashed. A bruise showed above Burgess' eyebrow.

But it was Great-Uncle Hubert that sent fear through her heart. He was gasping painfully, a feeble hand at his chest while his other hand, white and bony, clutched the end of the cane.

"Uncle Hubert," she cried, and rushed toward him, grabbing his arm and steadying him. His wild eyes held hers as she struggled to bring him to the hall chair. "I'll call Dr. Helmer." She turned to rush to the black telephone on the table, but Hubert's hand latched around her wrist with a surprisingly strong grip. She looked at him, wondering.

"P-pocket—" he rasped.

Pocket? Her eyes dropped to his coat. She reached inside and found a small bottle, unstopped it and shook out some pills onto her trembling hand. His shaking finger placed the medication under his tongue. They stared at one another, each wide-eyed and trembling.

Please God, don't let him die, she prayed urgently. *Please—* she had horrid images of the police coming again and this time…

Behind her she heard her father stirring, but he made no move to come to her side.

A timeless moment later, Hubert was breathing easier and the fear had left his face. His tightly grasping fingers on her wrist eased, leaving red marks. Sharlotte too eased her hold of him. She swallowed hard and closed her eyes. He was going to be all right.

When she opened her eyes, Hubert was watching her with a strange expression.

"Shall I...shall I call the doctor?" she whispered.

He shook his head no. "I'll be all right," he breathed. "Call my chauffeur to take me home."

She stood shakily, went to the heavy front door, and ran out into the strong wind. A gust went through her clothes, chilling her sweating body. She felt emotionally exhausted as she walked toward the black limousine. The chauffeur came toward her, removing his cap.

"Mr. Ashford is ready to go home now," she managed calmly. "He's had an attack and taken his medication. Please tell his nurse. She may think it wise to notify his doctor."

"Yes, Miss Ashford."

When the limousine pulled away, Sharlotte remained on the front veranda watching until it disappeared down the avenue. The fading summer roses dropped petals onto the garden bed.

When she went inside the house, her father had already left the hall. The butler was cleaning up the broken vase and mums.

"Mr. Ashford went up to his room, miss," was all he said.

"Thank you, Owen."

She went into the kitchen and waited a moment until she was certain the butler was still occupied, then she entered the side pantry, drew a wooden stool across the floor, and climbed up.

Sharlotte removed the empty canister from the top shelf, lifted the lid, and placed her jewelry inside to keep company with Kace's glove that she'd put there when first arriving from Long Island. She replaced the canister, climbed down again, and walked out of the pantry into the kitchen with a can of powdered cocoa.

Some minutes later she carried a small pot of hot, sweetened chocolate upstairs to her room where Amanda waited.

"Did I hear an argument?" Amanda asked worriedly.

Sharlotte set the tray on the table between them and poured, hoping her sister didn't notice her shaking hands.

"It's all right now," she said. "Uncle Hubert went home, and Daddy's resting in his room."

"Is he going to loan us money?"

"No."

"I didn't think he would…" Amanda sipped her cocoa. "Better enjoy this," she said with a wry smile. "The time may come soon when we won't have the luxury."

Sharlotte wasn't listening. Her heart weighed like lead, and it was all she could do to swallow. It had been horrid, absolutely horrid…her father storming up to Hubert and grabbing him from behind—Hunnewell swam before her eyes.

Her memory went back to Long Island on that stormy night of the canceled picnic. Once again she was standing in her father's room while the raging wind blew in the rain from the open terrace. The sound of her father's footsteps coming up the fire escape echoed in her mind. He had gone after the glove—but why? It had turned out to be Kace's. Again, there was something all wrong about this, but Sharlotte couldn't think what it might be.

"What are you troubled about?" Amanda asked warily. "You look as if you've just witnessed a murder."

Sharlotte glanced at her sharply. She said nothing and drank from her cup.

While Amanda talked, Sharlotte's thoughts turned to Clarence. She must marry him soon. Yes, very soon. Strange that he hadn't called her in a week. Like George, he must be busy.

∽

In the days following, the servants were all dismissed and the Ashford brownstone mansion was put up for sale. Although Sharlotte understood the debt, she could not fathom the depth to which her father had brought them. He behaved like a prisoner awaiting the guillotine.

One evening his fellow banking friends came to call on him, and not wishing to be seen, they arrived at the backdoor to conduct a hushed and sober meeting.

Her father was aging before her eyes. She was sure his health was failing.

She faced him in his bedroom, worried. "Uncle Hubert's doctor called this morning. He's recovering well enough, though bedridden. Please don't worry anymore," she said, for she naturally assumed he was burdened by guilt at having caused his uncle's heart attack.

He looked at her with glassy eyes, and Sharlotte wondered if he even saw her. "Daddy, you've got to explain things to me so I'll know what to expect."

He walked out and stood on the veranda. Despite the growing chill in the weather he wore no jacket. "This need not be your burden, daughter. I'll manage to salvage our name and our fortune, but I'll need a little time. I'm leaving for Texas tonight."

Texas! She hurried to him, her eyes searching his. Texas seemed to be the last place to go for money. "Daddy, I'll be able to handle things while you're away. And don't worry; I already know what you're afraid the police will learn. Kace told me on Long Island. You might as well tell me everything so I can prepare Amanda. She's taking all this harder than I am."

His gaze sharpened like an eagle spying a field mouse. "Kace told you? Told you what!"

She shook her head, helpless to add details because she didn't have them.

"Explain," he demanded again in a low voice that frightened her. She had never seen him this cold and adamant before. There was no getting out of it now. Perhaps she shouldn't have mentioned it.

"About—" she paused, and then whispered, "your bootlegging."

He stared at her. The chill wind struck them, causing her to shiver. Her hair tossed, like the dying golden leaves fluttering to the flagstones.

He laughed without humor. "Bootlegging? Is that what Kace told you? That I was a bootlegger?"

She wanted to cry with humiliation. "Yes," she admitted painfully. She reached both hands to hold him. "It isn't true, is it? The gangsters in Chicago—Al Capone, the others..." her voice trailed.

He laughed again. The sound between them turned her hands clammy. His eyes became like smudged glass, concealing the sanctuary of his soul.

It is true, she thought, astounded, horrified, *but why is he amused?* She knew if she recoiled that he would never tell her anything. She struggled against her runaway emotions.

"Uncle Hubert knows too, doesn't he? That's why he was so angry. He thinks you've invested Ashford money in the rackets."

Once more he gave that strange, brittle laugh. "Is that what you think? Bootlegging?"

"I didn't believe it. I thought Kace was only trying to insult us. I'm not sure I believe it yet..."

"You'd be wise not to. If Clarence's family suspects a breath of scandal, whether true or not, they'll back out of the engagement. I know that bootlegged liquor for the East Coast is brought in from Canada. I confess I've had a few small investments in the enterprise, but I am an honorable man. Those who cry the loudest about the evils of bootlegging all have scotch in their private bars and wine at respectable society dinners. They're hypocrites."

"You mean... that isn't what Uncle Hubert is outraged about?"

"No." His mouth thinned.

"Daddy—" He turned and walked into his bedroom. Going to his wardrobe, he removed a suitcase and began to pack. Sharlotte followed, watching, dismayed. "How long will you be in Texas?"

"A few weeks, no longer. I'll also have words with Kace about this absurd idea of working with Capone."

Kace hadn't mentioned the gangster in Chicago, but she didn't tell her father that. She felt relieved, prepared to believe what he had told her because she desperately wanted to. But actually, he had told her very little.

Unknown fears swooped about her. She turned swiftly to face him. "Daddy, let me go with you."

"No, you take care of Amanda while I'm gone. She needs you. I'll return before the Christmas holidays."

She walked up to him and he patted her arm. She felt like a child he was ushering off to bed so he'd have time alone to read his newspaper.

He paused, then: "We have a new lawyer now, a Mr. Wilkins. I'll have him arrange for your travel to the estate in Vermont. I'll telephone or write before I return on the train." He fumbled in his jacket pocket, found a card, and handed it to her. "If you need anything while I'm away, call Wilkins."

"Yes, Daddy." She kissed his cheek goodbye, and he smiled tightly and showed her to the door. Sharlotte reluctantly returned to her room.

Everything was gone except the house in Vermont, along with whatever money he had managed to keep from the hands of his creditors. And, she had her jewels. He must have forgotten about them.

"Maybe I'll awake tomorrow and find this all a nightmare." She slumped into a chair with dismay and glanced about at the furnishings, rugs, and draperies. Her wardrobe bulged with expensive clothes and elaborately fashionable evening gowns. Would she need to sell them to maintain the basics of life? How she had taken material things for granted! Never in her worst nightmares had she imagined it could all slip through her fingers like water.

Little remained except the rubble, the dust of bewilderment, the confusion. How would she begin anew? How was she to sort through what had been her life? Added to sudden ruin were the unknown years that waited in the dim future.

She felt incapable of dealing with this now. Like her father, she needed time to think her way out. There must be a way of escape from this maze, she decided, because believing there was not brought her to the edge of an abyss.

She went to bed dry-eyed and emotionally bankrupt. She lay there watching the watery, pale moonlight on her windowpane. The threat of the long, icy winter sounded in the whining wind. Her thoughts wandered to God. She had prayed, asking that Great-Uncle Hubert not die. Had God answered that cry, or had it been a coincidence that he survived?

Once again she wondered what He was like, whether or not He really existed. Why did she want to pray to God now? Because she was stuck in the mire? If the stock market hadn't crashed in October, if her father wasn't in some mysterious trouble, would she have prayed? If there really was a great God who ruled supreme over all His creation, what would He think if she came running to Him now?

"Don't be a little hypocrite," she heard her father's voice echoing from the past.

She'd been fourteen when he'd said that to her, and newly home from a summer in Texas. She had written out a prayer because she didn't know how to go about talking to God in the comfortable way Uncle Sherman did. Her father had discovered her in the process of writing it and had scolded her.

"There's no God," he had said flatly. "If you want anything, you ask me. I'm the only provider you have. Your clothes, your food, your existence comes from me."

His face had shown disappointment and she had blushed as he read her prayer. From then on she feared that her father would ridicule any talk of prayer as childish activity. All of her provisions would come from Mr. Burgess Ashford, including her fiancé, Clarence Fosdick.

But now! Her father was not the sure foundation she had believed him to be, but a man in trouble with the law and as frightened of the future as she was.

Sharlotte gritted her teeth and sat up, angrily brushing the tears from her cheeks. *I feel like a child again, crying in bed for*

Mummy and Daddy. I must grow up. I must learn to face the bitter winds of life.

The window hadn't been shut all the way and a gust of wind swept the drape outward. She shivered, tossed aside the sheet, and went to close and lock the window. As she did, she glanced up at the sky. The night was unusually clear, and a thousand or more diamond stars gleamed and winked at her. A thought came across her mind: *If your father was wrong about so many things, if he couldn't foresee the ruin threatening the foundations of his family, then was he wise enough to declare that there is no God? What if he's also wrong about that as well?*

The thought grasped her heart and held tightly. How simple.

Yes! He *could* be wrong! And if he's wrong, then there was hope. Her father did not know everything there was to know—he could not speak with certainty saying there was no God.

She made up her mind to start reading the Bible. It was late when Sharlotte at last fell asleep, only to awaken to hear the engine of her father's motorcar come to life. She threw aside the covers again and went to the window. He was leaving now for the trip to the Landry ranch in Texas. The car's headlights flared brightly as he drove toward the private gate. What would he tell Aunt Livia and Uncle Sherman? Would Kace be there? Again she wondered why he would even wish to make such a trip. The Landrys were far from wealthy. What, if anything, could they do for him in this hour of financial need?

She went back to bed. Tomorrow she would need to tell Amanda to make plans for their train trip to the country estate in Vermont.

〜

The following day her aunt by marriage, Cecily Van Dornen, arrived with cousins Pamela and Sheldon. Mrs. Van Dornen was dressed in black and wept: "He actually jumped out the window. It was horrible. I'll never get over the sight, never, never, never." Aunt Cecily always repeated emotional outbursts in threesomes.

She wept into her handkerchief while her bejeweled fingers, tanned from a winter vacation in Bermuda, shook.

"Really, Mother." Sheldon said, bored, "You hardly knew the fellow. You carry on as though he were a family member."

"It doesn't matter, Shelly, it was gruesome. To see a man so depressed, so discouraged that he'd jump…"

Sharlotte could see why Cecily was so shaken. Worried about their fortune, her aunt had gone to Wall Street with Sheldon to see her broker. During the morbid meeting in his high-rise office, the broker had committed suicide.

"I feel so guilty, as if somehow it's my fault. Perhaps if I hadn't gone yesterday he'd still be alive."

"Oh, Mother, nonsense. You were fair with him. The little rat pilfered your funds."

She looked at him, her eyes still filled with tears. "Do you think I was fair?"

"Certainly." Sheldon strolled up to Sharlotte, who sat on the edge of the divan in the sitting room. "The broker was misusing Van Dornen money. We've lost half our holdings because of him." He looked back at his mother. "Look, if he had lived he'd have to do time in the penitentiary."

Pamela, who had said very little so far, looked white and tense as she felt in her skirt pocket for a pack of cigarettes and a gold lighter. "I think I'd rather do time behind bars than jump. There wasn't much of him left." She shuddered as if a snowy blast struck her.

"You saw it too?" Sharlotte asked, feeling a wave of sympathy.

Pamela nodded and blew smoke. "I was totally shocked. I mean…totally." She placed a hand over her heart. "One moment he was pacing as he tried to explain the losses, the next he just walked over to the window, then—kaplop!"

"Please, Pamela dear," her mother moaned, "don't."

Pamela got up and moved to the fire. "Sorry, Mummy."

"Uncle John is quite calm about the crash," Sheldon said. "Makes me wonder if the dear old gent didn't pull the family assets out of the market before Black Tuesday."

"Calm? My dear, Uncle John is in shock," Cecily said.

Sharlotte knew that Cecily thought everything of Uncle John Van Dornen. After her husband had died some years ago, she had depended completely on her brother-in-law. John had never remarried, and Cecily, Sheldon, and Pamela lived and catered to his every whim.

If only Uncle Hubert were like John, Sharlotte thought wistfully. Both men were bachelors, both had recently turned eighty, yet John Van Dornen was generous and adored his nieces and nephews. Neither Pamela nor Sheldon would need to worry about their future as long as Uncle John managed to keep the Van Dornen fortune intact. But Great-Uncle Hubert…

"Poor John hasn't the fortitude to meet with his lawyer yet," Cecily said. "We've lost a *huge* amount I'm sure, but we'll be all right." She looked at Sharlotte with veiled pity. "I suppose Burgess will need to begin selling Ashford heirlooms? I can't bear to think of the losses affecting so many of our family and friends. It's like attending funeral after funeral to visit them. It's Hoover's fault, naturally. Who else's could it be? I thought I'd seen everything after President Harding's Teapot Dome scandals. But this. Do you suppose it's all part of the Red scare?" she asked of the widespread alarm over a Communist takeover through the unions.

"Don't be silly, Mother," Sheldon said with a mild laugh. He looked at Sharlotte with a wink. "Mother thinks everything is a conspiracy hatched by Lenin." He turned to his mother. "The Red scare they talk about is nothing but hysteria. This isn't 1917 in Russia, but 1929 in the good old u.s.a. The market will pull out of this slump by next year. Wait and see if I'm not right."

"Well, I hope you're right Shelly, dear. But don't forget that Communists set off that bomb on Wall Street a few years ago. The police even found a note written by some Slav or whatever, demanding the release of the Communists in jail or he'd kill everyone. You even saw the scars from the bomb yesterday."

"There will never be another war. Europe is at peace. Germany has learned her lesson. The German people will never turn to another Kaiser."

"What do you intend to do now, Sharlotte?" Cousin Pamela suddenly asked as she leaned against the fireplace, smoking. "If Uncle Burgess must sell this house, won't you and Amanda need to go back to Long Island?"

The catlike stare with which Pamela looked at her was troubling. *She's more curious about the reaction that Clarence and the Fosdick family will have over Ashford losses than anything else,* thought Sharlotte.

She couldn't bring herself to tell them that the Long Island estate would also be sold to debtors.

"Oh, we'll get along well enough," she said airily.

"She's coming home with us, of course," Sheldon said.

"Yes, that's one of the reasons I came by, Sharlotte," Aunt Cecily said, standing and gathering her mink stole and handbag. "You'll always be welcome at our house. John has always liked you, and he feels such sympathy for sweet Amanda, poor child. What a dreadful time for her to become ill and lose her mobility. Oh…did Burgess ever order that new wheelchair yet?"

"Yes," Sharlotte said dully. "About moving in with you— thank you for the invitation, Aunt Cecily. Tell Uncle John we're also grateful for his offered help. However, Daddy already asked us to go on to Vermont for the Christmas holidays. He'll join us there. And by then," she said with a false air of confidence, "things should be getting back to normal. He has other assets we can lean upon until…until things on Wall Street are back to normal again."

"I'm pleased he does. Still, the invitation stands."

"At least join us at the Connecticut lodge for skiing on New Year's," Sheldon said. "All our old university friends will be there.

It's going to be quite a celebration. The end of the Twenties and the beginning of the Thirties and all that. Clarence will be there too. He's already accepted the invitation."

Sharlotte hid her surprise. Clarence had said nothing to her about spending the holidays at the Van Dornen lodge in Connecticut. Nevertheless, she wouldn't admit it in front of Pamela.

"It should be a jazzy holiday," Sheldon went on, apparently oblivious to any strain over Clarence.

"This time, Sheldon, leave that empty-headed twitter, Bitsy, in Queens where she belongs, will you?" Pamela protested.

"Humbug. I'll do nothing of the sort," he said as they walked toward the front door. The shiny limousine waited out front, the chauffeur smoking by the forlorn rosebushes. When he saw them come out he walked toward the car and opened the doors. Sharlotte was struck by the fact that the Van Dornens still had servants and ritzy plans for the season. She could imagine the pity on Aunt Cecily's face if she knew that her father had already dismissed the servants and driven his own motorcar to catch the train.

"Can't you find someone of your own caliber?" Pamela was saying, still protesting Bitsy.

"I could," he said jovially, "but Bitsy does the Charleston so well," and he winked at Sharlotte, showing he enjoyed ribbing his sister in return.

"Oh, you're such a headache," Pamela groaned.

"Your sister's right, Shelly," said Aunt Cecily with grief. "Uncle John refuses to have that awful gum-chewing girl around."

"Dear old Uncle isn't going to Connecticut, so it doesn't matter."

"He's threatened to disinherit if you become engaged to her."

"I've no intention of getting married. She's a good time, is all."

"You're twenty-seven. It's time you became serious about Constance. She's a delightful girl. She's patiently waited for you to settle down for three years. Her parents will soon be looking elsewhere for a match. I hear they fared well in the crash, which means Uncle John is going to begin cracking down on you."

Sheldon sighed. "All right, all right. Give me this last skiing holiday with Bitsy, then I'll jump through Uncle's hoops. Anything to make him happy. At least Constance's father is heavily invested in shipping. They even have a house in Bermuda, where I'm going to win the yacht race. Just wait and see if I don't."

When they had finally departed, Sharlotte stood on the porch staring dismally at the privet hedge lining the drive. Discouragement, like a heavy blanket, draped over her spirits. Rain, sprinkling down from dark clouds above, caused her to move indoors.

I'm out of everything, she thought, amazed. *I no longer belong.* It was astounding and terribly frightening. She felt as if she were in a trance.

The mansion was silent again except for the popping sounds coming from the red-hot log in the fireplace. Had past conversations been this shallow? Except for the short time they'd faced the reality of the broker's suicide, it didn't take long to merge back into the old grooves. For the first time she was struck by the futility surrounding her. *It must be my mood,* she thought.

Sharlotte climbed the stairs. Once she reached Vermont, she might get Clarence to agree to a Christmas engagement, but there was still Lady Fosdick to get around, not an easy prospect.

Two days later Mr. Wilkins, the lawyer, arrived, explaining to her that her father had been forced to relinquish *all* of his holdings to pay off his stock market debts.

"That's not possible, Mr. Wilkins," she protested. "My father had millions."

"Not 'millions,' Miss Ashford. A million and a half in various assets, which included two houses and the Ashford valuables—such as rare paintings, family jewels, etc., etc."

At the mention of jewels, she grew silent.

His knotty fingers drummed annoyingly on the briefcase sitting on his lap. "Unfortunately, he found it absolutely necessary to convert those assets into cash to meet his margin calls. I suppose he told you before he departed upon his travels that this house must be vacated immediately, as well as the Long Island summerhouse, etc., etc."

If he says "etc." one more time—

She stood, plucking at her handkerchief. "I'm well aware of all that, Mr. Wilkins. We do still own the country estate in Vermont though, is that correct?"

"Well, yesss," he admitted, dragging out the word doubtfully. "Nevertheless, it's my duty to tell you that taxes will be coming due on that piece of real estate next year." He cleared his throat. "He'll need to come up with back taxes as well, but we need not overburden ourselves with that matter now." He stood, briefcase in hand. "If you need a little more time to organize things here, I can certainly speak to the brokerage house and attempt to arrange the matter. You may give my secretary a call at the office."

"How can I possibly know what to send ahead to Vermont in a week?" Sharlotte realized her father had left her with the overwhelming burden. "What of the dishes from France, the silver, the paintings, the furnishings? Some of these can be sold—"

"Fortunately—or rather, unfortunately, Miss Ashford—you won't need to sort through the heirlooms. You see, the paintings and other artistic valuables were included in the arrangement for selling the house. You'll only need to gather the family's personal belongings."

Sharlotte was speechless.

He looked about the large room with its paintings. "A tragedy," he hissed and walked toward the door. "A terrible tragedy. Nevertheless, prosperity is surely just around the corner."

She heard the front door close, and the finality of that sound echoed in her memory for months afterward.

17

Sharlotte arrived at the Vermont estate with Amanda in late November when the fall display, reminiscent of warm honey and cinnamon, was turning the woods into an autumn wonderland. She breathed in healthful, if chilly, country air. The unrushed atmosphere of the countryside was a soothing balm for her wounded heart.

"Isn't the sight magnificent?" Amanda whispered, as the Model T stopped in the driveway. Finney, the caretaker, had been waiting for them at the train depot and drove them home to the big white house dressed in green shutters. Sharlotte got out of the car, and Amanda sat in the backseat looking toward the golden-red woods.

"I remember riding on days like this. How the leaves stirred beneath the mare's hooves. Is Duffy still here?" Amanda asked, looking up at Finney with his good-humored wrinkled face and pointed nose.

As a child, Sharlotte recalled having once named him Mr. Prune. Now his face was comforting, carrying her back to a happier time.

"That mare never gives up. She's raring to run now, almost as much as she was when I had to lift you into the saddle."

Amanda sighed. "If only I could ride her one last time. I suppose I'll need to be content to bring her sugar cubes."

"She'll love that, or an apple from the orchard." Finney struggled with the wheelchair, and Sharlotte helped to lift Amanda into the seat. Finney went around to the back of the car for the two suitcases. Their trunks would arrive tomorrow. Instead of entering the house at once, Sharlotte moved Amanda toward the radiantly colored trees, laughing as she ran, the wheels spraying leaves that crackled beneath her feet.

"Doesn't smell like New York," Sharlotte said with exaggerated cheer.

"I think I'm going to like it here. I'm glad we came."

Sharlotte wheeled her down the narrow country road. She deliberately kept up the chatter and laughter. Stopping for a minute, she scooped up some leaves and tossed them toward Amanda.

Amanda laughed and threw some back at her.

"You just wait till the snows come," Amanda warned.

Soon the afternoon wind heralded the setting sun, and Sharlotte turned the wheelchair, and they started slowly back. With the wind behind them she paused a moment just to look at the house that was to be their only home. Amanda was right. They were going to settle here. Sharlotte, too, was glad they had come. This would be the one home she would not relinquish, no matter what, she told herself. If need be, she would fight whoever tried to take it away from them.

She started on again, pushing the wheelchair, her jaw set.

⁓

Each day that passed Sharlotte waited to hear from her father. She at last wrote a long-delayed letter to Aunt Livia. While waiting for a reply, she and Amanda received a wire from Burgess.

Matters have brightened. Our troubles will soon be over. I'll be home for Christmas.

Father

Sharlotte looked at Amanda and they both broke into smiles. They clasped each other around the neck. "You see?" Sharlotte cried, laughing, "Didn't I tell you it was too soon to surrender our dreams?"

The good news cheered them all, even Finney, and they planned their Thanksgiving dinner with bright holiday spirits.

"Let's write to Clarence and George and invite them to come up and stay the holiday weekend," Sharlotte declared on sudden impulse.

"Yes, let's!" Then Amanda's eyes lost their blue sparkle. "But will they even want to come? Especially Clarence. You know how demanding Lady Fosdick is. She may not approve of his absence at the yearly holiday dinner."

"Yes, I'd forgotten Lady Fosdick." For a moment Sharlotte's spirits sagged, then she recovered her optimism for her sister's sake. It was important that George came to see her even if he couldn't make it for Thanksgiving. As for Clarence, she would at least write him. "We'll send them invitations anyway. Maybe they can drive up after the family gathering."

Within a week they had their replies. Both men would be there to spend the weekend, arriving on Friday.

As the day came around, Finney chose the best fowl from the henhouse, and Sharlotte wheeled Amanda to the wild berry vines where they managed to glean just enough for a last pie. There were pumpkins from Finney's garden, and sweet potatoes, and when the day came it was full of cheer. It didn't seem to matter that the fowl was a little too dry and the berry pie a bit too tart. No one wanted to notice and the conversation was on a high level of optimism. Even the stock market enjoyed a brief rally before dropping again.

The weather also cooperated and, despite being chilly, the sun was shining. After the meal, Sharlotte and Clarence went for a walk in the woods where the leaves trickled slowly downward like huge reddish-gold snowflakes while George took Amanda down to the pond. Sharlotte could hear Amanda's laughter and guessed that George was once again entertaining her with some of his wild tales of stunt flying.

Clarence held Sharlotte's hand. They walked slowly along, not needing to express how they felt because they both knew what they wanted. They came to a slope covered with leaves that dropped off into a small creek that by next month would be frozen until the late spring thaw. There was a log nearby, and they sat down to enjoy the sounds of the wood: a songbird, the sighing of the wind playing amid the leaves, a scampering squirrel gathering acorns.

Clarence reached for her left hand and removed something from his pocket. Sharlotte caught her breath. He held out to her a diamond engagement ring, its stones reflecting spires of sunlight filtering down through the branches.

"Will you marry me, Sharlotte?"

"Oh, Clarence…" He slipped the ring onto her finger and stood, drawing her to her feet and into his arms. They embraced and kissed, and tears wet her eyes.

After the wonderful weekend, Sharlotte wrote to her father and Aunt Livia, telling them the happy news of her engagement. "Our marriage will take place much sooner than either Clarence or I first anticipated. I'm so happy."

All her worries about the future fled like shadows in a room where sunlight poured through the windows. Amanda would have her specialist. Somehow she would regain the brownstone in New York, maybe even the Long Island summerhouse—though Hunnewell's death had cast a pall of gloom upon it. There would be a new summerhouse, maybe in Edgartown. Even worries about her father and his mysterious behavior no longer appeared so important. Marrying into a great fortune mended her frayed insecurity, and fear once again became a stranger.

By early December, about the time Finney hauled in a huge fragrant Christmas pine, Sharlotte's confidence was again restored. She even sold a diamond brooch from her secret stocking to order the clothes she would need for her wedding, some long dresses for Amanda, and a new coat and hat for Finney. She called her French dressmaker to discuss her wedding dress, and Monsieur Fontaine happily promised to come out to Vermont in the latter part of January to bring cloth samples and a dozen new catalogs straight from Paris.

The first snow arrived on Sunday. Sharlotte awoke to a glistening purity that contrasted with the purple shades of daybreak that tinted the white snowdrifts. She and Amanda reverted to their youth and built a snowman and threw snowballs at each other. Life was carefree again and rich with a hundred dreams.

A telephone call from their father was expected that afternoon to let them know what time his train would arrive. And Clarence and George were coming to stay the weekend. They would decorate the pine tree in the huge country parlor and usher in the holiday season with a Christmas sing.

Finney offered to go into town to buy the ingredients to make the traditional fudge, and the corn was ready to pop and dye red and green. Amanda was even feeling strong enough to supervise Finney in making gingerbread dough for the tree cutouts that she'd been making since she was eight years old.

At three o'clock the telephone rang and Amanda, who was next to the stand, leaned over from her chair to answer it. Sharlotte hurried in from the parlor where she'd been gathering boxes of ornaments for the Saturday decorating spree.

Amanda smiled. "Hello, Daddy! An early Merry Christmas! Where are you? What!" She looked at Sharlotte and made a disappointed face. "You're still in Texas! Oh…but you'll be here next week? Splendid! We miss you terribly. Yes, everything's fine,

Daddy. Maybe we should wait to decorate until you arrive…yes, I'll tell her. Yes, everything is just fine. Sharlotte's still walking about in a trance. She's all giddy over her engagement ring."

Sharlotte made a face at her. Amanda said: "She's right here, want to talk? Oh. All right…then we'll see you next Saturday. Yes, I will. 'Bye, Daddy, love you."

Sharlotte watched Amanda replace the phone to the cradle. "What happened? Why is he late?"

"He's clearing up some important business. But he said he'd be here at the end of next week and not to worry. Everything is going to be all right."

"Well, our little party with Clarence and George goes on. Daddy never liked decorating the tree anyway. We'll give Clarence and George a chance to show off their creativity."

"Yes, and a week more isn't long," Amanda said. "Maybe we can even have a few presents under the tree when he comes home. Did I show you what I was making George and Daddy?"

"Yes," moaned Sharlotte, "at least ten times. But I don't think Daddy will go for argyle socks. But dear George will love his— especially that airplane you embroidered on the front." She tried not to smile.

Amanda beamed. "Clever, wasn't I? I even have George as a stick figure walking on the plane's left wing."

"Very ingenious. We'd better get to the kitchen. I hear Finney hollering about the oven getting too hot for your gingerbread men."

"Oh no! It's got to be a certain temperature." Amanda briskly wheeled herself to the back kitchen.

When Clarence arrived late Friday afternoon, George was not with him. Amanda was still in her room, putting finishing touches to her hair.

Clarence kissed Sharlotte briefly. She couldn't help but note the tension in his body. She looked at him, wondering. His eyes were somber. He looked toward the stairs. "Where's Amanda?"

"She'll be down in a few minutes. She's dressing. Why?"

"There's been an accident."

A despairing suspicion began to tighten her chest. "Oh, Clarence, no…"

"He wanted to surprise Amanda. A photograph was supposed to be taken of him in a daredevil stunt, standing on the wing of Skip's plane."

"Oh no," she repeated, clutching him tightly.

"The engine stopped somehow and…it crashed. Skip is still in the hospital with multiple injuries, but George was killed."

∿

It was late that same night as Sharlotte sat beside Amanda's bed stroking her forehead while the sedative Clarence had thoughtfully brought was putting her to sleep. Amanda's eyes were swollen from crying, and she murmured over and over, "George… poor darling, my true love, George, I need you…need you…"

Sharlotte's tears flowed again as she leaned over her sister. She felt Clarence's hand on her shoulder.

"She's asleep now," he whispered. "There's no more you can do, darling. Come, you need some rest."

Amanda was at last in slumber. Sharlotte eased herself carefully from the side of the bed.

Words were useless. Sharlotte knew she had no comfort to give, for what comfort could she offer Amanda at a time like this? What hope had she acquired from her father to offer the broken-hearted? What wisdom from the philosophers' speculative dissertations? The vain wisdom of the world seemed like the mad laughter at a circus.

George had been a wonderful friend with a sunny personality, and he'd been a source of cheer to Amanda as few people could. Sharlotte believed that he had already proposed, but because she was only seventeen they had needed to wait until the socially appropriate time, and they had said nothing. Now it no longer mattered. George would never bring his smile and funny jokes into their lives again. Yes, he had been the reckless sort, but who believed that he would actually get killed? He was gone, forever.

The words of Billy Sunday came back to Sharlotte as she stood in Amanda's room. "All the gold in the world could not open the grave and put a child back in his parents' arms."

Looking down at Amanda with the tears drying on her pale cheeks, Sharlotte's throat ached. Death had closed and locked the door to their dreams…and who had the key?

She turned away toward Clarence, and he put his arm around her and led her from the room.

Clarence returned on Sunday to New York and his law office, and Sharlotte, feeling very alone, waited anxiously for the arrival of her father on the following Saturday.

Each morning she woke up and for one sleepy moment was again the unencumbered daughter of the wealthy aristocrat, Burgess Ashford II. Then reality would come pouring in with a rush. The day weighed heavily upon her shoulders before she got out of bed.

One morning after being up late with Amanda, whose declining health worried her, Sharlotte came wearily down the narrow staircase. Finney came from the kitchen wiping his gnarled hands on a red-checked cotton towel.

"Morning, Miss Sharlotte. I've kept some scrambled eggs and coffee warm for you."

"Thank you, Finn. But just coffee right now. I've a terrible headache." She rubbed her temples.

Finney frowned. "If I may say so, you're beginning to resemble the scarecrow I put up in the cornfield in season."

Startled, she gasped: "Finney!"

"Sorry, miss, I don't mean any impropriety, but if you don't start taking care of yourself, you're not going to have the health to look after your sister. If you both take to bed pining away with illness, I might as well just pull the quilt over my head too and we'll all just go permanently to sleep."

She stared at him, prepared to counter his audacity, but instead looked at his rolled up sleeves and his long legs in canvas trousers that were too small, and she realized how much she had come to depend on his amiable moods, and that her affection for him was growing by the day. She dimpled, trying to keep from laughing, and the more she tried, the more he frowned.

He walked toward her with his peculiar light-stepped gait and tilted his head. "You're exhausted, that's what. Poor miss. We'll both be glad when Mr. Ashford gets here. I'll get your breakfast on the table."

"Oh dear," Sharlotte said, wiping her eyes. "I'm not doing very well. I fear you're right."

Finney had stopped at the window on his way to the kitchen.

"What is it?" she asked, standing and straightening her skirt and smoothing her hair.

"Someone's coming—looks like your father—"

"Oh!" she started in a rush for the door.

"No, no, miss, sorry, it just looked like him…He's coming closer. We'd better be careful. Hoboes are coming around these parts now. There was a robbery at the Hickersons' place the other day; some bum from the freight trains. Times are growing worse."

A robbery! Sharlotte peeked out the window. The man wore a gray suit and hat and looked well able to handle himself in any situation—why, it was the inspector from Long Island. The man who'd questioned them after Mr. Hunnewell's accidental drowning! Her heart leaped. What was he doing here? He had no jurisdiction in Vermont. Could he possibly be here on a friendly visit? No sooner had the thought flashed through her mind than she realized that it was quite unlikely. There had been no friendship during that short period last summer.

"It's all right, Finney. I've met him before. He's a policeman."

"Ah, the robbery at the Hickersons."

"No, it couldn't be that. He's from New York."

"Wonder what brings him here then?"

"We'll soon find out. Go get the coffee ready, will you, Finney? And a headache tablet if you can find one for me."

"Sure, miss, right away."

⁓

Sharlotte was seated in the living room with police Inspector Browden. She waited uneasily as he sipped his steaming black coffee, seemingly in no hurry to explain the reason for his visit. She glanced him over, noticing his heavy paunch, his drooping brown mustache, his shiny head. His prominent eyes were lashless, staring at her from under straight heavy brows. She shifted uneasily in her chair.

"Sorry, Miss Ashford."

"Sorry? About what, Inspector?"

He had a sheepish grin. "My presence seems to upset you."

"Don't policemen usually upset people?" she said, trying to smile.

"You have a point."

"They only come around after robberies or if someone's been…killed."

He looked at her. "Yes, usually. I…er…have some news. I wanted to tell you myself, though Vermont is outside of my jurisdiction. I hope you don't mind."

She twisted her engagement ring round and round. "I don't think so, unless it's bad news. I suppose it is."

"What makes you think so?"

"Why else would an inspector from New York come all the way to Vermont?"

He set his cup down and leaned forward, staring at her evenly. "You're right. We're reopening the Hunnewell case."

Her hands turned icy cold. She swallowed. "But...why? The inquest determined that the drowning was accidental."

"So it did. *I* think Hunnewell was murdered."

She stared at him.

Inspector Browden rose to his feet. "I regret telling you this, Miss Ashford, but new evidence points to your father.

*Murder...Daddy! No, no, it can't be...*She closed her eyes briefly, gripping the arms of her chair.

He paced slowly. "And we have reason to believe he's embezzled funds at his bank. We're looking for him now."

Sharlotte fought a wave of sickness that washed over her. Every fear that she had struggled to bury in the recesses of her mind now leaped upon her with mocking savagery. She jumped to her feet. "No!"

"I'm sorry, Miss Ashford. This brings me no pleasure. I had hoped it wouldn't turn out this way."

As she stared at him, the professional mask gave way just enough for her to see the sympathy in the depths of his eyes. "Please sit down."

He helped lower her into the chair and handed her a cup of coffee. She took it absently, almost spilling some on her lap. Browden offered her a cigarette. She shook her head no.

"May I?"

She didn't answer. He struck a match.

He walked slowly about the room, giving her time. After a minute or so, he looked over at her. "When was the last time you heard from your father?"

Her confused mind ran in all directions. "What? Last Sunday."

"He was still in Texas?"

So they knew. "Yes. He...we expect him Saturday on the train." She turned in the chair. "Inspector, you've got to be wrong. My father wouldn't deliberately take another life. He and Mr. Hunnewell were friends. You must be mistaken."

"There's no question about the embezzlement charges, Miss Ashford. And we've reason to believe there was no friendship lost between your father and his attorney, either. They had a savage disagreement last year over money your father owed Hunnewell."

"My father owed Mr. Hunnewell money?"

"Yes, quite a large sum. Some business deal that he didn't make good on. I believe it was the same way with Kace Landry. Did Landry tell you that at Long Island?"

She turned her head away, closing her eyes again. "Yes, he told me. But I hadn't heard about Hunnewell. Are you sure, Inspector?"

"Certain. Your father is no longer in Texas. Your aunt, Mrs. Landry, told law enforcement that he'd gone with Kace Landry to view the property where Landry wants to drill for oil. Your father was to have invested in that enterprise. Do you know anything about that?"

So that was why her father had gone there. "No, I didn't know."

"Didn't know what, Miss Ashford?"

"I knew my father was an investor in the exploration, but I didn't know he had gone to see Mr. Landry."

He walked up and faced her. "Neither man has been heard from since they left the Landry ranch. We're also looking for Kace."

Her eyes quickly searched his. "You're not suggesting my father may have forced Kace into something?"

He smiled. "I don't think Kace could be forced to do anything he didn't want to do. Have you heard from him recently?"

Sharlotte's eyes dropped to her left hand where the engagement ring stood out.

"No. Not since last summer." She looked at him. The inspector had noticed the ring.

"Did Kace give you that ring the last time you saw him?"

She realized he thought she was engaged to Kace. She felt a blush warm her face. She also remembered that Kace had put on quite an act of their romantic fervor last time Inspector Browden had seen them together. Explaining now that she was engaged to Clarence was awkward. But if she held back it would make him more suspicious.

"No, I'm going to marry Clarence Fosdick," she confessed.

Browden said nothing. He sat down again and made an attempt to appear to be taking notes.

"Would you mind telling me why you've decided you're not in love with Kace Landry?"

"Really, Inspector!"

"You and he did convey at Long Island that there was something serious between the two of you."

"I've never considered marrying anyone except Clarence," she said. "It's, um, true that Kace and I had a youthful romance once, but we've both outgrown that."

He watched her face. She felt foolish, as though he thought she was frivolous. "If you don't believe me, ask Mr. Landry. He's going to marry Elly McCrae."

He wrote down the name. "What is the date of your wedding to Mr. Fosdick?"

"September."

"Where's Mr. Fosdick now?"

"New York. He's a lawyer in his uncle's firm, Fosdick, Hutchinson, and Meade."

"I'll need to talk to him. I'm sorry. It would save time if you'd give me his address."

She did, but she was now so dazed that the remainder of his questions could not be recalled after he'd left. After what seemed to her a grueling hour, he apologized again for bringing the painful news and requested that she get in touch with him if she heard from either her father or Mr. Landry. He gave her his card and then bid her a "very good afternoon."

When he left, Sharlotte glanced up the stairway with trepidation. There was no possible way in which she could tell her sister, nor did she want to face Finney. She knew he had overheard.

Was Inspector Browden right about her father having been with Kace? Sharlotte's brow puckered. How could that be? Kace was no friend of her father.

Sharlotte paced, wondering if she ought to telephone Aunt Livia to find out if they had heard from either Burgess or Kace, but she soon dismissed that idea. A telephone call would require a discussion of the shameful news. Sharlotte shuddered with horror. *I can't bear to talk to them about Daddy now.* Nor did she want to cry on the telephone. Maybe Aunt Livia would write to her instead. Letters were safer, avoiding a possible slip of the tongue, and requiring long delays between probing questions.

Sharlotte left the house and sought the solitude of the woods. She ran toward the road as fast as her exhausted body would carry her, taking no thought for the icy wind or gathering clouds darkening the noon sky. She ran until she had to walk to breathe, then, having caught her breath, ran on again until her lungs burned.

She came to the slope where she and Clarence had walked on Thanksgiving Day and sank to the log in defeat, gasping from exertion and the cold wind. Murder!

Here, on a happier day, Clarence had placed his engagement ring on her finger. Here, she had heard the laughter of Amanda and George drifting up from the pond. Now, decaying leaves, so much like the loss of the precious things in her life, covered the ground with a mantle of death.

Could circumstances be any more bleak? Her father was wanted for murder and embezzlement. George was dead. And Amanda was sinking into an abyss of illness that was slowly draining away her life. If Amanda learned the terrible news about their father, would she even wish to recover?

Her disillusionment seemed complete. She dropped her face into her palms and released her anguish in a torrent of tears. She wept until her throat was dry and her stomach muscles cramped from sobbing. What was left to rekindle even a feeble flame of hope?

∼

A snowstorm was blowing in as Sharlotte walked slowly back to the house. An icy wind tore at her thin blouse and skirt and sent her golden hair whipping across her face. She stumbled up the porch steps and pushed open the heavy door, a gust following her indoors and sending the papers on the table scattering across the floor. The door banged shut.

She stood there.

Finney came from the kitchen, a twisted look on his wrinkled face.

He knew. Yes, of course he would. He would have listened to the inspector from the kitchen. She didn't blame him. It wasn't every day that a New York inspector came calling to tell you your father was a suspected murderer. She looked back at him evenly. If he was going to make some excuse to pack and leave, he might as well do it now.

"I was beginning to worry, miss. I was about to go searching for you."

"I needed to be alone. I suppose you want to leave?"

"Leave? Now why would I wish to do anything so foolish, miss?"

He said nothing more, and stood there, making it clear to her that he would not be bringing up the muted question about Burgess Ashford.

Sharlotte couldn't bring herself to show any more emotion now. "Thank you, Finney," was all she said.

Dully, she walked past him to the stairway. As though too exhausted to climb, she took hold of the banister and struggled slowly upward.

Finney followed, plucking at his shirt.

"Should I call Mr. Clarence?"

She paused, facing straight ahead. "No," she murmured tonelessly. Her left hand was on the banister and she looked at her engagement ring. She knew the way these people thought, for until very recently she'd been one of them. The Fosdick family would never allow their son to marry the daughter of a man accused of murder. The engagement was over. It was simply a matter of time before the telephone call would come. She could not expect Clarence to give up his family fortune, his career as a lawyer, and a future in the House of Representatives. "That's what it would cost him," she murmured. Yet, she felt no anger. She felt nothing except profound weariness.

"No," she told Finney again. "Don't bother Mr. Fosdick. I'll… I'll be just fine, Finney. Just fine."

She walked up the mountainous stairs, growing dizzy as she looked up and saw the landing tilting like the deck of a ship in storm. She clutched the banister, her other fingers going to her eyes.

"Miss Sharlotte!" Finney called with alarm.

She felt his grip on her arm.

"I'll help you to your room, miss."

"I'll be all right." She drew her arm away and climbed upward. She reached the landing, then collapsed.

18

Sharlotte was wrong about the telephone call from Clarence—she received a letter instead, and not from Clarence, but from the matriarch of the family, Grandmother Fosdick.

Dear Miss Ashford,

My nephew Clarence informs me that he has decided to embark on a year's travel in Europe on business for his uncle, J.P. Fosdick of Fosdick, Hutchinson, and Meade. Due to unusual circumstances, we also believe it wiser for all concerned to call off his engagement with you. I am certain that while this decision is fraught with disappointment, it will prove best for Clarence in the end. It is Clarence's wish, and mine also, that you keep the diamond ring as a gift.

Respectfully yours,

Lady Hillary Elizabeth Fosdick

∽

The telephone jangled and Sharlotte lifted the receiver. "Hello?"

"Hey, tough going, kiddo. Just want you to know I don't believe a word of it about Uncle Burgess. Anything I can do?"

"No, I don't think so, Sheldon. Maybe later."

"Sure. Say, what you and Amanda need is a little skiing and a stiff drink—not at the same time, of course." He made a brief, uncomfortable laugh, then hastened: "Why not come up to Connecticut? We'll all do our best to cheer you."

"I appreciate your concern, but neither of us are up to seeing people right now. Anyway, Amanda is too ill for anything except rest."

"Poor kid." He cleared his throat. "Oh, by the way...Mother says to tell you she and Pamela would come down and be with you, but she's taking Pamela on this grand trip to Europe with a friend. Old Lady Fosdick arranged it. Nice work, huh? Well, kiddo, if you change your mind about the holidays or need a shoulder to cry on, just give me a call. I'll come down myself and bring you."

"Yes...thank you...goodbye, Sheldon."

"Merry Christmas, Peaches."

"Yes. Merry Christmas."

Sharlotte slowly replaced the receiver. She had no doubt as to whom this "friend" was that Aunt Cecily and Pamela would be traveling with to Europe: Clarence. Nice work indeed, and fast work too. She really wasn't surprised. Not with two determined women like Pamela and Grandmother Fosdick working together toward the same goal.

Sharlotte was miserable. Now Pamela's future was beaming brightly amid the storms of life while her own became submerged in an ever-darkening dilemma. The sun had set; the bleak winds of winter were howling at her heels.

Sharlotte remained by the telephone, staring at the engagement ring on her finger that Clarence had recently placed there and sealed with a kiss. How swiftly the ardor of his promise had transferred to another. And for no other reason than that she had toppled from her social pedestal. Abruptly she twisted the diamond ring from off her finger and clutched it tightly in her palm. She'd show him, and that went for old lady Fosdick as well! She'd send the ring back to New York just as soon as she could make a trip into town with Finney.

I'll starve before I sell it to put meat on the table!

As quickly as her indignation arose, however, despair once again set in. Glumly, she sank back down. *I'm right back where I started before the engagement,* she thought, grieved. Her mind tried to search for an answer to her predicament, but her frustration solved nothing and merely impaired her ability to think and plan carefully. How was she going to be able to look after herself and Amanda?

Yes…she still had her jewels, but how much could she get for them on today's market when everything was being sold cheaply just to make ends meet? And how long would the money last, with Amanda's expensive doctor bills sure to come? Probably not more than a year, maybe not even that long when she was pressed to pay taxes on the estate. After the money ran out, what then?

What then? The words ran through her mind with a new insecurity she had never known before. If her father had committed murder and went to trial, how could she ever show her face again to the strata of people she had known all her life? Who would want her and Amanda? No one. Her family, her friends—they would soon turn their backs on her the way Clarence had. Yes, even Aunt Cecily and Pamela. The fact that Sheldon hadn't done so yet was due to his contrary nature, not his wisdom. Sharlotte had little doubt that Sheldon, too, would soon be forced by his Uncle John to sever his relationship with her and Amanda. Eventually she and Amanda would drift on the wind like a balloon whose thread had been cut.

I've got to be strong. I've got to be able to do things I've never done before, would never dream of doing.

Whenever she needed to think clearly and find new courage, she sought the crisp outdoors where the great expanse of sky and vista of hills and woods cooled her frenzied mind. She found her long coat in the hall closet and went out the front door. There was a two-seater swing at one end of the porch and she sat down, bundling herself up and pushing her hands deep into warm pockets. She rocked gently, looking up at a sliver of moon cradled in the arms of an indigo sky.

If she could manage to hold onto the country estate, they would at least have a roof over their heads. The land, too, was a blessing, because she and Finney could grow food in the summer. Then, there were horses in the stable, geese by the pond, laying hens in the coop, some cows, even a few sheep somewhere out in the field. She'd never given these things a passing thought before. Now, with her world upside down and the promise of hard times ahead, they mattered a great deal. Every chicken, every egg, every apple, and every berry. She'd ask Finney about their treasures in the morning at breakfast.

She knew about the nut orchard though she'd never paid attention to what kind they were. And she remembered that Finney had always relished his summer vegetable garden and fall pumpkins and squash. She would have him plan to increase the garden size and quantity of foods planted, adding potatoes and onions. He also knew how to preserve most of what they could grow for the winter. Finney was turning out to be a windfall of experience. She knew she would be relying on him heavily in the year to come.

Potatoes and onions. She couldn't believe she was thinking this way. Desperation can cause one to reach to the depths of one's resources and discover traits never known to exist. Here was the once-rich and beautiful debutante of 1929, now worrying about harvesting onions, potatoes, and cabbage. Sharlotte would have laughed if she hadn't felt so frightened, so alone.

A handsome, rugged young Texan came intruding into her thoughts, but she gritted her teeth and refused to think about him.

"Thank goodness Amanda and I have plenty of clothes, shoes, and essentials. We can get by for years with our wardrobes, even if they go out of fashion. And we won't need to concern ourselves about invitations to dinners and balls," she murmured wryly, "unless they need a maid." For a moment Sharlotte imagined herself bringing in a tray of hors d'oeuvres to Lady Fosdick while Clarence and Pamela waltzed, gazing into one another's eyes.

Yes, she decided, if they could keep the house and its property they could survive the snowy winters for several years. By then, perhaps what the newspapers were now calling the "Great Depression" would be on the way out, and a plentiful economy on the rise. Regardless, Sharlotte didn't care to venture any further into the future than the problems confronting her right now. The present burdens were more than enough.

She supposed that poverty could be borne with honor and dignity, but a father accused of murder and bank embezzlement? She shuddered each time the word murder intruded into her mind and shut the door against it. Doing so became easier the next time until she could almost convince herself that Inspector Browden had made a mistake. Someone else had murdered poor Mr. Hunnewell, but who?

An unexpected longing swept against her, as strong and bold as the December wind among the frost-laden branches. This time it was not to be denied. If only Kace were here. She'd even settle for his teasing innuendoes if he brought comfort and concern for her burdens. For a moment she allowed herself to dream of being held in his strong embrace again while he helped her sort through her options. He had always looked out for her when she was in Texas, and again on Long Island he had cared enough to voice his concerns. He had also warned her that she needed to take precautions with her jewels. If he didn't care, even a little, would he bother? She didn't think so. In spite of Elly, he must care.

He might help, if she asked…she bit her lip. Asking wasn't that simple, though. How did she go about it without making a fool of herself?

Now that she had thought the unthinkable, she realized that she'd secretly been struggling to silence the desire for weeks, perhaps longer: from the time the stock market crashed and the Ashford fortune had collapsed in rubble.

She knew one of the main reasons why she hadn't called him. Kace could have gotten in touch with her on his own by now if he had wanted to. He could have called soon after Black Tuesday to ask her how the Ashfords had fared in the crash and offered his sympathy. That he had not spoke for itself.

Sharlotte cringed as she remembered their last meeting when he'd tossed aside her jewelry and walked out, ending the stormy relationship. There was little doubt she had treated him scornfully, but his accusations against her father had angered her. Elly would never get upset and throw things, she thought. Elly was a great lady, the noble daughter of a pastor, while she—

Frustrated with herself, with her quandary, she stood abruptly from the swing. *You're a little coward, Sharlotte Ashford. In a moment you'll be running to him and wetting his shirt with your tears like a blubbering baby. How he'd laugh at that. He might even be waiting just to see you come crawling back so he can reject you the way you rejected him.*

She squirmed at the thought of his distant, amused green eyes. Well, she would stand on her own two feet. Before this is over, Kace would be admiring her tenacity. *I'll survive here, with Amanda, and show him—all of them, Clarence and old lady Fosdick included.*

~

With the passing days, the tidal wave from the economic storm continued to sweep across America from Wall Street, wrecking sections of the economy that seemed far removed from what had taken place on Black Tuesday. The newspapers and magazines wrote of hard times for increasing numbers of Americans who had lost everything and were out of work with no job in sight to provide for their families.

Men became hoboes, drifting from state to state by hopping rides on freight trains. The old and sick begged or sold pencils and apples on street corners. Many without honor turned to crime. The papers were loaded with horrid tales about mobsters, about bootleggers, about Al Capone strengthening his grip in Chicago. And there were new gangsters: Baby Face Nelson, John Dillinger, Ma Barker and her brood of bank-robbing sons, Bonnie and Clyde, and the list went on, spewing murderous tales of men gunned down on the streets and bank tellers being shot and killed.

There were reports with pictures of long, dreary bread lines, soup kitchens set up by Christian charities, and defeated men with no place to go and no change in sight. The list of new fore-closures grew each week, becoming longer and more pitiable, from businesses to farms to tenement houses. Sharlotte was grieved to see a woman who had been evicted from her tenement room in the city because she couldn't pay rent. She sat on a chair on the sidewalk by her dresser and a small dog with no place to go.

She read of men going into cafés and ordering a cup of hot water because they couldn't buy anything, then adding catsup to make "tomato soup."

That could be me and Amanda, she thought apprehensively.

Finney added to her fears by warning of the many robberies going on by hoboes passing through.

"The tracks run near the back property line, Miss Sharlotte. Hardly a day goes by that I don't see somebody jump off before the train gets to town. The woods around here make a fair place to hide out and camp. A good shot can get himself a rabbit or even a possum. I heard the people in the Old South eat possum all the time. Possum pie—"

"Finney, do you know where my father's old rifle is kept?"

"In the cabinet in the library. All it takes is one hobo with bad blood to turn robber, miss. So we need to be careful."

His warnings did little to aid her ability to sleep. Every creak of timber or rattle of a windowpane made her listen for someone trying to sneak into the house.

Thereafter, as soon as the sun set and the wintry darkness mantled the woodlands, Sharlotte would insist that Finney join her on a nightly tour of the big house while they checked every window and door to make certain it was barred and bolted. "What we need is a dog," she said.

Sharlotte wasn't the only one afraid of every stranger and every creaking floorboard. The newspapers told tales about the very rich who had survived Black Tuesday with their fortunes intact. Mindful of the French Revolution and the king and queen who had lost their heads for indulging on cake when the poor had no bread, the American elite were fearful that a new American revolution might occur based on Lenin's Communist revolution in Russia in 1917, and that they might be the objects of rage.

"A poor population without work, without food, and without shelter," they whispered, "might turn against us or even overthrow the government. They might encircle our mansions and break in!"

There was a quiet panic that motivated individuals in wealthy neighborhoods to take stronger steps to guard their domains from angry mobs.

"If the dollar becomes worthless, then gold is the thing to have," they said, and there were suggestions that many were sending their money out of the country for safe keeping.

"No, diamonds are better than gold. You can carry them on your person if you need to flee into Canada."

After reading about such scares, Sharlotte agreed with Finney that they must be prepared for anything.

"Do you know how to use the rifle, Finney?"

"I can drill a dime," he said confidently.

She doubted his boast, but let it pass. "If you know how to shoot it, you can teach me too."

Thereafter, Sharlotte would go out with Finney in the mornings after breakfast for her shooting lesson. With every squeeze of the trigger the stock would recoil against her shoulder, jarring her. That night she went to bed bruised black and blue. The next day Finney set up a target, and Sharlotte wore padding to protect herself. More often than not, both of them missed the bull's-eye.

"But if a mob surges in on us," she joked, "we're bound to hit somebody."

Sharlotte was also worried about her jewelry. She had learned that certain wealthy people didn't trust the banks with their valuables. Every day new banks had to close their doors and go out of business because they were unable to pay their customers. People had begun burying their money and other valuables in their backyards for safekeeping. Sharlotte decided it wasn't such a foolish idea after all.

She went to her bedroom and collected the silk stocking that held the Ashford and Chattaine jewelry and placed it inside a metal box. This done, she secretly brought it out to the woods and under cover of darkness she buried it beneath a crooked pine tree. She had this treasure, at least, that no one would ever be able to take from her.

Besides the buried jewelry, she still had money left from the sale of the diamond brooch and decided to stock the pantry with canned food in case there was a siege.

"We'll go into town tomorrow and buy all we can carry in the Model T," she told Finney.

"The motorcar is out of gasoline, miss."

"Can't you get some?" she asked, impatient over such mundane details. She was used to limousines and chauffeurs always ready to bring her wherever she wished to go. How odd to be worrying about where she could buy gasoline.

"We're likely to get stuck between here and town if we try. It's at least thirty miles. I'm thinking it'll be wiser to take the horse and wagon," he said apologetically. "I'll bring a container for gasoline, though, and store it in the shed for next time."

Horse and wagon, what a gaff! Would anyone recognize her? Then she remembered the police were looking for her father, and when she did remember, the humiliation was so strong that the idea of riding in a dilapidated wagon didn't seem so embarrassing after all. She sighed. "Very well, we'll use the wagon."

The next morning she was up early for the ride into town. A quick look out the window brought a scowl. Another very windy day. And those had to be snow clouds too. She and Finney had better hurry. She dressed in a split riding skirt with matching jacket and boots.

Amanda was still asleep when Sharlotte softly opened the bedroom door to peek in. No use waking her. Sharlotte had told her the night before that she and Finney would be going to town for supplies. Sharlotte also wanted to surprise Amanda by buying her a Christmas present. Maybe a good book would help cheer her.

When she went downstairs, Finney was not in his usual spot in the kitchen. In fact, the coffee hadn't been made, nor the eggs scrambled. How strange. Finney was always up by four. Was he ill?

That's all I need! More problems, she thought crossly.

The kitchen window rattled in the wind, otherwise the deep silence of the house set her on edge. Finney slept in a servant's bungalow behind the house, so she donned her heavier coat and stepped out into the wind.

If he was ill enough to remain in bed he might have something seriously wrong. In which case she might need to ride into town alone to locate a doctor.

She trudged through the wind to the cottage door and knocked. "Finney?"

There was no answer. She called his name several times before finally trying the door. It was unlocked. She stepped in. "Finney?

Are you all right?" His bed was neatly made and his clothes hung, his slippers in place, but he was not there. Odd, that he would go about his other duties before entering the kitchen. Had he gone into town without her, seeing that the storm was blowing in? Hardly. She had the money.

Standing by his small window with its shade drawn halfway up, she thought she heard running footsteps, but when she looked out she saw nothing except the old hickory tree, its limbs swaying in the rising wind.

The door creaked on its hinges. She whirled, feeling a shiver up her back. It was just the wind. She quickly left, shutting the door firmly behind her. Her alarm increased. If something had happened to him—

The morning was blustery with dark clouds. She pulled her hood over her hair and started across the yard toward the stables some distance away, her boots crunching over powdery snow.

Just maybe he had changed his regular routine this morning and, knowing they were going into town, he might have started early to hitch the mare to the wagon.

Five minutes later she neared the stables with the big doors wide open. Her relief brought a sigh. Finney had the wagon out and one of the younger horses already hitched. Another mare was also out of her stall, saddled, and tied to the post.

"Finney, we'd better leave for town now. I don't like the look of those clouds. What did you plan to do with Amanda's—"

She paused in the doorway of the stable, greeted only by shadows and the smell of animals and hay. Finney was not there.

Sharlotte hesitated, then cautiously walked inside looking about, wanting to make certain he hadn't fallen or become ill. She saw his sweater lying across a rail as though he may have gotten too warm while working.

"Finney?"

The other horses snorted a greeting, still in their stalls and eating morning hay. He may have gone out to the fields, though she couldn't imagine why, but her alarm was rising to such an extent that she wouldn't be at peace until she had checked.

She went to the mare and untied her. If he had gone far, he should have taken this horse that was already saddled, but since she couldn't be certain, she mounted, turning the reins to ride toward the apple orchard and beyond to where their cows and sheep grazed.

Last night he had mentioned something about one of the sheep being sick. He may have had some notion of isolating it from the others, or bringing it with them in the wagon to the veterinarian in town.

She rode into the headwind, following the dirt path that skirted the edge of the encroaching woods. She hadn't forgotten for a moment Finney's tales of hoboes riding the freight trains, and she trotted the mare along with an uneasy eye as she scanned the tall shrubs and trees. The train tracks were not far behind the mound, hidden by underbrush.

Sharlotte pulled her hood lower against the wind and drew near the bend in the road splotched with shadows. She had never enjoyed horseback riding as much as Amanda had, or Kace and Tyler, who not only rode exceptionally well due to their upbringing, but bred and tamed them.

The cold wind blew through the dark woods, causing a moaning rush through the swaying tree tops. Oh no! She drew rein. Ahead, Finney was sprawled on his stomach in the path. What had happened to him? A heart attack? She remembered Great-Uncle Hubert.

She stopped and swung down, running toward him. "Finney!"

Finney jumped to his feet. Except it wasn't Finney. The man's face belonged to a young stranger whom she'd never seen before. She gasped.

"I won't hurt you." He moved toward her. "Can you spare a little change, miss?"

"I...I don't carry money." She moved backward. Could she reach the horse and get away? Her heart thudded. His coat and hat were Finney's, the ones she'd seen only late yesterday afternoon hanging on pegs in the back porch. Then this man had been all the way up to the back kitchen door.

"Sure am hungry. Haven't eaten in days. Just passin' through. Hear the freight train rides through here into town."

His eyes were active and desperate. His fingers kept moving up and down the buttons of Finney's old work jacket.

"Wait here. I'll…have one of the workers bring you something to eat." She inched away.

"That's a fine lookin' horse."

She turned and ran. He was just behind. She got her boot in the stirrup, grabbed the pommel and was up in the saddle. She snatched the reins, wheeling the startled mare. He grabbed her arm, ripping the reins free. She dug her heels into the horse's sides and she reared, whinnying. It was no use. Sharlotte felt his bruising fingers latch hold of her, dragging her from the saddle. She clawed at him, kicking, fighting with every ounce of strength. A shocking pain splintered through her jaw as he struck a blow—

19

Charlotte awoke on the road. Something soft, cold, and fluffy settled on her face. Her eyelids fluttered open. Snowflakes swirled above her. Her brain weaved dizzily and pain stabbed through her jaw and her head. Was it broken? She tried to open her mouth and found that her lip was swollen. Slowly, her hand lifted to touch her jaw, following its contour up to her temple. It felt whole and she took heart.

She moved slowly, managing to get on her hands and knees, then tried to push herself up onto her feet. She swayed, but retained her balance.

Which direction to the house? She squinted through the snow, unable to focus clearly. She was remembering...

With a start of horror, she looked around her. The horse was gone. She felt her clothes. The buttons and zippers were all in place, everything was untouched. Tears filled her eyes. *Thank You, God.* She took a few steps, then sank to the path again, too exhausted to go on, while snowflakes danced gently about her like white butterflies.

She, Sharlotte Ashford, was sitting bruised in the snow, having been robbed and left unconscious. And who would ever know of her ordeal, much less do anything about it? Sharlotte, whose every whim had once been catered to, whose every desire had once been granted by the affluence of a rich family, had now come to *this*.

Cold reality forced itself upon her and demanded full attention: she might as well face the cruel truth that her father would not be coming back. A new world bid her enter its fearsome halls, a world whose rigors she was not well prepared for.

The wind crooned eerily through the leaves and blew the swirling flakes into her eyes so that she could hardly see more than a few feet ahead of her as she struggled painfully down the path.

Can't go on…must stop…and rest again…must sleep…

No, a voice seemed to say. *Keep moving. Just a little while longer. Rest, warmth, and comfort are waiting just out of reach.*

Comfort—she stumbled onward. Suddenly, she thought she heard a voice. She cried out. The voice shouted: "Miss Sharlotte, it's you!"

"Finney—" she cried.

The older man ran toward her, his long dark coat flapping like raven's wings.

"I was afraid you was lost. Where's the horse, miss?"

"Stolen."

"Stolen? What's this world coming to?" He stopped, sucking his breath in. "Child, you're hurt! My oh my, I've got to get you home! But I don't dare leave to get the wagon. Here, miss, lean on me. We'll get there. And when we reach the road I'll put you in a safe place till I go get the wagon. Come along now, that's it, slowly now."

Slowly, Sharlotte thought, her mind weaving in and out as the cold, whitish-gray world swayed in all directions. *Just one step at a time.*

〜

Finney reported the stolen horse to the police. A local deputy came out to ask questions of Sharlotte, who was in bed and being seen by a doctor.

"Come in, Ed, but go easy on the young woman," the doctor told the deputy. "She's still in shock and needs rest."

"I won't disturb her long, Doc."

The doctor patted Sharlotte's hand. "You're a lucky young woman."

"Is her jaw broken?" Amanda asked, worried, pale, and thin as she sat in a chair beside her sister's bed.

"No, but it will be tender and swollen for a few days. Your face will turn black and blue," he told Sharlotte, "but don't let that frighten you. And there may be a neck sprain or whiplash. There's also the possibility of neck pain and headaches for the foreseeable future, but I'll leave you something to take for that. Too bad we didn't catch the beast, but that's your job, Ed."

"We're looking for him."

In the days that followed the ordeal, the country house and grounds were silent. No visitors came to call, the road became deserted during the snowstorm, and whatever distant neighbors there were in the area were all unknown, having deliberately been kept at arm's length in the past. Even Finney, loyal to his employer, had absorbed some of the family smugness and had avoided friendships in order to guard Ashford secrets.

But now, with segments of the nation in turmoil, once-curious neighbors were content to stay within their own boundaries. The times bred fear, and when word circulated of the attack on Sharlotte, people were even more inclined to stay to themselves, reluctant to reach out and afraid of the unknown.

Then, on one mortifying day, Amanda came wheeling into Sharlotte's bedroom with a deathly pallor on her cheeks, the morning newspaper on her lap. "Sharlotte, Daddy's in trouble. The most horrid, *preposterous* charges—"

"Yes, I know," Sharlotte murmured miserably. "The police inspector came here last week. Let me see—" she reached feebly for the paper.

"Last week? You didn't tell me."

"No. You were too sick."

"Oh, Sharlotte," she said sadly, "I've been so selfish, pitying myself about George and my health, and all the time you were left to bear this burden alone. Well, it's going to be different now. Somehow I'll look after you."

Sharlotte hurt too much to smile and tried to focus on the article on the second page of the paper.

"Bank president Burgess Ashford II of New York is wanted for questioning on possible murder charges of his lawyer, B. B. Hunnewell."

Sharlotte groaned and let the paper drop on the bed, turning her head away. "I don't...want to think about it."

"I'm going to telephone Aunt Livia," Amanda said worriedly.

"No...don't. It will make matters worse."

"I don't see how."

"Because that was the last place Daddy was. If he's still there, hiding on the ranch somewhere, the police may learn you called. They may think Aunt Livia knows where he is."

"I hadn't thought of that. Do you think Daddy's there?" she whispered.

"He was last seen with Kace...and Kace hasn't been seen or heard from either. Who knows where either of them are?"

"I'll be careful about asking her any questions. But I think she and Uncle Sherman ought to know what happened to you by that despicable hobo."

Sharlotte was in no condition to continue to protest, and after a few minutes of silence, Amanda drew a blanket over her older sister protectively, removed the paper with its bleak headlines, and wheeled from the room, leaving the door open to the hall.

It must have been some twenty minutes later when Sharlotte heard Amanda on the telephone: "Aunt Livia? Oh—it's you, Elly. Yes—hello."

Elly? thought Sharlotte, coming alert. What was she doing answering the telephone at the Landry ranch house? Sharlotte managed to raise herself to an elbow, trying to listen, but Amanda's voice grew muffled, and she couldn't hear what was being said.

It wasn't until Amanda came back to her room later that afternoon that she was able to hear the news from Texas. Amanda wheeled in, followed by Finney bearing a tray with some hot tea and chopped chicken gizzard sandwiches. The thought of tea was appealing, but the gizzards made her gag.

"Gizzards?" she gave a laugh. "Has it come to this? Oh, woe is me."

"Now, now, miss, there's more in chicken gizzards that's good for you than meets the eye."

"Well, I'll take your word for it, Finney, but some other time, thank you. Just tea."

"Shame on you. You'll ne'er get well if you don't eat."

"My jaw is too sore to chew," she said, finding the excuse silenced him. She smiled and leaned back against the pillows, sipping the cup of tea. "Ahh," she teased, "being spoiled again may have been worth a crack on the jaw."

"What I don't understand, Finney, is where you were during the time Sharlotte was looking for you," Amanda said, nibbling a sandwich.

Sharlotte, watching her, felt a ray of hope. Since she'd been laid up in bed, Amanda had snapped out of her depression and actually had some color in her thin cheeks again. That seemed to be the one good thing to have come from the horrid incident.

"Well," explained Finney, "it was like this…"

He went on to tell them that he'd been suspecting that the hobo had gotten off the freight train boxcar a week ago and had been sleeping in the woods. He didn't want to frighten them, so he'd kept it to himself. The hobo must have seen the lights in the farmhouse windows at night and crept over to check out the area.

"That's when the buzzard must've stole my work jacket and cap. Well, the morning we was to take the wagon to town I got up a little earlier because I knew I was going to have some trouble with the wagon. One of the wheels was wobbly, and I wanted to fix it before we took off. I got things done all right, but by then I caught a whiff of wood smoke drifting from the field where the cows were. I got suspicious. I returned to the house for the rifle."

Sharlotte recalled having heard the vague sound of running footsteps. "Then that was you I heard. The sound spooked me and I left for the stables."

"And that was when I must've been inside the house looking for the rifle. It took me awhile to find it."

Sharlotte felt a little guilty. She had brought it up to the gun rack in the hallway by her father's bedroom, feeling better about having it at hand when she retired. She'd forgotten to tell Finney, who had expected it to be back in the library.

"That was my fault," she said. "Sorry, Finney. We undoubtedly missed each other by moments."

"I should have gone straight to where I'd smelled the wood smoke, but by then it was snowing and, well, I let the matter go. I knew you wanted to go to town and we'd need to rush to get back before the storm hit hard. And, being an old fella, I admit I was a little scared to go down and chase the hobo away, even with the rifle. So I fixed breakfast instead," he said sheepishly. "When you didn't come down, that's when I begin looking for you. The field was the last place I thought of, 'cause I never expected you'd have a reason to go there. And I didn't go back to the stable until I went there to get the mare to make a thorough search and found her gone. That's when I feared you'd smelled that wood smoke too and went there yourself. Then, I went a running."

Sharlotte assured him it wasn't his fault. "Next time we'll all be more careful."

"Let's make sure there isn't no next time," he said. " 'cause next time I'll shoot any stranger who comes nosing about uninvited, thinking to steal another horse or a sheep. That blasted thief killed the sick lamb and roasted it. That's what I was whiffing that morning."

"Maybe he'll get sick himself," Amanda said. "That would be poetic justice."

"It would," Sharlotte said, "but whatever that lamb had, I wouldn't wish its disease on anyone, not even that miserable hobo. I just hope he's long gone from here."

When Finney carried the tray away, Sharlotte asked Amanda about her telephone call.

"Did you speak with Aunt Livia?" she asked casually.

Amanda's expression became blank, as if wishing to conceal something from Sharlotte.

"Is Daddy there?" Sharlotte inquired.

"No…no, he's not."

"Then they haven't heard from him since he and Kace went to the oil property?"

"No," Amanda repeated, while fingering the buttons on her collar.

Something is wrong, Sharlotte thought. "I thought I heard you speaking to Elly."

Amanda gave her a guarded look, then sighed resignedly. "Well, yes I did."

"Was she there visiting Livia?" Sharlotte inquired, keeping her voice calm.

"No, not actually."

"Was Kace there too?" There. She had finally asked.

"No, but Elly said he was due back for supper tonight."

So, Kace was at the ranch after all. Then where was her father? It also became clear that Kace probably knew all about what had been happening to the Ashford fortune recently, yet he apparently had no concern whatsoever about how she was faring.

But then, why should he? She had made it clear the last time she'd seen him in her parlor that she wanted him out of her life once and for all. It appeared as though she had gotten exactly what she had asked for.

"Livia said there's a bad drought setting in. She said Kace is concerned the cattle business might fall on hard times."

Sharlotte felt her heart deaden. Most everyone in America had fallen on hard times.

"There's foreclosures too," Amanda went on grimly. "Livia said that smaller farmers and cattlemen are permanently out of business. It's hard on them to see lifelong neighbors and friends lose their land to debt. They have no place to go. She said there were nightly prayer meetings at the church. But, guess what!"

Sharlotte could only look at her.

"Tyler got married last month."

She sat up, forgetting her discomfort. "He didn't! To whom!"

"A rancher's daughter. Abby Hutchins. Remember her?"

Sharlotte tried to recall the name, and vaguely remembered something about a girl named Abby who had been too busy working on her father's ranch to come to the dances and barbecues.

Now I know how she must have felt, Sharlotte thought.

"Anyway," Amanda said, "Tyler's running his father-in-law's cattle ranch now."

Sharlotte thought again of her own near marriage to Clarence, and a wave of self-pity welled up. Her injured pride stung. If she ever got her hands on Clarence...*maybe his ship will sink*, she thought. *No, not that. Aunt Cecily and Pamela were also aboard.*

"Speaking of marriage, Pamela will end up marrying Clarence," she told Amanda wryly. "She finally won."

Amanda wrinkled her nose. "Yes, the little conniver. Well, Clarence deserves her. In fact, they deserve each other. I never much cared for Clarence, if you want to know the truth. I'm glad you didn't marry him."

Sharlotte wondered if her sister really felt that way, or was just trying to mollify her disappointment.

"Sometimes I think you were just willing to marry him because the family expected it of you. Especially after Daddy began having all those financial setbacks. Oh! Daddy, poor Daddy. Where do you think he could be?"

"I've no idea, and I know it isn't right—but, well, I hope the police don't catch him yet. Not until he can prove his innocence."

"You don't think he's guilty?"

"Absolutely not. Daddy had his weaknesses to be sure, but I know he wasn't a…he wouldn't harm Mr. Hunnewell."

Amanda looked sick and lapsed into reflection. "There was something odd about the happenings at that picnic outing…but I just can't put my finger on it."

Sharlotte rubbed her neck. Her head ached too terribly to think about it now. She looked at her sister warily.

"What else did Elly tell you?"

Amanda's gaze swerved back. She sat up a little straighter in the chair, brushing her red hair from her forehead. "I'd better tell all, I suppose…"

"Yes. You'd better." Sharlotte's heart began to pound with a premonition.

"She was visiting Aunt Livia to have measurements taken for her wedding dress. Elly doesn't have a mother, you know, and Livia learned years ago to be an excellent seamstress. So…"

Sharlotte felt her watchful, pitying gaze, before it dropped to her lap. "Sorry, Sharlotte. I have always known you had feelings for Kace. Looks like we both lost the real men we wanted. George, and now Kace—"

"I don't want Kace!" her mouth trembled, and she bit her lip to keep back tears. Her hands formed fists as she pounded the bed. "I hate him, hate him—" tears splashed down her cheeks, and she fell back to smother her crying in her pillow, defeated.

Amanda blinked hard, but also ended up wiping salty splashes from her face.

"Look at us," she said with self-derision, "two little rich girls fallen from their pedestals, eating humble pie. We've lost everything. Money and men. We'll probably end up being here all alone and live until we're ninety."

"Oh, hush," Sharlotte said, her voice muffled in the feather pillow.

"The wedding's September 18."

Why that cad, Sharlotte thought. *That's the very same date I wrote Livia that Clarence and I would marry. He probably talked Elly into that date.* She sniffed and sat up irritably, blowing her nose and wiping her eyes.

"Well, they can have each other," she said stiffly.

"Yes," Amanda agreed, "just like Clarence and Pamela deserve each other."

"Yes. What do we care?"

"We don't," Amanda agreed.

"That's right. We do not." Sharlotte threw the covers aside and, holding to the bedpost, managed to stand, chin lifted. "I feel better already. I'm getting up. If anyone thinks I'm going to snivel and crawl into my shell, they're wrong."

"Good for you," Amanda echoed. She reached for her crutches. "Me too. I haven't tried to walk since George was killed. He wouldn't like that."

"No, he wouldn't. If he were here he'd have scolded you. 'If you really care about me, Mandy,' he'd say, 'you'll not give up. Keep trying, keep believing.'" Sharlotte looked at her, determined. "And with God's help, we shall."

Amanda's winged brows shot up. "That's the first time I've heard anyone in this family say: with God's help."

Sharlotte glanced at her, holding to the bedpost with both hands. "Daddy was an atheist, but that doesn't mean he was right. He was wrong about a lot of important things."

Amanda didn't say anything for a moment, then just shrugged. "It's all right with me. Honestly, I rather enjoyed Uncle Sherman's little Bible talks when we were girls. You know what I liked best about him? His determination that Kace and Tyler believe the Bible. He took a real hand in guiding them. At the time, we sort of snickered, but now that we've grown up, it doesn't seem trivial anymore, does it?"

"No," Sharlotte said. "There were a lot of things the Landrys did when we were young that don't seem odd anymore."

"We sound like two old fogies," Amanda said with a wry grin.

"I feel ancient," Sharlotte groaned, and made her way back to the edge of her bed.

They were quiet and thoughtful, then Amanda said reminiscently: "The story I like to remember the best is the one about the four friends who brought their crippled friend to Jesus on a stretcher. Remember that one?"

"Yes…"

"They actually got up on the roof and tore it apart to lower the stretcher down in front of Jesus," Amanda went on. "And Jesus told the crippled man that his sins were forgiven and to get up and walk. And he actually did it."

Sharlotte thought about it but said nothing. She limped to the mirror. Every muscle in her body seemed sore. She gave a cry of dismay as she saw her black-and-blue face and her long tangled hair. "Jeepers! Who is that witchy-looking thing in the mirror!"

Amanda grinned. "Ready for your coming out ball, Miss Debutante?" Amanda hummed a Rudy Vallee love song, holding herself up by her crutches and swaying as if dancing in a ritzy ballroom. "Think Mr. Right will come along from out of the misty moonlight and sweep me off my crutches to waltz in shimmering silk somewhere?" She laughed shortly. "No? I don't either. Oh, well." She moved back to her chair and lowered herself, out of breath. "I'm too tired anyway. Maybe next time."

Sharlotte laughed, pointing at her image. "What a gaff! Clarence should see me now. He'd be convinced he made the right decision. Debutante of the year, ha! You mean *clown* of the year. *Fool* of the year." She began to cry again.

No, not a fool, at least not recently. Experience had convinced her that hardship and loss were more painful for the wealthy than for those who had always struggled with life. Perhaps it wasn't such a blessing to be rich, after all. Maybe Kace had been right when he'd teased her one day by telling her the Lord didn't have any spoiled children. All His children were blessed, but God didn't pamper any of them.

Thinking of that, Sharlotte decided that if the worst befell them, she might be able to get a job in a downtown piece-rate sweatshop where she'd heard from Finney that if a girl could sew two weeks for long hours she could make twenty dollars. It would mean moving back to New York or Chicago, though. She knew in her heart she couldn't do that. She wouldn't leave the neat, white farmhouse in lovely Vermont. She and Finney would just need to get out to the fields in the spring and sow for a fall harvest.

20

Except for the discoloration along Sharlotte's jaw and up the side of her face, she was recovering rapidly. It was the morning of Christmas Eve, and clouds of silver-gray hung over the woods. They had finally decorated the tree, and Sharlotte was thinking of picking wild holly for the Christmas table.

Amanda was in one of her dismal moods, having momentarily surrendered her "do or die" attitude.

"I thought for sure Daddy would be in touch," she said.

"He dare not." Sharlotte wondered where he was hiding.

"You'd at least think Aunt Livia and Uncle Sherman would send us a fruitcake."

"You know you loathe fruitcake," Sharlotte reminded her, gathering a basket and shears to cut the holly. "Besides, they're broke," she said pointedly.

"Everybody's broke," Amanda said. "There's nothing exhilarating to do. Maybe we should have taken Sheldon's advice and gone to Connecticut."

"And be pummeled with questions about murder and embezzlement by all their society friends? Oh, no. Besides, he drinks too much. They all do. And I don't want pitying looks from our old friends as they whisper about Pamela stealing Clarence away. Let's just make do with what we've got."

Sharlotte went to the front door and opened it.

"Where are you going?" Amanda asked, alarmed.

"To gather some wild sprigs of holly I saw growing alongside the property by the woods."

"The woods! After what happened with the hobo?"

"I'm not going to hide indoors for the rest of my life, afraid of what might happen next. Besides, such an incident would never happen twice."

"So you say. At least take the rifle with you? Please, for my sake."

"Oh, very well." Amanda's sad face made her regret her curt response, so she said humorously: "And if there are any freight-train 'strays' sneaking about, they'd better take cover. I'm in no mood to be roughed up again," and she went out.

Sharlotte understood why Amanda was in a dour mood. This was the first Christmas the family had been separated, and memories of past holidays filled with family, friends, and festivity brought a wave of nostalgia. Sharlotte felt it as well, but she didn't want to give in to it. *We've got to keep busy. Maybe we can make fudge tonight if Finney can dig up enough sugar.* They still hadn't made that wagon trip to town for supplies.

Sharlotte walked to the spot she had in mind and set the basket down by the gray-green bushes. She began to cut clusters of green leaves and bright red berries when she thought she heard a noise. A twig snapped beneath someone's shoe—

She turned sharply around to see a clump of snow fall from the embankment. She dropped the holly and froze, then remembered the gun. She grabbed the rifle leaning against a pine tree. No, not again. She had thought she was brave, but now panic seized her as a hobo in black clothes stepped from behind some trees. Fear caught at her heart. The man was returning—

Sharlotte raised the rifle and with trembling fingers squeezed the trigger. The crack of the bullet whizzed and smashed into a tree. The man had fallen flat down about the same time she had fired.

She knew he wasn't dead. "Next time it's between the eyes, mister," she called, keeping her voice as calm and steady as possible. He scrambled quickly behind a tree.

"You got one horse. You won't get another," she added.

"Annie Oakley, I presume?" Kace called from behind the tree. "I promise to surrender if you hold your fire."

Sharlotte's breath caught. Kace! Oh no. The rifle suddenly felt too heavy, and she set it down against the pine tree.

Kace cautiously stepped from behind his tree, coming forward with his hands behind his head in exaggerated surrender. He stopped, looked at the rifle, and then gave a low whistle. "I can see the headlines now, 'Dangerous Debutante Seeks Revenge.'"

Sharlotte silently fumed, but beyond her embarrassment, a great tide of relief and excitement rolled over her. Seeing him again sent her heart pounding. Her feelings about Kace had always proved puzzling because she could care so strongly about his presence and yet also find him so irritating. She was drawn to him, and never more than now. He wore a dark jacket, Levis, and boots, and his gray-green eyes were especially noticeable against his tanned features. He smiled suddenly and she realized she'd been standing there studying him. Embarrassed, she diverted her attention to the rifle, picked it up, and slung it over her shoulder.

"I'm looking for a princess," he said. "A Miss Sharlotte Ashford—a well-bred and elegant young debutante with snobbish ways and pride as thick as dried cowhide. Have you seen her recently?"

"So! You've come to gloat."

"Not gloat, but I am enjoying myself at the moment. Do you realize this is the first time we've been on equal footing?"

"Well, money doesn't make a great lady, and—"

He laughed. "Now that's a first coming from you. What was it you used to enjoy telling me in Texas? Money and social standing go together in order to make great ladies and gallant gentlemen."

"Oh!" she stamped her foot. "If you have nothing more important to say to me, Kace Landry, I shall bid you a good afternoon." She turned, as though she would walk away.

"I have a great deal to say once you hand over that rifle. I didn't come all this way to be hunted as a horse thief. I can find better breeds in Texas."

"You're lucky I didn't take your ear off."

"Or worse. Good thing you missed. It gave me time to drop."

He went back and snatched up his hat, knocking off the snow and settling it comfortably on his head.

"I didn't miss," she stated. "I hit the tree as I intended. Anyway, you should have made yourself known instead of sneaking about the woods."

"I wasn't 'sneaking about.' I was trying to locate your house. I jumped the freight train." He reached for her rifle. "It's amazing what a change of circumstances can do to a debutante's finishing-school training."

"Indeed? Well, I happen to maintain discriminating tastes, though I can't speak for yours."

"And did you acquire these discriminating tastes through good blood and proper breeding?"

His deliberate rebuke stung, but she said nothing and handed him the rifle.

"I'll teach you how to shoot some day. But all in good time. It's Christmas Eve. I'm tired, cold, and hungry. Can you afford to take a poor stranger in? I've traveled a long, hard way to get here after I—" he stopped abruptly.

She looked at him thoughtfully. After he what? After Amanda had told Aunt Livia about the attack from the hobo? Did he really come because she'd been hurt? The thought soothed her wounded vanity, and she dimpled for the first time.

"Why, Kace, you really did come to see how I was faring."

"Let's see the side of your face."

Embarrassed, she nonetheless allowed him to turn her head. His caring touch was warm and gentle. She tried to pull away. "I'm all right now. It was nothing."

"Looks as though you really took a hit. Good thing he's not around. He'd be picking up missing teeth from here to Dallas."

She laughed nervously. Kace was angry. She loved seeing his concern. He must still care a little bit. And if he still cared even a little, that meant—

"Don't look so smug," he said with a slight smile as though he'd read her mind. "There's another reason why I came. First, how about that coffee you offered me?"

Against her will she smiled again. "If you promise to be a gentleman."

He bowed. "Thank you, kind lady. I accept your Christmas generosity."

He picked up her basket and handed it to her, and they walked slowly back toward the house. Sharlotte found his presence reassuring.

"Did you really ride a freight train to come here?"

"Most of the way."

She laughed again, trying to imagine Kace lying in a boxcar with his hat over his face.

"Think it's funny, do you? Between the rattle of the wheels and the hard boards it's a wonder I got any sleep."

"Poor Kace."

"I went hungry too. Until I...um...got some eggs from a farmer."

"Your conscience bothers you, of course."

"He had me treat an injured horse before I left, so I figure I earned them."

She smiled. "Maybe I can find some work for you. I've some laundry you could scrub on a washboard. Finney's getting too old." She glanced at his muscled arms. "You look like you're perfectly suited for the job."

"Whose Finney?"

"He's worked for my father for years. Recently, he's been like a grandfather."

When they had reached the front porch, Sharlotte opened the door and entered, Kace following.

Amanda cried: "Kace!" She tried to get up.

He crossed to the wheelchair and lifted her up off her feet, kissing her cheek. "Hello, Precious."

Amanda was beaming a smile. "It's about time you got here."

Sharlotte folded her arms. "Well, what's this? Is there something going on I don't know about?"

Amanda laughed. She turned to Kace. "I didn't think you'd come."

"I always answer the call of a maiden in distress."

Sharlotte looked from one to the other. Had Amanda asked Kace to come? She remembered the telephone call to Aunt Livia and grew suspicious. So that was it. Amanda had been worried about her after the injury and must have said something to Livia about sending Kace. Still, it was surprising he had come at all, considering his own troubles.

"You'll stay the holidays, won't you?" Amanda pleaded, looking at him anxiously.

"I wish I could," he said gently.

Sharlotte watched them. *He probably speaks gently to Elly like that too. I'm the only one he enjoys goading.*

When Amanda wheeled into the kitchen calling for Finney to set another place at the Christmas table, Sharlotte told Kace in a low voice: "Why do you always talk nicely to my sister and not to me?"

"Not jealous of a kindness toward your little sister, are you?"

"Certainly not," she bristled.

"Some girls deserve to be treated with special consideration." A hint of amusement showed in his eyes.

"Oh, they do, do they? And I suppose *I* do not?"

"You do indeed. Any girl wild enough to pop bullets off at me also deserves special consideration."

Finney came in with Amanda, who introduced Kace Landry as their cousin.

Sharlotte, miffed over his airy remark, swept toward the stairway. "I'll show you to your room first, 'Cousin' Kace. I do hope you'll be comfortable."

"I'm sure I will," he said pleasantly. He bowed. "You're most gracious, 'Cousin' Sharlotte."

Sharlotte knew the compliment had been prompted by her complaint, but Amanda took it at face value and raised her brows. Sharlotte waited on the stairs as he came up. Her eyes met his evenly and found amusement there. "This way," she offered.

Kace followed. She led the way to one of the rooms, entered, and made a pretense of making sure everything was in order. "The bath is in here. There are towels and soap. And dinner is early tonight because of Christmas Eve."

Kace tossed his traveling bag on the rug-covered floor, removed his jacket, and glanced about the cozy room. "Looks like I've made a good investment after all."

She had walked to the door, but paused to look back curiously. "Investment?" she asked. "I don't understand."

He maintained his casual demeanor as he loosened the buttons of his shirt and pushed the mattress with his hand to see if it was soft. "Yes. Real estate is a good buy now that prices have dropped, but this is perhaps not a very good time to sell."

Real estate was a good investment, but...her lashes squinted as she walked back into the room, studying him with extreme caution. "What do you mean?" she inquired.

"This country estate—is mine," he said. "I own the deed on it."

He owned the deed?

She smiled suddenly. "Yes, of course." She laughed and walked toward him, hands clasped behind her. "You're such a terrible tease, Kace, I should have known. Anyway, the house isn't for sale." She walked about slowly, touching heirloom furnishings dating back to the 1880s. Her jaw set with determination. "We've lost both our home in New York and the summerhouse on Long Island." She looked at him, her violet-blue eyes sparkling. "This is all Amanda and I have left of the Ashford estate, and I intend to keep it."

Kace glanced her over thoughtfully. "I was afraid that might be your response. Unfortunately, I was serious when I told you it's mine. I hold the deed. Your father signed it over to me in Texas."

Shocked, she just stared at him. No, it couldn't be true! He was just saying these things, but she could see that he wasn't teasing.

Her mind shouted the words, shouted that he must have deliberately weaseled the property from her father, who was under duress and in no condition to do business. She was sure Kace had done so just to show his mastery over the Ashford name. Oh, he could be such a skunk sometimes!

"Maybe you'd better sit down," he said. "You're looking a little pale."

She very nearly picked up a book on the dresser and threw it at him. Instead, she sank down onto the edge of a chair. He couldn't do this to her now. Not after all she'd been through. How could he be so cruel?

Kace glanced around the room again, as though surveying the condition of his new investment. "I hold the deed until your father's debt to me is paid in full. An amount far beyond your present ability to pay." His brow lifted as he scanned her. "And there's still the matter of back taxes due on this property. Your father, it seems, was a bit of an undisciplined fellow. One who procrastinated on more than fixing old boathouses."

Her eyes swerved to his. How could he bring up that horrible situation on Long Island now?

"I've been able to scrimp together enough to pay off what was due over the past several years. You may not know it, but if I hadn't gained control of the property, you'd be facing foreclosure by early next year. So," he said suavely, "you have every reason to thank me."

Sharlotte leaped to her feet. "Thank you?" Frustration threw her mind into confusion. She'd tell him at once to leave her ancestral house and never come back. Then, dismay struck her and her indignation fled. What if he actually *had* paid the back taxes? Far worse, if he actually held the deed, what could she do about it? How could her father have been so shortsighted as to have done such a thing?

Realizing that he was watching her response, she struggled to gain some measure of control. He had wanted this revenge for a long time, and while she could do nothing except smart with humiliation, he could enjoy his advantage over the Ashfords.

Sharlotte was determined to keep her dignity intact and refuse him the satisfaction of seeing her go to pieces. Nor would she entertain him by begging, if that's what he expected.

His meditative gaze offered no clear suggestion as to his feelings. Just what did he want? Or did he want anything at all? Could it be that he was doing this to receive satisfaction for the selfish way she'd treated him in the past?

Sharlotte readily admitted to herself that she had treated him badly, but some leeway should be given her because she'd been so young. All of nineteen, she no longer considered herself a "girl" but a mature woman. But what Kace thought of her now was unknown, as were his motives. He seemed to want to keep it that way. Not that she blamed him completely.

"You can't be serious, Kace. My father would never turn the deed to this property over to you. The estate belonged to my grandmother on my mother's side. My mother left it to me."

Kace didn't appear surprised by the news. Had he already been told this by her father? He leaned back against the long carved-wood table with matching rose-colored glass lamps on either end.

"While your father told me about that, there's something he never explained to you. Before your mother took that fatal train trip, she agreed to turn over this estate to her dearly beloved husband. Things were arranged and signed before she left."

Sharlotte's heart pounded so hard she could scarcely breathe. It couldn't be, her mind kept repeating, but Kace's unrattled nerve and the confidence with which he spoke were gnawing swiftly away at the foundation of that belief. The unthinkable might just be. If so, there was little she could do to thwart him.

Sharlotte recalled something with a start. "He paid that debt you claim he owes you," she protested. "We had lunch together in New York just in September, and he told me so."

Kace didn't appear concerned about her protest. "Did he? I think he may have told you a lot of things that were far from true. Then again, he may have had this deed in mind and just hadn't explained."

Reality settled like a rock in her stomach: If she ever expected to keep the estate, then somehow she must pay what her father owed Kace. That, of course, was impossible, unless she sold the property, which she wasn't about to do. But it now appeared that she never even had a say in the matter. Something else occurred to her.

"You wouldn't sell the Ashford Estate!" she cried.

"Not unless I must. I can imagine what this place means to you, especially now. But there's oil on that land of mine. It could be worth millions one day. If it's a choice between this farm and oil—well, you get the point."

"I won't give up this house," she stated, more determined than ever. "I don't care what my father did giving you the deed, it belongs to me. And I intend to get it back."

"Your determination is noteworthy, but you'll need more than the sound of bugles to win your cause. You'll need money. A lot of it. But that's not impossible. There may be a way out for both of us. There's something I need to discuss with you, but now is not the time." He looked at his watch. "Why don't we meet after dinner?"

She drew in a breath and said suddenly: "Suppose I buy the deed back from you?"

He watched her alertly. "Where would you get that kind of money?"

She paced, stuffing a strand of hair into place. "I'll think of some way."

She felt his strong fingers close about her wrist, pulling her around to face him. He lifted her left hand, rubbing his thumb over the finger where Clarence's ring had been. "No engagement ring dripping with diamonds from the noble Mr. Fosdick? Now what could have happened to change things?"

She masked her irritation. The skunk...he knew, of course. The loss of money and respectability.

"I'm sure my uncommon trial amuses you, however—"

"'Uncommon' trial? Now, that's a euphemism if I ever heard one. You mean that your empty bank account doesn't appeal to the Fosdicks."

"I suppose it gives you a feeling of superiority to laugh at my misfortune?"

Looking unperturbed, he smiled. "I know this may rankle you, Sharlotte, but I've never felt inferior to you. It was your snooty belief in the Ashfords and Van Dornens that convinced you of your self-importance. Nothing like a stock market crash to put one and all in the same soup line."

"Soup line, indeed. I'll get the money back one day, you'll see."

"I don't doubt it," he said airily. "In fact, that's one of the things I've come here to talk about. I told you I had some good news too, remember? But your plans to *marry* into it will likely fail, now that Burgess Ashford has toppled from his financial pedestal. It's a strange malady that afflicts many of the very rich—once one of their own loses either money or power, the inner circle can no longer acknowledge his worthiness to continue as a member of their class. Case in point? Consider how the gallant, pure-blood aristocrat, Mr. Clarence Fosdick, has responded to your misfortune." He released her hand. "Now that he thinks you've hardly a penny to your name, he's conveniently decided to tour Europe."

How did Kace know about the voyage? It was all Sharlotte could do to remain calm. "Let's not talk about Clarence. Let's talk about *you*, Kace."

There was an ironic gleam in his eyes. "My, how you've changed. It couldn't be because I hold the deed to this property? You are much too sincere for that."

Sharlotte turned her head, her lashes narrowing. So that's what he thought of her. She walked away, folding her arms.

"Forget a loan from dear Clarence, if that's what you're thinking. I wouldn't accept it."

She cast him a glance, her brow arched. "I've no intention of borrowing from the Fosdicks or the Van Dornens. As you said, Clarence left for Europe, along with his grandmother, who never approved of me anyway." She paused briefly. "Pamela is with him too."

"So she won."

She was surprised that he understood how Pamela had been trying to win Clarence away from her. He must have noticed Pamela's interest when they were all on Long Island.

"You're better off without him. If he'd had an ounce of fortitude he'd have politely informed his family that he'd already made his choice about the woman he wanted."

"His future political career was at risk," she said wearily. "Can you imagine the headlines should my father be arrested for—" she couldn't bring herself to speak the unthinkable.

"Yes, I can imagine them. So you've no scheme to get Clarence back?"

His tone was casual enough, nor did she have any reason to think he wanted to know her plans about Clarence because of his personal interest.

Miserably, Sharlotte sank down onto the chair again. "No. I've no further plans, or 'schemes' as you so honorably put it. All I want is to get this horrid matter of Mr. Hunnewell behind me and manage to put my life together again. That's why I must keep this house." She stood and walked toward him.

"As I said, there may be a way out." He met her halfway, looking down musingly.

She looked at him hopefully. Thinking he meant her ability to raise the sum, she admitted: "I do have some money…it might be enough to buy back the deed."

He watched her with curious interest. "Oh? If not Clarence, then whom? Don't place any hopes in your great-uncle. He'll turn you down too, would be my guess."

She remembered the last time he'd come to the New York house and the argument that had ensued between him and her father, resulting in his heart attack.

"No, he's another Uncle Scrooge. He even has the white hair and whiskers," she said glumly.

"Yes, he's a scoundrel all right. Equal to your father. Are all the Ashford men so selfish and shrewd?"

"And who are you to call the kettle black? You're willing to take my house!"

"You're better off in Texas at the ranch anyway. After the recent attack by the hobo, you need someone to watch out for you and Amanda. As for this house, I won't sell it unless I must, to pay off your father's debt."

"I won't hear it—I said I'd pay you for the deed, and I will. You can trust me."

Kace smiled. "With what?"

She was surprised. What had he meant by that? And why did she think he wasn't thinking money when he said it?

"All right, tell me about this sudden windfall of cash you've collected." He shoved his hands in his pockets.

She wrung her hands. "Not exactly cash."

The corner of his mouth curved down. "That's what I thought. You're stalling for time. The best thing you can do is pack your trunk."

"Wait—Kace, I'm not trying to deceive you. I have my mother's and grandmother's jewels."

He paused and studied her thoughtfully. "Ah, so you heeded my warning and hid them from your father in time? You have me to thank for that."

"*And*, for *stealing* my house and probably *kidnapping* my poor father to browbeat him into signing over the deed!"

He laughed. "You are never more amusing than when you come up with these fantastic defenses. Kidnap! Steal! Ah, well, it's Christmas, and I'm in a fairly generous mood...so let's see your jewels. Just remember, I don't want to give you false expectations. I may decide the goods aren't worth the sentimental value you place on them. I've no interest in baubles and bangles. Neither does the bank."

"Baubles, ho," she countered. "Why some of the pieces are worth this house and much more."

"I doubt that. You have a tendency to exaggerate. Let's see your stash."

"I have a pendant from Great-Grandmother Charlotte Chattaine in Paris."

He gave her a pensive look. "My, you didn't tell me you had French blood in you. Did you say Chattaine?"

"Yes, why?" she asked, noting his thoughtfulness.

"My father knew—" he stopped. "Oh well, it doesn't matter...I thought you were straight New England tonic, an icy blue blood. Let's have a look at Grandmother Chattaine's pendant and whatever else you're willing to put up."

Sharlotte walked to the window and drew aside the drapery to look out. The day was gray and overcast now, with deepening shadows towards the trees.

"We'll need to go for a walk," she said evasively.

"A curious invitation. Looks like snow by nightfall, but if that doesn't bother you, it doesn't trouble me. Do you have a coat and gloves?"

"Yes. Give me a few minutes, then I'll meet you downstairs."

He watched her with a smile as she hurried from the room.

Once in her bedroom she put on her riding clothes and boots, added a hat, caught up a pair of gloves, and went downstairs.

Kace was waiting for her on the front porch with jacket and hat.

"We'll need a shovel from the garden shed," she said, and marched down the steps and around the side of the house. The snow crunched under her boots. She removed the shovel and handed it to him with a smile.

Kace gave a sound between a laugh and a groan. "Sharlotte, you didn't."

She flushed at his amusement. "Didn't…what?" she said defensively, but knew what he meant.

"Bury it. You didn't bury your jewel box in the woods?"

"And it was a good thing I did too. In case you've forgotten, Mr. Landry, a hobo attacked me. He came right up to the back porch the night before and stole Finney's work jacket and cap. What if he'd come into the house at night? No one may have heard him until it was too late. He might have stolen the jewels and murdered us all."

Kace winced. "All right. I get the picture. But buried treasure…" he laughed again, leaning on the shovel. "You win. Direct the way to the pirate's loot, my captain."

"As for *thieves*," she said meaningfully, walking along, "the worst kind do their stealing lawfully."

"If that's intended for me, I'll have you know I've never stolen a dime in my life. That streak runs in your family, not mine. And the biggest crooks are in the banks."

She quickened her pace to walk in front of him.

"I hope you remember where you buried your goods," he said.

"Of course I remember. It will take us a few minutes to get there."

"Why so far? Once you buried it, it was safe. In fact, there were plenty of ingenious places inside the house to hide it. I think you'd be a good deal warmer if you had."

"This way," she ordered. "And I really don't need your advice."

"That's where you're wrong."

She ignored him. "I've wondered about your mother," she said unexpectedly. "What was her name and where did she come from?"

"You're sure this is the right direction?"

"Positive. What's the matter, can't take the snow? You prefer dust and heat?" she laughed shortly.

He laughed with her. "After the heat of the oil field, this feels like a deep freeze. All the more reason to sell the place. The heat will do you good. Melt some of that frosty blue blood."

"I'm never going back to Texas," she scoffed. A moment later, "You didn't answer my question about your mother," she said casually.

"I don't remember her. Her name was Ann. She was French...a Chattaine, actually."

Sharlotte stopped, turned and looked at him in amazement. Yes, she thought, taking in the dark hair, the earthy good looks..."You never told me."

"Would it have made a difference?"

She flushed, turned, and trudged on through the trees and over the snow. "Yes, to my father," she said quietly.

Kace made no response.

Now and then she would stop and look in all directions, then walk on, avoiding his gaze.

"You're lost," he said. "Didn't you even draw your pirate's map?"

"Oh, do hush. The snow makes the trees look—well, different."

"Yes, it would," he said dryly. "Just where did you bury it?"

"Under a tree."

"There are many trees in the woods, my sweet. Did you think to mark it?"

"This tree was different. It was crooked," she said, biting her lip and looking about her.

"A crooked tree," he repeated smoothly. "That helps a great deal."

She stopped and turned to face him, near tears. "Yes, a crooked tree. Anything wrong with a crooked tree?"

Kace wore a faint smile as he tossed the shovel down. "Not a thing. Except there's about fifty crooked trees." He leaned back against a pine, hands in his jacket pockets, watching her with restrained amusement. "I hate to discourage you, but I've a suspicion you won't find your uniquely crooked tree with its buried treasure, so we might as well go back. You'll need to come up with the money some other way. I told you, I have some information worth listening to. Even when spring comes, it will be difficult to find your hiding place. You have my profound sympathy—"

She sent a splat of snow against his chest, turned and marched on. "I've got to find it. I will! My mother's and grandmother's heirlooms—" she rushed ahead, but the snow was deeper and she stumbled. She picked herself up and ran ahead to a crooked pine tree. "Over here, Kace, hurry. This is it. You see? I told you I'd find it."

Kace straightened, then slowly picked up the shovel and followed.

She pointed to the ground beneath the trunk. "There."

He cleared the snow until he came to the dirt, then dug for several minutes until he stopped and looked at her, one hand on his hip.

She peered into the empty hole. "But it's got to be here—somewhere." She avoided his gaze, and drew in a breath. "Very well, we'll start over."

"Now wait a minute—"

She pointed back toward the house. "I…think…yes, that's it, I should have turned right instead of left at the holly bushes."

The afternoon slipped away while Sharlotte grew more and more desperate. Oh, what a fool she'd been to not draw a precise map, but at the time it had appeared so obvious.

After numerous trees, Kace said: "All this digging has accomplished nothing except increased my appetite. It's Christmas Eve. I think I've earned my turkey leg and plum pudding."

Sharlotte was sitting on a tree stump, frustrated and in tears. "We're not having turkey. It's too expensive."

"Whatever it is, I won't complain. Just as long you don't feed me frog legs. I hear folks from Vermont love them."

She looked at him. "Where did you hear that?"

"Now, a little rattlesnake meat, that's all right. Come along, Sharlotte, game's over." He reached for her hand. "Up."

She stood. "Kace, it's here, I tell you. You've got to believe me."

"I do believe you. But finding your jewels will need to wait until you remember where you stashed them. You can't expect me to scour the woods digging under every tree. Looks as though you hid them so well, not even you can find them now."

The thought was horrifying, and as though he'd realized her anguish, he added more gently: "In the spring, honey, when the snows melt, you're likely to locate it."

She couldn't wait that long and he knew it. She'd return tomorrow and search again.

21

Sharlotte paced her bedroom floor. *So Kace hasn't come here because he was concerned about what happened to me, but to claim his property! And that teasing amusement in his smile tells me he's enjoying this tremendously.*

The jewels were lost. Impossible! Impossible! She fell hopelessly across her bed. She must keep searching for the metal box with her jewels. Kace was right, why hadn't she drawn a map? It was the snow. The blanket of white made everything appear all the same. She wished ardently that it was summer again, but when she got up from the bed to peer out, it was snowing, sending a fresh covering of white across the woods.

Sharlotte eventually calmed enough to bathe and dress for Christmas Eve dinner, and because Kace was there, she dressed up, choosing a shimmering violet-blue gown that matched her eyes.

This year, Sharlotte had considered lighting candles and reading the Christmas story from the Gospel of Luke. After the disappointing afternoon and the incident with Kace, she wondered if she should. She had behaved badly. She feared that reading from her mother's Bible now might make Kace think her hypocritical. If only she could be sweet-tempered and kind like Elly!

Sharlotte came downstairs, hiding her dreary mood for Amanda's sake.

Finney had made a special dinner of fried chicken, mashed potatoes, gravy, and greens. A sweet potato pie finished the meal, sprinkled with nutmeg and sweet cream from Lady Bertha, Finney's favorite cow. Afterward they enjoyed fresh eggnog, coffee, and minted tea. Kace complimented Finney's cooking: "If you grow tired of the snow, Finney, you can come to Texas and work for me. I'll soon have a house on my land, and after working in oil from sunup to sunset, we could use someone like you."

"Why, thank you, Mr. Landry. I'll remember that."

Sharlotte was about to say that Kace wasn't allowed to steal her loyal jack-of-all-trades, but then she remembered that Kace would be selling the estate if she didn't come up with the money. Offering Finney a job in Texas could turn out to be a goodwill gesture.

Sharlotte served the cookies she had baked on her own the day before when the outlook had been brighter.

"I didn't know you could bake cookies," Kace told her innocently.

"Of course I can bake," she clipped.

"Amazing."

Amanda glanced up sharply from her glass of eggnog and looked inquiringly from Sharlotte's face to Kace's. Her brows drew together in a puzzled frown and she hastened: "Sharlotte, isn't it time we enjoyed the Christmas tree and sang the carols you planned?"

The Christmas tree stood in the middle of the room, six feet tall, and the fragrance of pine pleasantly filled the air. Sharlotte went to the piano and sat down. She and Amanda had once discussed selling the piano, and she was now glad they'd delayed the decision. Her fingers moved easily across the keys and the words to Charles Wesley's, "Hark the Herald Angels Sing" filled the room with peaceful relief:

Christ, by highest heav'n adored;
Christ, the everlasting Lord;

Late in time behold Him come,
Offspring of the virgin's womb.

Veil'd in flesh the Godhead see;
Hail th'incarnate Deity!

Pleased as man with men to dwell:
Jesus, our Emmanuel!

Hark! the herald angels sing,
Glory to the newborn King.

She followed with all the traditional carols, ending in a duet of the "Coventry Carol" with Amanda. Their sweet voices sang out softly:

Lully, lulla,
Thou little tiny child,
By by, lully lullay.

O sisters too,
How may we do
For to preserve this day
This poor youngling
For whom we do sing,
By by, lully lullay?

Herod, the king,
In his raging,
Charged he hath this day
His men of might,
In his own sight,
All young children to slay.

That woe is me,
Poor child for thee!
And ever morn and day,
For thy parting
Neither say nor sing
By by, lully lullay!

How long the journey until a rainbow lightened the stormy sky with hope? she wondered. Was Christ Himself the hope?

The rest of the evening was pleasant. When it was time to retire, Kace carried Amanda up to her room and sat her on the side of the bed. "You sang beautifully tonight," he told her.

Sharlotte was just entering the room as Kace came out. He said quietly, his gaze, serious: "I need to discuss something with you alone in the library. I've news about your father."

At once, her heart began to pound. "I'll be down in fifteen minutes."

She wondered why he was just now mentioning it. After he went downstairs, Sharlotte, uneasy, entered Amanda's room. She put on a brave smile, walked over, and kissed her good night. "Merry Christmas, Sis."

"Yes, Merry Christmas." Amanda squeezed her hand reassuringly, and her thin face grew sober. "Don't be angry at Kace."

Sharlotte laughed a little. "What makes you think I am?"

"It was pretty obvious at dinner. I suppose it's his praise of Elly that's troubling you."

Sharlotte hoped her face was blank. "I've nothing against Elly. It's just that Kace is always touting her character. It makes the rest of us seem a little inadequate. You'd think she was a saint."

Amanda frowned. "Yes, I'm surprised he's saying all these things. It's not like the Kace I remember. Even when he had it bad for you, he was sparse with his compliments. The strong, silent type, if you know what I mean."

Sharlotte knew exactly. She might have told her about Kace's real reason for coming, to claim ownership of the house and property, but she couldn't bring herself to end Christmas Eve on a glum note that might make her ailing sister worry all night.

"Looks as if he dotes on her all right." Amanda shook her head. "Well…you must admit Elly is a wonderfully sweet girl."

"Don't you start in too," Sharlotte said wearily. "Better get some sleep. Good night, Amanda."

"Oh…I almost forgot." She lifted her pillow and pulled out their mother's Bible.

"I was wondering where it was," Sharlotte said. "I looked for it earlier to read the Christmas story."

"Oh dear, did you? I hope I didn't ruin your plans."

"No," Sharlotte sighed. "I probably wouldn't have had the courage with Kace looking on. He still thinks I'm spoiled, you know. A princess, and all that. Elly could have read it, but I'm afraid he'd scorn me if I tried."

"I'm not sure…he seemed rather impressed when we were singing the carols you chose. He watched you. Anyway, you can read it to me," Amanda said, handing her the Bible. "We're both on the same footing—sinners."

Sharlotte smiled. "Do you really want me to?"

"Yes, what better way to end Christmas Eve?"

Sharlotte drew up a chair and searched laboriously until she finally found the second chapter of the book of Luke.

"Uncle Sherman always prayed first before reading," Amanda said. "Shall we?"

Sharlotte shifted uneasily. "Aloud?"

"That's what he does."

"I know, but…um…you do it, Sis."

"Well, all right," she said doubtfully, and glanced toward the open bedroom door as if afraid someone would hear her feeble attempt. "I'll try." Amanda bowed her head and cleared her throat. "God, help us to understand Your word. Amen."

It wasn't much of a prayer in comparison to Sharlotte's memory of Uncle Sherman's, which sounded as though God were his Father, and that he'd just left His presence, but Sharlotte couldn't have done much better.

She read the passage slowly and deliberately, trying to use drama in her voice for the various parts about Mary, Joseph, and the angels. Amanda listened attentively, munching on some cookies she had smuggled up. Sharlotte concluded:

"And, lo, the angel of the Lord came upon them, and the glory of the Lord shone round about them: and they were sore afraid. And the angel said unto them, Fear not: for, behold, I bring you good tidings of great joy, which shall be to all people. For unto you is born this day in the city of David a Savior, which is Christ the Lord. And this shall be a sign unto you; Ye shall find the babe wrapped in swaddling clothes, lying in a manger. And suddenly there was with the angel a multitude of the heavenly host praising God, and saying, Glory to God in the highest, and on earth peace, good will toward men."

Sharlotte stopped and closed the Bible, and peaceful silence wrapped about them like a warm, cozy quilt while the snow flitted against the outside windowpane. She looked at Amanda. "Good news for *all* people. A Savior."

Amanda grinned. "And not just for sweet-tempered people like Elly, but for you and me." She sighed. "I wish George could have heard this story before he was killed." She looked off toward the window where the snow danced gently, silently.

Sharlotte too was silent. The night was still. They sat together, yet they were separate in their own thoughts, desires, and broken dreams. Eventually, Sharlotte set the Bible on the little table by the bed and stood.

"Mother's Bible belongs to both of us. I'll leave it here. Good night, Amanda."

Sharlotte went quietly away, closing the door.

Outside in the hall she paused, her mind fluctuating between spiritual thoughts and material problems, and she wished ardently she could somehow merge them into one. Yet to her they appeared worlds apart. Was God involved in everyday life?

She walked down the hall to the stairway. She thought of Kace again, and her new problem about keeping the house came swirling in. What did he know about her father? She peered over the banister to see if he waited and saw that a light burned in the library. He stood in the doorway, a dark silhouette. She came down slowly.

Kace had intimated there was much more to discuss than the ownership of the house and property. What other shocking tidbits of news did he have? Did she even want to know?

Her heartbeat increased as she went down to join him.

≈

It was after ten o'clock, and hot coals were glowing in the hearth. A pink-shaded lamp cast a warm radiance in one corner of the room. Heavy brocade draperies were drawn open at the rectangular windows, revealing the flittering snowflakes peeping shyly in from the darkness outside.

The room was warm, and Kace had removed his jacket and loosened the collar of his white shirt. He shut the door quietly and turned toward her, all lightheartedness gone.

He drew out a tapestry-upholstered chair. "Better sit down."

Oh no. Whenever he told her she'd better sit down there was trouble enough to convince him she might faint.

Her eyes searched his for some sign of woe to come, but they were now deliberately veiled. She sat, her hands tightening around the arm rests.

"You know where my father is, don't you," she declared.

Kace's voice was level, but his eyes were thoughtful. "Yes."

She started to rise, but he laid a hand on her shoulder. She stiffened her spine, determined to stay calm no matter what the news.

"Something is wrong," she whispered.

"Depends on the outcome. Considering the quicksand he led us both into, matters could be worse."

She could have protested and rushed to her father's defense, but to do so seemed ludicrous after all that had recently happened.

"I'm listening. Please go on."

"Are you aware that he came to Texas to contact me about the property I bought a few years ago?"

"Yes, Inspector Browden told me. I thought it odd he'd seek you out, considering."

"Not so odd. Your father and I had a long discussion."

She wanted to squirm. "Yes?" she asked uneasily, "about what?"

"A lot of things, including the crash on Wall Street and what it meant to him and everyone else in the country. But we'll get to that part later. He wanted to hire me to get him safely across the border into Mexico. In return, he promised to eliminate the debt on the oil land. Considering the financial jam I'm in with the bank ready to foreclose, I took a second risk and decided to accept his offer."

Her lips parted with surprise. "He's in Mexico?" she whispered. "You brought him there?"

Kace went on speaking in his even voice. "I got him safely across the border to a little village where he has a rancho."

This was the first she'd heard of her father owning property inside Mexico! Why had he never mentioned it?

Kace read her expression. "I take it you didn't know about the rancho?"

"No. Is it large?" she asked hopefully.

Kace smiled. "Nice size, about half as large as the Landry ranch. But you wouldn't stay there long. The weather is the same as Texas."

Her interest melted. She picked up on something else he'd said: "What do you mean you took a 'second' risk on my father?"

"Isn't it obvious? If I hadn't trusted him the first time I wouldn't be up to my ears in debt."

"But you did help him get to Mexico. I suppose I should be grateful for that."

"Don't get any wrong ideas about why I agreed to get him across the border. It wasn't done out of sentimentality toward your father, or you, for that matter."

Why did he think she might think so?

"Bringing him secretly to the rancho was no guarantee I wouldn't turn him into the Texas Rangers once our financial deal was transacted fair and square. I told him that, and he agreed."

"What new financial 'deal' did you make with him?" she asked stiffly. "You're not saying he's going to give you more money? I have always doubted this 'debt' you keep harping on. What if I told you I think this debt is the result of your camaraderie with untrustworthy oil friends?"

"Those so-called 'untrustworthy' oil friends are no match for crooked Wall Street tycoons," he drawled smoothly. "As for your analysis, it's way out in left field. The truth is, he owes me. He knows it, and we came to a bargain. The snag develops where you're concerned."

She resented the idea that he thought of her as a snag.

"For the plan to work out successfully, you must be involved. That's the part I balked at, but in the end I had no choice."

She looked at him, confused. "What about me? Surely you don't need me to sign anything over to you concerning this property? You said he had already given you the deed."

"It doesn't concern this house. As I told you earlier, what I could get for this place, if I sold it, is a small portion of what I owe the bank."

She jumped to her feet, insulted. "Small portion? This house, this property?"

"I realize you're sentimental about an old country estate that belonged to some saintly Ashford, but it doesn't come close to paying the debt I owe the bank for Texas oil land. It will help, of course."

Her face fell. "Then you were serious upstairs when you said you'd sell?"

He watched her. "If I must, yes."

"You scoundrel!"

"Anything else?"

"Yes!"

He winced. "Sharlotte, I'm quite willing to help you if I can—"

"Oh really?"

"And I already mentioned there may be a way, but you'll need to cooperate."

She picked up the needlework pillow from the chair and threw it harmlessly. "Help me? Why, you're the nasty culprit trying to steal the roof over our heads!"

"Come now, let's not resort to exaggerated dramatics. If I need to sell you won't be without a roof. As I said earlier, Livia wants you both on the ranch. So does Sherman."

She paced, frustrated. "I won't go. I don't like Texas," she said flatly.

"You've made that quite plain in the past. In the end, it may not matter what you like, but what's feasible, what works. 'Them's the times,' as they say."

"Heat, dust, flies—" she turned to face him.

His laughter cut her off. "It will do you good. Take some of the spoiled immaturity out of your system and tame your runaway conceit."

"I am not conceited, nor immature, and I will never go to Texas."

"Never say never. Would you be willing to go to Texas for a bag full of gold?"

She stared at him, wondering if he were jesting or if there might be some morsel of truth in his words.

His smile was sardonic. "I thought that would put some color back in your cheeks."

"Gold? A bag full?"

"Isn't it surprising how heat, dust, and flies no longer matter when the rich glitter of gold shines on the Texas horizon?"

She walked toward him. "What do you mean, gold?"

"Ah, yes, gold. Ashford gold, no less. All legal—I hope."

Ashford gold…all legal. Her heart leaped, and all her objections evaporated. Gold, to pay off debts. Gold, to secure this house from Kace. Gold, to send Amanda to the best doctors. Gold, to—

Kace smiled, his gray-green eyes flickering. "Now, are you ready to listen?"

Her answer, of course, was yes.

22

*G*old, Sharlotte thought, dreaming of all she could recover if she had a bagful.

Kace watched her, and her violet-blue eyes must have shone, for his dark lashes narrowed. "What a man might give to have you look at him like that."

"Hmm?" she murmured absently.

"Gold," he said sardonically, and jamming his hands into his pockets, he walked to the fireplace and leaned his shoulder there. "If your father isn't exaggerating, or outright lying, there's enough in gold to solve both of our financial woes. Are you interested in cooperating with me, or need I ask?"

Sharlotte smiled sweetly. "You need not ask, my dear Kace." She picked up the little pillow and walked up to him. "I'm all ears. Are you going to explain the details, or must I burst?"

He smiled, scanning her. "Suddenly sweet Sharlotte. All right, you'll need to come to the Landry ranch. From there we'll ride into Mexico to the rancho."

"Why Texas? Why not just go straight to the rancho from here?"

"Because it's far easier to cross the border from the El Paso area."

"You mean my father has gold at the rancho?" she breathed.

He glanced at her. "Not exactly on the rancho," and when she looked at him bewildered, he added easily: "Don't worry. I'll find it."

"Find it. You mean you don't know where it is?" she inquired anxiously.

"We'll discuss that later," he said airily. "The truth is, I told you the news wasn't all bad, remember? When your father realized he was about to lose his fortune, he had Hunnewell buy gold in London when England went off the gold standard. Burgess knew that London was the financial capital of the world, and that Great Britain was in big trouble. Its stock market crashed before ours, in January of this year. British banks were reeling from losses on bad loans. And Britain was loaded with U.S. stocks. It was clear to your father that they would begin selling everything at once, toppling the market. Naturally, he didn't expect Black Tuesday, but he did expect a sell-off, and that's why he had Hunnewell turn some of his cash into gold."

"Hunnewell?" the idea surprised her.

"Yes, it was Hunnewell who arranged contacts in London, who had it shipped out of Europe into Cuba and then to Mexico. It's not a millionaire's fortune, but it will be enough to allow you and your sister to sit pretty—at least until you can land a rich husband. Who knows? You may be able to lure Clarence back with it."

She could ignore Kace's sarcasm now that her mind was happily on the bonanza that had unexpectedly tumbled into her lap.

"I suppose it's in a Mexican bank?" she said anxiously, hoping it was safely guarded.

"That's the most feasible place to keep it, but with your father, things are never that simple," he said dryly. "That's part of the problem we'll have. He didn't tell me where he had Hunnewell stash it. You can be sure it's in a safe place. Some out-of-the-way spot. I've always thought that piracy ran in the Ashford blood."

She bristled like a porcupine. "I resent that, Kace. *Your* father, I understand, was a scoundrel, an adventurer—"

He laughed. "I won't argue that."

"But my father *must* know where the gold is. He'll tell me when we get there."

"That was the idea, yes, if things in Mexico go as planned. I've an idea where it might be, and I'll keep that to myself for now. But there is one small glitch to this sudden boon: you and I need to come to a bargain about more than this Vermont property."

She folded her arms suspiciously. So…"You're not audacious enough to suggest that you should have a cut in the gold?"

He too folded his arms and looked at her musingly. "Without me, my Sweet, there won't be any gold for anyone. You need me. Desperately."

She smiled whimsically and scanned him. "Do I?"

He smiled. "Yes. It's just a matter of when, and on what terms, you awaken to that reality."

"Perhaps I can locate the gold myself," she challenged.

He laughed shortly. "Greedy, aren't you? I can see it now." He glanced at her fragile gown. "You wouldn't last a day roaming about on your own in silk and ribbons."

Silk and ribbons! As if she didn't know how to take care of herself in the Texas wilderness.

"I'll buy boots and a six-gallon hat if necessary. I'll even hire someone to go with me and protect me."

"You just did. Me, whether you like the idea or not. Your father insisted. You wouldn't disappoint him, would you? Just keep it in mind that part of that gold belongs to me. And I aim to get it, with or without your approval. However, if you cooperate like a good girl, we'll be able to get this done quickly and successfully. Then you can leave Texas for good. It'll be, 'adios, señorita.'"

She glared, but the finality in his voice troubled her more than she cared to show.

"Well, do we have a bargain?" he asked after a moment of silence.

She turned and walked to the other side of the library, still holding the pillow. "Yes. We have a bargain."

"So I thought. Once we bring Amanda to the ranch, you'll need to travel roughly for a few days on horseback. You won't back out halfway across the border when things get a little uncomfortable for your spoiled tastes, will you?"

"Absolutely not. You underestimate me."

"All right, we have a bargain." He straightened from the mantle and walked over to her. "Now, better sit down. I have one last thing to tell you. Unfortunately, it's dark news."

He pulled out a chair and gave her a level look.

She tore her gaze from his challenge and sat down obediently. She thought she knew what was coming, and she braced herself for the onslaught. He knew that Inspector Browden believed her father guilty of Hunnewell's death. Had he arrested him after all? Her palms felt damp.

"So you've spoken to Inspector Browden," he said.

"Yes. What is it, Kace?" she urged.

"Did I mention upstairs that I've an appointment with him on Monday?"

Sharlotte showed her alarm. "You? But won't he hold you on charges?"

"No. As a matter of fact, I've been cooperating with him all along, even on Long Island. I told him everything from the beginning, including my suspicions of your father. He thought I might learn something more by keeping silent. You see, we weren't sure how much you knew. You might have been keeping important information back, so he wanted me to try to find out."

She sucked in her breath and stood. "You mean you *used* me deliberately to try and gain information?"

Kace looked at her lazily. "Yes, something like that. You didn't think I was going to keep back information from the police for the benefit of the Ashford name, did you? I notified him as soon as I found Hunnewell."

She was hurt and miffed. "Is that why you questioned me so much at the boathouse?"

His gaze refused to yield to her accusing stare. "Yes."

"Then I wasn't far wrong when calling you 'Inspector,'" she said coolly.

"Come, Sharlotte, I never suspected you had anything to do with it."

"What then?"

"I think you know," he said quietly. "We wondered if you might have seen your father and Hunnewell together and were concealing the fact to protect him. Don't worry," he said. "None of this will interfere with our plans for Mexico. My meeting with Inspector Browden concerns Burgess. Did Browden mention that your father was embezzling funds from his bank?"

The warmth of humiliation pinked her cheeks. "You need not repeat any of that, Kace. It was sufficient to hear it the first time—if it's true. The inspector could be wrong."

"He's not wrong, Sharlotte. Not about embezzlement charges, and certainly not about Hunnewell's death. Burgess is guilty of both."

She turned her back, horrified. "I don't want to hear—"

"I know that, and I'd rather not discuss it either. But it's best if we do. It will help you understand why matters have ended as they have in Mexico."

Ended? She turned slowly, a horrid premonition rising in her chest. "He's been arrested?" she asked in a small voice.

"He was always a gambler," Kace said tonelessly. "He thought he could make a mint in the market. All he needed to do was play it right. If he did, he'd be able to pay off his margins, plus make up for some big losses of the past few years. Things weren't so simple, though. They never are. The market took a bad tumble several times this year. Each time it went down, he received new margin calls from his broker. Each time his stocks were sold at large losses, leaving him in appalling debt. He soon grew desperate. He dipped into bank funds, and Hunnewell found out. Some of that money your father used belonged to Hunnewell himself. He came to confront your father on Long Island."

"Hunnewell's money?" she gasped. "He knew at Long Island? Then that must be the reason he was upset at the picnic."

"What made you think he was upset?"

"He seemed agitated. At first I thought it was because of the argument between Clarence and Stuart. Even Bitsy and Sheldon mentioned it. They were all there, discussing the possibility of you and Uncle Sherman becoming millionaires in oil."

Kace smiled. "I was suddenly acceptable."

"I think...yes, there may have been something in Hunnewell's hand. Something that looked like a piece of stationery. The reason I remember is because of the way he'd been clutching his briefcase, using both hands. He'd done so ever since he'd arrived. He wouldn't let it go. Sheldon even made a joke about it, saying he must have his life preserver inside. But he did let go of the case—because he had that piece of paper in one hand and the briefcase under his arm. I just happened to notice." She looked at Kace despairingly. She wondered that there was no surprise on his face. "Did the police ever find the briefcase?"

"No." Kace moved about the room, musing. "You were right about his being agitated. He'd just received a message to meet your father at the gatekeeper's cottage."

"How? I'd have seen if someone entered the front door and delivered a message to him. No one came. And the phone didn't ring. Nor did Hunnewell make any phone calls."

"There's a backdoor to the club, isn't there?"

"Well, yes—but how do you know Hunnewell received a message?"

"It was something Stuart said about a boy on the jetty."

She recalled that Stuart had mentioned the boy to her that same afternoon.

"The boy was sent to the backdoor to deliver an envelope to Hunnewell. The message? To meet your father at the gatekeeper's cottage instead of the picnic. Hunnewell may have been smart as a lawyer, but he was naïve about the depth to which his client would go to protect himself from arrest. He went to keep that appointment."

Sharlotte closed her eyes.

"But how did you know the boy delivered a message at the backdoor to Hunnewell?" she persisted a few moments later.

"Again, it was Stuart."

"But Stuart couldn't say just why something about the boy made him curious."

"No, but he told me the boy was playing with a paper airplane on the jetty. Stuart complimented him, and the boy showed it to him. It was made from an envelope from your father's desk, with your father's name printed in gold. It was the gold print that had caused the boy to keep it."

Sharlotte sighed.

"So I used George's roadster to visit the stable. As soon as the boy's father told me someone anonymously left a sealed envelope for his boy to bring to Hunnewell, I knew it must have been Burgess. Hunnewell removed the message and tossed the envelope on the back veranda of the clubhouse. The boy picked it up."

Yes, she could see it all…

"Your father arrived at the gatekeeper's cottage, and Hunnewell produced his evidence in the briefcase he had been clutching. As I said, your father had not only embezzled bank funds, but he'd dipped into Hunnewell's own account as well. Evidently that was the last straw for Hunnewell. They argued. Burgess, desperate, promised to pay Hunnewell back. He tried to get Hunnewell to juggle the papers and give him more time. If I recall, the market was rising during that period, and he thought he could make things right if he had more time. He may have also mentioned the gold in Mexico, but Hunnewell already knew about that, having arranged for its shipping to the rancho. He may have stored it away for your father in an unlikely place. If you look a little deeper into Hunnewell's past you'll find out he was tainted too. He was afraid of getting his hands sticky with your father's embezzlement charges, so he refused to cooperate. He snatched his briefcase, and turned to leave. Burgess was panicky. He grabbed him. They had a tussle—Burgess picked up the candlestick holder on the mantle and struck in rage."

Sharlotte stood shakily, unable to speak. No, her mind wanted to scream.

He looked at her a long moment. "I'm sorry."

She held her head in her hands. "How can you be so sure?"

Kace went on in a quiet, unemotional voice as though he didn't hear her: "Now he had to get rid of the body. There could be no accidental death if Hunnewell was left sprawled on the cottage floor. Burgess remembered the recent complaint of the handyman about the rotting jetty at the old boathouse. It was worth a chance—so he managed to bring Hunnewell there and drop his body into the water. Hunnewell may actually have drowned at this time if he was only unconscious, which could explain Dr. Lester's diagnosis. Afterward Burgess broke the step and rail to make it appear as though he'd fallen. Then he went back to the gatekeeper's cottage, retrieved the briefcase, and returned to the house unseen. After cleaning up, he had his chauffeur drive him down to the clubhouse. That's when he met you on the road."

She remembered her father's appearance and the bruise on his hand. "No," she whispered, grieved, sinking to the chair again. "He hadn't cleaned himself up very well. His—his watch was broken— and a button was off his jacket. He gave the gold watch to the chauffeur and joked about his selling it and investing the money in the market." Her head dropped into her palms.

Although Inspector Browden had already informed her that her father had probably killed Hunnewell, Kace's stark explanation of what may have happened was brought home to her with nauseating clarity.

Kace reached down and drew her up into his arms. "It's all over now."

This time his embrace held no challenge. He simply comforted her, stroking her hair. After a moment she raised her head to look at him, her wet eyes like violet-blue jewels, tears on her face. Her palms rested briefly on the lapel of his jacket. His eyes warmed and his hold tightened as his gaze went to her lips. Her heart fluttered. For a moment she expected to feel his kiss, but quite suddenly he released her and stepped back. The depth of her disappointment surprised her. Afraid he knew, she turned away and walked to the window. She stood there, clutching the window sash in her hand.

She watched the snowflakes gently coming down, burying everything in sight. It was the dead of winter. It felt like the winter of her life.

"There's no proof," she whispered again, after a moment of silence. "You—you may even be lying to me about who killed Hunnewell." She turned, staring at him.

He frowned. "What reason would I have to lie to you?"

She swallowed, her fingers tightening on the sash. "I can think of one," she said in a low voice.

"The gold." He gestured airily. "If I had plans to cheat you, Sharlotte, I wouldn't have needed to waste my time jumping trains all the way to Vermont. I could have forced Burgess to talk and stashed the gold some place in Mexico. But I'm not likely to commit murder for money. I'm only a Landry," he said meaningfully.

Her eyes flashed. "*Another* insult to the Ashford name—"

"Yes, where your father's concerned. While he was embezzling funds from his bank he was insisting you were to have nothing to do with the likes of me when you came to spend summers on the ranch. I wasn't good enough for the mighty Ashford name."

She turned away, dismayed, refusing to admit the truth. "I wasn't thinking of the gold when I said you may have murdered Hunnewell."

"Now I am curious."

She turned back slowly, watching him warily. "The glove," she said tonelessly.

Kace grew silent. Except for the rustle of wind outside the window stirring the holly bush, there were no other noticeable sounds. Sharlotte saw with a tightening of her heart that a slight change had come over his face.

"You see, I found a glove in the gatekeeper's cottage, and it wasn't Hunnewell's or my father's—it was yours."

He made no move to deny it or even to show surprise, but his green eyes were fixed on her.

"I still have it. With your initials on it. I could show it to the police. You'd have a great deal of explaining to do."

He observed her for an icy minute. A look of anger tensed his jaw. "If you found it, why didn't you show it to Browden?"

She dare not admit that she had held back because of any attachment to him. "At first I thought it was my father's, so I went back to retrieve it, but when I did, it had your initials on it." The irritation he showed over her assumed doubt interested her. *He does care what I think of him.*

He gave a short, unpleasant laugh. "So you think I murdered Hunnewell, do you?"

She didn't, but she was upset enough with his attitude to refuse to immediately deny it.

"Why not take this scenario a step further?" he said coolly. "I may have eliminated Hunnewell and have been trying to pin it on your father." Kace walked toward her. "I also may have known that you found my glove at the murder scene. And so this tale about gold is a clever plan to lure you away to Mexico and force you to marry me."

Her brow lifted provocatively, and her lips turned into a little smile. "But dear, sweet Elly wouldn't like that."

He cupped her chin and lifted her face toward his. "Oh, I don't know. If I'm the scoundrel you think I am, then it's you and I who deserve each other."

She caught her breath and jerked away. "Of all the nerve—"

He laughed. "Cheer up. I didn't clobber old Hunnewell on the head and dump him in the sea. And I didn't do in your father."

She sobered, as though icy water had splashed her face. That her father had committed that very grotesque thing brought a hideous shudder. She turned away, resting the side of her face against the drapery. "No," she said, her voice scarcely audible. "I know you didn't do it..."

Kace grew still and silent. A moment later he said: "Well. You have my glove."

"Yes. And I have wondered how it got in the gatekeeper's cottage. I remembered that you didn't have any gloves when we walked there. So you must have dropped it earlier..."

"You mean you can't figure out how it got there?"

She had imagined several different ways, but refused to entertain them in her mind. "My father wouldn't have—"

"Ah, so you have thought of it, and you're correct. Because he didn't leave his bedroom in the rainstorm that night only to search for his glove. He already realized he had left it and wanted to replace it with false evidence. He went out by way of the fire escape carrying *my* glove. That he thought about doing so was cunning on his part. Especially if the police had searched the gatekeeper's cottage and found it. Thanks to Dr. Lester's diagnosis, there was a short period of time when the police actually believed Hunnewell's death was an accidental drowning or a suicide."

Yes, she had secretly contemplated whether or not her father might have planted the glove, but the idea had been too ugly to endure for long. Even now, at this late stage, she recoiled. But then she remembered vividly that when she'd been in the cottage someone else was there too, someone who had gone out without seeing her. Still, she didn't want to believe it.

"It's not reasonable, Kace. How could he have gotten hold of it?"

"A simple task, really. My jacket hung in the cloakroom in the hall, with my gloves in the inside pocket."

"But how could he know you wore gloves similar to his?"

"Not similar. Identical."

"That seems farfetched, Kace."

"Not at all. And he also knew my initials were engraved. It's simple really. You see, Aunt Livia ordered gloves for every man in the family last Christmas, including her brother, Burgess. I remember she sent a pair to him, because she was packaging it for the mail. She had a scarf for you and asked me if I thought you'd like the color."

Sharlotte remembered the package, with scarves for her and Amanda, and—a pair of gloves for her father.

"I became suspicious of your father taking my glove because of something Amanda had said. You asked her where your father was. And she said: 'I saw Daddy hanging up his coat.' I knew he couldn't have been hanging up his coat in the hat room when she saw him there, because when he came in a few minutes later to see the inspector, he was still wearing it."

Sharlotte felt ill. She sat down slowly.

"Is that why you went to search his room that night?"

"That was part of the reason. I was aware he'd left by the fire escape because I heard him leave. I searched, hoping to find something that would explain his fear of Hunnewell. If I found my glove, all the better, but he'd already taken it with him to the cottage."

"But if he wanted the police to suspect you, wouldn't he have suggested they search the cottage?"

"His plant was a safeguard should things go wrong for him. His first hope was that the police would think the death was accidental. And they did, even after the inquest. It wasn't until Black

Tuesday and the eventual discovery of his embezzlement that Inspector Browden reopened the case."

"When did you notice your glove was missing?"

"When I took George's roadster to talk to the stable boy at the club. I also went to see your great-uncle. It was he who suggested I warn you to secure your mother's jewelry."

She was surprised. "Why didn't he tell me himself?"

"The personality quirks of your great-uncle belong to your side of the family," he said cheerfully. "I went there hoping to interest him in investing in the oil company, but he balked like a mule. He also reiterated his refusal to involve himself in any of your father's debt."

Sharlotte had no reason to continue her protest. "It's all dreadfully convincing, but how do you know all this in such detail? You speak as though the facts had already been given you."

Kace frowned, as though confronted with an unpleasant task. He reached into his pocket and removed a letter. "You're correct, Sharlotte. Your father wrote this in Mexico. I'll be bringing it to Inspector Browden. It's a confession."

A confession! She stood and looked at him, frightened. "Where's my father now? You said he was in Mexico."

"He is," he admitted quietly. "But I didn't say he was alive. He shot himself after he'd written this letter. I was admiring one of the white palominos on his rancho when I heard the pistol go off. I ran to his office, but he was already dead. He'd left this letter on the table."

She pressed the back of her hand to her mouth. "Oh—" she dropped her head.

Sharlotte could not hold back her tears. He had murdered Mr. Hunnewell, embezzled bank funds, and now he'd taken his own life. What a tragic irony for a family that had set such importance on a bloodline and a position in a society that believed itself the higher class. The family had ostracized Livia for her marriage to

Sherman Landry, and Sharlotte had refused Kace for a man who had a higher calling to fulfill in society. And now!

Kace frowned, passed her his handkerchief, and held her quietly again. He said nothing for several minutes.

When at last she could control her tears, she pulled away to wipe her eyes and blow her nose.

"I'm sorry I had to tell you tonight, but there wasn't much choice. I've got to get back to New York to see Browden by Monday. This letter has to be delivered. But I wanted you to know what happened first, before reading it in the paper next week."

Startled, she looked at him. The thought that she would be left alone to adjust to such dark, depressing news, especially at Christmas, was like being forsaken in the middle of the wilderness.

"Leaving?" she choked.

"Yes, I've got to catch that freight train that comes through at dawn," he stated wryly. "It's a long way to New York, and even longer to Texas."

She said weakly, "You can't mean you're leaving me to get to Texas on my own?"

"Yes," he stated matter-of-factly. "You have money for the train trip, don't you?"

"Well, yes, but—I'll need to tell Amanda the news about our father and arrange for the journey," she said, and it all seemed so horrendous.

"After waving that rifle around this afternoon, I have every confidence that you'll manage." He grinned at her. "In fact, the rifle is again with Finney. I'll meet you at the ranch in, say, six weeks?"

She took his manner for indifference. "I don't think it's very chivalrous of you to abandon me!" she said, annoyed.

"Now, that's a switch. Chivalrous. If I recall correctly, just this evening you've labeled me, among other things, a scoundrel."

"It looks like I was right the first time. All right, go. Catch your old freight train. I'll get along without you just fine."

She rushed toward the door. Kace caught up with her, leaning there before she could open it. He wore a grim smile. "One word of precaution."

"I don't need your advice."

"But I'll give it just the same. Until this matter in Mexico is taken care of, it's best not to mention the gold, or your father owning a rancho there, to anyone. Not even to your sister. It's wiser, and safer, to keep it between us. That goes for those in Texas, as well as your relatives and friends here in the East."

She searched his face, wondering, but found nothing that would explain his caution.

"And...I realize what's happened with your father is a matter of profound grief, but I'd like to leave you with another thought. By confessing, he avoided a drawn out murder trial that would have ended in a guilty verdict and a death sentence. There was no way he could have permanently escaped the authorities, even if he'd stayed in Mexico or went to Cuba. You don't have to wonder about him any longer. It's finally over."

Sharlotte remained silent. Yes...it was over. The wealthy lifestyle, the plans she'd had to continue down that same path. All was over and gone forever. Even gold wouldn't change that, or restore esteem and honor to her family name. Though she suddenly became rich again, she would be shunned by people like the Fosdicks. The short, barren days of winter seemed like her life: frozen, bleak, without the faintest stirring of spring. Not even Kace cared for her any longer.

He watched her. As though convinced she was in control of her emotions once again, he stepped back and opened the library door. "I'll see you in Texas."

She pulled her gaze away and walked across the dimly lighted hall to the staircase. She ascended, her shoulders straight, and didn't look back.

Sharlotte knew when she was beat. Perhaps if she cooperated with Kace now, she would manage to come back to the country estate and find her buried jewelry. She had nothing to gain by opposing him, and perhaps everything to lose.

With that in mind, she explained to Amanda her plans for going to Texas for a few months, leaving out the matter of Mexico as Kace had requested. Surprisingly, Amanda's eyes brightened.

"It will be good to see Aunt Livia and Uncle Sherman again. And Tyler too. I never thought I'd be anxious to go back to the ranch, but time changes everything."

The weeks passed dismally slow. As Sharlotte began to make arrangements for their travel, a letter from Kace arrived in the middle of January. Sharlotte frowned as she read it through.

Amanda, sitting up in bed, must have noticed her disappointment. "What is it? Is it from Daddy?"

Daddy. Sharlotte inwardly recoiled. She still hadn't informed her of his suicide. Now, she must explain, for they would not be going to Texas as soon as she had first thought. She feared that she had already waited too long to explain. Amanda had to know, and Sharlotte could only hope and pray she would be strong enough to accept the new burden. She sighed. "Looks like our trip to Texas has been delayed until June."

"June! But why so long?"

"Kace injured himself drilling for oil. He says they'd built a derrick and were sending 'tempered steel bits corkscrewing hundreds of feet into the earth's crust to tap into pools of oil' when he fell." Sharlotte's fright showed in her voice. What if Kace had been killed in that fall? She had an unexpected desire to grab him and hold tightly.

"Hurt? Badly?" Amanda was pale, and Sharlotte suspected she was thinking of her own fall from the horse and how it had crippled her.

"He insists he's all right, but you know Kace, he wouldn't go into details anyway. He'd suffer in silence." Suddenly she wished she were there, dust, heat, flies and all. "But he's laid up until his leg has healed."

So no trip on horseback into the rugged terrain of Mexico, she thought. *Not for a while. Will this accident change our plans altogether?*

"Well, I hope his hard labor pays off and he hits oil. I can just imagine him showered with all that black goop, can't you?" Amanda grinned.

Sharlotte slowly folded the letter and glanced at her. She dreaded this moment. "Amanda, there's something else I must tell you. Something quite painful. It's about our father…"

⟨⟩

When the snows began to melt in April, Sharlotte began a long and tedious search for the tree with the buried treasure. She even let Amanda and Finney in on the project and Finney, with shovel in hand, aided her in the fruitless search. It appeared as if the tree had gotten up and walked away during the night. The jewelry remained hidden in the darkness of the earth. Perhaps the little chest would never be found until someone in a future generation discovered it while digging to put in a road or build a house.

As the month of May came around, Sharlotte groaned to Amanda: "I just don't understand it. Unless—unless someone saw me hide it? And came for it later?"

"That doesn't seem likely, but it's a possibility."

"In which case I may have come back to the right tree after all, and it just isn't there."

Whatever the reason, she at last accepted defeat. Maybe some other time she could search again, but for now, the shovels must be put away in the shed and their trunks packed for Texas.

June arrived, and with Finney agreeing to stay on and look after things, Sharlotte arranged for her and Amanda's train trip. She wrote letters to Great-Uncle Hubert and her cousin Sheldon, telling them they were going to spend a few months with Aunt Livia and Uncle Sherman. Then, on Monday, June 3, 1930, she and Amanda boarded the train for West Texas.

The night before their departure, Sharlotte had read a verse from the epistle of James, and the words continued to churn in her mind, keeping time with the rush of the wheels on the track—

"Go to now, ye rich men, weep and howl for your miseries that shall come upon you. Your riches are corrupted, and your garments are motheaten. Your gold and silver is cankered; and the rust of them shall be a witness against you, and shall eat your flesh as it were fire. Ye have heaped up treasure together for the last days."

Part Three

West Texas

How much better it is to get wisdom than gold!
And to get understanding is rather to be chosen than silver!

Proverbs 16:16

23

The Ashford girls finally arrived at the Landry ranch after a three-year absence in the blistering heat of summer. The severe drought was turning the stunted leaves a shriveled yellow, and a film of dust painted everything. The wind blew incessantly.

Sharlotte settled into her old bedroom in the comfortable, rambling, double-story ranch house that was full of youthful memories. For several days she struggled to adjust to the climate and what she knew would be a difficult change in culture. Sometimes she wanted to escape.

Outwardly, the ranch had changed little. The hired hands were still riding the range keeping the cattle, but overall there was an uneasy calm, as though everyone knew the good times were ending. An inevitable reckoning was blowing in the wind.

Uncle Sherman was becoming concerned over the condition of the grazing range, and Sharlotte noted weariness in his face. Despite Aunt Livia's suggestion he slow down on his responsibilities, he insisted that he had no choice but find new range areas and attend meetings with the other ranchers to discuss the drought and new expenses for cattle feed.

Sharlotte heard that the cattle ranches and cotton farmers who generally borrowed from the banks each year to meet their ongoing needs were facing bleak times. Banks were closing at an alarming rate. Many of those institutions held mortgages on their lands, and when they shut down they took property and savings accounts with them.

Everyone talked about the heat, drought, dust, and the threat to their cattle or their crops. Hearing all this only made Sharlotte more desperate to make the trip to Mexico to gain control of her father's fortune in gold before it was too late.

Waking up suddenly in the middle of the night and finding herself lying in the house she had once determined she would never come back to, she would listen to the sounds of the wind whipping across the plains and wonder with some amazement how her life could have undergone such a drastic change in so short a time. In just a few months she had lost everything! Her father, Clarence, social prominence, and affluence. Then she would remember the gold waiting in Mexico! Bright, yellow gold would set her free again. She could buy back the deed to the country house in Vermont from Kace, and she and Amanda would return East where they belonged.

When Sharlotte thought back over the last year in New York and Vermont, she found it difficult to clearly recall the details of all that had happened to drastically alter her life. Events, sorrows, and disillusionments were a cloudy mixture of confused memories that were too unpleasant to dwell on or discuss in detail with Aunt Livia and Uncle Sherman, yet too life-changing to totally forget.

Her new life on the ranch was not easy to adjust to, even though she knew what to expect. Though she was familiar with her bedroom from past summers, the polished wood floors, the pine walls and beamed ceiling, the wood furniture, and even the plain blue curtains all seemed heavy and very rugged. There were no frills and lace here, and no pink satin coverlets and soft rugs that graced her bedroom in Vermont. Still the bed was large, like everything else in the ranch house, and the braided rugs, though a utilitarian blue, were very thick and pleasant under her bare feet. And the big wooden dresser held all her odds and ends and dainties with room to spare.

The ranch house and its environment reeked with masculinity, and since there hadn't been any daughters, the male world had conquered and now controlled. And Aunt Livia wouldn't have had it otherwise. She had always managed the big house and tons of cooking with the help of several Mexican women who lived on the ranch with their husbands and children. All events centered around the busy outdoor schedule of the three men in her life to whom Livia dedicated her waking hours: her husband, Sherman, whom she loved more today than she did when she married him, and his two rowdy, good-looking nephews, Kace and Tyler, who were equally dedicated to her well-being. It appeared as if no one would have changed things even if they could have.

When Sharlotte was younger, she'd been so preoccupied with her own schemes and dislike of Texas ranch life that she hadn't noticed the close family or felt the care that each member had for the others. Now, she could see a warmth and harmony of purpose.

Even so, she would have left for Vermont the first chance she could have. And once she had her father's gold from Mexico and the deed to the Vermont house in her hands, she would board the train just as quickly as she and Amanda could pack. The masculine world reminded her of Kace and made her uneasy. Kace would be marrying Elly this year in September, and though he hadn't discussed it recently, she felt she *had* to be gone by then.

Breakfast too was heartier here and noisier than she would have preferred. Although Amanda joined in the talk and laughter and seemed to enjoy it, Sharlotte wasn't accustomed to chattering like a happy bird so early in the morning. She liked her tea in peace and solitude while she slowly awoke to the burdens of a new day. Until she became fully alert, she wanted no demands placed upon her. Least of all did she look forward to sitting across from

Kace at the huge dining room table every morning as the wedding day grew closer. So far, she hadn't needed to worry, because Kace was not at the ranch when she arrived, and Elly was too busy helping at her father's church to come calling to welcome her arrival. Sharlotte found herself hoping that Elly would stay busy. She didn't think she could endure Elly chattering about sewing her wedding trousseau. No one had mentioned Elly yet, not even Aunt Livia.

Sharlotte consoled her injured vanity by telling herself over and over that her circumstances were only temporary. The gold waited. And that gold meant security. Gold meant a new start far from the Texas ranch in the middle of nowhere. Yes, nowhere, to her way of viewing things. There were no street addresses; in fact, there were no streets because there were no neighborhoods. She pictured streets with pavements and sidewalks shadowed by big, shady trees and neat houses, white and clean. Here on the ranch there were shade trees, of course, planted years ago when Aunt Livia and Uncle Sherman first built their home, and Livia had always loved flowers and vines. There were elms, mulberry, oak, native mesquite—lots of mesquite and lots of grazing land—as far as the eye could see, and more flat land beyond that. Land that stretched farther west to El Paso, to the Rio Grande, to the border between Texas and Mexico. But, regardless, this was not Vermont, and Sharlotte believed she could never grow accustomed to Texas or to its very different culture.

The ranch with its numberless acres had plenty of landmarks for identification to those who worked the cattle. But Sharlotte would often get lost trying to find her way around the numerous cattle runs and old Indian trails that led along the Pecos River with cut-offs that wandered aimlessly to certain creeks. The vastness and ruggedness made her uneasy. It either questioned and intimidated her culture with parentlike amusement, or it boasted it would capture her heart at last and mold her into one of its own. At times Texas was like Kace, and she was determined to avoid its mastery.

Although she viewed the ranch land as being in the middle of nowhere, there were other localities. Vermont would have considered these distant enough to be considered part of another state, but here the hamlets or ranches of neighbors were "just over yonder." Unfortunately, "yonder" to Sharlotte was a day's journey on horseback that ended with sore muscles and heat exhaustion.

The localities didn't mean much to her, either. To the east of the ranch there was Big Spring and Abilene, and a little further north, there were names like Jacksboro and the Graham area that was booming in oil.

No sooner did she make up her mind that the ranch was somewhere near Midland, than someone mentioned Odessa, or "as far west as Pecos." She was never quite sure exactly where the Landry land began or ended. It all looked the same to her—a prairie wilderness that, aside from cattle grazing, was good for little except dust devils, jackrabbits, and prairie dogs—that is, until the prospect of oil began to circulate in the talk around the dinner table. Then she began to wonder.

When she had first arrived, Kace was away from the ranch house working on his property. She heard that he had recovered from his fall off the oil derrick and was again working from sunup until past sunset. Sharlotte thought of riding out to his property to see the oil exploration work for herself and to ask about their journey into Mexico, but she had no clear idea where Kace's land was located. One day she casually broached Aunt Livia on the subject without telling her the reasons for her interest.

Aunt Livia bore the Ashford appearance, with hair once as golden as Sharlotte's, but now it was mostly gray. Her pale blue eyes with few lashes reminded Sharlotte of her father, and so did her height. She carried herself well. Most of the time she dressed casually in jeans and plaid shirts and was rarely without a pair of boots. But she always changed into a fashionable dress with jewelry for the evening meal. Sharlotte guessed it to be a holdover from her youth in New York.

"I've never seen a man so sodden with dirt and in need of a good soaking as Kace is when he comes in from working on those oil derricks."

Sharlotte smiled in spite of herself. "Exactly where is his land?"

"Not far. Between Midland and Pecos, near the river. You can't miss it, dear. Maybe twelve miles from here."

Sharlotte laughed. "Between the jackrabbits and the sagebrush?"

"You've got it, dear. Very nice land, very nice indeed. Of course, he's hoping to convince Sherman to explore for oil as well. If the two lands could merge one day, he and Tyler would own a big hunk of Texas when we pass on."

I'll settle for Vermont, Sharlotte thought. *All I need is Daddy's gold.*

Did either Livia or Sherman know that her father had invested in Kace's land? She didn't think so. They hadn't even mentioned her father's awful crime or his suicide. She knew their silence was out of sympathy and kindness. She was impressed by their restraint. Had they been her New York elitist friends, they would have looked down on her.

Twelve miles west of the southern end of the ranch. *Wouldn't Kace be surprised if I managed to ride there on my own? After all the mean things he's said about me being spoiled, this would prove him wrong! It would also show him I'll be no problem riding with him into Mexico. Could that be the real reason for the delay, that he doesn't think I can survive the hardship?*

Sharlotte managed to slip unseen into Uncle Sherman's office where she'd noticed the big map of Texas on his wall. The map was like a big chart in which Uncle Sherman had drawn an X showing where certain groups of cattle were moved at certain intervals throughout the year. Water holes were also marked, some with favorable months and seasons. She could see how the ranchers were completely dependent on rain. Without it, their livelihood was doomed to failure.

Sharlotte studied the perimeter of the ranch and was surprised by its size. She knew she was in good fortune when she saw that her uncle had also drawn the boundary line of Kace's property west of the Landry ranch near the Pecos River. The journey was marked off in miles, with other words scribbled in that she had no notion of trying to understand now. She did understand a skull and crossbones, but decided that spot was far to the south of where she planned on riding.

I'm a good horsewoman, she thought. *There's no reason I can't ride there. I'll start at dawn and leave a note on the dining room table. I'll be back before anyone even misses me.*

It all seemed so simple as she laid out her boots and riding outfit that night after supper.

Sharlotte could hardly sleep, she was so excited about her plans. By eight in the morning she was wide awake, dressed, and determined to prove herself Texas worthy. She imagined the look on Kace's face when she came riding in alone and capable. Her bravery would surely win his admiration, something she had never received from him before. Even Elly couldn't do better.

The yellow sun was climbing above the wide flat horizon when Sharlotte waited near a cattle trail wandering west. As she had arranged the evening before, the small Mexican child, Tony, who was related to the older boys working the stables, arrived with a saddled horse. She smiled and gave him a quarter and put a finger to her lips. "Shh," she whispered. "Say nothing."

He grinned, enjoying the secret, and held the reins while she grabbed hold of the saddle horn and stepped into the stirrup, swinging herself into the creaking leather saddle.

"Señor Kace has rancho that way," he pointed down the dusty path.

Sharlotte took the water canteen he gave her and a big hat he called a "longhorn," made of straw and good for hot, sun-laden days.

"Gracias," she told him. She turned the reins and trotted west down the well-beaten way, its dirt as fine and dry as cornstarch.

By mid-morning the sun was brilliant in the clear brassy sky. She came across dry creek beds and rock-studded, dun-colored hills where tough prairie grasses grew sparsely. There was cactus in profusion, and what she remembered as yucca and creosote bushes. The drought had worsened and the land seemed more harsh and dangerous to her than ever.

The heat was scorching, stinging her eyes, and the dust that arose from the horse's hooves clung to her perspiring skin. The wind was parching, burning her throat and causing great thirst. How much farther? How far had she ridden? She hadn't yet seen a marker designation for anyone's ranch, let alone what the little boy Tony called Kace's rancho.

Two vultures swept along above her, two lonely looking black spots in a colorless, heat-hazed sky.

I've made a mistake, but it's too late now. I must keep going.

The morning wore on and the sun climbed higher toward noon and the heat became more unbearable. She stopped her horse by a large rock hoping for a little shade, but shadows had not yet appeared. She took her canteen and drank thirstily, using a small amount to dampen her handkerchief and wipe her sweating face and throat. Her skin dried within seconds and so did the cloth. Dry brush rustled, and not even insects appeared to be using their energy. The horse whinnied nervously and shied away, tossing his head up. Sharlotte steadied him. Then she saw what the animal had evidently noticed: a diamondback rattlesnake curled close under the small ledge of the rock, keeping out of the heat of the day. She shuddered, her skin crawling. Quickly she turned the horse and rode back onto the cattle trail and didn't stop until at last she saw two big posts and a cross beam. A wood sign hanging by two short chains creaked in the wind: "K.L. Oil."

Sharlotte let out a deep breath of relief. She had never seen anything more beautiful than that sign announcing she was near.

She had made it on her own, and now that she was here, she was safe.

She rode past the sign. Oil, it had said. She smiled. He certainly was determined. And he had faith too. He had, perhaps, a fifty percent chance of striking oil.

The two-hour trip that Aunt Livia described had taken Sharlotte three and a half hours.

As she rode slowly toward the camp, she saw a handful of Mexican and Anglo workers, and off in the distance, a few pieces of oil drilling equipment. Someone shouted something and everyone present turned in her direction and stared as if she were a mirage. Sharlotte bravely rode forward, keeping her dignity intact. She stopped her horse, and her gaze glanced across the curious, disbelieving faces of men young and old.

"It must be a vision," someone said.

"Yeah, heat's cooked our brains. It was bound to happen."

"Then let me dream on, boys."

Sharlotte smiled. "I'm looking for Kace Landry. Is he here?"

The men exchanged glances and smiles. Then one older man stepped forward and gestured with his thumb. "He's out on that rotary rig, yonder."

Sharlotte looked off toward the derrick but didn't see him.

"I'll go git him, if'n you want, miss," said another, and spat tobacco juice from the corner of his mouth. "An who do I say is, er, callin'?"

"Miss Ashford."

She looked about the camp at some tents, trucks, horses, and mules. In one area an Indian with gray pig tails wore an apron and was busy broiling what appeared to her to be some jackrabbits. A huge coffee pot simmered on a cookstove, and under a canvas roof there were long tables and benches. She wondered who the Indian was. She remembered that Tyler once told her that in the days of the U.S. Cavalry this had been Apache territory.

Sharlotte turned as she heard laughter. She saw Kace walking toward her with the men, some of then grinning at him and saying something. When he saw her, he stopped. She intercepted his surprised stare. They evidently hadn't told him who his visitor was.

She hardly recognized him as he strode up in rugged jeans and a dirty, unbuttoned shirt, his wide-brimmed hat sweat-stained and beat-up. He stood there, hands on hips.

Sharlotte was uncomfortably aware of the strange excitement she felt whenever she saw him. *It's because we're going to Mexico for the gold.*

He left the men and came up to the side of her horse, his green eyes actually flickering with unconcealed joy in seeing her.

"Why Sharlotte! I don't believe my eyes. You actually rode out here alone to see me?"

His response took her by surprise and she smiled warmly and laughed. "I thought I'd shock you. Now you owe me an apology. All those mean things you've said to me about being spoiled and such all these years."

"And, of course, you're not," he said, but his tone was pleasant and it might have been a compliment. So she smiled again. He was so masculine and handsome that her heart fluttered.

"You're a sight to cheer a man. You don't know how tiring it gets looking at these greasy men across the table three times a day. It's like feeding time at the zoo. But, you!" His glance swept her. "You're like a breath of fresh air. Here, let me help you down. I'll need to get you into some shade."

Sharlotte's skin tingled over his praise and the warmth in his look.

He reached for her, but Sharlotte smiled and wrinkled her nose, leaning away. She used the handle of her small horsewhip to gently prod against his chest. "You'll ruin my outfit. You're covered with oil."

"If it were oil, honey, I'd embrace you anyway, from sheer joy, and buy you a dozen new outfits. It's only grime and sweat, but you'll need to get used to it."

He didn't suggest why she would "need" to get used to it. "See that rig?" he gestured. "We hit water again. One of these days it's going to be the real thing."

She climbed down unassisted to the hot dusty ground, feeling the heat sprawling up around her throat. She followed his gaze and imagined oil gushing out like a fountain and spraying everyone in sight.

"Take a good look around you, Sharlotte. This land is filled with oil. All I need is the right equipment to get it out of the ground. Unfortunately, very expensive equipment, big rotary rigs. Not the one you're looking at now. I got it cheap, and it's ready for the graveyard. But one of these days a wildcat well is going to explode. And when it does…" he looked at her.

She smiled a little. "And when it does?"

Surprisingly, this time he was the one who didn't accept the challenge. "It will be just the beginning."

The wind blew against her, stirring up the dust. It was hard to believe in oil when all she could see was sagebrush and creosote bushes. But as she turned and looked at him, she saw something else: an individualist with strength of conviction to endure in a harsh, hostile environment. Somehow Kace seemed to her to be inseparable from the land. If she were to believe in him, she must accept the land that meant so much to him.

But the blazing wind, the fine film of dust she could taste, the relentless sun beating down upon her—this world was too foreign to ever fully love and embrace as her own.

His eyes appeared a brighter green than usual, contrasting with the tanned skin and grime. She smiled. "You can have your oil. I'll take my father's gold."

"Ah, I might have known," he mocked a sigh. "The woman hasn't braved the uncivilized land of cactus and rattlers to brighten my day. The woman has gold on her mind...and Vermont."

"Hush, they'll hear you. Or is it all right to speak about it now?"

"No, not all right. It's a very risky topic, so keep your lips sealed. Come along, there's shade over here."

The tent had a roof spread across some poles with screening on three sides to help keep out dust and flies. "Welcome to my office," he said, and pulled out a canvas chair, dusting it off. "Have a seat. Care for coffee?"

"I think I'd prefer water."

"Would you like ice with that?" he asked with a smile. He walked to the opening. "Hoover! Water for the lady. And bring the coffeepot!"

"Hoover?" she asked.

He smiled. "Our Apache likes that name. The men don't, of course. They told him it could get him into the White House. It's his dream to walk Pennsylvania Avenue in full Apache regalia at the next inauguration, probably Roosevelt's."

Sharlotte smothered a laugh. The Indian came in carrying coffee, a tin of lukewarm water, and a roasted jackrabbit.

"Care for some?"

She grimaced. "Really, Kace, how can you eat that thing? It looks disgusting all skinned like that. It's burned black too."

He laughed. "When a hardworking man is hungry, my dear, he'll eat anything. Even rattlesnake meat tastes like chicken."

"You could have at least taken its ears off. That would have made it look more like meat instead of a cute little rabbit."

He scanned her. "Hand me that knife, will you?"

She did so, making a grimace as she watched him cut off a hind leg and part of the rump. Hoover had carved several sticks to make sharp prongs. Kace, piercing the hunk that he'd cut, sprawled comfortably into a chair to eat.

"I wouldn't think of making you eat unless you were hungry," he drawled. "Even though you're missing a treat."

She *was* hungry and he knew it. Stubbornly, she refused. The hot wind pulled at the screening and moaned around the corners of the poles. A lizard, evidently accustomed to Kace's men, sauntered across the floor. She drew her boots up on the chair. Kace looked amused. "Still squeamish of harmless critters. I suppose you check under your bed every night?"

She sipped the lukewarm water, making a face. "Not all of them are harmless. I saw a rattlesnake riding up here. Do tell me, Kace. When are we leaving for my father's rancho?"

"As soon as possible. But that can't be for another six weeks."

"Six weeks! Why so long?" And then she remembered. "You're injury—I forgot. You're recovering, I hope?"

"I hardly notice it now. No, there are other reasons for the delay. It's interesting you should come here today, because it's my last day here for a time. I was leaving for the ranch tomorrow. The next morning I'm heading for El Paso. Something has come up."

He had mentioned El Paso as the route they would take to her father's rancho. "Then why six weeks? Won't I be going with you now? You said we'll need to pass that way into Mexico."

"If lizards and rattlers unnerve you, sweetheart, I don't think you'll be happy making camp underneath the stars with Mexican bandits roaming the prairie. In Chicago the FBI would call them gangsters. Here they're just bandits. That should sound a little less frightening to you."

"Bandits!" It didn't sound less frightening at all. She remembered the ordeal she'd undergone when confronting the hobo. "Are they anywhere near?" she gasped, thinking that she had ridden all morning alone.

"No. They're gone by now, but they'll be back. They come across the border." He stood, refilling his mug. "The ranchers in this area are having their beef stolen."

"Bandits," she repeated, unnerved, trying to imagine such a thing.

"We've had trouble for as far back as I can remember. It's gotten out of hand recently. A friend was shot while riding range over on Snowcroft's ranch toward Pecos. So we've decided to do something to crack down on the rustlers."

"Rustlers," she said. "In 1930!"

"We generally call them poachers now. They're after expensive bulls for breeding. They drive them across the Rio Grande and keep them a year or so until they've got a nice-sized herd. Then they run them to market in Mexico City, with some of the best white-faced herefords shipped to Argentina. If they can steal a few quarterhorses along the way, they'll have all the more reason for a fiesta."

Bandits roaming the area! No matter how much she wanted to claim her father's money, the thought of running into them on the long journey to El Paso and beyond to the rancho gave her second thoughts.

She stood. "I'm not about to take the chance of meeting bandits. How long until the police find and arrest them?"

"That depends."

He didn't say on what. Why, it might be months before they could go to the rancho. "But, Kace, what about us!"

He looked at her, a glimmer of a smile in his eyes. "Us?"

She stepped back quickly, embarrassed. "Mexico," she said.

"I'm afraid it will need to wait awhile. I'll also be taking Pastor McCrae and Elly to the Christian boys' orphanage, but I shouldn't be gone longer than six or seven weeks."

The Christian orphanage...That Elly and her father were dedicated to such a noble cause for God's glory that they would risk bandits to reach the orphanage pricked her conscience. Kace too was putting aside his work in the oil field to bring them, and no doubt involve himself there for a few weeks. She admired him for doing so. Her personal occupation with her dreams and goals appeared to her to be shallow in comparison.

She felt a blush warm her face, and she walked over to the tent opening and looked out as though interested in the scenery. A dust devil stirred the drought-stricken plain. She struggled between personal disappointment and approval of the work on the Christian ranch. Almost two months...such a long time. She straightened her hat, feeling his gaze study her. She held back the emotion that would have protested the delay.

"Well, I admit the work Pastor McCrae is doing, and...Elly... needs to take precedence over my plans to return to Vermont..." her voice trailed off.

"I'm glad you see it that way."

She turned, intercepting his thoughtful gaze. Sharlotte grew confused, for in catching him off guard she found a hint of admiration in his eyes, something she had never seen before. It surprised her, and she wondered about it as she returned his long look.

Instantly he recovered and the old glimmer of amused tolerance was back. "I'll come back for you as soon as I can. Remember, I've a stake in that gold too. It will help pay for the expensive equipment I need and buy more time from the bank. I can just hear the foreclosure papers shuffling on the president's desk."

"Then you ought to know how I feel about the Vermont estate you hold the deed to," she half accused.

A lifted brow told her he knew exactly how she felt, but he still had no intention of relinquishing the deed.

She walked up to him. "Really, Kace, aren't you being a little unfair with me?"

A faint smile concealed what he may have thought as his gaze went to the gold medallion around her throat.

"A little hard on you, but not unfair. I thought I made it clear last December that your father left me holding the debt on this land while he wasted millions in the stock market."

Remembering Inspector Browden's statements about her father embezzling funds sealed her lips, and she dropped the painful subject. "Very well, Kace, you win—" she smiled sweetly, "for now. But once I get my hands on that gold, I expect you to turn over the deed."

"Of course," he drawled smoothly. "What would I want with the place?"

It still irritated her that he shrugged off the Ashford heritage. She quipped: "The jewels, perhaps." And she turned away glumly, reliving the frustration of trudging daily to the woods with Finney and the shovels. "I still haven't located them," she confessed.

Kace only laughed.

"I don't think it's funny."

"So you're still determined to go back to Vermont?"

She turned, surprised. "Why yes, Kace, of course I want to go home."

"Sounds dull and cold. If you had that mansion back you'd have a difficult time keeping it up. You can't afford servants."

She glanced at him. He was watching her response alertly.

"You'd have to close off most of the rooms and live in the kitchen to keep warm," he said. "You wouldn't be able to afford utilities."

"The kitchen! Very amusing."

"Best room in the house," he said with a grin. "Seriously, Sharlotte, what would you do if you went back? If old Finney gets arthritis, are you going to chop wood for yourself and Amanda and keep the cows and chickens milked and fed? You'll need to do it all, remember. I can't see you getting up at four in the morning to milk a poor cow. Somehow I think you sleep until 10:30, then loll between satin sheets sipping tea and leafing through magazines."

"Oh!"

He smiled. "Not only that, you grow faint at the sight of a little lizard."

"Never mind. I can get used to lizards."

"I'll believe it when I see it."

"Nor am I afraid of a little hard work," she said firmly.

"My, but you have changed. I can't imagine what you'll be like in a few months or a year. This is getting interesting. So you won't mind weeding your sweet potato patch?"

"I'll wear gloves, and a sun hat—" she smiled suddenly. "Maybe I'll talk you out of this longhorn hat before I go."

"That I've got to see. The lovely Sharlotte Ashford, sweet, dimpled debutante of the year, weeding her potato patch in a longhorn."

"Maybe I'll even get a job. I could become a seamstress—maybe open my own shop one day."

"And stick your fingers with needles, no doubt. I can't see you bending over a machine all day, either."

"Evidently you can't see me doing a lot of things. That simply reveals how prejudiced you are about me. Just what *do* you see me doing, pray tell?"

"What you're good at. Breaking hearts and looking more beautiful than any woman has a right to."

"I think you're impossible to understand," she said, but smiled, pleased that he thought so. "Once you give me back the deed I'll invite you to Vermont just to see how well I'm doing. After all, didn't I ride out here on my own, facing lizards, rattlers, and who knows what else I was blessed to not notice?"

"Yes, and to my chagrin what do I learn is the *real* reason? Gold. And to think I was hoping you had missed me at the ranch and were anxious to enjoy my stimulating company."

"Oh, but I did miss you—"

"You missed the promised trip to Mexico, señorita. So don't go batting eyelashes."

She quickly changed the subject. "I read in a New York paper before I left that Boston seamstresses get paid twenty dollars a month. I could work. But I shan't need to do any of those things. The money will last me and Amanda until I marry."

"What makes you think you can win Clarence back from Pamela?"

"I wasn't thinking of him," she said with a little frown.

"Have you anyone in particular in mind?"

"What a question!" she refused to look at him, afraid her eyes would unmask her secret thoughts, thoughts that not even she dare bring to a conclusion in her mind.

"But an important question, I would think," he said. "Whom you marry is one of the most important decisions you can make. Unless you're back to your old ways of doing things. In which case, I imagine your criteria will be based on social status and money again. You'll haul down the old social register and make a list of names of who survived the stock market crash."

She knew he was teasing, but his poor opinion of her hurt more than he realized. To cover her feelings, she turned away and said airily: "You're being nasty and unfair. I won't discuss this with you anymore." She walked to the table where she'd left her hat and horse whip and gathered them up. "I only came to learn when I could expect to be brought to the rancho." She turned and looked across at him. "I have my answer, and now I'll go."

"I intended to go to the ranch tomorrow, but if you want to wait until sundown I'll drive you back in the truck tonight. We can't have you undergoing the trauma of meeting up with another lizard."

The idea of returning in the truck was a great relief, but she was still hurt by his amusement over her perceived inability to survive what Texans considered "the mundane," when Elly was willing to chance bandits to serve the Lord.

"I prefer to ride the horse, thank you." She snatched up her riding gloves, slipping them on. "Good day," she said with dignity and went out into the hot, glaring sun.

If anything, it was hotter. The sweat ran down between her shoulder blades. The horse was waiting and she untied the reins and mounted easily. She swung him around to ride, glancing back to where Kace had come out and stood. He watched her with a lazy interest that rekindled her secret hopes.

She rode back through the camp and picked up the cattle trail back toward the Landry ranch.

Sharlotte hadn't gone more than a mile or two before she regretted her decision. The dust blew against her and her eyes hurt from the brilliant reflection of the burning sun. Her entire body ached from jostling in the hard saddle, and she was hungry, having gone without breakfast and lunch.

I'll make it, she thought, and surprised even herself by the determination that gripped her. A year ago she would have accepted defeat readily, with the excuse that the hardship wasn't worthy of her status. She knew better now. Now, the determination to trust God, to grow by means of hardship, to press on despite discouragement, were the prickly gifts from an eternal Hand that wanted her best. She must believe this if she stood any hope of ever becoming like Elly.

Elly! How absolutely astounding that Sharlotte Ashford wanted to become like the pastor's daughter.

Were her motives pure? At the moment she couldn't endure the searching lamp of God's Spirit moving through every secret passageway of her soul. Kace had something to do with her will to mount the heavenly ladder. But there was also a hunger to please God, however small the flame that had been lit.

24

Aunt Livia sent word to Tyler that Sharlotte and Amanda were at the ranch. He had ridden over from the Hutchins' place for the weekend with his new bride, Abby, who came to make her friendly acquaintance with the two nieces of her husband's aunt.

"Tyler's managing his father-in-law's ranch now," Livia told her before their arrival. "He'll likely inherit it. Old Will Hutchins is the very last of the Hutchins' clan, all of whom raised cattle from the time the Civil War ended. He's a widower, and Abby's his only child. Matters look good for Tyler. I wish things were going as well for Kace."

Sharlotte was rather surprised that Livia seemed to know about Kace's debt. She could have alleviated some of her fears by telling her about the gold, but remembered what Kace said about keeping silent on that touchy matter.

They were in the kitchen gathering dishes and utensils to set the dining room table for supper. Rosita, the Mexican cook, was working at two large stoves, and her younger daughter Tina, who was Amanda's age, was helping. Tina kept peering out the window as if expecting to see someone who obviously interested her. Her mother whispered something in Spanish that sounded like a rebuke.

Probably a boyfriend, Sharlotte thought. She had seen a number of Mexican cowboys on the ranch, called "vaqueros." As boys, Kace and Tyler had enjoyed their company and picked up many of their skills with horses and cattle, as well as some Spanish.

"Kace is sure there's oil on his land," Sharlotte told Livia.

Livia sighed. "For his sake, I hope so. He's got his heart set on it. Sherman would hate to see him lose it. He's put so much work into wildcatting."

"What if he does lose it?" Sharlotte asked on impulse, not that she believed he would.

Aunt Livia's forehead puckered with concern.

"He'd probably come back to raising cattle, but he wouldn't enjoy it as much. He's different than Tyler in that respect."

Sharlotte couldn't resist satisfying her gnawing curiosity about Elly. Ever since Sharlotte arrived at the ranch, she'd been asking questions about her, always careful to sound casual and merely interested in Kace as the cousin-like friend she'd known since girlhood.

"What does Elly think of his dream?"

Aunt Livia smiled to herself, as though the mere mention of Elly's name evoked reasons for thanks. "I'm sure she's very supportive of Kace in everything he does. She's the kind of girl who'll always stand by her husband's side."

Sharlotte felt a pain as sharp as a knife gouge into her heart. She had never really supported Kace's dreams, but had always been pushing for her own fulfillment. She lacked a submissive spirit too, and she knew it. It had never troubled her before, not until she'd been convicted when reading what God said a Christian woman should be like. Her submissive and quiet spirit was said to be of great value to God.

Sharlotte felt guilty and lapsed into silence.

Livia stirred the chocolate pudding simmering on the fire. She laughed to herself. "I'll admit Kace is a little bossy sometimes. He takes after his father, Austen. He was quite a soldier. But he expected everyone else to follow his orders too. So does Kace. But I've heard her disagree with him on occasions. Even so, Elly's soft-spoken about disagreements. That gets to Kace every time, so that he respects her and always listens."

So he always listens politely, does he? The green hornet of jealousy stung. *He never treats me that way!*

Sharlotte bit her tongue to keep from saying anything. It would never do for Livia to think she had a crush on Kace.

I need to pray about all this, she thought, suddenly grieved by her conduct. *It must be from reading Mother's Bible every morning. I'm learning so much. Yet to obey is such a struggle. Will I ever be as sweet-tempered as Elly?*

Sharlotte glumly cut slices of bread from the big loaf that was still fragrant and warm from baking and placed them on the platter. She covered it with a quilted warmer as Livia had shown her.

"We'll set the table now," Livia was saying cheerfully. "We've a large group of ranchers coming to supper tonight. Kace is bringing them in for a meeting with your Uncle Sherman."

Sharlotte supposed the meeting would be about the problems of running the cattle business.

Tina rushed to the kitchen window at the sound of horses. "They're here now, Señora. Señoritas Elly and Abby are with them too."

"Then Kace must have met them at the Hutchins' place first." She removed her apron and went to greet them on the porch. Sharlotte hesitated. Her stomach wanted to flip. Elly…for the first time ever, the unpleasant sensation of inferiority gripped her. Here was a girl who had won praise without the best clothes, finest education, or the loveliest face and figure. Here was an ordinary Christian girl whom Kace esteemed highly enough to marry. The evening stretching before her felt like it led to a precipice.

Sharlotte heard cheerful voices and laughter out front. *Don't be a little coward*, she told herself. Reluctantly, but forcing her lips into a smile, she joined Aunt Livia on the porch.

"Hello, love," Livia greeted her husband, Sherman. "You're just in time for supper."

Uncle Sherman came up the steps, brushing a customary kiss on her cheek. "You hear no complaints about that. Come on in, fellas."

Sherman was a big, amiable man with graying hair and a leather-brown face. He had a slight paunch that hung over his belt, its silver buckle engraved with his initials over a Texas long-horn steer. Sherman had always been kind to Sharlotte and she never appreciated it more than now.

"Well, well," he said with a warm grin, taking both her hands into his, "my favorite Eastern rosebud, all decked out in pretty finery!"

Sharlotte smiled up at him, wondering why she'd never fully realized before how much she liked him. Nor had she ever told him how much the Bible stories had made an impression on her while visiting each summer. She would be sure to do so at the appropriate time.

"Hello, Uncle." Suddenly, she felt ashamed of the past. Impulsively she threw her arms around his neck, drew his head down, and kissed his prickly sun-hardened cheek.

"Well, if this isn't the best birthday present I've gotten in years," he teased.

"It's your birthday?" she cried.

"Next week. But I'll take another kiss then," and he winked. "Now, child, you just settle in and find some happiness. This is your home now too."

Sharlotte intercepted Kace's glance and noticed that he'd watched the exchange between her and Sherman as though it pleased him.

"Where is Amanda?" Sherman glanced around for her.

"She'll be down for dinner," Sharlotte told him. Amanda was actually keeping out of sight in the parlor so Sharlotte could help her surprise Tyler. She wanted to greet him and Kace without her wheelchair or crutches.

Sharlotte noticed a half dozen cattle barons in the yard, most of them Uncle Sherman's age. They congregated below the porch, talking and removing their hats in greetings to Livia. Sharlotte slipped back into the house and went to Amanda.

Her sister waited behind the parlor door. "Hurry, Sis," Amanda whispered.

"You're sure this isn't going to tire you too much?" Sharlotte asked, concerned.

Amanda smiled weakly. "No, I'll be just fine. Here, help me stand…"

Sharlotte grabbed the crutches and gave them to her, then as Amanda placed them under her arms, Sharlotte struggled to help her to her feet.

After Amanda gained her balance, they moved step by step to the parlor doorway.

"All right?" Sharlotte whispered when Amanda paused.

Amanda nodded, then drawing in a deep breath she handed Sharlotte first one crutch, hesitated, then released the other. Sharlotte hovered, prepared to catch her should she fall, afraid Amanda's legs were too weak. But Amanda stood straight, without weaving. Slowly she turned her head and smiled at Sharlotte. "I'm taller than you again," she joked.

Sharlotte smiled back, but felt a tug at her heart.

"Here, let me fluff out your skirt." She stooped to shake out the long silky folds that covered her legs, then stood and arranged Amanda's red hair so that it draped prettily over one shoulder.

They heard voices and bootsteps. Sharlotte darted out of view, keeping to one side of the door. She watched Amanda with an encouraging smile, but inside she felt pain. Since Amanda had learned about their father's crimes and suicide, she had once again suffered a decline in health. She was thinner, and there were dark circles beneath her eyes.

"And after all the things he told me about how George wasn't good enough to marry into our family," she had wept.

Something must be done to get the best doctor in Texas who could handle her spine problem, Sharlotte thought, but to find such a doctor would require money, lots of it. Again, she thought of Mexico. Six weeks was a long time. And how much time after that would it take to get hold of the funds and be able to use them?

If I hadn't insisted Amanda and I trade horses that day, it might have been me, not Amanda, who took that fall. It's my fault...

"Amanda," Tyler called from the next room, genuine surprise and pleasure in his voice. "You're standing again!"

Amanda grinned, her eyes taking on a sparkle that Sharlotte hadn't seen since before George was killed.

"Hello, Ty. Fancy meeting you here," Amanda said with a small laugh. "How's that horse of mine? You gave him to me, remember? I want to ride him again!"

Sharlotte winced, closing her eyes, for the desperation in Amanda's voice spoke the truth of the heartbreak that was just behind her outward smiles and bravery.

"Amanda," Tyler said, and there was a sigh in his voice.

"I'm serious," Amanda insisted, still smiling. "I want to ride again, to feel the wind in my face and hair—you'll take me?"

Sharlotte bit her lip and found that her fingers had tightened.

Tyler came into the parlor. His brown hair was bleached lighter by the sun and his handsomely boyish face was tanned, emphasizing his clear gray eyes.

Sharlotte felt alarm when she saw Amanda's expression.

"Are you telling me you can walk?"

Amanda smiled, folding her hands in front of her. "I can stand," she admitted ruefully. "I just had to greet you and Kace properly after all these years."

Tyler seemed about to kiss her cheek, but halted, then reached behind him, taking Abby's hand and drawing her around to greet Amanda.

"It's…good to see you again, Amanda," he said, and Sharlotte saw him swallow, trying to mask his emotion.

"My, you've changed, Ty!" Amanda said with feigned cheerfulness. "Marriage must be good for you."

"Yes, this is Abby, my wife. You remember each other?"

Abby was tall and athletic looking. Her dark hair was uncut, worn in braids. Her eyes were quiet and brown, and her plain face, though not pretty, bore a healthful glow. The difference between the two young women was startling. Sharlotte was remembering Amanda before her accident. She too, had been full of boundless energy, sparkling eyes, and pink cheeks.

Abby put forth her hand, taking Amanda's, and smiled with genuine warmth.

"Hello, Amanda, how nice to meet you at last. Tyler has told me so many nice things about how you and your sister spent summers here on the ranch. I don't know why I never had the privilege of meeting either of you." She laughed. "I guess Pa kept me too busy with the horses."

"Yes, that must have been the reason," Amanda said, and the earlier glow faded.

Kace walked into the parlor. Sharlotte didn't recognize him from yesterday. He wore a fastidiously pressed white shirt, black string tie, and black trousers. He didn't hesitate to hug Amanda and comment on her feat, but he also didn't appear to think it wise, for he swept her up and carried her back to the wheelchair without asking, as though it were the most casual thing in all the world to do. His manner showed the biggest difference between him and Tyler.

"So you want to go riding? We'll arrange something if you eat all your supper tonight."

"We've got a bargain," Amanda said with a grin.

Elly must be with Livia, Sharlotte thought, remaining to one side of the door, watching.

Kace turned from Amanda and saw Sharlotte holding Amanda's crutches. He walked up as she managed a casual smile, glancing him over.

"I see you've emerged from the tar pits."

He leaned his hand against the wall, keeping her there in the corner, his eyes briefly taking in her white linen dress with lace. Their eyes held.

"And you braved the lizards and snakes to get back safely."

"Yes, and I've changed my mind. I'm leaving with you and the others in the morning for El Paso."

"That little ride you had yesterday is nothing compared to the distance we'll travel to the boys' orphanage. True, I'm taking you to Mexico to the rancho, but I've made leeway for the extra time you'll want."

"I can do without the extra time the same as Elly—"

He smiled. "I doubt it. Anyway, those bandits haven't been caught. That's why we're having the meeting tonight."

She was still mulling over what he'd said about Elly needing less help.

"Now, Kace, don't be difficult. I've decided I'm willing to risk bandits, just like everyone else in your party," she said in a low tone. "I need to go now, Kace. I can't wait for that money—"

"Hello, Sharlotte," Elly's voice came from a few feet away.

Sharlotte turned guiltily, but Kace turned leisurely.

"Elly, you remember Livia's niece?"

"Yes, of course I do. How wonderful that you've come, Sharlotte."

She can't mean that, but as she searched the girl's eyes, Sharlotte was surprised by the sincerity she found. Elly was smiling, reaching out both hands to enclose Sharlotte's in a warm greeting of acceptance and friendship.

"I've told Tyler and Kace so many times I wished you'd come back and visit. I'm so sorry it's under such sad circumstances."

Sharlotte would have taken that latter comment as false sympathy from her rivals in New York, but not from Elly.

"Thank you," she replied simply. "We're slowly getting adjusted to the shock of losing everything, plus our father."

Elly looked genuinely troubled. "I admire your courage. It must be very difficult to survive a traumatic shaking in your life and be the only one surviving. I've often thought the one surviving has the biggest trial of all."

Sharlotte stared at her. Elly admired her? But it was supposed to be the other way around. She wondered if Kace had caught that word courage, but she didn't want to look at him.

"I don't know how long Amanda and I will be staying. We may go home by January." She put a slight emphasis on "home."

"You're not staying permanently? That's our loss. Tyler said you and Amanda would make your home with Livia and Sherman."

"They've generously offered, but my sister and I both want to return to our grandmother's ancestral home in Vermont."

"That's understandable."

"Not that we don't appreciate staying on the ranch," she added.

"Well, at least we'll enjoy your company until next year," Elly said. "I shouldn't say we, as I'll be working at the orphanage most of the time, though I'll be home for Christmas."

Sharlotte glanced at Kace. His bland face told her nothing. Did this mean Elly would continue the Christian work after September when she and Kace were to marry?

Sharlotte saw an opening and took it: "I wanted so much to go on the journey to El Paso, but Kace won't let me." She sighed. "I'm so disappointed."

As she glanced at Kace she saw his jaw harden and a flicker showed in his eyes. As expected, Elly turned to him, surprised. "Oh, but why, Kace?"

Sharlotte covered a smile and said sadly, "He thinks I'll slow everyone down and be a terrible burden. I promised I wouldn't, but he just won't hear of it."

"Kace," Elly said as though she couldn't believe he would be so thoughtless. "If Sharlotte wants to come see the work, it seems so unkind to tell her no like that." She turned to Sharlotte who kept her eyes lowered, plucking at her handkerchief.

"I'll ask my father to speak to Kace. I think we can convince him."

Sharlotte smiled at her, ignoring Kace's glittering gaze. She was relieved when Tina appeared shyly and announced that supper was being set on the table.

"We'll discuss the trip later, Sharlotte," he said politely. Too politely.

She knew she was in for a verbal thrashing when they were alone, but she was amused that she had gotten the best of him through Elly.

"Yes of course, Cousin Kace," Sharlotte said, and saw the corner of his mouth twitch.

Kace beckoned Tina aside for a moment, but Sharlotte was not to know what was spoken. Elly was walking beside her into the dining room, talking in a warm, friendly fashion about the El Paso school.

"My father's here tonight too," Elly said. "You remember Pastor McCrea?"

"I do, but I was rather hoping he wouldn't remember me."

"Oh! You don't mean it."

"Not the way you think," she hurried on. "You see, I often gave your father a terrible time and I'm ashamed. I'm afraid I wasn't a very good listener during his sermons when I was young."

Elly smiled. "Oh that..." she made an airy wave of her hand. "My father understands the restlessness of young people."

She sounds as if she's so much older, but she can't be more than three years my senior.

"Kace wasn't much better," Elly said with a laugh. "Thankfully we've all grown up and matured in faith since those years. Father will be pleased that you're back. He's working hard to bring attendance up at the church, so the prospect of gaining you and Amanda will make him happy. You will come, won't you?"

"Yes, I've every intention of coming."

Soon they were all seated at Aunt Livia's huge table that was covered with a sparkling white tablecloth and dishes. Supper was a grand multi-course affair as was customary at the ranch: broiled steak, cottage potatoes with onions, stuffed red and green peppers cooked in olive oil and more onions, some kind of small beef tamale with raisins in the cornmeal, two vegetables, the grits that were served at every meal, including breakfast, big flaky buttermilk biscuits with gobs of butter and molasses to the side, and some kind of an omelet. Dessert would come later with servings of pudding, peach pie, and pound cake.

Aunt Livia said, "Well for goodness sake, Kace, I don't believe it. There's not a smidgen of grime on you. You look as if you've just come home from the university in Richmond again."

Everyone laughed.

"There was just enough water left in Hutchins' Creek to steal a bath and change my clothes. I knew you wouldn't let me eat supper unless I did."

"Probably left a ring in the creek, too, Pa," Tyler joked, speaking to his father-in-law.

"If my cattle die, Kace, I'll know who poisoned my water," Will spoke up.

"There's not enough water left in that creek to satisfy a hundred cattle," Kace was saying seriously. "Drought's worsening, Will. Better think about drilling for oil instead of raising cattle."

"I'm thinking," Will Hutchins said. "Thinking seriously. Ty tells me we're losing cattle every day now. Not from those poachers from the Rio Grande, but sickness."

A light omelet appealed to Sharlotte, who wasn't that hungry. She took a large spoonful from the platter that passed her way, and put it on her plate with a fluffy biscuit. She was adding salt and pepper when Kace said: "Should we let Sharlotte know what she's eating, Ty?"

Sharlotte looked up cautiously. She knew that tone of voice. She saw the smile breaking on Ty's face.

"Scrambled eggs," she said.

"Delicious, my girl," Uncle Sherman said. "Eat up. Duck eggs and scrambled cow brains. Go together like potatoes and gravy. It took a while to get Livia to eat them when we were first married."

"I *still* won't eat them," Livia said. "It takes everything out of me just to cook them. Push them aside, Sharlotte dear. I keep telling these men that we women, at least, are civilized."

"What do you mean? Abby eats 'em," Tyler said with a grin, looking at his wife.

"I was raised on them," Abby said. "Look, you're turning Sharlotte green."

Sharlotte lowered her fork. She swallowed hard.

"Here, try this," and Kace handed her a warm platter of thick, juicy, filet mignon steaks.

The steaks were huge. Sharlotte cut one in half, taking the smallest portion.

"Look at her," Kace said with feigned gravity. "The girl never eats. How are you doing, Amanda?"

"Enjoying myself," Amanda said taking a big bite of steak.

Perhaps this is the cow that had its brains scrambled, Sharlotte thought. Nevertheless, once she took a bite she couldn't stop until she'd finished her piece.

Kace turned the conversation back to oil. It took a while for Sharlotte to understand that when he spoke of a "gusher" it meant a productive oil well. From what Sharlotte picked up from the conversation, oil had been an ongoing topic of discussion at every meal for the last few weeks. It appeared as if Kace were trying to interest his uncle in drilling for oil on the ranch, but Sherman was reluctant.

"We've been cattlemen from the days of Sam Houston."

"I know that," Kace said. "One thing about oil, though. You won't need to worry about drought, cattle disease, or poachers."

"He's right about that," Tyler said wearily. "Two years without rain is telling hard on the land. That wind's starting to blow too. It could take the topsoil. And as far as poachers—"

Kace turned toward his cousin. "How many sick cattle were discovered?"

"One too many. It's making me worry."

"What the whole of West Texas needs is a prayer meeting," Sherman said. "How about it, Pastor McCrae? When are you holding those meetings again?"

"Soon as I get back from El Paso. I hope to see all of you in your places in the pews, gentlemen. You too, ladies. And we'll be sure to give the two Miss Ashfords a warm and proper welcome."

Elly smiled across the table at Sharlotte and Amanda.

"This time, Pastor McCrae," Sharlotte said with a smile, "I promise to listen to your message. I'll even bring my notebook and pencil."

"We couldn't ask for better than that," the older man said with a smile. "I can't guarantee our Lord will send rain, but I'll guarantee you'll hear His Word."

Uncle Sherman said, "Well, Ben, the pastureland is exhausted. If the Lord doesn't send rain, we're going to lose the livestock. Many of us aren't going to make it into 1933. Make no doubt of that. If this curse continues we'll need to start shooting the cattle, or sell 'em as cheaply as we can to the packinghouses."

"Livestock are already congesting the packing houses," Kace told him soberly. "Beef on foot is selling as low as a penny a pound. The state is too broke to grant aid."

Sherman sighed. "Drought, cattle disease, wind—what's next?"

"Foreclosure," one of the cattlemen named Clyde said sadly, and shook his head. "This year, we can manage. But come the next, and it's anyone's guess."

"Surely there'll be rain by then," Aunt Livia said, dismayed.

"Even if there is, it won't help pay the bills yet."

"I don't recall ever seeing a time like this when God held back the rain for so long," Livia said to Pastor McCrae. "It's frightening, Ben. What do you think the future holds for America?"

"It should give us all much to consider. Along with the stock market crash, and lines of people going hungry in the cities, I can't help wondering where America is headed in the 1930s."

"For trouble," Sherman said. "Unpleasant things are happening in Europe too, especially Germany. Who is that young man leading—what were they called—? Nazis?"

"Hitler," Kace said.

"Yes, that was it. Strange man, if you ask me."

"Well, we've enough problems here at home," Will Hutchins said.

"The Scriptures have a great deal to say about the chastening hand of the Almighty," Pastor McCrae said.

Everyone respectfully listened.

"Lack of rain—sometimes too much rain, locust plagues, loss of wealth—God uses all these things to get our attention. He's trying to get us to see how desperately we're dependent upon Him and to turn from our sins to Him."

Sharlotte moved uneasily. Loss of wealth…she glanced around the table, feeling conspicuous, but no one was looking at either her or Amanda.

"Did you see the Brazos, Kace?" Tyler asked. "It's way below normal in some places, and this is not just taking place in Texas, but I hear of it in Oklahoma and Arkansas too."

"We approach fall with the prospect of hiring the railway to haul in tanks of water," Will said.

"But how long can we do that?" Uncle Sherman frowned.

"If the drought doesn't break, the only clouds we'll be seeing in the Southwest come next year are dust clouds," Kace said. "Some of the wildcatters are thinking of joining me in doing what Oklahoma and Wyoming wildcatters are doing. Instead of drilling for oil, they're tapping into underground water supplies. I spoke to a geologist in Fort Worth who says West Texas has plenty of it beneath the earth's crust."

"If that could be done," Sherman said, "you'd save us all from bankruptcy."

There was silence. Sharlotte, who knew little of raising cattle, had no difficulty in seeing the dangers ahead of the ranchers and farmers. For the first time she considered how the range sustained and replenished their way of life. They were independent among men, but acknowledged dependence upon God. They displayed the same strength to endure as the harsh, often hostile environment. She saw in Uncle Sherman, Tyler, and the other men at the table the same spirit that she had always noticed about Kace. She began to think it was present in most of the Texas cattlemen and oilmen—and in their women.

She studied the faces of Aunt Livia, Abby, and Elly. They looked on gravely with quiet confidence. Livia had been right earlier when she'd said of Elly that she would stand by Kace no matter what. The same could also be said for Livia and Sherman, and Abby and Tyler.

Sharlotte again felt her admiration growing, with a wistful longing to be that kind of a woman. She saw herself as she had been: at times self-centered and sometimes vain, building her life on the sand. She had never shown Kace anything except her selfishness and flirtatiousness. No wonder he had forgotten all about her and loved Ellie.

Although her heart knew a persistent ache, she accepted the painful truth, choosing to believe that the thorn on the rose that the Lord had placed in her hand would somehow bring growth.

She glanced at Amanda, wondering if she might be thinking some of the same things. Her sister had hardly spoken, but she was listening and looking from Tyler to Abby.

Yes, she does understand, Sharlotte thought.

25

After supper, while the table was cleared and coffee was served outdoors on the long, wide porch, Sharlotte wheeled Amanda to her bedroom for the night. She helped her get ready for bed and moved the wheelchair and crutches within her reach. Before she left the room, Sharlotte went to the open screened window and looked out.

Off in the distance there were bunkhouses for the cowhands. Perhaps two dozen smaller cabins were situated farther away, reserved for the ranch help that had families. A few lights glowed in the windows from kerosene lamps. Fragrant wood smoke wafted on the wind.

Far in the distance, though she could not see them now, she knew that there were a number of corrals and stables, and beyond that, endless miles of dry, dusty range.

"Dusty badlands" beyond the Pecos River, as Kace and Tyler used to call the territory. West Texas was rough land, fit only for the most rugged. Some areas supported only grasses, cactus, yucca, and creosote bushes. Aunt Livia had told her that ranches out here, considered average by the big cattle barons, ran to 100,000 acres.

On the opposite side of the road, closer to the ranch house itself, the orchard trees grew, once in plentiful supply but now withering. There used to be peaches, plums, apricots, and walnuts. Sharlotte hadn't liked those trees until now. Now they represented the struggle they all faced. They also brought memories of youth... the honeysuckle arbor was located there, where Kace had first kissed her.

Yes, unless the rains came, the drought would kill most everything.

Nearby there grew a large plot of Aunt Livia's precious strawberries, now brown and brittle, rustling in the wind. The Landrys loved this land, but they weren't the only ones who had dreams connected with the soil and the culture that went with it. She thought of the Ashford estate. Like Uncle Sherman, she too had her heart set on a piece of land that meant almost as much to her as this ranch did to him. Why couldn't Kace understand what the Vermont property meant to her and sympathize? She feared Kace would proceed to sell the country estate if anything interfered with their getting the money her father had sent into Mexico.

The stars were gleaming, and the moon was coming up over a low hill. Uncle Sherman had always joked about that small hill, saying it wasn't a hill at all, but a Texas anthill. "Everything grows bigger in Texas," he used to tease them when they were young. "Even the ants. Why, I once saw one at a picnic that carried away a whole watermelon." Sharlotte smiled to herself. She had believed him too. She turned away from the window to look once more at Amanda.

"They looked happy, didn't they?" Amanda said wistfully. "Tyler and Abby, Kace and Elly. I noticed though that Elly doesn't wear an engagement ring. Isn't that a little strange?"

Sharlotte didn't respond at first. *What a ninny I am! Why didn't I think to look at her left hand?*

"You're certain?" she whispered.

"Certain she didn't have his ring...but maybe Kace just can't afford one right now."

Sharlotte's spirits dropped again. "Yes, that's probably it. Everything he owns is poured into his land and drilling equipment."

Amanda sighed. "It's wrong to be envious, but it's hard sometimes not to wish to be like Elly or Abby. I don't think I'll ever meet someone else like George. He loved me as I am, not as he wished me to be. Sharlotte?" her eyes showed pain and self-doubt. "Do you think there is someone for me? Someone who'll see beyond my inability to walk?"

Sharlotte reached over and squeezed her hand. "Why, of course there is." Secretly, she wondered. Clarence's love had been shallow. He'd walked out on her at the worst possible moment in her life. *I should have hung on to Kace,* she thought miserably. Kace offered emotional encouragement, but it was too late now.

"I was talking this afternoon to Aunt Livia," Amanda said thoughtfully. "She said we both needed to wait on God's timing, that His ways are not our ways, nor our thoughts, His thoughts. His ways and thoughts are so much higher than ours that we don't always see what is best for us. We only know what we want, and sometimes those emotions are immature. She seemed to think God's purposes for each life are unique. We can't compare our lives with someone else's and say, 'why can't I have what she has?' God has a plan that won't fit anyone else the way it will fit you."

Sharlotte considered, and tried to smile. "It's good you listen to Aunt Livia. She's studied the Bible for years. As for plans—I still intend to go home to Vermont, to dear old Finney, and...to a new life. Both of us."

Amanda didn't smile this time the way she usually did. She looked at Sharlotte sadly. "I wonder if I'll ever return to Vermont."

Now why did she say that? "Things will work out eventually, you'll see."

"I didn't mean it that way..." she turned her head on the pillow and looked toward the window. The shade was pulled up and the moon could be seen shining brightly in the sky. "I meant...never mind, Sis. Don't pay any attention to my mood. I'm just tired...and a little depressed, I guess. I keep thinking about what I would have been, and done, if it hadn't been for that accident."

Sharlotte understood her sense of loss, the disappointment, but she saw the gold waiting at the rancho as the answer to their problems.

Amanda looked at her worriedly. "Maybe we both should be thinking about what God wants us to become now. Like Aunt Livia said, if God has closed the door behind us, then the one before us is open."

Sharlotte thought, *I've still got my heart set on getting a good doctor for you. I won't let anything stop me. Not even bandits.* She took a deep breath. "If I tell you a secret, will you promise not to breathe a word to anyone?"

"Yes, what is it? Not more bad news?"

Sharlotte smiled. "No, good news. Daddy left us an inheritance in gold. It's safely in Mexico, and Kace is taking me there to claim it."

"Gold!"

"Shh," Sharlotte warned. "Things are going to turn out all right. And you," she said with a smile, "are going to get better again."

Amanda smiled back at her, but her eyes questioned. "How did Daddy get gold into Mexico?"

"Mr. Hunnewell arranged it all. It's best not to discuss it now. I'll tell you everything when I get back. I'm afraid it may be longer than expected, though. Now that you know why I'll be away, do you think you can keep trusting and waiting?"

"Of course I can. Livia will be here, and Rosita too. She's a kind woman. I'll be praying for you. And...you behaved well tonight too. I just wanted you to know."

Sharlotte was encouraged that someone thought so. She reached over and turned off the small lamp. She didn't want to say goodbye and walked to the door, pretending it was just another good night. She looked back at her. Amanda smiled tiredly.

"God be with you, Sharlotte," she said quietly.

"And with you. I'll see you—in a little while."

"Yes, just a little while."

Sharlotte closed the door and stood there for a moment thoughtfully. Then she slowly walked away to what lay ahead.

≈

She returned to the dining room. The men were taking coffee out on the porch, and Aunt Livia, Elly, and Abby were in the parlor discussing a church project. Elly and her father had gathered food and clothing to distribute to some families from across the Rio Grande. They were camped in the open land near the boys' orphanage. It was the same orphanage, Elly said, where Kace had spent almost two years after his father was killed in France. Elly was explaining that a mission organization Kace knew of in Fort Worth had sent a team to run the compound.

Sharlotte slipped quietly through the screen door onto the porch, hoping for a word alone with Kace about going with them to El Paso, but the men had moved to the side of the house to the flagstone patio.

The night was hot. The wind, bone dry. She walked softly to the end of the porch facing the patio and heard their voices.

"What happened in October will have more effect on the whole of America than even the war in Europe," Pastor McCrae was saying. "Who knows what it will take to get America back on its feet? We've sown to the wind, and we'll reap the whirlwind. God's truth is not mocked."

Sharlotte felt her fears prickle her skin. She saw millions of American faces from all walks of life oblivious to the danger that waited like a tiger ready to spring.

America had thrown off all moral restraint and had rebelled against belief in God and the Bible. Had the decade of what was recently labeled the "Roaring Twenties" met up with God's judgment with an economic crash? Perhaps it was just the beginning of a long, dark, arduous road, as the pastor said.

Someone brought up their neighbors in need, and what would likely happen if they couldn't sell their livestock. Feed was too expensive. Foreclosures were threatening. Was there any way to create a financial pool to help out? Uncle Sherman insisted he would begin a fund through Pastor McCrae's church. "Let's give in the name of the Lord so that the glory goes to Him."

How different these people are from the Fosdicks and Uncle Hubert, Sharlotte thought, amazed. Until now, she'd never thought about it and had never even noticed. Had she been blind?

In time of trial, Clarence and his family had turned their backs on her. Other close social associates, yes, even cousins Sheldon and Pamela had forgotten her. With the loss of wealth had come the end to her social standing and her so-called friends.

But these wholesome church people and dear Uncle Sherman were different. She thought of the old Bible he carried in his saddle bag wherever he went on the range. She had once thought Sherman silly for taking out that Bible and sometimes reading passages to the Mexican cowboys. Now, she knew differently. The fear of the Lord was the beginning of wisdom, and Uncle Sherman was a wise man. He cared about the souls of the men who worked for him.

Tyler was talking now, telling them that word had come from farther east of the foreclosure on the largest cattle ranch in all East Texas, the Burroughs Ranch.

"I don't know what the answer is," Tyler said. "Things are going from bad to worse and it doesn't appear as if the man in the White House knows what to do about it."

"Now, don't go blaming the president, son," Sherman said. "There were wide cracks in the financial institutions of this country before he ever took office. He inherited some of the mistakes of past administrations."

"Come on, boys, enough of politics," someone drawled.

"Yes, we've the matter of Santana's poaching to discuss."

"What makes you think it's Santana, Crawford?" Will Hutchins asked.

Sharlotte drew closer to the porch rail to hear. Santana? Was he the leader of the bandits?

"Snowcroft claims one of his men saw him before his foreman was shot and left for dead," Kace said.

"That can't be, Kace," Pastor McCrae said worriedly. "Tomas gave me his word he'd stay camped across the Rio Grande. He promised us both."

"That's what we want to find out, sir. Whether or not Tomas has gone back on his word. My opinion is that he has."

"Look, here, Pastor," Will Hutchins said. "You know we all think the world of you, but we've worried a long while about your kindness to that passel of poachers he heads up."

"Now, Will, not every man associated with Tomas is a poacher. We've bought that property next to the orphanage to turn it into a Christian boys' ranch. Eventually the squatters will leave, but we don't want to round them up like a bunch of troublesome coyotes. Not when we represent the Lord. We must move cautiously. Give them nothing to find fault with us about."

"That's all mighty fine, Pastor," Will said. "We're all behind you. The work you and your congregation are doing down there is commendable. But if Crawford's right, and Santana's infiltrated the squatters, then we've no choice but to get the law into this. Like Kace suggests, he may be posing as one of the poor farmers during the day, and poaching the ranches at night."

"Now let's not rush to judgment," Uncle Sherman said. "Most of those folks are decent. They have families. All they want is a job and a chance for a better life in Texas."

"He's right, Will," Tyler said quietly to his father-in-law. "If the law goes busting into the camp looking for an outlaw, someone's bound to get hurt, and it's likely to damage Pastor McCrae's work."

McCrae pleaded: "We're just now gaining their trust. Elly's been at the orphanage for the last two months with the mission group out of Fort Worth. They've even got a Bible class going now. Our congregation took up a collection last Christmas to have Spanish New Testaments printed for distribution. We'll be bringing them down now. Asking us to risk all this work just to flush out one man—when we're not even sure he's guilty—"

"Now, Pastor McCrae, we're not asking that at all," Crawford said in a low, patient voice. "I've been talking to Kace about this. He has an idea I'm interested in if you're willing to hear him out."

"Certainly, Kace, speak your mind."

"There's a way to find out if Tomas is involved without making a raid on the camp. I know one or two of those young men. If I can guarantee them and their families safety from Santana's revenge, I may be able to get them to talk secretly. I'll be going down with you and Elly on the pretext of helping with the distribution. With Crawford giving us time, we'll be able to avoid an ugly incident."

There was a moment of silence, then low voices.

"Sounds like the best solution if you can do it, Kace. Especially if Crawford says it's legal. Is that so, Bill?"

"I've told Kace I'll go along with it under certain circumstances. What do you say, Sherman?"

"You know I've every confidence in Kace," Uncle Sherman said. "I do have one request, though. Don't worry the women about this. What about you, Clyde? Are you signing on to the plan?"

"Fine with me too. Except I keep thinking about that cowhand shot on Snowcroft's ranch. The fella's dead. That right, Tyler? You've been in Pecos recently."

"Pistol shot through the head," Tyler said quietly.

"That's it, then, as far as I can see," Will Hutchins stated, anger in his voice. "No matter what we agree on here, the hornets' nest has been stirred up. The local authorities down there will be scouring the area for bandits crossing the Rio Grande. Snowcroft's bound to be heated over this and pushing for action."

"Tyler's already taken care of that," Kace said. "He's talked to Snowcroft and the law. Better explain, Ty."

"Uncle Sherman knows the local police there," Tyler said. "So Kace suggested we talk to them last week when all this came up. They know Santana once worked for Uncle Sherman. They've agreed Kace's help will be beneficial. They'd rather not raid that camp until they hear from him. Snowcroft's willing to give us time too."

"Well then, looks like it's settled…or just beginning," Will said gravely. "Better be cautious, Kace. Santana's known to turn on old friends."

"I'm aware of that. He's done it before."

They began to break up the meeting. Sharlotte slipped into the shadows of the porch, intending to go inside the house, but as she reached the screen door the women were coming out of the library. If they saw her now, they would wonder where she'd been all this time. They might even guess she'd been listening.

The crunch of boots walking across the patio gravel alerted her that the men were nearing the porch. Sharlotte hung back in the shadows where the bougainvillea rambled along the trellis as they came up the steps and began to enter the door. As Kace approached she stepped forward and plucked at his sleeve. He turned.

"I must speak with you alone," she whispered, glancing toward the door to see if anyone had noticed. Apparently no one had, and she drew back into the shadows, where there was a two-seater swing.

He followed, and in the light coming through the window she could see that he guessed she'd been listening.

"You overheard? Maybe I should say 'eavesdropped.'"

But she took heart when he didn't seem particularly upset about her actions.

"I didn't intend to," she admitted meekly. "I wanted to talk about going with you tomorrow to El Paso."

He lounged back against the rail. "Yes, a clever little move of yours tonight getting Elly on your side."

He would bring that up now. "Now, Kace, please don't be difficult—"

"Me, difficult!" he laughed.

"Do hush," she wheedled, but kept her voice pleasant, and laid a palm on the cuff of his shirt. "We haven't much time before they miss us..." she whispered. She could see them gathering for the cookies and cake Rosita brought in from the kitchen.

Kace glanced down at her hand on his wrist. Slightly embarrassed, she removed it as he said, "All right, what's on your mind. I'm a very reasonable man."

"You already know. I want to go with you and the others. It will save us time, and I'm quite up to the ordeal if that's what concerns you."

"That's debatable, but we won't get into that. If you heard the ranchers tonight, there's no reason to talk around the subject. You know about Tomas Santana."

"Yes. Since when did you become friends with bandits?" she teased.

"He worked here for Sherman when Tyler and I were growing up. He wasn't a thief or a killer then; at least, I don't think he was. He wasn't much older than we were. He taught us things that only the vaqueros know. He's excellent in taming wild horses and roping steer. Then he turned rotten. He shot a horse I thought the world of just to get even with me. He accused me of trying to steal his girlfriend. We got into a fight—one he insisted on, and then he ran away. Later I found my mustang dead."

"Oh, Kace, I'm sorry..."

"He's been drifting in and out of Mexico ever since, poaching cattle and trying to turn the Mexican cowboys on the various ranches against their Anglo bosses. He'd like to form some kind of gang and control the borderland near the Rio Grande. But he made his final mistake by murdering the foreman at Snowcroft's ranch. We probably would have ignored his poaching if he hadn't turned killer."

The idea that Santana might be living secretly among the families on the orphanage property was disturbing, especially when she knew that Kace was going there to locate him.

She glanced toward the parlor, seeing Mr. Crawford, a ruddy-faced man with graying hair and wide shoulders. "Who is Crawford? You and the others were concerned that he approve what you were going to do."

"My dear, Crawford's the law. He's been given the go-ahead to swear me in as a short-term deputy. That means I can carry a gun, which I intended to do anyway, once you and I crossed the border into Mexico."

She remembered how he had also worked with Inspector Browden about Hunnewell. "Then I don't see any reason why I shouldn't come along. We'll all be quite safe, especially if Crawford rides with us. Kace, I need my father's money to care for Amanda. She's getting worse."

He frowned, glancing off toward the house. "Yes, I noticed tonight."

"I've got to hire the best physician I can find for her. So you see, the trip to Mexico *can't* wait. Please, Kace, I'll be dreadfully disappointed if you refuse."

He considered for a long moment. "You're certain you want this? We'll be at the mission compound for a week or more."

She thought she knew what he meant, that she would be with Elly, both on the long ride and at the compound. "A week or so won't matter as long we leave for the rancho when you and Mr. Crawford have finished your job."

"It won't be longer if I can help it. Remember, I want my share of that gold too."

"You'll get your share if I get the Vermont deed."

"Ah yes, the deed. Keep your end of the bargain and pay what is owed, and I'll turn it over with my blessing."

"Then you agree that I can come?"

"I'll chance it. Pack lightly. Bring only what you absolutely need. And be sure you include riding clothes, boots, and the biggest hat you can find."

"I'll be ready," she said with a smile.

"You'd better get some sleep then. Tomorrow will be a long day. Be downstairs by four."

Uncle Sherman and Tyler were still talking with the other ranchers when Sharlotte left him near the parlor and went upstairs. It was settled! She would soon be at her father's rancho in Mexico!

26

It was nearing dawn. Sharlotte took a final look through the things in her one small bag that were to make do all the way to Mexico and back. How she had fretted about deciding what to bring with her.

"Be practical," Aunt Livia had said when she came up to her room.

Kace had told her Sharlotte was coming with them, and Livia wanted to make certain she brought the necessities. Sharlotte suspected that Kace had asked her to come up and make certain she had packed properly.

Livia told her: "Once across the Pecos River, the area is known as the badlands. It can be treacherous to someone unaccustomed to its savage environment. Wear comfortable clothing, dear. Make sure it completely covers your skin. And never be without your sombrero. Believe me, you wouldn't exchange it for all the hats in Paris once you get out there in the summer heat."

Aunt Livia had some other odds and ends that she placed in her bag, along with some headache tablets. "You're likely to need one at the end of the day. That glare can be dreadful. Oh, and did you bring skin lotion?"

"Yes, gobs. And a pair of sunglasses."

"Good. Looks like you're all set. And Elly will be sure to share anything you may have forgotten to take. There's breakfast on the sideboard. Now, I don't want you to worry about Amanda. Sherman and I will do all we can for her."

Sharlotte knew they would and kissed her goodbye.

The dawn was lighting the eastern sky to a bright orangey glow when she came down the stairs. Kace was waiting for her in the doorway of the dining room. He had a plate heaped with thick flapjacks oozing with butter and syrup, and he ate while standing. "You're late," he said easily.

Sharlotte laughed. "How can you eat that syrupy mess this time of night?"

"I'll have you know that birds are singing and dawn is brightly shining, and you call this night? Better eat. This is your last chance until we dine amid sagebrush and lizards."

"I'll just have tea, thank you. With one lump of sugar."

"The Ashfords are a strange breed."

She noted that the dining room was empty. "So I'm late, am I? Why, the others aren't even up yet."

"They were up an hour ago, ate, and went on to get their baggage. They have two trucks loaded with goods for the orphanage. They'll meet up with us at the Pecos River."

"Oh," she said meekly.

He smiled at her expression. "You see how generous I am with you? I even let you sleep an extra hour."

"Your consideration overwhelms me."

"But you'd better get used to big changes. On the journey you'll need to keep up with the rest of us."

She smiled and drank her tea. "Just wait. I'll show you."

He finished his coffee and set the mug down. "Ready, señorita?"

"Ready."

Two horses were saddled and waiting. He tied her bag to the side of the saddle, and she mounted, slipping on her gloves. It was then that she caught sight of the rifle on his saddle, and the pistol in his belt. A strange excitement, mingled with incredulity, swept through her already charged emotions. What was she getting herself into? Turning their horses, they rode west toward the Pecos River.

∾

It was nearing sometime in the afternoon. Sharlotte was already exhausted from the heat and glare—her eyes smarted, and her skin burned as though she had a fever. And she was hungry. The thought of flapjacks with butter and syrup now made her mouth water.

True to Aunt Livia's words, Sharlotte wouldn't have traded her sombrero for every pretty hat in Paris. She was learning that fashion was not worth very much when survival was the key in a harsh and hostile environment.

The open range stretched before her in all directions, flat land that seemingly possessed no visible horizon. She hoped her misery was not too obvious to Kace, though he apparently had little difficulty in seeing through her front. How could he know her so well when their thinking was often worlds apart?

"You'd do better if you stopped fanning yourself with that lace gadget."

Gadget! Her thirty dollar Belgium lace fan!

"Nothing you say surprises me, but really, what's wrong with my fan?" she asked.

"You're using up needless energy. And that perfume you've soaked it in draws yellow jackets and flies as well. Better save it for some promenade down Fifth Avenue."

She swished her face more rapidly. "I happen to enjoy the fragrance. How much farther?"

He smiled. "Honey, we just started. All day. We'll camp at the river tonight—unless you think you're going to faint on me."

"I am *not* going to faint. You needn't worry I'll slow you down. I think you take some sort of malicious enjoyment in seeing me like this," she said stiffly.

"You flatter yourself. My eyes are busy watching for rattlers. I hadn't thought about seeing you at all."

Her lashes narrowed. "I'm thirsty."

"And hungry too, probably. You should have listened to me. There's a canteen on the back of your saddle. Go easy, though. We can't refill it until tonight."

Sharlotte thought of the river they'd come to where she could wash away the dust and sweat from her skin when they camped.

He studied her for a moment. "We'd better stop at the next tree. There's a mesquite up ahead. It'll offer a handful of shade."

She would have protested, but she was so sore from the saddle that even a fifteen-minute stop seemed a luxury.

He helped her down to the ground, and they took respite in the blessed shade. Sharlotte fanned herself and looked about despairingly.

"Don't melt," he said.

"I'm quite all right. I suppose you think there's oil in all of this wasteland."

"I'm not the only one. All the big oil companies are moving in, especially around the Graham area farther east from here. I'd wager there's oil all over Texas and Oklahoma. Mexico as well. It takes discipline, though, to find it. But all you need is one break."

He unstopped the canteen and handed it to her. She drank sparingly. "Is that all you think about, discipline? Enduring? Proving you're able to survive in this awful place?"

"Sounds like I should have let you sleep another hour. As to your remark about discipline, I hadn't thought about it, really. It's simply a way of life that one gets used to because if you don't, survival is in question. For you, this is misery, I suppose. You've lived all your life pampered by luxury, by quiet Long Island breezes, in a bubble of false security. Not just because of your father's money, but because your name is Ashford."

"Are you back to that again?"

"Your kind expect too much too easily, and they take it for granted."

"If this is all there is to your reality, you may keep it."

"Reality is often placed upon us whether we want it or not. I think your father believed life was automatically obligated to see to his wants. He didn't believe in God, but he did believe that some Power was in the business of making his class rich and powerful."

She couldn't argue that. "If some are rich and powerful, as you say, it's because they—they—" she halted. Recently she didn't know what she believed. The world had turned upside down.

"Were you going to suggest that the rich deserve their positions of power? I'd agree, if they worked for it. Most of the time it's all handed down from generation to generation, until disaster strikes. But while the Ashfords lost everything, don't deceive yourself. Thousands more, like the Van Dornens, made even more money on the rubble of other peoples crumbled hopes."

She knew that was true too. Some who had gotten out of the market before it crashed had come back in recently and bought up shares of companies at a fraction of their original cost. One day they would see those shares triple in price, adding more to their already stuffed bank accounts.

"Maybe you're right," she said. "But they deserve to rake in the bounty."

"Because someone gave them a tip that the market was likely to hit bottom? I've heard even Hoover quietly withdrew all his stock market investments around three weeks before it crashed.

That goes for Coolidge, too, and the Kennedys. They all got out. Did you ever ask yourself how they knew?"

"Maybe they were just smarter," she protested.

Kace looked at her. "Sure," he said dryly.

Sharlotte handed him his canteen. "Anyway, I'll have my father's gold. My rightful inheritance. And I'm not putting it in any old bank."

His eyes glinted with wry humor. "You prefer to bury it under a tree?"

The skunk. "I suppose you have a better idea?"

"Now that you ask, yes." He smiled.

"Well, I don't want to hear it. What do you know about money?"

"If I'd been an Ashford instead of a Landry, I'd never have lost your estate. As for the gold, if it were mine, I'd invest it in the oil land around Graham or Jacksboro."

"Might as well cast it to beggars in the London streets."

"You don't need to go to London. You can find a throng to cast it to on any street in America."

"Even if you had it to invest in more oil land, what would you do with your smelly old cows?" she laughed.

"Sharlotte, honey, how many times must I tell you that they are not 'cows,' but steers?"

"A cow is a cow."

"Uncle Sherman doesn't want to admit it, nor do any of the other ranchers, but the drought and failing beef prices will make raising cattle a poor investment for the next few years, maybe longer. It depends on the dust storms. I say oil is the next big bust in Texas. If you were smart, my Sweet, you'd invest in it. One day you'd end up an oil heiress. Believe me?"

She pursed her lips thoughtfully. "Well…maybe, but it's a risk I won't take right now. I'm going to bring Amanda back to beautiful Vermont." She sighed.

"You can invest in oil without living here. If you keep the gold it will soon be used up. But if you invest it, you can double it, even triple it."

"And I suppose you'd like me to turn it over to you to invest?"

"Sure, why not? We could be partners. I'll give you half of everything I've got and do all the work. You can just hang around waiting for the big black geyser to come bursting forth from beneath the good Texas earth."

She knew he was teasing her, that all his bantering was taking her mind off her misery, but she detected a faint seriousness to his offer as well. For a moment she imagined sinking her gold into his land, making it possible to expand, and to buy all the equipment he needed. His own share of the gold would pay off all the remaining debts her father had incurred. What if it worked? What if he did strike oil?

She glanced at him thoughtfully. "And I suppose you are going to become a wealthy oil baron? Swaggering, conceited, loud, and obnoxious?" She smiled.

Kace was unperturbed. "I've never been loud. I like the distances surrounding me, the quiet. There's freedom of thought and action in not allowing one's self to be pressed into familiar molds. That's the one thing that's irritating to me about you, Sharlotte."

"Only one?" she raised a brow.

"You expect me to conform to your precise estimation of the man you dream about—"

"Oh, really? Aren't you being a little conceited? What makes you think that you know what kind of man I want?"

"I do. The insufferable Clarence Fosdick the Second."

She smothered a smile. "The Third."

"All right, the Third. But you do get my point."

"Yes, you want to rob me of all the gold, not just your share. Maybe it's not bandits I need concern myself with after all, but one Kace Landry."

He laughed shortly. "Come along, Charmer, we need to keep moving. Keep in mind what I said about investing in oil. I may even allow you to buy into my company."

"I wouldn't even think of it unless I own an equal share with you."

"Partners?"

She glanced at him. "I'm going home to Vermont," she said firmly.

~

They arrived at the Pecos River at sundown. A wide sweeping splash of rose and gold settled over the western horizon and the first evening star was beginning to gleam like a brilliant diamond. It wasn't much cooler by the river, and the ground and rocks continued to hold the heat of the day, but the relief that came from escaping the sun's rays was something to be thankful about. The others had already arrived and a camp was set up near the river. Sharlotte saw that the trucks, laden down with goods, were parked and still, and the horses and mules were relieved of their burdens and tied some distance away to take nourishment from the sparse range grass.

"How do they expect to get all that across the river?" she asked Kace as they neared the site.

"Boats. The trucks belong to the church congregation. We'll be leaving them here and using mules to pack the supplies. Three of the company will be returning to Midland."

He came around to help her down. "Think you can walk?" he teased.

"Just barely. Thank you…" His strong arms seemed to effortlessly lift her from the saddle and set her gently on the ground. For a moment they stood close together, his hands on her waist and hers on his broad shoulders. He was the first to turn away.

He unstrapped her bag and handed it to her, then proceeded to unsaddle the horses. "Elly will show you where you can bathe," he said. "But don't wander too far, and watch the shrubs for poisonous snakes...ants the size of grasshoppers."

Grasshoppers! She laughed at him and walked ahead as Elly came to meet her.

"Poor dear, you made it. Bless your heart. Are you all right? Come along, I've hot tea just for you and a big tub of cool water inside my tent. You can have all the privacy you need."

"Oh, I've reached paradise."

Elly laughed. She waved at Kace. "Coffee's on, Kace! And Pa's got a stew you won't believe how tasty."

"I'll be right there, Elly. After putting up with Sharlotte all day you come off as either a saint or an angel. I haven't made up my mind which."

Sharlotte paused, turned around, and looked at him, her lips parted over his temerity. But he continued to smile and led the two horses to the grass.

Elly laughed. "He enjoys seeing you get all indignant."

Later, Sharlotte sighed contentedly as she snuggled into the round tub of water and closed her eyes. *I think I'll just go to sleep here,* she thought. When she opened her eyes at last, ready to get out of the tub, her gaze fell on the tent floor. In the shadows, cast by the one small kerosene lamp, she saw a scorpion and a tarantula in battle for supremacy. She swallowed the panic that rose in her throat and sank lower into the water. "Elly!" she screamed at the top of her voice. "Elly!"

Elly came tearing into the tent, eyes wide. Sharlotte pointed.

Elly halted, made a grimace, but went calmly to get the broom and sweep them into a dust pan. Holding the pan out as far as she could reach, she muttered "ugh" and crept out the tent with them. Outside she heard Kace asking Elly what had happened.

Sharlotte gingerly stole from the tub and dressed as quickly as she could, all the while staring at the floor. *And I'm supposed to sleep on the ground tonight? What if another spider comes creeping in? What if I awoke with one of those things crawling over my face?* She shuddered with revulsion.

That night around the campfire, after a hearty meal of beef stew and hunks of bread, Pastor McCrae read from the Bible and Elly led them in singing several hymns. Sharlotte quietly listened to the words, deeply stirred by their truth and their message for her own life. Oh, how she wished her father had heard them and heeded their message. She sang with the others:

> Years I spent in vanity and pride,
> Caring not my Lord was crucified,
> Knowing not it was for me He died on Calvary.
>
> > Mercy there was great, and grace was free;
> > Pardon there was multiplied to me;
> > There my burdened soul found liberty, at Calvary.
>
> By God's Word at last my sin I learned;
> Then I trembled at the law I'd spurned,
> Till my guilty soul imploring turned to Calvary.
>
> > Mercy there was great, and grace was free;
> > Pardon there was multiplied to me;
> > There my burdened soul found liberty, at Calvary.
>
> Now I've given to Jesus everything,
> Now I gladly own Him as my King,
> Now my raptured soul can only sing of Calvary.
>
> > Mercy there was great, and grace was free;
> > Pardon there was multiplied to me;
> > There my burdened soul found liberty, at Calvary.
>
> Oh, the love that drew salvation's plan!
> Oh, the grace that bro't it down to man!
> Oh, the mighty gulf that God did span at Calvary.

> Mercy there was great, and grace was free;
> Pardon there was multiplied to me;
> There my burdened soul found liberty, at Calvary.

Sharlotte wiped her eyes and was glad she was seated in the shadows. The words repeated themselves in her heart: "Years I've spent in vanity and pride, Caring not my Lord was crucified."

Was Jesus Christ *her* personal Savior?

She felt drawn by a sweet, gracious longing and bowed her heart before Him. "Oh, Lord Jesus, if I've never received You into my life as my only Savior from the penalty that I deserve for my sin, I do so now. Come and live in me and own me as Your child."

Now I've given to Jesus everything, now I gladly own Him as my King, the words sang on in her mind. Had she yielded everything? Including her ambitions? There remained strongholds in her life that provided areas for strong temptation and attacks by the wicked one. She needed to turn these areas over to the control of God's Spirit. She must open her clenched fists of all the trinkets she held onto so tightly. One thing kept coming before her mind: the love of gold, the belief that it would answer the need to her longings. Did she trust in it too much?

She agonized in a spiritual struggle. *But I need that gold, Lord! I need it for Amanda.*

Is it really for Amanda, or for you?

"Yes, Lord, for Amanda. So she can get well again and walk again. Once my sister is cared for, after that—yes, after that, Lord Jesus—I'll do whatever you ask of me.

After that…But God must be first. Seek *first* the Kingdom of God and His righteousness, and all these things shall be added to you.

Despite her prayer she was troubled by a gnawing restlessness.

When she crawled into her bedroll that night she didn't worry about spiders and scorpions creeping into the tent. She had more important concerns. She tossed, wide awake, too warm, while Elly slept next to her as peacefully as a contented child. Sharlotte raised herself to an elbow and looked over at her. *You don't seem to worry about very much. You're not even resentful of me spending so much time with Kace. If I could be like you, I would crawl out of my skin at once. Will I grow more spiritual as time passes, as I learn of His Word and yield to God's truths?* Sharlotte laid down again and listened to the wind. *Maybe He doesn't want another Elly...maybe He wants me. As for weaknesses, His strength alone can undergird. He alone can subdue the restless spirit that demands to reign in willfulness. It is my part to yield...to lean on Him, rest in His provision, and trust Him in darkness.*

The wind moaned and sighed and tugged at the tent flap, even as a longing seemed to knock patiently at the door of her innermost heart. She had opened that door to her life and Jesus had come in. Now, if she were to enjoy fellowship with Him, she must submit all her plans and desires to His holy gaze. The dross must be burned away by that purifying fire, and then only true gold, silver, and precious stones would remain.

27

On the other side of the Pecos River they all mounted horses and, with a dozen mules laden down with the goods for the orphanage, they began the slow and oftentimes tedious journey westward toward the Rio Grande.

Sharlotte found the western part of Texas beyond the Pecos River a mostly barren land, with jagged brown mountains, dry riverbeds, stark mesas, and vast horizons. The beauty had a majesty all its own, quite unlike anything she was accustomed to in the East.

Elly told her that the land her father's congregation had bought to expand the orphanage into a boys' ranch was located near the river, a little south of El Paso.

"The orphans come from all over Texas," Elly explained as they rode along side by side. "We even have a few from Santa Fe, New Mexico. Nate eventually wants to expand the orphanage to include girls, but that dream lies somewhere in the future. We'd need to build a separate dormitory to keep them and hire more help."

"Nate?" Sharlotte asked.

"The minister from Fort Worth, Nate Caldwell. The Southwest Mission Organization sent him to run the new ranch. He's had plenty of experience, and he's doing a marvelous job, but we need money if we're to include girls. With hard times coming, I don't know where we're going to get it. A fine lack of faith I'm showing! 'With God all things are possible.'"

During the journey, as Sharlotte had expected, Elly proved herself an example of patience and charity. She didn't complain about the heat, nor about the long days beneath the burning sun. At evening when they stopped to set up camp, Elly was the first to begin cooking supper and the last to turn in. She waited on the men, bringing them coffee and food, and she was always there to refill their mugs. If anyone could hope to measure up to the virtuous woman of Proverbs 31, Sharlotte thought, discouraged with herself, it was Elly.

Sharlotte watched her and tried to emulate her attitude of serving others instead of herself. She began to assist Elly in cooking breakfast and supper, and she took over the task of bringing the coffeepot to the others in the evening as they gathered around the campfire. Sharlotte greeted each man with a sisterly smile and asked how he was faring under such hard labors. She even offered to wash their shirts if they needed her help.

A little while later, Kace met her with a disarming smile. She should have known he was up to something when his gray-green eyes sparked with amusement.

He handed her his shirt. "Need any soap?" he asked, his voice smoothly innocent.

She struggled to keep back a smile. "I have enough to share."

"You're generosity overwhelms me."

She took his shirt down to the creek and scrubbed it clean, then came back and hung it up to dry near his tent.

By mid-morning the next day they neared their destination, and by afternoon arrived at the orphanage with its new expanse of church-owned land. Sharlotte was immediately introduced to the handful of dedicated missionaries. The boys who lived there numbered eighteen in all, and ranged in age from eight to fourteen years.

Pastor Nate Caldwell was a lanky young Texan with sandy hair, a ready smile, and alert brown eyes. He was warmhearted and friendly and welcomed her as though she were a traveling missionary who had come to stay among them.

Sharlotte settled into the mission compound and the next three days went by more quickly than she would have expected.

She enjoyed the communal mealtimes with the staff and boys. There was daily chapel with singing, Bible study, and prayer time. At sundown there were outdoor sporting games: baseball and football for the boys, with Nate, Kace, and the other men joining in.

She went with Elly, a missionary named Lorna, and a Mexican girl named Maria to visit the families camped some distance away near the river. Here, they visited with the women and handed out soap and other commodities, including dried rice, beans, flour, and coffee. There were clothes for the babies and things as simple as safety pins, so appreciated by the beaming mothers who had come across the Rio Grande with as little as the clothes upon their backs.

Sharlotte even managed to ride with Kace and Pastor McCrae to where the men had gathered to receive the Spanish New Testaments. Pastor McCrae spoke a brief message of hope and grace in Christ, freely offered to all, and then when the men, old and young, lined up for the New Testaments, she saw Kace walk to the end of the line where two young men waited. He spoke alone with them. Was he asking about Santana?

She didn't get a chance to ask him on the way back. Pastor McCrae was telling her and Kace about all the good plans they had for the land. He pointed out the area where the horse corrals and a bunkhouse would be built. A large schoolroom was needed too, one with partitions to give the older boys their own quiet area to study from the textbooks.

"And then one day it's our hope to have a place for abandoned girls as well."

"I would think girls would take priority," Sharlotte said. "Girls are in more danger on the streets when they're not wanted."

"You're right," Pastor McCrae said. "Maria was such a girl. She came from the cantina section of El Paso about a year ago. She's doing better since she's come here to help with the cooking. But we need a more encompassing program to help many, many more like her."

When they returned to the main compound, Sharlotte was hoping to speak to Kace and ask whether he had gotten the information he needed on Santana, but he had gone to find Mr. Crawford, and neither of them showed up for supper.

Sharlotte inquired secretly from Pastor McCrae where the two had gone, but he didn't seem to know any more than she did. Nor did Elly. They still hadn't returned by nine o'clock.

It was a lovely evening, though extremely hot even by the Rio Grande. The boys had gone to their bunks as curfew set in, and Sharlotte walked back across the yard toward her tiny cabin near the river.

She walked slowly, trying to cool herself in the wind. She had to admit that she'd enjoyed her stay so far. Working in a cause that had eternal results was a far cry from worrying about her coming out balls, or listening to Cousin Sheldon telling his like-minded friends about some yacht race. She was moving and breathing in a whole different world she hadn't even known existed.

So much had changed. Sharlotte herself was changing. She was beginning to measure her life's accomplishments not by what she had lost in New York, but by the insights she had gained since coming to Texas. Still, she had a long way to go before she could compare with Elly. She reminded herself that she hadn't even completed reading the whole Bible through.

But I will, she thought with determination.

A utility side road divided the land in two. On the other side was a long line of trees shading some cabins.

Sharlotte stood at the edge of the dirt road and gazed out into the evening darkness. In thinking of ways to help her sister, she remembered her father's secret rancho. Kace had intimated that it was far from being an estate, but could it be sold for a good price? Now, more than ever, Mexico was the key to the chest that held the gold to fulfill their future plans.

They would both be happier in Vermont. She could find a church to go to and make new friends. She could forgive Clarence and Pamela for their betrayal, even tell Sheldon about the Lord. Yes, surely God *wanted* her to go back home.

Sharlotte's rambling thoughts were interrupted by a young woman's tearful voice coming from the trees—or had it come from the cabins?

The voice ended abruptly. Sharlotte frowned and quickened her steps in the direction from which she though it came. She had heard that woman's voice before, just last night, for her cabin window faced the river and trees. She had little doubt that the couple either worked at the compound, or were among the squatters on the other side.

Moonlight filtered through the trees onto the neat furrows of tilled earth. Sharlotte followed the path until the voices grew louder, this time in heated debate. She couldn't understand what was being said because they spoke in Spanish, but it was clear that they argued.

Now the woman burst into tears again, followed by a man's rebuke, then running footsteps. Sharlotte stopped. A girl's shadowy figure ran through the trees, a mere silhouette against the backdrop of the full moon, her long black hair flying behind. For a second she paused, seeing Sharlotte, then ran on.

Sharlotte couldn't see her face at this distance, but she was sure that it was Maria.

Maria fled toward the cabins and disappeared behind a big tree. Sharlotte waited a moment to see which cabin she would enter, but the girl never reappeared. She must have slipped away into still darker shadows.

A lover's quarrel, Sharlotte decided. Should she mention this to Elly tomorrow, or let it go as none of her affair? Maria might be in trouble with no one to turn to for help.

All turned quiet and she put it from her mind. She walked toward her own cabin. She wasn't anxious to go into the warm room. Where was Kace? Had he returned yet?

She slowed her steps to look at the heavens, mostly black with shades of indigo. Even though she longed for home and much of what was forever lost to her, she had to admit to herself that there was nothing quite like a big glowing Texas moon on a clear silent night, illuminating the plains. Nothing like the sighing prairie winds hustling along like a herd of wild Spanish mustangs through sagebrush and range land. And the Rio Grande moving along with rushing sounds that filled her ears.

In time, there came a new sound. Footsteps. She looked toward the river and shrubs, darkly shaped and mostly indistinguishable. The footsteps halted as though she had been noticed standing there so silent and still. Then, cautiously, the footsteps came closer. A large figure moved from the shadows into the moonlight. The man wore a poncho that hung to the hips of his breeches along with a vaquero hat.

Maria's boyfriend.

"Good evening, Señorita Ashford." He walked slowly forward, hat in hand, and offered her a sweeping bow. She did not recognize him as one of the men she'd seen that day, but then, she couldn't recall them all. He was young, not much older than Kace and Tyler. His strong features shone in the moonlight, and his even white teeth gleamed against a dark mustache. There came a flash of reckless smile.

"How do you know who I am?" she asked, keeping her distance. Had Maria told him?

"I remember you from three years ago, señorita."

Three years? "You—remember me?"

"What man could forget such a beautiful woman with so unusual color of eyes?"

His boldness set her on guard. This was not one of the men in the camp, who were all the essence of polite deference.

"When Señor Kace was only a boy, I taught him how to break a mustang without ruining its spirit. That was before Señor Sherman brought him to the ranch house and made him a son. Now he is no longer my friend. He turns the señorita against me."

Maria…

"'A bandit,' he tells her. 'A thief!' And does she believe me? She believes him!"

Sharlotte took a step backward. Santana.

"I enjoyed your summer visits, señorita. I watched you from afar. I often laughed to myself at how you flirted with Señor Kace. Then you refused him!"

Sharlotte glanced toward the compound with its lighted windows.

"If you're looking for food—" she began, but he cut her off with an abrupt wave of his hand.

"I am looking for much more than a handout, señorita. Cattle, horses, perhaps gold? What is that glimmering around your pretty neck, eh?"

Sharlotte had worn her gold medallion to dinner and it must have caught the moonlight. It was just one small piece of the jewelry she still owned. It was not worth much, but her father had given it to her on her fourteenth birthday and she cherished it, especially now when she knew she would never see him again.

Her hand went to her throat. Horrid memories of the hobo near the tracks sent her fears running wild.

"If you take one step toward me I'll scream from here to Mexico City."

He threw back his head and laughed.

In those seconds when he was off his guard, she turned and fled, crying for help. Would anyone hear her at this distance?

Her boot heel turned inward on a small rock and caused her to break her stride. She ran on, but he overtook her. His hand grabbed her arm, swinging her around to face him.

"The fine haughty lady from the East! Showing herself off on the Landry ranch. And now here! You are no lady. You are no different than Maria." He grinned, his black, robust eyes moving over her. "But prettier." He laughed roughly, pulling her into his arms. "Lord help me," she prayed, fighting fiercely to free herself. She kicked and clawed, screaming all the while. He spat furious words at her. She bit his fingers that tried to silence her. He let go and grasped the gold medallion at her throat. In one swift jerk he yanked it free, breaking the chain. Her skin burned as though a whip had lashed about her neck. She turned to run. He grabbed her arm again.

A click of a rifle brought swift release. Sharlotte nearly lost her balance. He spun around in surprise.

"Let her go, coyote," Maria spat, holding the rifle aimed at his chest.

Sharlotte ran to her side, sweating and gasping from the struggle. Maria must have expected trouble and went for a rifle.

He gritted, saying something insulting in Spanish, took a step toward them, but Maria raised the barrel. Her flowing rebuke of fiery words followed. His eyes narrowed into slits of fury.

Voices came from the compound behind them, and Santana turned and fled toward the river.

Maria slowly lowered the rifle, then looked back over her shoulder. Some of the older boys were coming across the field.

"They must not see me here. I must go," she whispered earnestly. "*Please*, señorita, please say nothing of this, especially to Señor Caldwell and his sister."

A woman called anxiously to Maria from the door of a distant cabin. Elly, thought Sharlotte, recognizing her voice.

"I must hide the rifle. I will come back for it when they are asleep."

Sharlotte saw her rush into the trees and scramble up the nearest trunk. She came back down, then was calling in a calm voice across the field to the boys. She even laughed. Whatever

Maria had told them, they were convinced, for they stood for a moment, then turned slowly and walked back toward their bunkhouse.

"I told them you were afraid. You squealed because you saw a tarantula—and there is one—right there on the path."

Sharlotte moved back, revolted by the sight that turned her skin to goose bumps, her courage to jelly.

It was a tarantula, a huge one! Creeping along in the dust, its body bigger than her fist, it only magnified her terror. She knew from past experience that they had long hairy legs and a weird network of eyes. In her phobia-stricken mind it appeared to be willfully coming toward her, as equally forbidding as Santana himself. Her fear caused her to break into a sweat as she watched it, now unable to move.

Other voices were heard coming from another direction, followed by running footsteps.

Maria took hold of her, her eyes pleading. "Please, say nothing. I will explain everything tomorrow." She ran across the field toward the cabin where Elly waited, unaware of what had happened.

Sharlotte's gaze was transfixed by the tarantula. It inched forward.

Kace ran up. Crawford followed.

"What happened?" Kace took one look at her face, then took hold of her, drawing her to him. "What is it?"

Sharlotte gripped his arm and pointed.

Kace followed her stare. His breath eased in exasperation. He released her and stepped back, hands on hips. "You scared the daylights out of me when you screamed. We broke the fifty-yard dash getting here." He threw up his hands and looked at Crawford. "A spider," Kace explained simply. But that one word contained a full dismissal of her scream of terror.

Sharlotte was too sick at the sight to even speak. Her throat felt as if a vice had closed her vocal chords. As if in a trance she stared.

"I'll let you handle that eight-legged critter. The one I'm interested in has two," Crawford was saying.

"Everything all right?" Pastor McCrae called from across the road.

"Yes!" Crawford answered. He smiled at Kace, then walked back toward McCrae.

Kace watched her, scowling. "Say, that little thing actually intimidates you. Honey, it's nothing," he soothed. "Look, I'll show you—"

"Don't—" she choked, backing away, hands at her throat. "If you come near me with it—" She gave a sob, turned, and fled.

She had reached her cabin door when he stopped her. She squealed hysterically, her fists beating against him.

"Sharlotte, honey, don't!" He pulled her into his arms, drawing her head against his chest, stilling her hands. "It's all right," he soothed. "It's gone now. It won't bother you."

Sharlotte struggled to control her emotions. His embrace was comforting, and she wanted to stay there forever.

"You've got a phobia," he said softly. "I hope I didn't cause it when I put one under your pillow years ago. It didn't enter my mind that it would affect you so badly. It was just a silly boyish prank. I had a terrible crush on you, and little boys like to hear girls squeal."

Sharlotte clung to him, paying scant attention to what he was saying. Her only thought was to take advantage of his comforting strength.

"Here," he soothed, "let's dry your eyes. Do you have a handkerchief?" He handed her his.

He was being so kind, so lover-like in his touch that she was forgetting the creature and everything else in the hot night except his nearness. Her head fell back, the moonlight shining full on her face and throat.

"Kace, I—"

His breath caught. He stared. He reached a finger and touched the welt where the chain had bruised her skin. He glanced back to the path where the spider had been crawling. His gaze swerved to hers.

"That isn't what you screamed about," he said very quietly. "You were wearing a gold medallion tonight. Where is it now?"

The pleading voice of Maria rang in her ears.

Kace glanced thoughtfully toward the squatters' camp.

She owed it to Maria to keep her secret, yet how could she keep the truth from Kace? He and Crawford were here to find Santana.

"Someone…came from the orchard when I was out walking. He demanded I give it to him. When I refused he grabbed me…it was awful, worse than that hobo." Her voice gave way to her churning emotions.

"Come," he said with unexpected gentleness, holding her close again as though he would never let her go. "Come, now. You're safe."

After a few moments of silence, he said against her hair, "Did you see his face?"

"There was nothing memorable…he wore a hat…a poncho."

"Have you seen him before?"

"No." She pulled away a little and forced herself to look at him.

"Certain?"

"I'm certain. That is…I don't remember having seen *him* before, but he remembered me."

He breathed in sharply. "From where? Today?"

"No, Uncle Sherman's ranch." She sighed, and it all came out in a rush. "Maria met him tonight in the trees by the river. The girl is frightened and begged me not to say anything. I felt as though I should protect her since she came with a rifle and threatened him. That's when he ran off. He told me he'd worked at the ranch in the past. Even taught you horsemanship." She shuddered. "He called me by my name. And said insulting things. When I asked him if he wanted food or clothing, he mocked me. He said he was only interested in cattle, horses, and gold."

He looked toward the cabins. "I learned about Maria tonight from one of the young men at the camp. He said she was Santana's girl. I was on my way to tell Crawford when I heard your scream. What else did Tomas say, anything?"

"No, I ran away. That's when he caught me. Kace, can't you wait and talk with Maria tomorrow when she's alone? Elly's with her. Maria's afraid she might ask her to leave."

"She won't be requested to leave. This mission exists to help people like her. She may be able to pass on information about that cowhand who was shot on Snowcroft's ranch. Tomas likes to brag. If she does know something, it can't wait."

"What about Santana?"

"By now his horse is galloping with the wind. He'll know Crawford and I are here. He may cross the border. Come, let's get you in the cabin."

Sharlotte was too exhausted to protest. Kace opened the door. Heat like an oven greeted her. A moment later he lit the kerosene lamp. He glanced about, looked in the small closet, then walked back to the door. He checked the bolt to make sure it locked securely.

Sharlotte sank to a hard chair. "After you talk to Maria, will you and Crawford ride out to find Santana?"

"No. I doubt if we could find him. It could take months to track him down. He's well acquainted with this area. I'm sure Crawford now will have the information he needed, proving Tomas is the one who entered Snowcroft's ranch and killed his foreman. My work is done here. The rest will be left up to the Texas Rangers."

"You mean we're free to go on to my father's rancho?"

"Yes, unless you'd rather call this off and go back to Sherman and Livia."

"No. I'm going on, Kace."

He watched her for a moment as if making up his mind. "All right. I want to be with Crawford when he questions Maria. We'll start for your father's rancho tomorrow afternoon. That will give you a little time to recover."

She smiled wanly. "I'll be all right. I'm glad you're not going to confront him."

He looked at the mark on her throat, frowned again, and made no reply.

"What will we tell Pastor McCrae and the others?" she asked a little shakily.

"The truth. That your father left you a small rancho in Mexico. I'm bringing you there to look it over, so you can decide if you want to sell it or keep it." The gold, of course, would go unmentioned until they accomplished the task and were safely back at the Landry ranch. "Sweet dreams, Sharlotte." He went out and crossed the room to bolt the door.

She closed her eyes and rested her forehead there a moment. It would soon be all over.

"Heavenly Father, thank You for rescuing me," she prayed.

28

The blistering land was a treeless, short-grassed country. Tall cactus plants and now and then a gnarled tree were the only landmarks Sharlotte could see.

They had crossed the Rio Grande at sunset and by dawn the next morning they were well inside Mexican territory. He was finally able to tell her that the rancho was located inland near El Sueco, another three days of travel. Sharlotte was jumpy, stirring at every unusual sound. She noticed he kept his gun on him, and the rifle near at hand.

By noon, as the sun rose in the hard blue sky, Kace chose a hollowed-out section in a small hill surrounded by rocks to make camp. They would sleep during the hot day and travel again in the moonlight. A pepper tree's big branches and lacy leaves overhung the opening and sent off a spicy odor in the squelching sun. With only one entrance, Sharlotte felt more secure. Exhausted, she soon fell fast asleep.

A drift of smoke and the aroma of broiled meat awakened her. Kace had a small fire burning and had added rocks to make a spit. A jackrabbit was roasting on a piece of wire she'd seen him use previously from his satchel. She was so hungry that even the thought of wild rabbit aroused her appetite.

"Sleeping Beauty has at last stirred from her slumber," Kace said, and handed her the canteen.

She groaned as she wet a cloth sparingly and tried to wash her face and hands. "How much farther to the rancho?"

"Anxious, are you? Two days. Maybe three. Depends on how well you hold up. And then you can take a cool bath and sleep between sheets while I arrange things at the bank."

She undid her hair and brushed it. "The bank?"

"You mean I didn't tell you?" came his casual voice.

Her brush paused and she looked toward him. His back was toward her as he turned the rabbit over the coals. "Tell me what?" she asked cautiously.

"I told you I didn't know where the gold was, but what I didn't tell you was that your father left you a letter at the bank. Naturally, to get it, you'll need to sign something and prove your identity. That's why I needed to bring you here. The letter either holds a key to a security box or information on where the gold is stored. Perhaps in the bank itself, but I rather doubt that."

"A letter! And you just *now* are telling me?" she crawled out of the hollow and pushed her way through the pepper leaves.

It was sunset, and the sky was aflame against a deepening blue. The wind was still dry and exceedingly warm, tossing her hair like golden threads.

Kace looked at her. "Here, have some coffee. It will be a long night." He poured a cup and handed it to her.

"Thank you…but you haven't explained why you waited until now to tell me."

"The answer to that is simple. If I had told you, you wouldn't have come to Texas at all."

"Not come—I don't understand."

"Oh, I think you do, though that innocent look is enough to convince me otherwise. If you'd known about the letter, you'd have left Amanda in Vermont and grabbed the first transportation available for Mexico, leaving me holding an empty bag. You've only cooperated with me because you thought I alone knew where to find the gold."

It was true. She had thought that only Kace would be able to lead her to her inheritance. "Are you suggesting I'd keep it all and not pay the debt?" she half accused. She sat down on a low rock and drank her coffee, watching him over the rim.

He lounged back with his cup while the rabbit sizzled. "I wouldn't have let you get by with it, though. I'd have come to Vermont looking for you. And you haven't forgotten that I hold the deed to the Ashford estate. That accounts for a good part of your recent well-mannered behavior. But you'd have come here alone. Maybe gotten yourself robbed."

"Indeed. And to think I was just beginning to believe you'd changed for the better. I see I've jumped to conclusions," she said loftily. "You're just as difficult as you ever were."

He laughed and scanned her. "I was just thinking the same thing about you, señorita."

He cut the meat and handed her piece on a stick. She hesitated. "I even cut the ears off just to please you. No excuses this time."

She smiled, in spite of herself, and took the end of the stick. When the meat had cooled, she ate in silence, dreaming of the gold, of cool Vermont. She glanced at Kace and found he was watching her lazily.

He stood, threw the bones into the fire and walked over to the horses, saddling them. Sharlotte finished eating, rinsed her fingers in a bit of water and cologne, then quickly braided her hair and pinned it out of the way.

Kace walked up and kicked out the fire, adding more dirt. "Ready?"

"Yes." She put on her big sombrero and grabbed her satchel. A few days to the rancho, Kace had said. Just a little while, and then!

The little Mexican village was dry and dusty. "Wind-blasted," Sharlotte murmured, "and quiet." Her instincts told her its stillness was a mere illusion. It was afternoon, siesta time. There were squat buildings of mud or adobe, most of them cantinas.

They rode on down the dirt street. An adobe building ahead of them stood baking in the sun. The road was lined with sleepy trees, thirstily drooping. The wind kicked up a small cloud of dust. A horse was tied to a rail along with a few burros. Some chickens scratched beneath a castor tree.

Sharlotte shaded her eyes. Across the flatlands she saw more small squat buildings, huts huddled together in what Kace called a barrio. A scrawny dog lay in some shade.

"We're not far now," he said lightly.

She glanced at him unhappily. "*This* is where my father bought a rancho?"

There was a faint smile on his mouth as though he knew what she was thinking. "Welcome to El Sueco, señorita."

Sharlotte sat rigid and silent as they slowly rode their horses through the tiny village toward a bend in the dirt road.

They must have traveled another half mile before Sharlotte saw a hacienda ahead, surrounded on the backside with eucalyptus trees.

Minutes later they halted their horses in some shade. There was a patio with bushes. The upstairs rooms had verandas, but the place was neglected, and there were cracks in the adobe. No one had been watering the plants. A few struggled on, but the others had turned brown.

Kace swung down and tied the reins to a hitching rail. Flies buzzed sleepily. Someone was there, thought Sharlotte, because the fragrance of roasting corn mingling unnaturally with the odor of animals drifted on the hot breeze to her.

Hot and disquieted, Sharlotte accepted his help as she dismounted. He steadied her a moment as the ground rolled beneath her feet and heat waves blurred her eyes.

"You'll be able to rest now," he said gently.

They walked toward the hacienda. As they neared, Sharlotte heard the slip-slapping of sandaled feet coming across the patio stones. A middle-aged woman appeared, her brow eyes reflecting uncertainty. She wore a shapeless dress with woven leather sandals, and her graying black hair was pulled straight back and tied.

Kace spoke to her in Spanish. Her eyes brightened with sudden recognition, then she spoke rapidly, her nimble hands flying in all directions.

Sharlotte tried to read Kace's expression. When the woman lapsed into uneasy silence, he spoke again. From his tone she could tell that he was asking questions. The woman dabbed at her eyes with her apron and kept repeating: "si, si…" then, "nada, nada."

The woman then turned and hurried indoors. Sharlotte took hold of his arm. "What's happening, Kace?"

"She says bandits have been here. They've taken the animals and the silverware and anything else that served their purpose."

Her stomach tightened. "You think they knew about the go—"

"Not a word about that."

"You mean they don't know?"

"We'd better hope they don't."

He didn't need to explain. The bandits would come back.

"Your father wouldn't have breathed a word about it to anyone here. That shiny secret would soon be whispered all over El Sueco."

"Then why did they come here? How did they know?"

"I'm hoping they didn't, and that the thieves just heard about his death and decided it was a good time to collect some free horses and animals and whatever else they could get their grubby hands on. We'll start with that premise, anyway. Come along, we've still got beds, food, and water. When it gets right down to it, that's what matters."

Sharlotte didn't see it that way. Raw disappointment threatened to overcome her. What if the gold was stolen? What if all this misery had been in vain? The heat, dust, weariness, frustration, and now bandits—they all caused her to give in to the demands of exhaustion and fear. What would they do if the men came back? Was there any real authority in this little out-of-the-way spot? If so, could it even be trusted? Except for Kace and the gun he carried, they were completely vulnerable, far from any Texas Ranger.

Her booted feet felt as if they weighed ten pounds each as she walked beside him across the patio and through the open front door.

The woman led the way, pointing, speaking in a rush.

Sharlotte breathed in the silky coolness, the sweet shadows that soothed her eyes from the glare, the delicious smell of Mexican cooking, and the refreshing chirp of caged birds. They followed her to a low staircase of seven or eight steps that opened onto a wider dining area and more rooms. Sharlotte almost collapsed.

Kace swung her up in his arms and carried her into the dimness. He spoke to the woman and she hurried on and opened a door into a bedroom. He laid her on the bed, then said something and the woman went out.

"Rest. I'm going out for an hour. We'll talk tonight at supper. I'll ask Theresa to bring you water and some tea."

He walked to the door and opened it. Sharlotte raised herself, still feeling dizzy. "You're going back out?"

"I want to find the local police to ask about those bandits."

"Kace?"

He turned and looked back, unreadable.

She smiled tiredly. "Thank you for getting me here safely."

"You can thank me when we're back at the ranch…counting our gold nuggets." He smiled and closed the door.

Gold nuggets. She sighed happily. Gold, surely the answer to all her problems. "Lord, help us to get the gold my father left me. You know my real trust is in You alone. But I desperately need the money."

~

That evening Sharlotte waited for Kace to return. She used the time to refresh herself and tour her father's hacienda. She decided it could be made into a charming place if she had the money for decorating and the desire to live in the small village, which she did not. It might be better to sell it, she decided.

It was the dinner hour and the smell of tortillas, beef, and chili drifted through her open veranda and mingled with the fragrance of honeysuckle. She tried to block out of her mind the memories the honeysuckle scent was reminding her of. She had soaked for an hour in a cool tub of water and changed into her only other clothing, a clean riding habit. It was attractive (which was why she had brought it along), a muted dusky blue with black ribbon trim and silver-coated buttons. She had even put on a dab of the perfume that she had managed to carry in her satchel. How good it felt to be clean and pampered again, if only for a little while. She thought of the long journey home and cringed. If only it was the fall instead of the middle of summer.

Where was Kace? she wondered again while loitering on the veranda. Had he found out anything about the bank to which she would go? Her brow wrinkled, puzzled. She hadn't remembered seeing any financial institution on the dusty little street when they had ridden through to the rancho. Did they even have a bank here? The people had seemed too poor for anything like a bank, but she assumed there must be some prosperous Mexican ranchers somewhere near in the area. Kace would be able to tell her more when he returned.

A knock. Kace!

Sharlotte opened the bedroom door. It was Theresa. She looked nervous, but perhaps she was still upset over the bandits breaking into the hacienda and making off with treasures, especially the animals. Animals meant food, and food was hard to come by. The woman could speak English after all. Why had she behaved as though she couldn't?

Theresa informed her that Señor Landry had returned from talking to the sheriff. He was now staying in her father's bedroom and would soon meet her for dinner in the inside patio. Sharlotte thanked her and a few minutes later went down to the patio room where it was a little cooler.

There were stone bowls waiting on a table smelling temptingly of Mexican cuisine. She lifted the heavy lids and sniffed each dish approvingly. Delicious. She had never been so hungry, so relieved in her life to be safely at her father's rancho for several days' rest, perhaps a week. She sighed contentedly and dipped a big spoon into the bowl of soup made with what looked like black beans, corn, tomatoes, and peppers. It was too hot for her liking, but palatable just the same. So Kace was back from the policeman. What had he learned?

He came in while she was nibbling on tortilla chips and a variety of sauces.

He had bathed, shaved, and was dashing again in clean clothes. His dark hair and gray-green eyes went well with black, she thought. She smiled. "Mi casa es su casa, señor."

He bowed. "Gracias, my lovely señorita!"

He came toward her, glancing at the doorway into another room where Theresa loitered.

"Well, I've good news. I was right. Your father left the letter at the bank. We'll go there tomorrow and sign for it."

"Splendid, Kace! Did you find out anything from the police about the bandits?"

"He assures me they've long disappeared. I'm afraid there's no hope of getting the animals back. You'll need to be content with your father's inheritance money." He toasted her.

Sharlotte smiled and raised her fragile glass. "To our bargain."

"And now, what's for supper?" He lifted the lids on the bowls to see what was there.

Kace didn't seem overly concerned about anything, and that soothed any worries she still had. While he filled his plate, she glanced toward the veranda where guitars had struck up below in the courtyard. She was going to ask Theresa about the players, but she had gone out to water some flowers she had growing in stoneware pots on the outdoor patio.

The sound of the music was soothing. Sharlotte crossed the tile floor to the veranda, her emotions a whirl of confusing and contradictory impulses. The night was warm, yet pleasant, the wind heavy with various odors and fragrances. Below in the yard she saw the group of musicians, well-dressed, strumming guitars and singing. They bowed toward her.

Kace joined her, leaning against the veranda railing and watching the guitar players.

After a few minutes she said unexpectedly: "I admire Elly. I'm glad I was able to spend some time at the mission."

She expected him to be surprised by what she said, and he was. He turned his head and regarded her for a long moment. She supposed he must be astounded she would admit such a thing. Here was Sharlotte Ashford admitting to the mirror on the wall that she was not "the fairest of them all."

"I think she'd be proud if she knew how you felt. I'm curious. What is it you admire most about her?"

"Do you really want to know?" she looked at him gravely.

"You've captured my curiosity. Why would you find someone you once thought drab suddenly admirable?"

She was thoughtful. "It wasn't all that sudden. I've had second thoughts about many things recently, including Aunt Livia and Uncle Sherman. Maybe I've just seen things for what they really are. The mask was removed from the people and society I grew up in, when my father—" she didn't go on. She knew he understood. "And it all seems shallow now, compared to what people are like here. The ranchers who met with you and Uncle Sherman for instance, being so willing to help their friends." She glanced at him, and found him watching her alertly.

"It's a far cry from the way everyone we associated with in our world behaved. They turned their backs toward me and Amanda after my father fell to such dismal depths of shame."

Thoughtfully, she plucked a honeysuckle blossom from a vine. "I also prayed and acknowledged my great need for God's forgiveness. It was that song Elly led at the campfire that night on the river. I asked Jesus to be my Savior. I *know* I'm a Christian now."

"That's the most wonderful news I could have heard." He walked toward her. "And yet you want to go back to Vermont," he said quietly. "Everything we've done until now is geared toward that very goal."

Yes, she thought uneasily. She hastened: "But I don't want to go back to what was, but to more comfortable memories…not everything in my life was empty. I still don't belong to Texas, Kace. You know that. I'll never truly belong. Not the way Elly does, or Aunt Livia, or Abby. I belong to Vermont. Amanda and I both belong there. That's why it's so important to pay the debts so I'll be free to go home."

Kace said nothing, and leaned against the rail again, looking down at the guitar players, deep in thought.

"Maybe you're right," he said at last.

"Just…maybe?" She smiled ruefully.

He looked at her without smiling. "You've only been here a few weeks. Texas might grow on you. Maybe the Lord doesn't want you to go back."

"Well…" she said doubtfully.

He smiled. "Maybe," he repeated.

"Turning the orphanage into a larger boys' ranch is a wonderful idea," she continued. "Elly said you were friends with the new director, Nate Caldwell."

He looked at her, and she sensed his scrutiny, as though he was wondering how much she knew.

"What else did Elly tell you about Nate?"

That's odd...why is he behaving so cautiously?

Sharlotte's curiosity grew stronger. She smiled at him and managed a casual shrug. "Elly just said you'd arranged for her to work with Pastor Nate and that you had even encouraged her to go there. Is that true?"

"Sounds as though she's told you a lot of things that weren't necessary. What else did she explain, anything?"

She sensed his alert gaze. She laughed, bewildered. "No, why do you ask? Is there some big secret I'm not supposed to know about yet?"

His pensive stare puzzled her, and she added: "I certainly don't mean to pry." She turned away, focusing her attention once again on the guitar players below.

For some imperceptible reason he was nonchalant once more, and chose to go on. "I've known Nate for years. We attended that orphanage together. He was two years ahead of me in school."

"Nate was an orphan? So that accounts for his interest in the orphanage."

"We both wanted to do something to improve things at the school. Nate believed he had a calling from God to enter the ministry, but I wanted to make money. Lots of it. So I could invest it in building the best boys' ranch in the States. Considering how things have worked out, it was rather naïve of me. I've helped Pastor McCrae get the property line extended and encouraged Nate to take over as director, but my big schemes of becoming wealthy enough to give Nate everything needed has fallen flat."

Sharlotte considered all this with some surprise. She had never imagined this tender and human side of Kace Landry.

"You didn't fail," she said quickly. "How were you to know the economy would fall to pieces when everything was going so well? And there's always tomorrow, Kace, and the tomorrow after that. You're young. And you're convinced there's oil on your land. Surely this depression can't last more than a year or so...then, who knows? You may actually have that oil shower after all!"

He laughed softly and came towards her.

"Why are you laughing?" she said backing away.

"Because that's the first honest compliment and encouragement you've ever given me. And I'm astounded! A little wary too. I find myself feeling like a hungry coyote circling a tempting trap, never knowing if one bite means my doom!"

"It is not my first compliment!" she said, shocked to think it might be. There were a hundred times when she had thought complimentary things about Kace. Had she kept them all locked in her heart? But she felt hurt too. He saw her as a trap! But could she blame him after the way she treated him years ago?

He was smiling as he stilled her hands against his chest. "Maybe you've developed a heart after all. Makes me curious to find out… if I wasn't just as cautious. Those violet-blue eyes can easily haunt a man's dreams…drive him to distraction if he's not careful."

Sharlotte wasn't thinking of violet-blue eyes, but green ones, with hard flecks of steely gray…

But unexpectedly something distracted him, and she lost his attention. He let go of her and turned toward the railing and the yard below.

What was wrong, she wondered. What had he noticed? She didn't know whether to be relieved or disappointed that he hadn't followed through on his first romantic intentions.

"What is it, Kace?" she whispered.

His expression was not tempered by guitars but by thoughtful deliberation.

"The guitars stopped," he explained. "And that song they were playing…I just realized where I'd heard it before."

She sensed his concern mingling dangerously with the scent of heated stone and dust.

"What has the music got to do with—"

"Did you recognize the song?" he asked in a low voice.

"No, is it important?" She looked at him curiously. What did it mean to him?

He didn't explain. He stood still for a moment in the darkness. She followed his gaze down toward the yard but she could see nothing out of the ordinary that hadn't been there all along. All was silent. The hot breeze stirred the trees, causing a dry crackling sound.

She came up beside him, and he took her arm and drew her inside the room. He quietly closed the veranda doors and drew the drape across.

Theresa was making sure the bowls of food were still warm. Seeing them, she smiled, bowed, and left them alone.

Sharlotte kept looking at Kace, trying to guess his next move.

"Better go up to your room and wait for me," he said. "Lock the doors and don't let anyone in, not even Theresa. I'll need to leave for a little while."

Fear coiled about her heart. Something unexpected had prompted him to an action that he hadn't intended to make yet.

"Let me come with you, Kace."

"No, honey," he said softly. "You're safer here. Don't worry so. I'll be back later tonight."

"Can't you at least tell me where you're going?"

He smiled. "To see a priest."

A priest! She stopped and stared at him.

He left the same way he came, unexpectedly, passing through a doorway into the shadows. She didn't hear him leave the house, quite possibly because he intended it that way. A moment later, with growing concern, she went to her room and locked the door as he had asked.

29

Sharlotte awoke with a start. The bedroom was stuffy with heat and in darkness except for the moonlight streaming in from the veranda. Not a whiff of wind stirred through the curtain. Her heart thumped. She threw aside the sheet and slipped on her father's cotton robe. Her bare feet felt the soft smooth warm stone as she moved toward the veranda to peer below—

Someone was in the room! How it was she knew this, she couldn't say, but her skin tingled with awareness. She heard no footsteps, but someone was there, standing near the veranda. She stopped, hardly daring to breathe, staring intently into the shadows.

Something moved, then an obscure shape came into the vague moonlight. Sharlotte tensed, and she opened her mouth to cry out, but a voice whispered: "I'm sorry I frightened you. I had to come in through the balcony. Don't make a sound." It was Kace.

She froze, then fury gripped her: "What are you doing climbing over my veranda!"

"Hush, Santana is somewhere below. I couldn't come in through the front door."

"Santana!" she grabbed him. His arms went around her reassuringly.

"I don't want Theresa to hear us talking. I found out she's his aunt."

"You mean she's on *his* side?" she whispered incredulously. "All that distress this afternoon was a show?"

"I could give her the benefit of the doubt, but doing so would place us in danger. We've got to leave without her knowing."

"But—how did Santana's aunt—?"

"I don't know the answer to that, except your father was exhausted when we arrived, the arduous travel was too much for him. He hired Theresa to care for him after I left. In snooping around she may have learned something about the gold shipment and passed it on to Tomas. He had no problem recognizing the name Burgess Ashford as soon as she told him whose rancho this was."

Sharlotte remembered his remarks at the orphanage. What had he said? Something about wanting—cattle, horses, and *gold?*

"Then he knew why we were at the boys' orphanage even before we crossed the Rio Grande."

"He's certainly had no trouble guessing why we're here," he stated.

She shivered at the thought of that night when facing him alone. She glanced anxiously toward the veranda. What could they do? How could they leave without Santana knowing?

A horrid thought mocked her hopes. "And the gold! How can we possibly get hold of it and escape?"

"For one thing he's not expecting us to leave tonight. My statement earlier about visiting the bank tomorrow was for Theresa's benefit."

"You mean you knew even then that she was his aunt?"

"I knew as soon as I was shown to your father's room. I searched his desk to make sure he hadn't left some message behind other than his suicide note. I found the name of his housekeeper scribbled on a piece of paper, Theresa Santana. By now she's probably passed the news on about the bank visit to Tomas."

"But how? She's been at the rancho since we arrived."

"She didn't need to leave. Remember the stable boy when we were on the veranda earlier?"

She recalled the boy speaking to one of the guitar players. So that was it. "He brought a message from Theresa?"

"That's my guess. And that song. Tomas played it often enough when he worked at Sherman's ranch. I've never heard it anywhere else."

The guitar players! And to think that they'd been standing in plain view on the veranda while Santana and his gang serenaded them! That must have caused him malicious mirth. She remembered how Kace had suddenly changed moods and mentioned the guitars and song. She looked at him. "That's why you—" she stopped, but not before a vague smile touched his mouth as he apparently followed her thoughts.

His gaze drifted to her lips, and Sharlotte, feeling the heat of embarrassment, realized his arms were still around her and drew back at once.

"But, Kace," she protested in a whisper, "if she tells Tomas about our going to the bank for the gold tomorrow he'll know and follow."

"True, but neither he nor his aunt is expecting anything to happen tonight. He'll be waiting for us to go there tomorrow during banking hours. By then, I plan to be out of El Sueco and on our way to the Rio Grande." He looked at his watch in the moonlight. "If we leave in an hour that will give us at least half a day's head start to reach the river before him. We'll need every minute of it as we'll have to travel at half his speed. That chest of gold will be heavy. We'll bring a burro, two if we can manage."

Sharlotte was bewildered. "Leave in an hour—but how! The bank's closed. We need my father's letter to convince the official to turn the gold over to me."

"The letter isn't in the bank. Neither is the gold. Burgess entrusted the envelope with the Spanish Mission priest—the last place anyone expected, including me. It was only after I spoke with the local sheriff—at least he goes by that title—that I guessed."

"The policeman knew the letter was with the priest?"

"He didn't. Tomas would have carved the information out of him by now. It was something the sheriff said that made me think. He said your father was a very devout man who went daily to the mission. It struck me, then, that your father would never have done that. But he did know that the mission and the padre were respected by everyone in town, even Tomas, and your father took that into consideration. He entrusted the envelope with the padre, asking that he hold it in secret until either of us claimed it."

Sharlotte remembered when Kace made the strange statement that he was going to see the local priest. Her excitement soared. "Oh, Kace, then the padre has the letter?"

"He did, kept safely in his vestibule." He reached into his jacket and brought out an envelope. "I've taken the liberty to open it."

Sharlotte removed the sheet of paper and brought it to the stream of moonlight, reading: Vera Cruz. Her brow wrinkled, and she turned toward him. "But he didn't tell me where the gold is."

"Oh, but he did."

"Vera Cruz?" she whispered, dismayed, picturing the city on the map of Mexico. "But that's a week of traveling from here, or even longer on horseback."

"It may be as near as a simple walk in the moonlight."

"You mean here?"

"I'm almost certain. Change, quickly, and pack. We'll leave before Theresa can send Tomas word by the stable boy." He went quietly to the bedroom door and slid back the bolt. Sharlotte was beside him, her excitement ready to burst. "You know where it is?"

"Patience, my lovely. I'll get my bag from your father's room and meet you back here in five minutes."

He closed the door, and Sharlotte, trembling with both fear and excitement, fumbled her way into her riding habit and boots.

She stuffed her other things into her satchel and was ready when he silently returned a few minutes later.

She followed him to the veranda. "Can't we get protection against Santana by going to the local policeman?"

"If this were any other reasonable village, probably," he said dryly. "It isn't. The sheriff's afraid of his own shadow. I asked him about the bandits breaking into the rancho. He claims he was sound asleep when they came through. By the time he could round up a few men with rifles, they were gone."

"You think he's involved with Tomas?"

"No, just a coward. He probably bolts his door and hides beneath his bunk whenever Tomas and his ruthless vaqueros come back across the border with stolen cattle and horses." He held out his hand. "The letter from your father?" She handed it to him. He struck a match and set it aflame.

"We're on our own. We'll need to leave the same way I came in. Wait a moment..." he stepped out onto the veranda, presumably to see if the way was clear. Sharlotte set her bag down on the tile, her legs feeling weak. Suppose they were caught. Suppose—

Kace returned. He looked at her.

Her heart sank. Something had gone wrong. "What is it?" she whispered.

Confused, she hardly knew what to expect when with determination, he pulled her into his arms. With his face just above hers he said: "I've never been one to leave an interesting project unfinished. Danger merely adds a little flare."

His arms wrapped around her tightly, and his lips were on hers, erasing her mind of gold, of bandits, of the hot dusty little village on the Mexican border.

She felt unsteady when his embrace loosened. She stared at him, catching her breath. He picked up her bag, took hold of her arm, and propelled her toward the veranda. "Now, we'll go."

The hot, dark night was quiet. The Spanish Mission of San Pablo del Rio sat still and white in the moonlight with two huge pepper trees shadowing the courtyard. Sharlotte followed behind Kace, walking along beside her horse and the burro from the rancho. *Where are we going? Back to see the padre?*

Yet Kace didn't turn toward the front of the mission, but carefully made his way past the adobe building to the gnarled olive trees growing in back. Beyond was a cemetery with innumerable white crosses. Statues were situated here and there, along with a giant statue of the Virgin, as though she looked out over the dead buried there.

What is he doing? she wondered, her heart beating too fast. Although she knew he carried a gun and plenty of bullets, she was terrified that she might actually hear the sound she dreaded: the running footsteps of Santana and his handful of thieves in hot pursuit. She kept glancing behind them, yet saw nothing but night shadows.

"Oh Lord, be with us," she kept praying. "Help us get the gold and escape before Tomas finds us."

Kace stopped and tied the horses and burro to the trees.

Sharlotte moved back between two huge olive trees with gnarled trunks and concealed herself, waiting. The stars above were like diamonds on a bed of black velvet. The leaves quivered along with her heart.

"Stay in sight," he said quietly. He reached for her hand.

Ahead, there was a gate, and she followed him through. To the left of the gate, as though on silent sentinel duty, stood a great statue shaded by an ancient olive tree. There were some benches and what appeared to be a flowerbed. Kace walked to the statue and surveyed the awesome, stark, cold figure carved in stone. Sharlotte peered too, and surmised he may have lived in the age of the conquistadors.

"Meet General Ferdinand Marcos of Vera Cruz," Kace murmured. "My hunch was right."

Sharlotte looked at him. Her heart leaped. She watched breathlessly as he removed a knife from his belt. Holding it low, he ran his other hand over the statue and down its base. He stooped to the ground and crawled to the backside. Sharlotte knelt beside him watching, intrigued. Near the base of the foundation he felt the rough stonework, pressing here and there, as if searching.

He took his knife and carefully inched about the Mexican tiles, until lifting one slightly out of the ground and gaining a finger-hold to work it loose, he drug it aside. He pressed the blade into the dirt and hit something solid.

"I always did say pirate blood ran in the Ashford family," he taunted. "Look, buried treasure."

Sharlotte was too thrilled to take offense. At the moment nothing mattered to her but the dark-looking metal box she saw in the hollowed-out hold.

"Hunnewell put it here at your father's orders, is my guess."

"Hunnewell!"

"Hunnewell waited here at the rancho until the gold sent from your father's secret friend in London arrived. Your father instructed him to bury it here. But Burgess was too ill when he arrived to do anything about retrieving it. The closest he came to his box of gold was to take daily strolls here in the garden. He must have cast glances toward this statue a hundred times. No wonder he acquired a reputation for being very devout."

Not even sadness for her father stole away her joy.

"Do hurry," she whispered.

He sheathed his knife, reached in, and lifted the heavy metal box out onto the ground.

"How much gold do you think?" she whispered. "Let's see. Oh! It's locked," she said anxiously. "We'll need to break it open."

"Not now, there's no time. Anyway, the noise would alert the padre, or worse."

Sharlotte's mind was in a whirl. She looked on as he set the stone slab back into place, shifting it into position. A few taps here and there and a dusting of the stone base with a little dirt, and the seam was nearly invisible. She smiled. "You're brilliant, Kace."

"About time you realized that."

He cleared their footprints with an olive branch, tossing a few olives here and there. He lifted the chest and, as silently as they had come, they slipped away in the darkness, Sharlotte running ahead to the burro.

30

By sunrise the next morning they were far from El Sueco. Kace found some shade beneath an oak tree by a creek, and they led the animals to water.

"Will Santana follow us?"

"Undoubtedly. We can't stay here for long. Thirsty?"

He took the canteen and handed it to her. While she drank, he looked at his watch. "We'll rest an hour. I won't be satisfied until I've a good twenty-four hours between us and Tomas. By now he still doesn't know we're gone. Theresa will think we're exhausted from the journey and sleeping in. Tomas will be keeping an eye on the bank to see if we come out with a satchel."

Sharlotte laughed. "We'll be safe in Texas before they ever realize we took my inheritance and vanished."

"We'll need to make do with this." He took some apples out of his saddlebag.

"Aren't you forgetting something?" she whispered excitedly.

Kace looked innocent. "Now what could that be?"

"The gold! Let's count it."

"Oh. That."

"Yes. That." She ran to where he'd put the chest beneath the tree. "How will we open it?"

"You mean you don't have the key?"

"The key? No, I—" she stopped and looked at him over her shoulder. She saw that he was teasing her. She smiled and stood. "Ah, but you're so clever, surely you can open it?"

He walked up. "And my payment for so difficult a task?"

"You're already getting enough to pay my father's debt in full."

"Stingy, aren't you," he said lightly. "Money mad, is the better word. I've noticed a change in you ever since you knew the gold was within sight."

She folded her arms and tapped her foot. "Such lectures. Well...all right. Maybe a few extra gold coins. You *did* get me here safely."

"And back, hopefully. I may yet have to use this gun on Tomas."

"Oh, let's not ruin the moment by thinking of that. Hurry, Kace, break the lock. I want to see it shining in the sun."

His mouth turned wryly, and he glanced at her. "As for extra payment, I may wish to be paid by some other means. A woman's charms, perhaps."

She drug her eyes from his to the box.

"How quickly a woman forgets."

She knew he spoke of last night when they had kissed.

With his knife and piece of wire he soon completed the task. Sharlotte knelt beside him as he lifted the lid. She gasped, her hands flying to her mouth.

"*Rocks!* Oh! Oh, no! No!"

Kace turned the chest over and dumped them on the dusty, dry earth. Rocks... ordinary rocks...

"We've been tricked," she wailed, forming fists and pounding her thighs. "Who would do such a wicked thing, who!"

"There's a letter," Kace said.

"From my father?" she asked hopefully, leaning over to read the brief writing.

"No," Kace said quietly. "*To* your father. He never opened the chest, so he never knew there were just rocks. He must have been assured that whoever handled this for him was completely trustworthy."

"Assured? Don't you know if he was?"

"My dear girl, was I involved in your father's friendships?"

"You brought him here." She jumped to her feet.

"At his request. And in kindness."

"Kindness? He's been robbed. And how do I know you weren't involved all along?"

He looked at her for a long moment, but this time there was no smile, no teasing glint in his eyes. "I wasn't kidding when I said the bright glitter of gold has gone to your head." He stood. "My part of this bargain was handled fairly and in complete honesty to you."

Bitter disappointment tore at her weary body like thorns. Days, weeks, months of hoping came tumbling down upon her head once again. No hope for Amanda. No getting the Vermont estate back. No money to pay Kace to save his land. Nothing but rocks!

Tears filled her eyes. She grabbed a rock and hurled it with all her strength. "Maybe you're the thief. You came and went last night. You had plenty of time to change the gold for rocks and hide the gold again."

"If I were the thief I wouldn't need to bring you here to Mexico. I could have spared myself the difficulty of putting up with your tantrums!"

"My tantrums? You're raising your voice at me."

"You deserve worse. You should have had a father who turned you over his knee and paddled you good instead of pampering you."

"Indeed!"

"Women," he said, frustrated. "A man risks his life and limb for them, waits years hoping they'll learn to love him, and what does he get for it?"

Devastated, she collapsed to the dust, head in palms. "A chest of rocks," she murmured tearfully. "All for nothing…"

"Enough said. Let's read the letter. I don't think your father ever saw it. I'm sure it will explain."

Kace tore open the envelope. "It's from Hunnewell," he said, surprised.

She looked up, her face smudged with tears and dust. "Hunnewell?"

"Listen to this—

> Burgess:
>
> *The final joke is on you. Surely you will agree that your long-owed debt to me is paid in full.*
>
> *B.B. Hunnewell*

Kace looked at her. "Well, well. That's a surprise. Evidently your father owed him a great deal of money too."

Sharlotte groaned and dropped her face into her blistered palms again.

Kace sat there a long moment saying nothing. He folded the letter and laid it on her lap.

"So much for our bright dreams," he said.

She sniffed loudly and felt in her pockets for her handkerchief. She didn't have one. Kace reached into his pocket and handed her his.

"Keep it," he said dryly.

Unexpectedly he smiled, he reached over and picked up a rock, looked at it, then laughed.

"How can you laugh," she said miserably.

"Better to laugh, my dear, than weep. Life goes on, with all of its tomorrows—and its debts." He stood, picked up his hat, and whacked the dust off. He put it on his head with a pat. He looked down at her with a smile, hands on hips.

"Well, Charmer, we're back where we started. I'm facing foreclosure, and you're destined to lose out on snagging a rich husband. We both had better get used to it."

She shook her head silently. "No...everything depended on getting my inheritance. *Everything.* There's no hope now, none at all. I'll never get used to it."

"Where's the new faith in Christ you told me about? Are you telling me you can't be content without gold? Money enough to give you an easy life?"

"I prayed...and He didn't answer."

"Maybe you set too much value on reclaiming what you've lost. Thousands of others are in the same boat, you know. They're out struggling day by day just to put food on the table for their families. I thought you told me just last night that you admired Elly and what she invested her heart and energies in?"

"I do..."

"So now you're bitter at God for not answering your prayer. He allowed rocks instead of shiny gold. But maybe He knew we were both letting our trust in money rob us of a greater faith in His provision."

Sharlotte said nothing. She remained seated in the dust beside the chest full of rocks.

Kace stood there for a moment, and then walked away to get the horses and burro.

She heard him come back some time later with the horses saddled. He mounted and walked his horse toward her, stopping.

"Get up, Sharlotte."

"I wanted the Ashford estate in Vermont more than anything. I wanted a doctor for Amanda so she could walk again. Now everything is gone."

The wind blew, kicking up a dust devil. The horse whinnied and shook its mane.

She looked up at Kace. He watched her evenly, and something in his face brought a cold shiver to her heart. Fear and confusion held her prisoner. As she looked into his eyes she knew without his ever saying it that something had died.

"Are you going to sit in the dirt waiting for Santana, or are you coming with me? I said I'd get you back safely. I intend to do so."

She stood slowly and went to her horse and mounted. Kace rode ahead and Sharlotte soon followed, her eyes looking back at the rocks in the chest for the last time.

∽

They arrived back in Texas at the Landry ranch several days later. The journey back had been one of prolonged silence. Sharlotte didn't know what to make of Kace. He had soon gotten over his anger and had treated her politely, even kindly at times, but after a day she began to miss his bantering, his compliments, the warm glint in his eyes that she would sometimes find when looking at him quickly and catching him off guard. Hurt and bewildered by his manner, yet too weary to consider how she could change things, or even if she ever could, she left him at the road to the ranch house.

"Aren't you coming up to the house to see Livia and Sherman?" she asked, when he turned his horse to ride on.

"No. I'll see them in a few days."

"Where are you going?" she asked, bewildered.

"Home," he said. Without another word he rode off in the direction of his oil land near Pecos leading the little burro.

Sharlotte looked after him until he disappeared, then slowly turned and rode down the long dusty road toward the ranch house.

The drought was worsening, she thought dully. The sky above seemed brass. The trees were nearly void of green now, and the earth appeared a perpetual carpet of moving dust as the wind blew and continued to blow.

The house seemed more quiet than usual. She eyed the front porch, expecting Aunt Livia to come hurrying out as she always did to greet her with a warm smile and the offer of a piece of fresh-baked pie and coffee. Livia didn't appear. Where was Uncle Sherman?

Rosita came from the side of the house. When she saw Sharlotte, she came hurrying towards her clutching and unclutching her apron. Tears were in her eyes and ran down the crevices in her cheeks.

"Oh, señorita, sad news."

"What is it?" Sharlotte slid down from the saddle, holding to the side of the horse.

Rosita pointed behind the house, then covered her face with her apron.

Sharlotte felt the same sickening terror beginning to cut off her breathing. She ran toward the back, her legs feeling weak but fear driving her on. "Lord, I've been so bad, I haven't trusted You as I should. Please—please don't chasten me—"

As she came around the house and faced the back property she could see far in the distance some people gathered, but she couldn't see who they were. Aunt Livia? Uncle Sherman? Tyler and Abby?

She began to run faster across the dust-blown field, her heart slamming in her chest, her throat dry and aching with fear.

They saw her coming and walked towards her. Uncle Sherman stopped the others and they stood waiting. He walked alone to meet her.

No, Sharlotte thought. *It's Amanda. I know it in my heart. Amanda's gone.*

Tears rushed, blinding her. She ran toward Sherman, and he came to her with open arms.

"Where's my sister—"

Uncle Sherman held her tightly and tried to soothe her, patting her back. "She's with the Lord," he choked. "We buried her this morning. That fever—it just sapped her strength away."

Sharlotte broke away and ran toward the small family cemetery. The others held back, watching. Sharlotte searched for the fresh plot with a small white cross and found it, her sister's name freshly inscribed:

> Amanda Ashford, 17 years.
> Now in the presence of her Savior, Jesus Christ.

Sharlotte's sobs broke as she fell to her knees. "Amanda—" her hand clutched a fistful of sod.

"But all the gold in the world could not open the grave and put that child back in his parents' arms." The words of Billy Sunday echoed in her mind.

But Jesus Christ can, she thought.

Therefore I love thy commandments above gold; yea, above fine gold.

31

In the long weeks that followed, Sharlotte remembered little of the jumble of seemingly unimportant incidents that took place on the ranch. Time and events swept her and everyone else along on a course that moved forward turning, twisting, but always moving onward.

Distant thunderclouds rumbled and flashed, yet never opened to drop their thirst-quenching rain to end the anguish of the drought. Dust storms were beginning. Long, thick, rolling clouds of dust that covered everything with an eerie Egyptianlike darkness that left the few remaining birds dead and cattle dropping in the fields from lack of water and food. Ranchers gathered for more meetings, many claiming disaster. Foreclosures were prominent. Some families were packing up what little they had left. There was talk of California and a new life.

But for Sharlotte the loss of Amanda, though she knew her sister was with the Lord, left the worst heartache of all, one that would not be easily mended. In the passing of her sister, who had shared her past way of life that no one else in the family understood or cared about, Sharlotte had lost her one true friend. Her final link to carefree, happier days was gone.

Kace occasionally came to see his uncle, but because he did not stay for supper the way he used to do, she never saw him except from afar. Then one day she walked out to the cemetery to Amanda's grave and looked up to see Kace waiting for her some distance away.

Sharlotte walked toward him, her heart knowing the first stirrings of feeling in what seemed a dearth of days.

"Hello, Kace," she said simply.

"I can't stay long. Old Will Hutchins died a few nights ago of heart failure."

"I'm terribly sorry…"

"Ty and Abby have decided to sell the ranch and leave for California."

"Leave?"

"Abby is expecting a baby. They want a new life. Ty's thinking of buying property in Southern California. He's heard they grow a lot of citrus there. He's had it with cattle."

"That will devastate Uncle Sherman, won't it? He's so accustomed to having you and Tyler as part of this ranch."

"The way things are going, even Sherman won't be able to hang on for long."

What about you, she wanted to ask, but she was afraid of the answer. Was he going away too?

"I stopped by to give you something," he said.

Her heart trembled. She watched as he reached into his pocket and held out an envelope. She looked at him, then at the envelope.

"Take it," he said quietly.

She did so, cautiously, wondering. "What is it?" she asked uncertainly.

The slight ironic smile was back. "The deed to the house in Vermont. I decided not to sell it. I wanted to give it to you before I left. It's yours."

The wind blew against her and ruffled the envelope in her hand as she stared at it. At last…at long last…and now she didn't want it. She wanted the man standing before her.

"I—I couldn't…"

"I never wanted it anyway. I always intended to give it back to you. I was just waiting for the right time. It never came. Now is as good as any."

"But Kace, I—"

"It's what you've always wanted," he said. "Now you've got it back. No need to be shy about it. There's nothing here now. You're better off in Vermont. I didn't think I'd ever say that, but time changes most everything."

Who else had said those words? Amanda…time changes most everything…

"But—what about you? Your land, the debt—"

"They foreclosed two weeks ago."

"Oh, Kace! I didn't know…"

He smiled, and there was the same determined look in his face, the fire in his gray-green eyes. "Texas is big enough for me to try again one day. It's not the end. One door closes, another opens."

His confidence and faith brought a lump to her throat.

"Goodbye, Sharlotte." He turned and walked away.

Panic seized her. "But, Kace!" She trailed after him at a loss. "I've changed my mind. I don't want to go to Vermont."

He walked on as though he hadn't heard her. She went after him. "Kace, wait, please—" she took hold of his arm. He looked at her, and Sharlotte searched his face for any sign that he cared at all. She saw nothing. "You once offered me a chance to buy into your company. I realize the land is lost—but as you said, there's new land. Lots of it in Texas! Kace, we'll sell the estate in Vermont. We'll buy more land. It's cheaper now. You should be able to have your choice—even the Graham area you talked about once. All I ask is—is a chance to invest in it."

He regarded her for a long moment until she felt the heat burning her cheeks. It didn't matter. She could be humble. She wanted to beg him to not go away. If he would just stay. She would have thrown herself into his arms, but she feared he would coolly remove her hands from him and keep walking.

What could she say to stop him? Would he listen to anything now? Was it too late?

"Where are you going?" she pleaded.

"To see Elly."

Sharlotte stopped dead in her tracks. Her heart fell to her feet. She froze as he walked on.

Sharlotte was still standing there when he had disappeared, too numb to feel the pain. She turned and looked back at Amanda's grave, then down at the envelope which held the deed to the Ashford property. His words came back to her on the hot, dusty wind: *This is what you've always wanted.*

Yes, she thought miserably. *It is what I always wanted. And now it doesn't matter anymore. I've lost Kace, and I've lost Amanda. And I deserve to lose them both. What a silly little fool you've been, Sharlotte Ashford. You had to lose everything before you realized what really and genuinely mattered.*

She walked slowly and tiredly back to the ranch house. When she came in through the back screen door into the big kitchen, Aunt Livia was boiling water for coffee. Her aunt had grown thinner and more drawn in her face, but her eyes still shone with her faith in God and His goodness.

"I suppose Kace told you about Ty and Abby," Livia said when Sharlotte stood there dully, saying nothing.

"He told me. I'm sorry."

"Well, perhaps it's better in the long run. They say California offers a new start. If the rains don't come soon, most of us will need a new start somewhere."

Sharlotte looked out the kitchen window. The sky had a dingy yellow appearance.

"Did Kace tell you the Rangers caught Santana?"

"No…"

"He's one less prickly piece of cactus that Texas needs to worry about. He confessed to killing Snowcroft's foreman."

Sharlotte accepted the cup of coffee that Livia brought her. The comfort of her motherly hand on her shoulder, gently pushing her toward the chair almost made her cry. Everything, recently, seemed to turn on her tears.

"My dear, what is it?" Livia asked gently.

"It's…" she whispered, "oh, Aunt Livia, so much has gone badly. I've destroyed everything."

"I don't believe that for an instant. You did all you could for your sister. Why don't you unburden your heart to me. Do you think I won't understand?"

Sharlotte wiped her eyes and shook her head. "It's not that. It's just—everything's so hopeless."

"It's not hopeless at all. Do you know what Paul the Apostle said about your heavenly Father? He called Him 'The God of all hope.' As long as the Sovereign God of this universe lives, there is hope. It's *never* so dark that God's light doesn't shine. He'll never leave us, never forsake us. His good plans for us cannot come to ultimate failure. He works all things out for good and for His eternal purposes. He offers us cheer and comfort and gives us the strength we need to carry on."

The words comforted her heart like a soothing balm. Sharlotte tried to smile.

Aunt Livia handed her a handkerchief. Doing so only reminded her of Kace. The tears started up again. Kace, what would she do without him? He had always been there when she needed him.

"Kace—" she said, then couldn't go on.

Livia looked at her for a long, thoughtful moment. "He told you he lost his land? Well, you don't need to worry about that one. Kace will always get back up on his feet when he's down."

"He's going away…with Elly…" Sharlotte lowered her head and arms on the table and cried unashamedly.

"With Elly? He told you that? You must have misunderstood, dear. He may be going to El Paso, but not to take Elly away, but to attend her wedding to Nate Caldwell. Didn't he tell you?" Stunned, at first Sharlotte couldn't move. Marry Nate Caldwell!

She raised her head and saw a sympathetic smile on Livia's face. "I see he hasn't told you. Shame on him. He kept it from you for some reason. Why, he's known since before you both went off to Mexico. Elly told me the night she was here with her father, Pastor McCrae. She gave her engagement ring back to Kace that night."

Sharlotte's heart felt as though it would burst.

"And Kace isn't leaving the ranch. Sherman needs him desperately and has asked him to stay. I think if Kace left him now, after Tyler's decision, your uncle wouldn't be able to carry on. He thinks of both of them as his sons."

"Kace is staying here? He's not going to marry Elly?" Sharlotte managed to stand to her feet, though her knees were weak.

"Kace is staying," Livia repeated with a smile. "It came as a surprise to me when Elly explained about Nate, but evidently Kace had known it for some time. She told me Kace was the one who introduced her to Nate. It was almost as if he hoped they would fall for one another, though he never said that, of course. He encouraged Elly to work with Nate. Well, she did. And she and Nate made such a good team that they soon discovered they cared for each other as well as for the work they were doing. Kace and Elly both agreed that they didn't believe God meant them for each other. They always were more friends than sweethearts." Livia smiled knowingly. "Now I wonder why he worked so hard to introduce her to Nate Caldwell? It was right after he saw you again at Long Island. Do you think he might still be carrying feelings for you?"

Sharlotte's hand brushed against the Vermont deed that was still in the envelope in her skirt pocket. "Aunt Livia, is he still on the ranch with Uncle Sherman?"

"No, I think he rode back to his place. Why, dear, did you want to see him?"

"Oh, yes, yes, at once!"

Livia got up and looked out the window at the sky. "More dust storms… it's too dangerous now, dear. Do wait until tomorrow? If you will, you can use Sherman's Model T. Can you drive?"

"Yes!"

"Then why not leave first thing in the morning? I wouldn't want to see you riding all that way in this weather. Here, Sherman keeps the key in the bowl up here…" Aunt Livia reached up and brought down a chipped blue sugar bowl. She handed Sharlotte the key. "You'll drive safely, won't you?"

"Yes, I'll be careful. I'll leave first thing in the morning." Sharlotte took the key and hugged her aunt, then ran upstairs to her room feeling giddy. He didn't love Elly! And he wasn't going to leave the ranch with Tyler and Abby. What words would she use to tell him how she felt about him? Was there any fire left in his heart for her? Would he listen? Could she convince him to give her another chance?

If only Amanda were here. How she would laugh and rejoice with her when she told her the news.

"Oh, Amanda, I miss you so…" she laid down on her bed and sobbed. "Lord Jesus, help me…"

The afternoon darkened with the storm, and Sharlotte soon fell into a fitful sleep.

How long she dozed she didn't know, but she awoke with a start, yet with a strange peace wrapped about her heart.

A thought flashed across her mind, startling her: *Whoever places their confidence in gold instead of the Lord will be left with a fistful of wind.*

A fistful of wind…

At that moment a gust of Texas wind rushed across the plain, whipping up the dust and shaking the house. She heard the timbers groan and the room trembled, and she trembled with its weakness. The mighty, old pepper tree that had grown in the yard long before Uncle Sherman had his ranch house built around it was little more than a tumble weed, should the wind decide to take it down. The wind could uproot the tree's proud stature and send it crashing to the dust. Instead, it chastised its leaves and branches and allowed it to stand.

Haven't you learned anything from your trials, Sharlotte? she thought. *Did not your father place his faith in uncertain riches and not in God? And where is your father? Where is the lover whom you dreamed about marrying for his riches and power? Didn't Clarence abandon you in your need? Where is the love of the Ashford family? Is it not those whom you despised who have taken you in now, to comfort and feed? To love and pray for you? Will you trust in gold, or will you trust in God with all your heart?*

"Jesus, I choose You!" she said tearfully.

She remembered something she had told the Lord when she'd camped with the others along the Pecos River while on their way to the orphanage. Elly had been leading the song, and Sharlotte's heart had been moved to surrender to God. "Once Amanda is taken care of, I'll do whatever you want of me," Sharlotte had said in prayer.

Amanda was now taken care of. She was safely at home in the presence of the Lord.

It's time, she thought calmly, *to yield my life to His purposes, whatever they are.*

From where she sat in bed she could see out the window, but it was dark, and the dust churned, seeping in through the cracks. Although it was dark, she knew the moon still shone brightly above, undisturbed by human events. Long after she had played out her life, the moon and stars would still shine on, a tribute to their Maker and His sustaining hand. The wind would still blow.

New honeysuckle blossoms would be sending off their sweetness to yet another generation of young lovers. Cattle would yet again be lowing in the fields. All because of Christ. Christ the Creator, Sustainer, Redeemer, whose faithful care kept the universe together, and life on earth intact. And who was she to doubt His care now and place her confidence in a fistful of gold? A fistful of wind! Without Jesus Christ, the gold was mere fool's gold. Without the man she loved, life was but a lonely shell. Would she continue to be a fool, or would she choose wisely? First, to do God's will no matter what. Secondly, to humble herself and let Kace know that she loved and wanted *him* for *himself.* He might reject her. But she would give him that opportunity.

Sharlotte slipped from the side of the bed and knelt to pray.

"Father, forgive me for failing to trust You. You wanted to answer my prayers all along, but in my blindness, I was asking amiss, to consume it upon my lusts. But You are not only kind and good, You are all-wise. You knew there was a need in my life that was much more important than just solving all my problems. What I was really asking for was a crutch to lean on, when all along what I needed was to know You better. It was in mercy You took away all the things I trusted in too much. You did it not to punish and hurt me, but because You love me with an everlasting love. You wanted me to see that I needed to find my all in all in You and Your Word. Now I want to grow as a Christian and become all You want me to be. I know it will be hard and difficult. I will continue to fail… but I accept the pain of growth with the promise of the rainbow after the storm. I commit my future to You alone."

She hesitated, wiping the tears from her eyes. "And Father, if it's Your will—enable me to convince Kace how much I love him. And if not…" she bit her lip, feeling the struggle of pain, of opening her clenched hand and releasing the sunbeam…"then Your purposes be done. I want what is truly Your very best for him."

It was late when Sharlotte went to the window and moved aside the curtain, looking out into the night. Although not a star could be seen shining, nor the moon offering its pale yellow light, there was light in her soul and peace in her heart. "The LORD is my light and my salvation...the LORD is the strength of my life." She knew that whatever tomorrow would bring, she would never face it entirely alone.

Kace too would be returning. Her heart knew the kindled flame of expectation. For beyond the night waited the dawn. She went to lift her mother's Bible from the stand where she'd left it, and as she did, it opened, and a piece of paper fluttered to the floor. Sharlotte stooped and read the verse written out in Amanda's handwriting. It was dated the day before she had passed on to be with the Lord.

Dear sister,

I've found the perfect verse for all woes—

"Weeping may endure for a night, but joy comes in the morning."

Weep no more, Sharlotte. The morning is fast approaching. And I'll see you then—in the morning light.

Amanda

Sharlotte looked at the words for a long moment, then she smiled. Yes, joy comes in the morning. No matter how dark the night, nothing can stop the glorious dawn from bursting forth in the sky. Not woe, but joy abounded in God's morning.

It's morning at last in my heart. And in the morning she would see Kace.

Epilogue

The next morning Sharlotte left the ranch house and drove Uncle Sherman's car down the narrow dusty road toward the land by the Pecos that, until recently, had belonged to Kace. She admired his tenacity in spite of disappointment and broken dreams. Knowing the manner of man he was, she believed that he would never quit. Perhaps one day he would see his hopes realized, maybe even strike oil.

It was mid-morning when she arrived at the property. She didn't see him anywhere. She brought the car to a stop and stepped from the running board to the dusty ground. There wasn't a cloud in the brassy sky and the birds had fled. The dried grasses crackled in the hot wind that was stirring up distant dust devils. The oil drilling equipment stood solemn and silent except for a clanking chain that swayed in the wind like a hangman's noose.

Sharlotte shaded her eyes and glanced about. The tents were gone and the men had already moved on, perhaps to Midland looking for work. They'd be lucky to find anything, she thought sadly. Where was Kace? Had he left for El Paso after all?

She hurried across the field toward the small cabin. Maybe he was resting, or packing. Would he be disappointed that she'd come? She thought back to the first time she'd ridden here, soon after she and Amanda arrived from Vermont. She remembered with a cramp in her throat how genuinely pleased he'd been to see her. But now he might respond to her arrival with little more than tolerance. Worse yet—suppose, oh suppose he rejected her outright as he seemed to have done yesterday?

Sharlotte paused a few feet from the rough-hewn cabin door. Never had a worn wooden hut appeared so inviting, as though the opening of its door could lead to the fulfillment of her heart's desire. She wanted Kace and his love. Nothing else on earth would matter much again, even if she never owned expensive new dresses or sat down to a glistening white tablecloth with china dishes. If Kace were near, if he loved her, she could be happy at a small wooden table with chipped dishes and a glowing lantern. The security of his love, his strength and understanding, was all she wanted now. She walked slowly to the door, her heart pulsing in her throat, and reached a trembling hand and knocked. The sound, breaking the silence, was like a toll that would either seal her lonely doom, or open to a garden of love.

She knocked again…No answer. Had he seen her coming and deliberately turned a deaf ear? Perhaps yesterday had been his final answer. She had disappointed him, rejected him. Was it now forever too late?

"Kace? Are you in there? It's me, Sharlotte. I've got to talk to you. Kace! Please open up!"

She realized he wasn't the kind to hide from her. He hadn't responded because he wasn't here. Relief swept over her like a gentle breeze. Yes, he had simply gone out on the property somewhere, perhaps to check some equipment or gather up some stray cattle to bring to Uncle Sherman. She tried the door handle, and finding it unlocked, stepped inside.

The cabin was hot and a bit dark, but she didn't mind it now. With joy she saw that his clothes were still here, along with his traveling bag, and there was a box of groceries sitting near a small cookstove as though he had intended to fix something to eat before being interrupted.

At once she had an idea...she would surprise him. She felt unexpectedly free and happy, even a little daring and giddy. She would fix his meal and have it waiting when he came back, surprised to see her!

Was she being too trite? Could she really expect their stormy and uncertain relationship to turn around with new hope and courage? A fresh start to make it together?

She poured water in the basin and washed the dust and sweat from her face and hands, then started to work, no easy task since she had little cooking experience except for the rare times in Vermont when Finney had been busy outdoors, and she had made her and Amanda some lunch...Amanda. She wanted to cry but she blinked it back. Amanda would be proud of her if she could see her now, she encouraged herself.

She worked swiftly, not knowing when he would be back. Her cooking skills were awful but she charged into her task with determination and a concentrated scowl. Soon coffee was boiling with a fragrant, welcoming aroma, and potatoes and eggs were cooking slowly in the one black iron skillet. She began to be pleased with her endeavor. She visualized Kace laughing with her as he had in the past. She was taking a risk, becoming vulnerable to awful rejection. It was frightening, but she told herself she was willing to endure his rejection if only she could make some improvement in how he felt about her.

At last the small table was set, the meal cooked, and the coffee too strong but ready to pour. She could add a little more water to it. Where was the sugar and cream—of course there wouldn't be any fresh cream, and that's right—Kace drank it black and he liked it strong.

She waited, struggling to keep everything hot, but not overcooked and dried out. Then a horrid thought came, what if he didn't return till sundown? The thought was so disappointing that she lowered herself onto a hard-backed chair feeling foolish and desolate. She had no reason to expect him to return this soon. Why had she allowed her emotions to get carried away? Then she heard horse hooves, and her heart jumped to her throat. She stood quickly, smoothed her hair, straightened her blouse and skirt, and bit her lip as she turned toward the door, staring.

At last she heard his bootsteps nearing the cabin door. He would have seen his uncle's car, but he would not be expecting her. Her heart did a flip-flop as she waited.

He appeared to hesitate outside the door, as if he knew it wasn't Sherman after all. The aroma of food drifted out through the open windows. Did he know it was her?

The door opened and he stood there, his rugged form silhouetted against the light. Her first inclination was to run to him, but wisdom gently warned her to caution. He wouldn't appreciate her throwing herself at him. He'd had women doing that for years. She must leave him to decide on his own.

The wind blew in, ruffling the hem of her skirt before he stepped inside. The door shut abruptly as their eyes met and held. Though she could see his surprise, it was reasonably restrained.

Sharlotte stood rooted to the wooden floor, waiting. Kace silently looked at her. The ticking clock seemed to stop as they analyzed each other's feelings.

Finally, he leaned back against the door, his glance scanning the table set with two plates, two cups, two forks, then the stove where the skillet was covered.

"I don't believe it," he said quietly.

Sharlotte's hopes surged. No rejection…not yet anyway. She dragged her eyes from his to look at the table as though it were the most natural thing in the world to have cooked his lunch.

"I—I made us something to eat," she said, and her voice sounded not like her own. "You must be hungry."

She felt warmth rise to her cheeks. Quickly she went to the stove, grabbed the blackened coffeepot and filled two steaming cups. "Looks strong," she managed desperately. "I think I boiled it too long. I—I can add some water if you want."

Still, he said nothing as he watched her.

She picked up the spatula and begin placing potatoes and scrambled eggs on his plate, her back toward him. Her eyes stung.

"There wasn't any bacon," she said weakly. Wasn't he going to say anything?

Then she heard his footsteps behind her and her eyes closed. His hands were strong, yet gentle on her shoulders as he turned her around to face him. He took the plate from her hand and set it on the table, took the spatula from her other hand and set it down on the stove. He lifted her chin and looked long into her eyes, looking carefully as though reading her very heart. Her tears brimmed over and wet her cheeks. She knew her eyes told all: her love, her fears, her apologies. But what would his response to her vulnerability be? She didn't need to wonder for long. With a flood of relief she saw a small flame of love and passion that stirred the embers to life in the depths of his gray-green eyes.

"Sharlotte…" Then his arms were tight around her waist and shoulders, and they held to each other as though to let go would mean to be torn apart forever.

"I love you," Kace said fiercely in her ear. Between kisses he was saying, "Desperately love and want you…I always have…but you wouldn't let me."

"Oh, Kace! I've been so blind, so foolish…because down deep in my heart I've always loved you too."

"That is what I wanted to hear." He kissed her once more.

Sharlotte tried to confess, "But I was too blind to realize how much I loved you. I was so full of foolish pride, I didn't recognize it until it was too late—"

"Not too late." He spoke very quietly, and raising her left hand kissed her palm gently, then her ring finger.

"There was so much keeping us apart…" she tried to go on, to say *I love you and will wait for you forever*, but she put her arms around him and kissed him tenderly instead.

"And now there is nothing between us," he said. The strength of his embrace gave her confidence. Their kiss was in defiance of anything that would ever come between them again.

"Nothing," she whispered giddily.

"Do you love me, Sharlotte, no matter what?"

"Yes, Kace, no matter what."

"Always?"

"Always."

The dry wind rattled the door and seemed to shake the little cabin. He held her for a long time, pressing her head against his chest, and they were content to let the moments slip by without further word.

"Kace, what will we do now? The future, I mean?"

"Tomorrow is Sunday. We can ask Pastor McCrae to marry us after the service. He's back."

"Kace, darling, be serious," she said with a laugh.

"But I am serious. In fact, tomorrow is too long. We can ride over there tonight."

She sighed contentedly and snuggled into his arms. "And after we're married, what will we do? Will we stay here and settle on the ranch?"

"Right now it appears we don't have much choice. Until the drought ends and the dust settles, if it ever does, Uncle Sherman will remain determined about raising cattle. But there's not much hope in that. The cattle are dying, the water is drying up, and there's no rain in sight. The soil is simply blowing away."

"At this moment all that matters to me is that I have you."

"For a few years it will be rough, but since God controls the future, we can proceed with confidence—no matter what."

She nodded and smiled bravely. "Yes, nothing can separate us from Him and His love. We can trust in Him and know that His plans for us are the best." After a moment she added: "I suppose you'll eventually want to drill for oil near the Graham area?"

He smiled at her, his eyes teasing her. "Are you willing to become a Texas oil woman?"

"I'll follow you wherever you go—even into a field raining down black muck."

"Black gold," he corrected. "Speaking of gold, the yellow kind, remember that treasure you buried?"

At first she thought he was merely teasing her again for hiding it too well. "Yes," she sighed. "Under a crooked tree."

"Yes, under a crooked tree. And it's still there, somewhere, unless old Finney found it and ran off to the Bahamas."

She laughed a little, imagining Finney under a palm tree sipping a cool lemonade. "He wouldn't do that. Not Finney."

"No, I suppose he wouldn't. Anyway, one day we may go back and spend a month looking for that tree."

"Oh, Kace, are you serious? Legally, you own the mortgage on the property. And I meant it when I said I wanted to sell the Vermont house and pay the mortgage on this property. If you say there's oil here, I believe you."

"I can't take your money. If something goes wrong, I want you to have that Vermont property to fall back upon. Then again, we've also got my uncle's land since my father owned half. All we need do is hold onto it."

"And don't forget our *lovely* rancho in El Sueco," she added with a glimmer of amusement.

"Maybe we'll go there for our honeymoon. Nothing like that long horseback ride across the Rio Grande into Mexico: jackrabbits, heat, rattlers, and sleeping out under the stars…"

She looked at him aghast, then she saw his smile and knew he hadn't meant it.

She threw her arms around him again and kissed him, then turned around looking at the cabin. "Why, we can stay here and fix up this cabin. Somehow, together, we're bound to get enough money to pay the bank."

"You're right. It's worth fighting for. And if it is, it's worth waiting for, for a very long time.

"But Sherman needs me at the ranch for the forseeable future. Would you mind living there for now?"

"As long as we're together I'll be contented," she said.

And meanwhile, we'll have seven sons and three daughters, like Job. And if they look anything like you, they'll be the fairest in the land."

"Ten?" she laughed. "Where will they all sleep?"

"One day we'll get this land back. And then we'll turn this little cabin into a grand house."

"You know something, Kace Landry?" she whispered. "I believe you."

He pulled her to him and his kiss promised more happiness than her heart could hold. For now the days were bright and happy again. The heat didn't matter so much after all, nor the constantly blowing wind, nor even the drought, the dust, and the uncertainty that wound into the future. She had Kace, and he was not afraid of the future. Hand in hand they would journey into the unknown, knowing that whatever waited, they would have one another, and that God had both of them.

Sharlotte looked up at him again, and there was even more than love in his eyes, there was something flickering in his gaze and showing on his face that she had always longed to see, and now, at last, it was there. Admiration and respect for a woman who had godly beauty within.

"Yes," he said very quietly. "Some things are worth waiting for, because their value exceeds gold and rubies. You, my beloved, were worth waiting for."

"Oh Kace…" she whispered.

Harvest House Publishers
Fiction for Every Taste and Interest

Gilbert Morris

JACQUES & CLEO, CAT DETECTIVES
Cat's Pajamas
What the Cat Dragged In
When the Cat's Away

Mindy Starns Clark

Whispers of the Bayou
Shadows of Lancaster County

SMART CHICK MYSTERY SERIES
The Trouble with Tulip
Blind Dates Can Be Murder
Elementary, My Dear Watkins

MILLION DOLLAR MYSTERIES
A Penny for Your Thoughts
Don't Take Any Wooden
    Nickels
A Dime a Dozen
The Buck Stops Here
A Quarter for a Kiss

Debra White Smith

THE DEBUTANTES
Heather
Lorna
Brittan

THE AUSTEN SERIES
First Impressions
Central Park

Susan Page Davis

Finding Marie
Inside Story

Susan Meissner

Blue Heart Blessed
Remedy for Regret
In All Deep Places

RACHAEL FLYNN MYSTERY SERIES
Widows and Orphans
Sticks and Stones
Days and Hours

Kaye Dacus

Ransome's Honor

Sally John

THE OTHER WAY HOME SERIES
A Journey by Chance
After All These Years
Just to See You Smile
The Winding Road Home

IN A HEARTBEAT SERIES
In a Heartbeat
Flash Point
Moment of Truth

THE BEACH HOUSE SERIES
The Beach House
Castles in the Sand
    by Trish Perry
Beach Dreams
Sunset Beach

Brandt Dodson

Daniel's Den
White Soul

COLTON PARKER MYSTERY SERIES
Original Sin
Seventy Times Seven
Root of all Evil
The Lost Sheep

Lori Copeland

Outlaw's Bride

Jerry Eicher

THE ADAMS COUNTRY TRILOGY
Rebecca's Promise
Rebecca's Return

Marry Ellis

THE MILLER FAMILY SERIES
A Widow's Hope

Linore Rose Burkard

REGENCY INSPIRATIONAL ROMANCE
Before the Season Ends
The House in Grosvenor Square

George Polivka

Blaggard's Moon

TROPHY CHASE TRILOGY
Legend of the Firefish
The Hand That Bears
    the Sword
Battle of the Vast Dominion

Craig Parshall

Trial by Ordeal
Rose Conspiracy

THE THISTLE AND THE CROSS SERIES
Captives and Kings
Sons of Glory

CHAMBERS OF JUSTICE SERIES
The Resurrection File
Custody of the State
The Accused
Missing Witness
The Last Judgment

Roxanne Henke

On a Someday
Learning to Fly
The Secret of Us

COMING HOME TO BREWSTER SERIES
After Anne
Finding Ruth
Becoming Olivia
Always Jan
With Love, Libby

B.J. Hoff

Song of Erin
American Anthem

THE RIVERHAVEN YEARS
Rachel's Secret
Where Grace Abides

MOUNTAIN SONG LEGACY
A Distant Music
The Wind Harp
The Song Weaver

Siri Mitchell

The Cubicle Next Door
Moon Over Tokyo